Vena Cork is from Lancashire, but has lived in London all her adult life. She attended Homerton College, Cambridge, where she was a member of Cambridge Footlights. She is married to the art critic Richard Cork and lives in North West London. This is her first novel.

Praise for Vena Cork:

'This gripping, edgy novel is good, believe me. For a first novel, it is rather better than good. The portrayal of life is awfully well handled and shrewdly characterised . . . she hooks her reader from the start. Well done, Vena!' *Colin Dexter*

'A compelling, dark-hued psychological thriller that eerily captures some of London's more sinister undercurrents and sense of menace' *Guardian*

'In her atmospheric novel *Thorn*, Vena Cork skilfully builds a sinister feeling of menace surrounding her attractive heroine'
Sunday Telegraph

'There's more to this psychological thriller than meets the eye. Look no further for a real sense of menace' *Daily Mirror*

'You'll be gripped as this persuasive thriller races

to its grisly conclusion' *Marie Claire*

'Vena Cork's perceptions of human nature are spot-on and the suspense is tangible when the small malevolent acts turn into something much more evil and sinister. This is a great start to what is sure to be a string of successful books' *Aberdeen Press & Journal*

'A tense pace combined with a tightly woven narrative makes this a surprisingly compelling debut from novelist Vena Cork' *Buzz*

THORN

Vena Cork

headline

First published in Great Britain in 2004
by HEADLINE BOOK PUBLISHING

First published in paperback in 2005
by HEADLINE BOOK PUBLISHING

10 9 8 7 6 5 4 3 2

ISBN 0 7553 2394 7

Typeset in Electra by Palimpsest Book Production Limited,
Polmont, Stirlingshire

Printed and bound in Great Britain by
Clays Ltd, St Ives plc

Headline's policy is to use papers that are natural, recyclable products made from wood grown in sustainable forests. The manufacturing processes conform to the environmental regulations of the country of origin.

HEADLINE BOOK PUBLISHING
A division of Hodder Headline
338 Euston Road
London NW1 3BH

www.headline.co.uk
www.hodderheadline.com

To Richard, Adam, Polly,
Katy and Joe, with all my love.

ACKNOWLEDGEMENTS

I would like to thank the following people for their invaluable help and support during the writing of this book: my editor, Martin Fletcher and the team at Headline; my agents, Lisa Moylett and Nathalie Sfakianos; my friends Nalini Chapman, Evelyn Cantor and Bruce Murphy; my cousin, Jean Hartley, and Helen Hamber and Lisanne Radice.

And last but never least, my wonderful family: Richard, Adam, Polly, Katy and Joe who have always loved, supported and believed in me, even when I didn't believe in myself, and without whom I could never have written this book.

28 *January*

Rob Thorn applied a touch of green to the bottom left-hand side of the canvas. Then he stood, scrutinised and, eventually, smiled.

'That's it,' he said. 'Finished.'

He dragged his eyes away from the painting. He always felt the same at the end: a deepsea diver, surfacing from oceanic depths to rejoin the real world. You had to be careful not to ascend too quickly or you'd get the bends. The room shimmered back into focus. His gaze wandered over the canvases stacked against the walls. So much work. And so much more to do.

But not today.

He glimpsed himself in the paint-splattered mirror. His face, with its prominent cheekbones and dark eyes, wore the emptied-out expression that told of work completed.

'Enough,' he told his reflection.

His body was stiff from crouching over the canvas. He took a deep breath, stretched, and gave a bellow of delight. Life was good. He looked out of the upstairs bay window. The late-winter world shone bright, cold and clear. In Consort Park across the road the snowdrops and crocuses vied for attention, their white and purple flowers glittering jewels scattered on the grass beneath the bare trees.

Near the tennis courts, Rob spotted two figures throwing a Frisbee: his children, Anna and Danny.

As always when fresh from the hermetically sealed world of his work, Rob caught his breath at the wonder of them. It was hard to believe such creatures existed and, moreover, that they owed that existence to him. To him and his pale, perfect Rosa. His White Queen. He banged on the window, but they were too far away to hear. He was overcome by an urge to be with them, to tell them how much he loved them.

To play Frisbee.

Well, why not? The painting was finished. He would go out there right now and join his children. He smiled as he watched them – gangling teenagers, regressing to childhood as they always did when out in the park with a ball or a Frisbee. He dropped his painting shirt onto the floor, put on a sweater and selected a track on his mp3 player. The mellow tones of Bob Marley filled his head with sunshine and nostalgia as he made his way out of the house. The sharp winter air hit his lungs, and he felt intensely alive, a sensate being in a world crammed with sensation. Tonight he'd take them all out for a meal. Somewhere trendy in the West End. He saw Anna floor Danny with a flying tackle and grab the Frisbee. He laughed and ran gladly forward, back into the land of the living.

'No woman no cry,' sang Bob, as Rob stepped off the kerb.

The boy driving the stolen Ford Mondeo was chatting to a fellow joyrider on his mobile. He felt a jolt and something dark passed over the windscreen like a cloud blocking the sun.

'Laters,' he told his mate, and accelerated out of the area at warp speed.

The Thorn children heard metal hitting flesh. They saw a lifesize rag doll describe an arc through the air before splitting open like a ripe pink watermelon as it hit the pavement outside their house. It took less than a minute for them to realise that their world had come to an end.

ONE

In the fading heat of early September, Consort Park resembles a young girl after a heavy night out – frowzy but still gorgeous. Golden afternoon light glints on the pooper-scoop bins, and in the distance I see Mary the Hologram dishing the latest local dirt into the avid ear of Singing Vic. Georges, Jacques et Jules are having a combative game of boules, and the artist who always paints the same tree is painting the same tree again. All is as it ever was.

As I walk I practise saying, 'I'm a widow.'

In the nine months since Rob's death I haven't yet come to grips with this particular sentence. No one queries your marital status at auditions. Everyone's a theatrical Miss. But supply teaching's different. There will be staffrooms and colleagues and nosiness. Particularly at Churchill Towers Comprehensive, if Jess is to be believed.

What tone should I use? Matter-of-fact? Brave little smile? Barely audible, in a low, musical timbre? The bronze statue of Albert, Prince Consort, stares down at me from his plinth at the top end of the park.

'I'm a widow,' I tell him.

'My wife was a widow for forty years,' he replies. 'Get used to it.'

Why am I going back into teaching anyway? That's easy: the money. A bit-part actress who hasn't worked for months doesn't bring in enough to support a gerbil, let alone a family of three.

'I'm a widow.' I try it again.

'I wish I was,' says an old woman on a bench wearing a scarf that doesn't quite hide a purple bruise on her cheek. 'I wish I was.'

No, you don't, old woman. You don't want your life destroyed by some idiot who, for all the police seem to care, is still on the loose killing innocent pedestrians. You don't want to hear that distinctive squeal of brakes followed by a muffled thud. And you certainly don't want to see the light of your life lying on the road with half his head missing, and quite clearly dead.

I leave the park, not by the gate where Rob died, but by the other one further up the hill. One day I'll go the quick way home, but not yet. Not while I can still see his brains spilling onto the pavement, and Singing Vic weeping as he tries to push them back in with his paisley handkerchief.

And Anna and Danny, motionless in the park, watching.

But we all have to move on. Tomorrow is a new day. The future beckons. My cup of clichés runneth over.

Churchill Towers Comprehensive is our future.

Rob would turn in his urn to know that Anna and Danny have swapped their independent schools for a comprehensive, but hey Rob, you should have left us the money for the fees, shouldn't you? And you should have looked before stepping into the road.

Anna's outside our gate talking to a stranger. They're both crouching down looking at something. It's a squirrel, flattened by yet another speeding car. It's still alive, but as we stare it gives a little sigh and is still. Maybe Rob gave the same sigh as he died. I must ask Singing Vic.

Anna's crying. 'Poor little thing.' She turns to her companion – whose cheeks, I notice, are also wet. 'I'll bury it in my garden.'

'Here,' says the man. He carefully wraps the squirrel in his scarf and hands it to Anna.

I'm touched by my daughter's devotion to dumb animals, but wish the dead ones didn't all end up in our garden. She has a special, ever-expanding patch that Rob called the Pet Cemetery. He said that when he died she could bury him by the cat, but on no account did he want to be anywhere near the goldfish.

In the event, he's in an urn at the back of a cupboard waiting for me to decide what to do with him.

'Anna, must you? There'll be no room for plants soon.'

Anna doesn't dignify this with an answer. She carries the squirrel into the house and I follow. The young man shuffles from foot to foot on the sun-dried pavement.

The house is cool after the sunshine. The walls are shaking and the decibel level is beyond imagination. Danny's playing 'Stairway to Heaven' on his electric guitar. With backing track. Even as his devoted mother I can tell he has some way to go before Jimmy Page needs to start worrying. Still, he enjoys it, and that's the main thing. Maybe his inexpert fumblings are a way of expressing his grief and loss, because he sure as hell hasn't let his feelings out in any other way. At first after Rob died, Danny was strong for all of us. I haven't yet seen him cry. I've tried to talk to him, to say that even though he's seventeen, it's still OK to be sad, but I can't penetrate the self-contained façade. Jess says it's because he's an adolescent male. Adolescent boys tell their mothers zilch. But what does she know? Her own particular adolescent male isn't exactly Mr Normal.

I make supper. Anna appears, flushed and sticky from grave digging. Blissful silence falls as Danny, seduced by the smell of lamb stew, packs away his guitar and comes down to eat. At the end of the meal, there's a pause. No one wants to leave the table and do what they have to do. Tomorrow looms. Out with the old. In with the . . . what?

We're all aware of the gap where Rob used to sit.

'Should we pack our satchels now?' I say. My children indulge me with faint smiles.

'I'm going to take an apple for the teacher. Oh, whoops – I *am* the teacher.'

'Give it up, Mum,' says Danny.

Later I put the rubbish out. Anna's Squirrel Man is still there, over the road staring at our house. I shout hello. Unsmiling, he acknowledges my greeting, leaning immobile against the park railings. A flurry of wind blows some dead leaves up the path. I shiver. Autumn's round the corner.

TWO

Grey Squirrel. *Sciurus carolinensis.* Grey squirrels affect an upright posture in order to observe their habitat, employing both sight and olfactory senses.

Squirrel Man is still there this morning when we leave the house to start our new lives. He stares at our house as if it holds the key to all things. When he sees Anna he smiles and calls out, but she's far too preoccupied to notice and stomps grimly up the road towards Churchill Towers. I wonder whether he's been there all night. Then I forget about mysterious strangers as terror kicks in. How will I survive classfuls of recalcitrant adolescents?

In the mid-nineteenth century, Alfred Churchill from Willesden in North-West London invented a special cog for use in the railway industry. This made him filthy rich and, deciding he needed a grand house to complement his newly acquired status, he bought a piece of land on a hill near Willesden, and employed a fashionable architect. Churchill Towers was the result. The architect worked unstintingly to produce a dizzying confection of turrets and crenellations that was a cross between St Pancras Station and a minor folly of Mad King Ludwig. Alfred only demanded one change: to replace one of the towers with an observatory. This was duly done, and he spent the rest of his life, spurned by both his social inferiors *and* superiors, sitting under the glass dome observing the stars and pondering the nature of existence.

After his death his widow sold up and moved thankfully back to the village, and the house became variously over the years: a hospital in World War I, a secret government department in World War II, a lunatic asylum and finally, in the 1960s, a school. Behind the turreted splendour of the original building, a glass and concrete obscenity was thrown up, and Churchill Towers Comprehensive was born. The 1960s was not good for either teaching or building. The hastily erected structure soon began to fall down, and the child-centred theories of learning which were all the rage ensured that by the time they were sixteen, most of the kids at Churchill Towers left the school as unemployable illiterates. But the school hung in there. It got by. Many aspirational parents who normally wouldn't have looked at it twice, were bamboozled by the grandeur of Alfred's turrets into thinking it was a grammar school.

The present Head Teacher has done more than most to encourage this notion. His chiselled features and open, yet intimate manner have made him the nation's pet rent-a-quote Head. He can be seen almost weekly on the television, either on the news, commenting on the government's latest education initiative, or debating the state of our schools in various earnest discussion programmes. His apotheosis, according to Jess, who is Head of English at Churchill, was appearing on *Any*

Questions with Kenneth Clark. His name is Leonard Ratchett, but he is known to all as Leo.

Except for Jess. To her, he's Ratshit.

And from today, he's my boss.

I'm not used to bosses. As a jobbing actor and home-maker I've always been my own boss. The teaching post is not permanent, thank God – just part-time maternity cover, three days a week till next Easter.

How will I cope after fifteen years away from the classroom? Jess says it's a piece of piss, but Singing Vic, a peripatetic music teacher at Churchill, tells a different tale. I could be in deep doo-doo. He's tried to retract some of his more distressing stories since I told him my news, but I'm not deceived. How could I forget the time his arm was in a sling for three weeks because a psychotic child slammed the piano lid down on his hand? Or the Friday his barber-shop quintet locked him in the music room and he wasn't discovered till Monday morning?

I'm as thrilled about this job as a turkey on Christmas Eve.

When I reach the gates, Anna has already disappeared into a frenzied whirlpool of adolescents. I turn to wish Danny good luck, but he's gone too. Neither of them is pleased that I'm joining them in the big adventure that is Churchill Towers. Having a mother teaching your mates Drama isn't that good for the street cred. But as I told Danny, beggars can't be choosers and I wasn't doing this as a cunning parental surveillance exercise. I'd rather be pursuing my chosen profession, not my rejected one. I only trained as a teacher to satisfy my mother's wish that I should have a proper job to fall back on when the acting work dried up. I don't regret it because that's how I met Rob: at college. After qualifying, I did a year or two at a school which was subsequently closed down – a fact I hope was unconnected to my crap teaching. I loathed it and swore that never again would I teach.

Moral: don't swear undying oaths. They may come back to mock you.

And never fall in love and make a life with someone, because they may die, and then where will you be?

I'm overwhelmed by a wave of such negativity that I want to vomit. Not a good start.

It's a fitting rebuke therefore when suddenly my ears are assaulted by a noise so loud it seems to encompass the whole known universe: the first four, ominous notes of Beethoven's Fifth are blasting forth from a PA system. As I watch, the maelstrom of bodies is sucked, as if by a giant Hoover, through various doorways into the building. When the last child disappears, the music stops, mid-phrase. I'm the only person left in the playground. My eardrums throb gently. I'm busy collecting my wits when the voice of God addresses me from on high.

'Ms Thorn, I presume.'

I look around. I'm alone apart from the creepy feeling that hundreds of eyes are watching me.

'Up here.'

I look up at the line of windows. I see children, loads of them, and they are laughing. At me. Please God Anna and Danny aren't witnessing my humiliation.

'Not there,' repeats the voice. 'Here. In the Observatory.'

I look up at the vast dome. A handsome man, immaculate in a pinstripe suit, smiles down. In one hand he holds a microphone into which he projects his beautifully modulated voice.

'Welcome to Churchill. We're so grateful you could join us at such short notice. I hope you and your children will be happy here. Danny and Anna, isn't it? Sixth Form and Year Nine? Great. Any problems, my door is always open. Just fix up an appointment with my secretary.'

Before I can respond, a set of electric blinds descends and I'm alone again. A screw of paper hits my cheek and I hear sniggering. I'm about to go home to cry when Jess appears.

'Fuck me, Rosa, you've missed Staff Briefing.' She sees me gazing at the blank white face of the Observatory. 'Ratshit doing his party piece? He loves freaking out new staff with his voice from the heavens routine. It's a control thing. Wanker.'

Jess hasn't recovered from Leo appointing Primrose Pepper as Deputy Head, having led her to expect the job was hers. Personally I'm rather taken by his unusual form of greeting. It smacks of a certain eccentricity – something I'm all in favour of in our homogenous designer world.

Jess gives the finger to the lowered blinds and ushers me into the building, where I spend a day of confusion, ineptitude and chaos. I'm introduced to the Head of Expressive Arts, Dave Alessi, who is young, funky and committed. He has a shaved head and a small tattoo on his neck, and quite clearly thinks I know a lot more than I do. His management style is casual, and leaves no room for questions. I'm given a pile of incomprehensible work schemes, pointed in the direction of my Drama room and left to get on with it. I'm then subjected to wave upon wave of children, most of whom think of Drama lessons as time out. The boys roll around the floor punching each other, and the girls do each other's hair and swap lipgloss.

Occasionally they take pity on me and listen.

Very occasionally they produce some Drama. If that's what you'd call it.

When half past three arrives and we're all leaving the building accompanied by the Overture to *The Magic Flute*, I completely forget to look out for my children. Stunned, I totter home alone.

From the Observatory, Leo Ratchett watched as Rosa Thorn walked across the playground, dodging footballs and fights.

'Pale as the moon, and twice as preoccupied,' he said. 'Interesting . . . Hope she ditches the widow's weeds soon. Women in black look so drab.'

He smiled. 'Maybe Churchill Towers will put the roses back into Rosa.'

THREE

Fox. *Vulpes vulpes.* The myriad shades of brown in its pelt, ranging from ochre to chestnut, along with the amber eyes and thick tail, make this creature uniquely recognisable.

When I arrive home I barely register Anna's new best friend, still outside the house. I'm in a state. I've made the biggest mistake of my life. Whatever made me think I could swan back into a classroom after twenty years away? I must be truly insane. I can't do it. I don't want to do it. I'd rather sell my body to a passing stranger.

I fill the kettle with trembling hands and try not to think about a particularly unpleasant child called Wayne, who set out to sabotage my best Drama games and succeeded beyond his wildest dreams. I also try not to think about Primrose Pepper, Deputy Head, swinging by at the moment when the whole of 7C were rolling round the floor kicking each other and shouting, 'Fuck!'

'How interesting. So good to have a real theatre practitioner with us,' she breathed. I told her it was a Trust Game. I don't think she was convinced. I hate her. I hate Churchill Towers, and I hate Jess for getting me this horrific job.

Damn you, Rob! If only you'd taken out life insurance instead of putting all our money into school fees. I know how you wanted the best for your kids after your own crappy childhood, but still . . .

I make my tea and eat three chocolate biscuits, trying to avoid the inescapable conclusion to which my mind is leading me. I need a regular income. Even if I front it out at Churchill Towers for the duration of my short contract, what then? Should I take a full-time job as a Drama teacher and forget acting? Do supply teaching and try to fit the acting around it? Even if, God forbid, I end up teaching full-time, it's not going to give us more than a very basic standard of living. Gone are the days when teaching in London was a viable proposition.

I need more money, and here comes the bit I don't want to face – there's one easy way of making it.

I could rent out Rob's studio as a bedsit.

I haven't set foot in it since he died nine months ago. I can't.

The same thing happens every time I try: I turn the door knob, my hand refuses to budge and I start to sweat. My heart thunders, my vision becomes blurred, I tremble violently and I can't breathe. Eventually I go away and pretend I never meant to go near Rob's room anyway.

Why am I so frightened?

I finish my tea and walk upstairs. I stare at the door, willing myself to open it. Nothing happens. Sweat trickles down the back of my neck. I grip the handle, commanding my fingers to turn it.

Minutes pass. Then I'm released from my paralysis by a blinding realisation. The work will have to be stored in the garden shed!

Before he died, Rob had turned the shed into his permanent studio. He was about to move in, the week he was killed. So I'm fully aware that it's ready. Even so I'm down the stairs and out of the door in less time than it takes to say 'panic attack'.

All is as it should be: a perfect studio for an up-and-coming painter with a growing reputation, who needs a bit more space and distance from his family. Pity he's dead.

I march back upstairs and fling open the door.

It's all still there. The canvases – finished, half-finished – the table neatly arranged with brushes, palette knives, paint rags. The familiar smells of linseed oil, turpentine and paint. The room is covered in thick dust and I see my footprints leading across the floor towards me. They aren't the only ones. A crowd of smaller prints trail back and forth, from the door to the fireplace at the end of the room.

In the hearth is a little shrine. Rob's photo – taken on our last holiday, only months before he died – stands in a silver frame between two candles alongside an incense burner and the small black urn containing his ashes, which I thought was at the back of my bedroom cupboard. I can't look at the urn so I pick up the photograph and look at my husband instead. He's laughing at the person taking the snap – me – and he looks . . . alive. His molasses eyes brim with mischief, and his black skin is burnished by sunshine.

Rob on holiday, the intensity of his work forgotten.

Artists are strange creatures. Their work takes them

deep into themselves, into another dimension. Their bodies are present, but that's all. As an experiment I once told Rob I'd fallen down the stairs and thought my neck was broken. He frowned sympathetically, said, 'Poor baby,' and carried on daubing.

That's why holidays were so important to us. Rob on holiday was fully present. He lit up our lives with his fun and laughter and love, pouring himself into us with the same intensity that he normally invested in his work.

It's Anna's altar.

So this is where she comes in the night. I've heard her creeping around when she thinks we're asleep. I know I should get up and see if she's all right, but I can't. During the day I try to be a good mother, but night is different. It's my time with Rob; when I put on his pyjamas, curl up in our bed and conjure him. I can't share my nights with anyone else, not even my own daughter.

But the thought of her coming here month after month, to commune with her dead father, is more than I can bear.

I survey the room again. Rob's painting shirt lies on the floor. I pick it up. A line of grime runs round the neck. I bring it up to my nose and there it is, faint but unmistakable: his smell. Sweat and musk and hair.

How can he be dead when I smell him so clearly?

I see myself in his cracked mirror: a scarecrow woman with wild red hair whose amber eyes glitter as she clutches a tatty old shirt as if it were the Crown Jewels. The afternoon sun, suffusing the room with light, suddenly disappears and I feel detached from reality. Floating. The smell is alive. Rob isn't. Then the tears come. And I curse him for dying, pounding my fists on the table, scattering brushes and paints. The bit that's still in control hopes Singing Vic isn't giving a music lesson next door, but mostly I don't give a toss.

Eventually it's over. I feel purged.

And the room is just a room.

A bolt of energy surges through my body. I have superpowers. Within an hour I've moved the large canvases. I decide to vary things a bit and move some smaller objects. I'm scrabbling about under the table when I see a grey metal box.

It's locked. I didn't know my husband had a locked box.

I'm torn between an urgent desire to break it open, and an equally strong impulse to leave it be – throw it away even. Is it a hidden stash of cash, or another Will leaving everything to a second family in Surbiton?

Pandora-like, with a knife and a hairgrip, I prise open the lid, but the box is empty except for a grubby pack of cards, some dice and a piece of paper that says *I owe Robin Thorn £2343*. It is signed *Vic Verdi* and dated a month before Rob died.

Singing Vic.

Rob, Singing Vic and Guy Gropius, our neighbour on the other side, used to have the occasional game of poker for fun, but I didn't realise they played for money. Rob always said it was for matches. So why the locked box? Maybe Singing Vic really did owe him £2343. In which case, why hasn't he said anything?

Or paid it back?

He knows how poor we are.

Singing Vic is a jobbing opera singer, who gives private lessons between gigs, plus doing a weekly stint at Churchill Towers. His real name is Victor Green, but he changed it to Vittorio Verdi. His father was a Liverpool docker and Vic has inherited his powerful, squat frame and barrel chest. He's a good-natured, straightforward Scouser. The only deception I've ever been aware of is the Italian accent he assumes for impressionable private pupils.

I thought I knew him. Maybe I don't. I know him as a good neighbour, not a close friend. And now he owes me money. If booty from a game of poker is something I wish to claim.

Anyway, I can't face raising the subject. It's far too embarrassing.

I'm in the kitchen looking for a box to store all the paints and brushes in, when I'm interrupted by a roar. It's Anna, back from school.

She's in Rob's room. Not for the first time, I'm struck by her strange beauty. Although she's only fourteen, Anna's already five foot nine and wand-thin. The combination of Caucasian and Caribbean has produced in our daughter a striking amalgam of features: blonde Afro curls, honey-coloured skin and luminous hazel eyes. Now these eyes are blazing. Anna looks like a Pre-Raphaelite angel barring the faithless from heaven with a flaming sword.

'You've no right to come in here and steal him. I hate you.'

I say that as his widow, Rob's urn is my property. Technically she has stolen it from me. I explain why I've dismantled the studio. I say that we'll recreate it in the shed, which was Rob's plan anyway. But she's implacable.

'You've destroyed him.'

'No. That was the bastard who mowed him down.'

'He was always here, and now he's gone.'

She takes the urn, the photo and the candles to her room. She stays there all evening, refusing supper, and I've no idea how her first day at Churchill went because she's not speaking to me.

The following morning she's gone before I'm dressed. As I peer through the curtains to check whether she's taken her packed lunch, I see her talking to the wretched Squirrel Man. They walk off up the road together.

He was older than Anna remembered. Late twenties at least. His skin was leathery and he had deep creases around his eyes, but the eyes themselves were beautiful: grey and clear. Lakewater on a wind-free day. In his left ear, a gold hoop earring, a tiny cross of seed pearls dangling from it, glinted as it caught the morning sunshine. His shoulder-length black hair made him look like the hero in one of those crap black-and-white movies on late-night TV.

'Want to see something good?' he asked her.

Anna thought of all her mother's warnings about strange men. Particularly strange men who asked if you wanted to 'see something good'. However, after the destruction of Dad's studio, her mother had forfeited any right to interfere. Besides, the man wasn't a stranger. He'd wept with her over the dead squirrel. Given her his scarf. Dad always told her to be open to life's adventures. If he were here, he'd be gabbing away nineteen to the dozen with Squirrel Man.

'What?' She crossed her fingers, praying that he wouldn't unzip his jeans and produce his penis. She wondered what to do if he did.

But his hands were nowhere near his flies. Instead he held them out to her, palms slightly cupped.

'Look.'

There, motionless, sat a strange, angular creature. It was brown and thin, all knobbles and joints.

'It's a stick insect.' The grey eyes met hers. She was shocked by their intensity. 'You'd never notice it, because it's like a twig. I found it on a broken branch. It must be an escaped pet. Stick insects don't breed in the wild here.'

Anna looked at the small creature. 'Stick Insect' was the name some girl at school had called her yesterday.

'I have to go,' she said, and turned away.

Squirrel Man fell into step beside her. All the way to school he talked about the life-cycle of the stick insect. At the gate he left her.

'Bye,' he said, and didn't seem to mind when she made no reply.

FOUR

For the next three weeks, Anna walks to school and back with Squirrel Man. I ask what they talk about and she tells me to mind my own business.

'You *are* my business. I don't want you striking up friendships with strange men.'

'If you can destroy Dad's studio then I can talk to strange men.'

'You're fourteen years old, madam—'

'Fuck off.'

'Don't you dare swear at me—'

But she's gone. Off to school early, with Squirrel Man who's set up camp opposite our house.

Finally, one day when Anna is closeted in her room, I confront her admirer as he lolls against the railings.

'What are you doing?'

I hadn't taken in his age, which is at least thirty. He has beautiful, smoke-grey eyes.

'Is Anna in?' His voice is soft, lilting, Irish.

'Why are you watching my house?'

'Could you be fetching her?'

'She's fourteen years old. Leave her alone.'

'Will you see if she'll come outside? I need to ask her something.'

'Aren't you listening to me? I said go away.'

'Is Anna in?'

'Will you please go away.'

'I want to ask her out. To the zoo.'

'Are you deaf? *Go away.*'

'She likes the zoo.'

'I'll call the police.'

He smiles. 'She loves animals.'

'Get lost.'

'Is she in?'

'Piss off!' I'm shouting. People in the park turn and look in the usual London way – indifferently curious.

'Is Anna in?'

I leave him. The man's a fruitcake.

Anna's in the kitchen.

'You mustn't have anything to do with that man, Anna. I've just been talking to him and I think—'

'You've what?'

'I asked him to go away.'

'You told my friend to go away?'

'He's not your friend. He's a total stranger.'

'To you.'

'He's not normal.'

'What's normal?'

'He's off-beam.'

'Don't know what you mean.'

'I've just failed to conduct a sane conversation with him.'

'You think that's *his* fault?'

'He's been lurking around for weeks.'

'You just can't leave things, can you?'

'Anna, the man is loopy.'

'Always on my case . . .'

'Listen—'

'I make a friend and you want to ruin things.'

'He's not—'

'Not middle-class?'

'Don't be stupid. He's away with the fairies. And he's at least thirty. You're fourteen.'

'He's a friend.'

'Oh, please. What exactly do you think a thirty-year-old man wants with a schoolgirl?'

'I'm not going to jump into bed with him. We don't all have your dirty mind. You're just jealous now you don't have a man of your own. You probably fancy him yourself.'

I see in Anna's eyes that she knows she's gone too far, and I realise that I want to go even further and thump her – something I've only done once when she was three and ran into the road without looking. Just like her father. Maybe if I'd thumped him, things would be different and he'd still be with us. We glare at each other and then once again – an increasingly familiar move – she flounces upstairs.

Danny appears, and with impeccable timing announces the news that he's forming a band with his new friends, Dwaine and Delroy, and can they use the shed for rehearsals.

'Of course not. It's your father's studio.'

'He's hardly going to be using it much.' Danny sees my face. 'Sorry, Mum. But it's true. And the shed's massive – there's room for me and the lads without going anywhere near Dad's stuff.'

'Those paintings are very valuable. I'm supposed to

be calling the gallery to talk about a memorial show. I can't risk them being damaged. Sorry, Dan, you'll have to find somewhere else.'

'Like where? Dwaine lives on the tenth floor of some shit block of flats and Delroy and his mum have a two-room flat.'

'You'll just have to use your initiative.'

'But I've already said it's OK.'

'More fool you.'

Danny has always been easygoing. Problems roll off him with a shrug and a smile. Even Rob's death hasn't made him lose his cool. He's been my rock during the past nightmare months, dealing with the funeral arrangements, reassuring me about the change of schools, looking after Anna when I was too low to get up in the mornings. Danny's been just about perfect. But it looks like the worm is about to turn. I've never seen him so angry.

'Do you know what it's like, starting a new school at seventeen?'

'I thought you liked Churchill. You said it suited you much better than Westminster. You were pestering for the change even before Dad died.'

'I do like it . . . but it's hard – breaking into things. Like they all grew up together, and they call me "Rich Boy" because of my accent, and I know more than they do, thanks to Westminster, so I have to pretend to be stupid in case they think I'm showing off. Do you get me? It's not easy.'

'It's no picnic for me and Anna either. But it will get better, I promise.'

'You've always told me to make the best of bad situations. Jamming with Dwaine and Delroy's the perfect way to make things work for me. They're good guys and we've got things in common – like music – and if we could just set up this band . . .'

I look at my son, so eager, doing his utmost to make things good, looking like Rob on a mission. Looking like Rob, the young Rob, the skinny boy with the big eyes that I first fell for . . .

What does a dead person's stuff matter compared to lovable, living Danny finding his feet at Churchill?

'OK. But there'll be hell to pay if any of you so much as breathe over those paintings. And it's deathly cold in there – you'll have to use our old electric fire, or you'll all die of hypothermia.'

My reward is a rib-crushing hug.

'You're a star, Mum.' He's out of the room, dialling his mobile.

'Danny . . .'

'Yeah?'

'Has Anna said anything to you about Squirrel Man?'

'No.'

'Don't you think he's strange?'

'What do you mean?'

'He stands outside our house for three weeks, he walks her to school every day and he's at least thirty. I spoke to him today – he's really weird – and she's so defensive – won't talk about him. What are we going to do?'

The light fades from Danny's face. He's suddenly older, bowed with responsibility. I'm hit by a massive twinge of guilt. What am I doing? I realise how much I've relied on his cool competence. Me, the great feminist, I've played the helpless little woman with my son like I never did with his father. He's not my husband.

He's not Anna's father. He's a seventeen-year-old boy who's lost his dad.

'I'll talk to him,' he says.

'No . . . it's just me being daft. Go on, disappear. Stardom beckons.'

'Are you sure?'

'You heard. Get lost, before I change my mind.'

I don't know whether I've convinced him, but he goes anyway and I make a resolution that whatever's happening between Anna and Squirrel Man, I'll sort it without Danny.

I turn on the news. The newscaster is announcing the discovery of a girl's body. In the Consort Park area of North-West London.

After giving the good news to Dwaine and Delroy, Danny went down to the shed. Wicked! It was perfect. His father's paintings were propped against the wall down one end, leaving loads of room for the band. In one corner was a plan chest, full of drawings. Danny preferred Rob's drawings to the paintings. They felt more personal. He pulled a sketch from the top drawer: his mother breastfeeding him. Her expression was one he knew well: a mixture of tenderness and mischief. She'd probably been teasing his father about something while he drew. She used to do that a lot. He sighed. Not any more. Lately she'd lost her sense of humour. He missed it. Like he missed his father. He didn't usually brood about missing Dad because there wasn't any point. It wouldn't bring him back. But being surrounded by Dad's work, he was suddenly overwhelmed by loss. His eyes burned with the effort of not shedding tears. Dwaine and Delroy were due any minute. It wouldn't do anything for his reputation to be found moaning like a baby.

FIVE

In the staffroom this morning there's a lot of talk about the dead girl. Apparently she was an ex-pupil – Susan Bradley. A little cow by all accounts, who was expelled in Year Eight for running an extortion racket to part Year Sevens from their lunch money. When one foolhardy child refused, she beat him up so badly he was in hospital for a week.

What goes around comes around.

The police haven't released details of her death. They're coming in today to talk to the students and staff who knew her. Rumour has it that she was found near Consort Park Station, with a slit throat. I feel shaky. I tell myself it's the thought of 8C, who broke three chairs and cracked a window in my lesson last week. In reality I know it's something else.

I need to talk to Jess.

She's in the English storeroom. Churchill has become a non-smoking school this term and Jess, never knowingly parted from her pack of twenty, has various little hidey-holes where she can pursue her vice undetected. Leo's other innovation for the new school year is a complex system of security cameras. He says it's to guard against intruders, but Jess sees it as part of his bid to win Control Freak of the Year Award, with herself as the system's first casualty. She's crouched in the corner under a tiny camera whose beady eye surveys the shelves of tatty Shakespeares and ancient poetry anthologies.

'Fucking undignified if you ask me, darling,' she wheezes. 'I'm too old for all this PC health bollocks. Most of the little shites smoke twice as much as us anyway.'

Jess is a charismatic teacher – passionate about her job and her students. She loves them all, however mad or bad, and they know it. That's why she gets away with her sewer mouth, when any other teacher would have been the subject of an Education Department tribunal before being banished from the profession. There seems to be a staff-pupil conspiracy to protect Jess and her profanities from the politically correct Thought Police for, unbelievably, no one has ever lodged a complaint against her. She always speaks her mind – loudly and forcefully – and she'd be a total pain were it not for her commitment, kindness and generosity. Her Achilles heel is Leo Ratchett. She thinks it's his mission in life to get rid of her, in spite of her unfailingly excellent exam results – the best in the school. She genuinely believes that his real reason for installing the cameras is to catch her committing some massive misdemeanour. This is why she's being uncharacteristically furtive about the smoking.

She and I met as students and have been best friends ever since. A shared sense of humour and a dislike of bullshit are the rocks on which our friendship is based. Over the years she's seen me through the vicissitudes of life and death with a temperamental artist, and I've picked up the many pieces of her invariably disastrous love affairs. I'm godmother to her son Lozz and she's Danny's godmother. I would trust her with my life. Since Rob's death I've been very bad at keeping up with friends. I haven't been able to face people. Jess is the only exception.

I tell her about my encounter with Squirrel Man, and my uneasiness about the dead girl.

'He's a sad little fucker who's got a crush on Anna. I can't see the harm in it if he just sticks to walking her to school.'

'There's just something about him . . . And now this dead girl . . .'

'You're such a drama queen. If he's been outside your house day and night, he'd hardly have time to go off and murder anyone. And if he had, unless he's completely stupid, he wouldn't hang around waiting for the police to crown him chief suspect. Anyway, Susan Bradley was such a little arsehole I dare say there's a queue of suspects a mile long who wanted to do her in. I was sorely tempted myself once or twice when I took her for English. We had a staff party when she was permanently excluded.'

I find this new term for kicking someone out quaintly bureaucratic. In my earlier teaching incarnation, miscreants were either suspended or expelled. Now it's temporary exclusions or permanent exclusions. There's something faint-hearted about it. Lacking in conviction. I can't imagine God, for example, permanently excluding Satan from Paradise. It doesn't have the same ring to it.

I'm pissed off by Jess's lack of sympathy.

'I'd like to see you being so casual if it were Lozz being stalked.'

'Lozz is different.'

Lozz has Down's Syndrome. He's Jess's only child, the result of a brief liaison with a married dentist. She adores him.

'Anna's a bright girl. If she thinks this guy is OK, you've got to trust her.'

'He's at least thirty. What's he want with a fourteen year old?'

'What does Anna say?'

'That he's just a friend.'

'Well then. Trust her. She needs friends right now.'

I hear something in Jess's voice. 'What do you mean? What's wrong?'

'For fuck's sake, woman, calm down! Nothing's wrong – nothing specific. Just a feeling . . .'

'You've known Anna since she was born. If you think there's something wrong, then there probably is.'

'Maybe . . .'

'Is she not making friends? Perhaps everyone's ignoring her.'

'Quite the opposite. The in-crowd have claimed her for their own. She's Ms Popular.'

'In-crowd?'

'Crystal Johnson, Athy Petros et al.'

'Doesn't sound like they're your favourite people.'

'They're terrific. Very lively kids – great fun. But not Anna's type.'

'What do you mean?'

'Bit loud. Bit brash. Bit in-your-face.'

'Like you and me? People often ask why a retiring little violet like me has a friend like you.'

'Oh ha fucking ha. I just thought she'd choose a couple of the quiet kids to chum up with.'

'I hope this isn't the start of the big teenage rebellion. I don't think I could hack it right now.'

'Perhaps that's what she needs – to do a bit of posing and posturing. What's she like at home?'

'Still blaming me for destroying Rob's room.'

'Does she mention school?'

I now add guilt to my other anxieties. I've been so absorbed in my own problems that my children's transition from pampered private school pets to inner-city comprehensive survivors has been pushed to the back-burner. Last night Danny had a go at me, and now Jess. Anna may be living it up with the wild bunch at school, but at home she's very quiet. No smiles. No jokes. She spends most of her time in her room. She hardly talks to me and Danny at all. And she's still wandering at night. I've assumed it's all to do with Rob's death. But is it? I should make more effort to talk to her, but it's as much as I can do to keep myself emotionally afloat and functioning, let alone anyone else. I stagger to the end of each day relieved that I haven't shattered into a million pieces.

I've been neglecting her. I must do something about it.

'What are those girls' names?'

'The last thing Anna needs is Mum-the-Teacher blundering into her new social scene.'

'I just want to put names to faces.'

'Promise you'll leave it?'

'Promise.'

'Crystal Johnson and Athy Petros.'

I know who they are. I remember passing Anna's

class lined up in the corridor one day. I didn't want to embarrass her by saying hello, so I was scurrying past, head down, when a small girl with pointed features and the olive skin of the East Mediterranean called out: 'Is that your mum, Anna?' And the pneumatic girl next to her said: 'She don't look like you – 'cept for the height. Is your dad black, Anna?' When I looked at them, they both beamed and chorused: 'Hi, miss.'

They seemed very friendly. A bit loud perhaps. But OK.

The lesson bell rings. Jess stubbs out her fag on the bottom of her shoe and slips the butt into a plastic bag hidden behind a stack of *Romeo and Juliet*.

'Tell you what – the fuzz are in asking questions about Susan Bradley. Have a word with them about Squirrel Man. Set your mind at rest.'

Leo Ratchett surveyed the security monitors in Fred Borrage's office. Studying the footage was his daily treat. He loved the feeling that his all-seeing eye could protect and guide the hundreds of souls under his care. He looked at the back-field monitor. Huddled under a tree, some boys were passing something around. Leo jotted down names. A visit to Year Eleven at some point today would be in order. On another monitor, a hunched figure scurried out of the front gate. Leo made another note. Time to remind staff that they were expected to stay on-site during their free periods. He turned his attention to a third monitor: Jessica Mackenzie emerging from the English stockroom with the new Drama teacher.

They were laughing.

Maybe at him.

After Mackenzie locked the door, she looked straight

up at the camera, gave it the finger and mouthed something. It appeared to be, 'Sit on this, Lenny boy.'

Leo sighed. Was the woman omniscient? How she hated him. He wished she'd resign. He'd thought that's what she'd do after she failed to get the Deputy Headship. But here she still was – flaunting her dislike, humiliating him whenever possible, making his life as difficult as she could.

If only she weren't so popular . . . He'd do anything to be rid of her.

He studied the two women. Laurel and Hardy – Mackenzie's flabby bulk forcing the pin-thin Rosa into the wall. They seemed very friendly. Wasn't it Mackenzie who'd suggested Thorn for the Drama job? If he hadn't been so desperate to replace Joanne, after her pregnancy bombshell, he'd never have considered it.

He must have been mad, giving Mackenzie another ally.

But then again, Rosa Thorn was something else. Lovely, in fact. And if he could get her on-side, maybe he could kill two birds . . .

On another monitor he studied the police officers handling the Susan Bradley business. So unfortunate that they'd connected her with this school. After all, she'd left some time ago. Why weren't they focusing on her present school which, if he remembered correctly, was miles away. It wouldn't do Churchill's reputation any good at all. Or his . . .

The police were outside the gym now. Why didn't they use the office, where he could have kept tabs on them? He didn't like them nosing around. It wasn't good. Still, they wouldn't find anything incriminating at Churchill. He was sure of that.

SIX

The heart beats on till
Sharp blade pierces creamy throat
And obliterates.

Anna had found the ideal place: a walk-in cupboard in the Science Block, once used to store laboratory equipment. The shelves were still stacked with defunct and broken pipettes, test tubes, Bunsen burners with decayed rubber hoses and other bits of scientific rubbish. There was just enough space on the floor for a cushion which she'd smuggled in from home. It even had a tap, if she was thirsty. No one was allowed in the laboratory corridor during lunch, so she was safe from discovery, provided she was quick off the mark at the end of morning school and able to slip in there without the Science teachers noticing. Today she'd started her special project. Plasticine was the perfect medium. She still had to collect the other things, but she could bring them tomorrow. Now it was time to leave. She hid everything under a loose floorboard and grabbed her bag. Usually she waited until the bell for afternoon school, but today she was desperate for the loo. She opened the door and slid out.

Straight into a police uniform.

'What's the rush, sweetheart?'

A pudding-faced policeman blocked her escape. Beside him stood a very tall man. Even taller than Dad. He smiled in the way grown-ups do when they think you've done something silly yet funny. She felt hot all over.

'I was getting something for my teacher.'

She knew this sounded feeble, but it was the best she could do. She looked up the corridor, thankful for the absence of security cameras, praying that Dr Ingleton, the truly terrifying Head of Science, wouldn't appear.

'What's your name?'

'Anna Thorn.'

'OK, Anna, we're asking about Susan Bradley. She used to attend this school.'

'I'm new.'

'Do you live locally?'

'Yes.'

The tall man produced a photograph. His voice was gentle. Anna winced. Don't patronise me, she thought.

'Recognise her?'

Anna saw a plain, plump girl with a bad case of acne.

'No. Can I go now?'

The Inspector pretended to think. He scratched his chin and deliberated. 'What d'you think, Sarge?'

'Dunno, sir. Looks a bit suspicious to me.'

'Yeah. It's the eyes. If they're hiding something, the eyes swivel from side to side.'

She was outraged. And worried. Did they know what she'd been doing in the cupboard? Surely not. Then she felt herself blushing. They were teasing her. She hated them.

'I need to find my teacher.'

The tall man smiled. Floppy fair hair covered one eye, but the other twinkled at her. 'Buzz off.'

Anna felt very small. She'd almost escaped when he called after her: 'Haven't you forgotten something?'

Why couldn't they leave her alone?

'What?' she said rudely.

'Whatever it is you were fetching from that cupboard.'

Anna was reminded of someone. Dad. For a moment the stupid man sounded like Dad.

It happened all the time. Most men she came across nowadays at some point said something that made her think of Dad. She gave the two men her haughtiest stare.

'It wasn't there. My teacher must have made a mistake.'

Then she ran and didn't stop till she was safely locked in the girls' toilets.

I see the police at various points during the day. One uniform, one plainclothes. They've been given Primrose Pepper's office, but they roam the school, talking randomly to staff and students alike. I'm having a bad teaching day. None of my classes wants to listen. The only Drama taking place is my histrionics over their bad behaviour.

And I've broken the photocopier.

Fax Max the Media Resources Officer says it's probably irreparable, but not to worry, he won't grass me up. He's trying to create an intimacy between us – the concealment of my cack-handed destruction being the glue that binds us together.

I don't like Max. He's a slimy creep who constantly drools over the young female teachers. His idea of courtship is Ordeal by Blue Joke. This week alone, I've seen at least three young women edging out of the Media Resources office to the sound of Max braying with delight at his own punchline.

He also smells: BO overlaid with strong aftershave. It's disgusting.

At thirty-nine, I'm over the hill and spared his worst attentions, but even so he squeezed my ageing bottom as I was scrabbling in the bowels of the wretched photocopier this morning. When I last taught, we used Gestetners and banda machines, and we teachers did everything ourselves. On my first day, I had to ask Jess what exactly a Media Resources Officer was, after Dave Alessi told me to find one to help me with my work schemes.

This particular one's repellent.

I noticed him having a word with the detective earlier. What could Max know about poor Susan – particularly since, like me, he's new to the school this term. I suspect he's one of those blokes who gropes the girls, but smothers the blokes in instant mateyness. Who likes a finger in any dirty little pie steaming in the kitchen.

At the end of school, I look for the police. Marion, Leo's secretary, says they've gone, but as I leave the building I see the detective talking to some girls by the gate. Crystal Johnson and Athy Petros are there. Maybe they knew the dead girl. As I approach, the group breaks up. The man's doing a seven-league boot routine, and I have to run to catch up with him. I don't normally run – it's against my principles – but this time I make an exception.

'I'm Rosa Thorn. May I have a quick word?'

Amused blue eyes lock with mine. Amazing eyes – pale blue with a deeper, almost violet ring around the outside of the iris.

'That's what we're here for.'

I feel wrongfooted already – literally. My ankle twists and I stumble. His arm shoots out to steady me.

'It isn't about Susan Bradley. At least I hope it isn't. Or maybe it is . . .'

'Oh?'

'There's a man bothering my daughter.'

Do I detect a fleeting look of ennui? If so, it's gone instantly, to be replaced by the courteous interest of the professional listener. Behind that, I sense I've done something he finds highly amusing. Nonetheless, I'm going to say my piece, even if he does see me as a capering fool.

I tell him about Squirrel Man and Anna.

'He's been standing outside our house every day for three weeks. I've tried to talk to him but he won't listen. Or rather, he doesn't respond properly. There's something odd about him. Disconnected. And when I heard about the murder . . .'

'It's unlikely he has anything to do with Susan Bradley's death.' His voice is steady and reassuring. Not London. Public school with a dash of something else. I'd like it if it weren't for that hint of mockery.

'How do you know?'

'I can't divulge confidential information, but the girl had problems. It's becoming less and less likely that anyone else was involved in her death.'

'You mean it was suicide?'

'I can't say.'

I feel a huge rush of relief. Squirrel Man's not a killer. I realise how much I've overreacted. As usual. However, he's still a stalker, and he's still very odd, and I want him gone.

'Couldn't you charge him with stalking?'

'Not if your daughter says he's a friend. Under the present legislation, we could arrest him if *she* perceives him as a threat. But it doesn't sound like that's the case.'

'*I* perceive him as a threat – won't that do? She doesn't realise how dangerous he could be. She's a minor and he's twice her age.'

'Has he made any sexual advances?'

'No.'

'Has he been violent?'

'No.'

'Then I'm sorry, but there's not a lot we can do.' He glances surreptitiously at his watch. I could kill him. Smug, self-important oaf. I want to cry. If the police won't help, what else is there?

I must be looking agitated, because he suddenly relents and asks, 'Where do you live?'

'Opposite the park.'

'I need to drop by Consort Park nick. You're on my way. I'll stroll down with you and have a word with him.'

He's not an oaf. He's a saint. I'm so grateful I have to stop myself from falling at his feet and kissing them.

When we reach home, Squirrel Man has chosen that day to be absent. I feel a complete idiot.

'This is the first day he hasn't been here,' I mutter. The policeman must think I'm a fantasist as well as a fool. His mouth twitches slightly.

'Not to worry. If he comes back, call Consort Park police station and they'll send an officer to have a word.'

A sop to the over-protective mother. He turns to go. I can't bear it.

'Why don't I make you a coffee? He *will* be back.'

He glances at his watch again. I do something I loathe: I beg.

'Please. Just for a few minutes. I'd be really grateful.'

I can see him weighing it up.

'Tea. Milk, no sugar.'

I take him upstairs to Rob's studio because it's easy to spy from there. As he follows me up the stairs I'm aware of his eyes boring into my back. I'm suddenly conscious of being alone in the house with him. This is the first time since Rob's death that a man has been up here. I feel a bit weird, even though he is a policeman. I wonder if I'd feel the same if he were squat and ugly instead of being, quite frankly, a bit of a hunk.

'Nice room.'

'It was my husband's painting studio.'

'Taken up trainspotting instead?'

'He died.'

The teasing glint vanishes. 'I'm sorry.'

'And it wasn't a hobby. He was an artist.' Now who's wrongfooted? 'I'm going to rent it out as a bedsit. Sit down. I'll go and make your tea.'

For the first time he smiles properly at me, without the teasing edge. It's a good smile – slightly crooked.

'Did you say your name was Thorn?'

'Yes.'

'I think I met your daughter today. Anna?'

'That's right.'

'She's like you.'

'Hardly.'

'Not physically, but there's a quality that's very similar. Or maybe it's that you both spend your lives blundering into people and getting cross about it.'

He's laughing at me openly now, but this time I don't mind. He tells me about his encounter with Anna.

'She must miss her dad,' he says.

'Yes.'

'Poor kid. I'm very sorry.'

I never know what to say when people commiserate about Rob. Do I say, 'Thank you,' or, 'It's OK,' or, 'Don't worry about it'? I always have the urge to make them feel better, to take away the embarrassment that death brings to the unbereaved. Not with this man though. I can see the word embarrassment isn't in his vocabulary. I also see dawning recognition.

'He wasn't Robin Thorn? The Doors man?'

Well, slap hand, Rosa, for assuming that Plods know nothing of Painters. Not that Rob hadn't achieved a certain small notoriety with the general public. As an artist who painted large detailed representations of closed doors, and nothing else, he'd had several 'But Is It Art?' moments with the tabloids over the last year of his life.

'Yes.'

The man's eyes glow with the fervour of a true enthusiast.

'I'm a fan – actually I own one of his small studies from the Barn Door series.'

I must be looking dumbstruck, for he laughs.

'Just because I'm a policeman it doesn't mean I'm a complete barbarian. Your husband was a great painter. It's a tragic loss.'

I feel a pricking behind the eyes and can only nod and rush off to make the tea.

Then we sit for what seems a very long time, during which there is neither sight nor sound of Squirrel

Man. I wish that I could be at my sparkling best – not only to keep him here until Squirrel Man returns, but also because . . . Because what? I don't know. But I can think of nothing interesting to say. I've shot my bolt getting him here and persuading him to stay. My head is empty of small talk – any talk. He doesn't feel the need to speak at all. He just leans back in his chair and gazes out of the window. I'm reminded of big cats at rest in a safari park. There's a contained power in the long limbs and a concentrated intensity on his face that speaks of the ability to move into frightening action at a split second's notice. Eventually he stirs.

'Gotta go. If he comes back, phone the nick.'

'Can I ask for you?'

'Sorry. I'm not based at Consort. I'm with AMIT up in Hendon.'

'What's that?'

'Area Murder Investigation Team. The local cops call us in to solve any murders on their patch.'

'Oh.' I feel strangely put out. 'I'm sorry to have wasted your time Mr . . . ?'

'Tom Brice. All part of the service, Mrs Thorn.' The mocking edge is back.

'I wasn't inventing it. He's been here every day for three weeks.'

'I really do have to move.'

'Sorry.'

I'm talking to a retreating back. He's down the stairs and out of the door, punching up numbers on his mobile before I can say *The Bill*. As far as he's concerned, my problems are already history.

I wish.

Squirrel Man will turn up again.

Like a bad penny, as my granny used to say.

'Something tells me I'm into something good.'

Tom Brice whistled the old 1960s number and felt that for once it was true. All the way up to Hendon he luxuriated in the unfamiliar feeling of happiness and well-being. He was still whistling when he entered his office, deep in one of the buildings of the former police college.

'You're a happy bunny today, guv. Won the lottery, have we?'

'You could say so, Steve. In a manner of speaking.'

As he made his way to the interview room where Kevin Binns waited to be charged with the murder of his two-year-old stepson, he felt that things were indeed finally slotting into place. New job, new flat, new life and maybe something else – bigger than all the rest rolled into one.

And yesterday's revelation from the builders that the flat had to have a new roof and a complete rewire, far from plunging him into despair had, today, given him an idea that would kill two birds with one stone.

Life was good. Life was perfect.

He opened the door to the interview room. The pasty face of Kevin Binns stared sullenly up at him. Tom placed the photographs of baby Jason's battered and burned body on the table in front of the young man. He was hardly more than a child himself, he thought.

'Morning, Kevin. Care to take a butcher's?'

Kevin's eyes slid sideways.

'Can't face it? Didn't seem to bother you when you were doing a spot of ironing on Jason's backside.'

'I want my brief.'

'He's on his way. Won't do you much good, though. You're in for the long haul, Kev my son.'

What had been going through the boy's head when he cracked open the baby's skull with the iron that he'd just used to make patterns all over the child's body? It was Tom's job to find out. Before the end of the day he'd know exactly what made Kevin Binns tick. He put to the back of his mind his plans for a wonderful future, and concentrated on the here and now: the bead of sweat trickling down Kevin's forehead, even though the interview room was distinctly chilly.

SEVEN

Fox. *Vulpes vulpes.* A vixen will often hide food for her cubs, but is content to share with an extended group if necessary.

Suddenly, Squirrel Man's gone. Anna pretends she doesn't care, I am ecstatic, and Danny, caught up in his band, hasn't noticed. He says I'm not to call it a boy band. It's a fusion of UK garage, drum and bass, and hard rock. He says I am to be particularly careful about boy-band banter in the presence of Dwaine and Delroy. In fact, he says, I'm to be particularly careful about any kind of banter with them.

I like getting to know my children's friends. It makes me feel we're not living our lives in separate universes. However I've obeyed Danny to the letter. I'm Mama Cool when they're around. As Delroy and Dwaine pad through the kitchen on their way to the shed we exchange grunts and that's that, and when I do utter more than two words, I try not to make them cringe-making attempts at teenage argot. I am, however, furtively insinuating myself into their good books by taking van-loads of food down to the shed at well-regulated intervals and casually dumping them on the table before slipping mutely away. As a result, they are beginning to come to me. Yesterday I noticed Delroy lingering in the kitchen, shifting from foot to foot. I asked if there was anything I could do for him. It was his mum's birthday, he said. What could he buy for her with £7.34? He and I were having an interesting debate about the merits of body lotion over frilly knickers when Danny came in and spoiled it all by hustling his friend off to the shed. As he left, Delroy gave me a brilliant smile, and I felt humbly grateful to be tolerated by such a nice young man.

Dwaine's a different kettle of fish: bright, funny, energetic. There's a lightning quality in him which could achieve great things – Danny says it's Dwaine who has most of the ideas for the group – but I've noticed that he finds it hard to focus his attention for more than a minute at a time, and I sense an anger churning away inside him.

I've started to wonder whether he's on something.

His dad left a year ago. Dwaine was Daddy's boy. Now he won't have anything to do with him. Dangerous waters. Dwaine's mum Charlene is the canteen supervisor at school. Maybe I should talk to her? But what do you say to a total stranger? 'Charlene, I think your son's on drugs.' 'Charlene, there's an indefinable current of rage flowing through your son and I don't want my son to be affected, so sort it.' I don't think so. If Danny found out, I'd be dead meat – and anyway, maybe the whole thing's my purple imagination. Perhaps I'm oversensitive at the moment. I must concentrate on the fact that Dwaine's one of the main reasons that Danny's now well settled at Churchill Towers.

Which is more than can be said for my daughter.

Since my talk with Jess I've been studying Anna, and something is very definitely wrong. Something unconnected with Rob's death, or the studio débâcle. Anna's basically a motormouth, like me. The two of us could natter on for hours. Rob and Danny would laugh at our appetite for endlessly viewing and reviewing problems. Not any more. I know she's angry about Rob dying, and that the studio business is a good excuse to unload that anger onto me, but it doesn't fully explain her behaviour. She looks dreadful, and most of the time she doesn't speak. Her silence isn't the muteness of suppressed anger but a terminal listlessness. She says nothing's wrong. School's fine, friends are fine, work's fine. And it's true that whenever I see her at Churchill, she's surrounded by exuberant teenagers, looking bright-eyed and bushy-tailed. It's home that turns her from Miss Jekyll into Ms Hyde. She says she's just a bit tired. I drag her to the doctor who prescribes a tonic. It makes no difference. It's two weeks now since Squirrel Man's desertion and I ask between gritted teeth if it's him she's missing. She tells me not to be stupid.

Life was simpler when my children were little: a straight question from me got a straight answer from them. Now it's like crawling through enemy territory on your belly in the dark, knowing one false move will blow everything sky-high.

Maybe Anna and Dwaine should get together and share their problems. I could lock them in a room and say, 'Let it all hang out, folks, so the rest of us can stop worrying.'

What is it with me at the moment? I'm now obsessing about Dwaine. I hardly know him, for God's sake!

Then I have one of those illuminating flashes that occur only too infrequently. The reason my justified concerns about Anna and now Dwaine are becoming irrational is that there's a free-floating anxiety permeating everything I do. It isn't connected with anything I can articulate. It's not confined to people – it's also seeped into my surroundings.

I've lived in Consort Park for nearly twenty years. Rob and I moved here after we got married and I've always loved it. It's my idea of the perfect London village: small, friendly, but not too friendly – with the bright little park itself and its Edwardian bandstand, and statue of Prince Albert, the jewel in the neighbourhood crown. But since Rob's death I've only once been for a proper walk in the park: the day before I started at Churchill. It took all my willpower and determination and I only lasted ten minutes before rushing home. I can't seem to dissociate it from the accident. That dreadful day is imprinted on my consciousness with a merciless clarity. Now I see the park as my enemy. Not wonderland but wilderness. Out to get me in some way. I go through it when I have to, but I keep my head down. What am I avoiding? The spectre of my former happy life, maybe, or the memory of that journey through the crocuses towards the children when I registered every gnarled tree trunk, every twist and turn of evergreen berried hedge, every blade of thin winter grass as the distance between us narrowed and I could see the crazy disbelief on their faces.

The familiar cast of Consort Park characters has also taken on a parodic unreal aura which leers and threatens. I avoid them all as I rush through the park on my daily business. Mary the Hologram, so called because of her ability to be seen gossiping at either end of the Park at the same time, now seems like the Angel of Death, scattering misery and misfortune in her wake. If I see her, I take a different path to avoid being pounced on. Jules, Jacques et Georges arguing over their morning game of boules have assumed the aspect of the Furies, spinning my fate as they crouch down in the dirt of the boules pitch, and Prince Albert, like Rob, untimely taken, looms over everything, darkly brooding. Singing Vic has twice asked me in for tea with him and his mother, and is obviously hurt at my refusal, but with him at least there's a reason for my avoidance. The knowledge of the IOU hangs over me like a giant question-mark. The days are shortening, and the leaves are falling, to reveal the skeletons of the trees beneath. Usually I love autumn in the park. It reminds me of when we moved here on a mellow October day when the copper and yellow leaves floated down and mingled with the long afternoon shadows and I felt my real life had begun. Now the bare branches of the semi-naked trees look twisted and ravaged, and the light is grey, not gold.

It's worse at night. Then the park's a whole other world where owls, foxes and rats lurk, predatory in the darkness, ready to kill and maim and eat. At night the city moves out and merciless nature moves in. Last night something happened which left me shaking and soaking wet with perspiration. I drifted into wakefulness, navigating the shoals of memory and misery which loomed out of my waking consciousness. The window was open and I stared out at the great forest trees creaking and bending in the darkness. I tried to morph into an altered state where somehow I'd find Rob. I fixed on the dark void beyond the trees, eyes wide and unblinking, willing a connection. It didn't happen. Instead I seemed to shrink and fade in my bed. I tried to touch my arm, but it felt as if my fingers were passing through it. There was nothing corporeal left for me to grasp. And as I became smaller, so the world outside the window grew and grew. It wasn't a windy night, but I became aware of a wave of cold air rolling into my room.

Except it wasn't air.

It was breath.

It was the world breathing.

And with every breath, I dissolved. I experienced, properly *experienced* – in my gut, not my brain – the vast indifference of nature, and with it the disappearance of everything that made me feel safe. Even the walls of the house were insubstantial. There was no barrier between me and the cold, meaningless universe.

I lay there, paralysed, till the terror receded and I was left quivering and quaking, back in my own sweat-soaked skin. Then I forced myself to move. Feeling the blood pulse through my fingers as I closed the window made me weep with relief.

I'm dreading tonight in case it happens again.

Consort Park was once a horses' graveyard, and recently I thought I heard faint whinnying. A dead brewer's nag, or one of the Four Horsemen of the Apocalypse? Famine, Pestilence, War?

Or the other one.

Death.

Or am I just falling apart?

I feel a lump of dread inside. I don't know where it came from, what it's about or how to get rid of it. To everyone in my life I'm Rosa Thorn, coping bravely with her husband's death. Rosa the mother, making the usual mistakes in her usual bungling way. Rosa the returned teacher, eagerly embracing pedagogy after fifteen years away from the chalkface. But I'm not sleeping, and my body's in a permanent state of adrenalin arousal. I'm waiting for something.

I just wish I knew what it was.

EIGHT

Glittering, gold girl
Blazing out on autumn day
Topaz eyes shine bright.

Spring forward. Fall back. The clocks have changed and I walk home from school in the dark. Our road is a black tunnel, intermittently illuminated by the faux Victorian lamp posts that Consort Park Residents Association campaigned for long and hard. The light they shed is strictly localised, and I scurry between the small yellow pools pretending I'm not nervous. I've been tramping the streets of London all my adult life, unaccompanied and with no fear, but now I can't swallow because my mouth is dry and my heart's hip-hopping behind my ribcage. It's been like this every day since the nights closed in. Anna comes home alone, and if she's later than me I try not to pace the floor waiting for the sound of her key. I know that as a young male, especially a young mixed-race male, Danny's more likely to be targeted, but in spite of my feminist beliefs I'm still more fearful for my girl. Or is it the spectre of Squirrel Man looming over us?

Tonight, as I reach my gate, the dread feels heavier than ever. The house is in darkness. I curse Rob for not installing the porch-light he promised for so many years. I doubly curse him because he's not there for me to say, 'I told you so.' If there's an afterlife I'll get some of my biggest kicks from being able to zap him with all the I-told-you-so's. My knees begin to tremble.

Someone's waiting for me, crouched down in the doorway. I'm not imagining it, because I can hear slight movements. I should run next door to Singing Vic, but my feet won't move. I clutch my keys in my fist, the tips between the knuckles as a weapon.

'Who's that?'

No reply. Just the sound of someone shifting their position.

'Who is it?'

I hear a soft exhalation of breath and I shoot back to the gate. The street's deserted. In the distance a police siren howls. The coldness of the metal gate under my fingers jolts some sense into me: my mobile.

'I'm calling the police!' I shout.

Nothing, except another almost imperceptible breath.

My shaking fingers refuse to go where my brain tells them and I drop the phone into the pyracantha bush whose prickles tear my hands when I try to retrieve it. I hear a laugh, low and threatening. Rage kicks in. How dare he lurk in the dark, trying to frighten me? I won't be threatened on my own doorstep. I run back to the porch. The noises are louder now. He *is* laughing at me. Furious, I lunge forward and fall flat on my face.

My hand is touching something warm and wet. It's

whatever's making the noise and the noise is not laughter. I feel hysteria rising . . .

Then I hear footsteps and a voice. Anna.

'Mum?'

Before I can stop her, she's helping me up, and opening the front door. Light floods out, illuminating the porch and I look down.

On the step lies my oppressor.

Not human at all.

A cat.

Its white fur is covered in blood, oozing from the spot on its head which once housed an ear. Next to it is a glistening, glutinous thing. I don't recognise it at first. Then my stomach heaves.

It's an eye, still attached to the bloodied socket by the thinnest of slimy strings. Every now and again the cat's mouth opens and it wails. How could I have confused that noise with laughter?

Anna screams.

NINE

WPC Black is from the North. Her manner is lugubrious.

'I'm from the Community Action Team.'

She peruses the cat from every angle before allowing Anna to take it inside and call the vet. She also examines the doorstep and the path for clues. There's nothing except the piece of purple material where the cat was lying.

'Isn't that a bit odd,' I say, 'to mutilate the animal so horribly, and then wrap it up like a baby?'

'When you've come across as many nutters as I have, nothing's odd. Can you describe the man you think might be responsible?'

'About five ten, dark shoulder-length hair, grey eyes, gold earring – looks a bit wild. Irish accent.'

I tell her about Squirrel Man and his disappearance after the death of Susan Bradley. I describe my feeling of foreboding that seems connected to him, but I sound feeble and unconvincing. I can see WPC Black wondering whether I'm as mad as the cat butcher. She asks to see Anna, who has to be dragged away from her patient and who is adamant that Squirrel Man is not responsible for the atrocity.

'Whatever Mum says, it's not him. He would never do anything like this. He loves animals.'

'How well do you know this man?'

'He's a friend.'

'But you only met him recently.'

'So?'

'What's his name?'

Anna scrapes her foot across the carpet. She can be as obstinate as her father when she chooses.

'Some friend,' says WPC Black, 'if he won't even tell you his name.'

'Anna,' I say, 'you must tell us.'

'I don't know anything.'

'What did you talk about with him?'

'Animals. He knows all about the wild animals round here. Like he says nowadays there are more foxes in cities than the country.'

'Where does he live?'

'Don't know.'

I can tell WPC Black would love to give Anna a piece of her Northern mind.

'Whoever did this is a nutter. Next time it might not be a cat. It might be your mum.'

For the first time Anna looks uncertain. WPC Black pursues her advantage.

'Your friend might have an alibi. Then he'll be in the clear.'

There's a silence. Then Anna mutters something unintelligible.

'Pardon?'

'He's called Mick.'

I can't keep silent. 'It would be a bit of a coincidence if it wasn't him.'

'Why?'

'He's the only odd thing to come into our lives lately.'

'Is he?'

'What do you mean?'

There's a look in her eyes that I can't fathom, but all she says is, 'Chill out, Mum.'

WPC Black interrupts. 'Anything else you can tell us that would help find him?'

'He travels about a lot. He mentioned various festivals he'd been to.'

'And you haven't seen him now for a couple of weeks?'

'No.'

Anna's lying. I can tell. So can WPC Black.

'Come on now, spit it out. You've seen him, haven't you?'

'No.'

I'm losing patience. The effects of the shock are beginning to wear off and I'm tired and ratty.

'For God's sake! If he's out to hurt anyone in this family you should realise where your real loyalties lie.'

If looks could kill I'd be well on the way to joining Rob.

'He didn't do it.'

'Then he won't mind us talking to him. If he's been watching your house he might even have seen something. He could help us catch the real criminal.'

WPC Black has cracked it. Anna's face lights up.

'Yeah.' She looks at me. 'Then you'd have to thank him.'

'Yes,' I say through gritted teeth.

'The day after that girl was found dead, I was walking back from school and he grabbed me. He looked really upset. He said he had to go away for a bit and would I still be his friend even though he wasn't here.' Anna looks ruefully at WPC Black. 'Some friend.'

'Did he say why he had to go?'

'No. But he was frightened.'

'Could it have anything to do with Susan Bradley's death?'

Anna's moment of goodwill passes.

'First you say he butchered the cat, now you're insinuating he butchers people. You are *so* wrong. Can I go now?'

I'm about to wade in, but a warning glance from WPC Black stops me.

'That's it for now. If your friend did nothing wrong, he needn't worry about us. Off you pop. I just want another word with your mum.'

After Anna has gone, WPC Black says, 'Keep an eye on her. She knows more than she's letting on. I've got all the details now. There's nothing more we can do tonight. I'll submit an incident report and if anything else happens let us know.'

'Is that all?'

'For now. I'll tell the other Home Beat officers to keep a special eye out for the next few days.'

'Will you try and trace him?'

'I'll have a squint at CRIMINT, the police computer, but if he hasn't any previous he won't come up. To be honest, from what Anna says, he sounds pretty harmless. I don't see him doing something like this.'

I can't help asking my big question again.

'What about him and Susan Bradley?'

'Him disappearing the day after she was found doesn't really constitute a connection. Anna said he travels about. He could be off with one of the fairs or anything. Besides, although we're still waiting for the post-mortem results on the girl, we're pretty sure we know what happened.'

'What?'

'Sorry. You'll have to wait till the inquest.'

'When will that be?'

'Months. Anything up to a year.'

'You're joking!' I can't exist in this state of uncertainty for up to a year. I need to know now.

'Please tell me,' I say. 'For Anna's sake. It may sound like she doesn't care, but underneath I know she's frightened. She thinks he might have had something to do with it, and that means every time she sets foot outside this house she feels at risk. We can't let that go on until after the inquest.'

Across WPC Black's plain features a battle rages between duty and sympathy. Eventually she sighs and looks round furtively to make sure her boss isn't concealed behind my sofa.

'If it gets out that I told you, I'd lose my job.'

'My lips are sealed.'

She frowns. I realise she finds my delivery a bit frivolous, so I assure her with all sincerity that we won't betray her trust. It does the trick.

'Her mum kicked her out and AMIT thinks that in a fit of depression she slit her throat. It's nothing to do with your stalker. I will check on him, though.'

'But basically, you'll do nothing.'

'No, Mrs Thorn, I said we'll look into it.'

All of a sudden, I feel very tired. 'OK. Thanks for your help.'

After I see her out I realise I'm starving. I'm dialling for takeaway pizza when Anna rushes in.

'I've found a vet. He'll see us now.'

I replace the phone. I'm so weary that this simple act takes up what remains of my energy.

'And who's going to pay for it?' I snap. 'Vets don't come cheap.'

One look at Anna's desperate face tells me exactly who's going to pay. I grab my purse and my car keys.

'Let's go.'

Anna sat in the back of the car with the cat. She stroked its blood-matted fur and willed it to survive.

'Poor thing,' she said. 'Poor little thing.'

She made herself look at the lump of flesh that had once been an ear, and the empty, gaping eye-socket.

Mutilated, she thought. Part of it's been ripped away. Like me.

TEN

The cat lives. And has become part of the family.

Everywhere I go, there it is, glaring malevolently at me with its remaining eye. It doesn't seem to recognise my part in its good fortune. It hissed at me earlier today. I whispered into its surviving ear, 'You're on borrowed time, sunshine. One false move and it's cat pie.'

It's worth it if Anna is comforted.

Not that there's much chance of that. She looks worse every day. I've questioned her till I'm blue in the face about school and she insists it's fine. I've also interrogated her teachers, and they think she's settled well and is popular, though a bit quiet. I've initiated conversations into which I cunningly insert questions about new friends and what she does in the lunch-hour, and how about joining some after-school clubs. But Anna can spot a subtext from five hundred paces. A couple of days ago, in desperation, I asked her if she'd like to bring anyone home for tea.

'When I'm ready, and only if you promise not to interrogate them.'

So I'm incredibly relieved that today she has, finally,

brought people home: Crystal Johnson, Athy Petros and another girl whose name I didn't catch.

They seem very fond of Anna. I watch them surreptitiously from the window as they walk up the road. Crystal has her arm around Anna's shoulders and Athy's linking arms with her, while the other girl skips in front, giggling. Now they're laughing and joking in the living room.

I take them some biscuits and drinks in order to have a little snoop.

'Anna, your mum's really nice,' says Crystal. 'My mum would never give us stuff like this and, like, wait on us.'

Anna scowls at me. 'Mine doesn't usually,' she says.

Athy screams with glee. 'You're so horrible to your mum, Anna,' she shouts, giving Anna a playful punch. The other girl giggles. Is that all she can do? I haven't yet heard her say one word.

'Did you want something else?' Anna looks pointedly at the door. I know an exit line when I hear it. I take my cue and leave.

After they've gone, I remark in an offhand way to Anna that they seem very nice.

'Yeah.'

'Who was the other one?'

'Laxmi Patel.'

'She seems nice.'

'Yeah.'

'I'm glad you've made some nice friends.'

'Yes. They're all very, very nice. Nice girls, nice friends. I'd love to chat but I've got loads of homework.'

Miss Jekyll obviously went home with the girls.

Trying not to sound huffy, I say that I too have things to do, and march off to make supper, which Anna doesn't eat. Then I go up to Rob's ex-studio. Or should I say ex-Rob's studio. Or ex-Rob's ex-studio.

I've given it a coat of brilliant white silk finish, fixed up some roller blinds, and Guy the Groper has done me a laminate floor and a cupboard. Guy's my next-door neighbour on the other side. He took a Double First in Philosophy from Cambridge, then decided the life of the mind was too taxing, and became a carpenter instead. His private life is a disaster area, with three divorced wives and at least seven children. His nick-name comes partly from his surname – Gropius – and partly from a tendency to be a bit touchy-feely with everyone, male and female alike.

Along with Singing Vic, he was one of Rob's neighbourhood buddies, although he's always been a bit wary of me. I have, over time, become friendly in a casual way with all his ex-wives and several serious girlfriends. Guy thinks they tell me things about him. He's right. I know more about the inner workings of his relationships than I do about my own. Consequently he steps around me with great caution.

I have to admit though, he's been great about helping with Rob's room. Every time he comes to the house I wonder whether to raise the matter of the poker games. Somehow I can't bring myself to do it, and have to content myself with praising his bevelled edges.

The room's looking good. Ready to let. I've been dragging my feet a bit because the thought of a stranger in the house is still something I can't get my head round. But the current bank statement arrived yesterday. Not good news. So tomorrow I start the ball rolling. I'll put up a notice in the staffroom first. See if there are any takers. I don't fancy a complete stranger.

Particularly after the past few weeks.

I'm off strangers.

WPC Black tells me that Mystic Mick isn't on the police computer, but that the police are keeping an eye out. However, I haven't noticed regiments of burly bobbies parading up and down outside our house. I haven't actually seen so much as one teeny tiny baby bobby. And there's no more news on Susan Bradley's death. Certainly no official announcement of suicide. The only thing the school has heard unofficially from the police is that the post-mortem revealed a cocktail of drugs in her body. As a result of this, Churchill Towers is to hold a Drugs Awareness Day for each year-group, featuring workshops, videos and pep talks from police, youth workers, bereaved parents and reformed addicts. I don't know what good this will do. The students are all too aware of drugs as it is, and horrific videos featuring people shooting up and then dying only serve the instructional purpose of showing them exactly how to apply a tourniquet and insert a syringe correctly.

My cynical thoughts have taken me over to Rob's window. Now the trees have lost most of their leaves, I can see into the park even at night. My heart jumps. There's a dark shape in among the trees.

Squirrel Man.

He's weaving his way from tree to tree, crouching and creeping, as if hiding. The gates are locked at sunset so he shouldn't be in there. I phone WPC Black. She promises an immediate investigation. I spend the next twenty minutes trying to keep him in sight. Eventually I see two figures near the tennis courts. I can't bear squinting out of the window any more, so I go downstairs and make a coffee.

The doorbell rings. WPC Black.

'The good news or the bad news?' she says.

'Just tell me what happened.'

'He's promised to leave you and your family alone.'

'And?'

'He's got a new job. As a gardener. In Consort Park.'

Being turfed off her tea-break to chase loonies round a park at night was not her idea of a good time. But if it got Rosa Thorn off her back, then all well and good. It also got her out of the canteen, away from Bill Wicks and his mates who'd been teasing her about Tom Brice. Now he'd moved from Consort Park nick to AMIT, they kept needling her about her supposedly broken heart – just because she'd been assigned to work with him more than any of the other WPCs. They couldn't be more wrong. She didn't remotely fancy these graduate, sensitive types. They were talking out of their arses, as usual.

As was Rosa Thorn.

The Irishman wouldn't hurt a fly. When she'd found him in the park he was crouched down behind a bush. When he saw her he put a finger to his lips and motioned her to watch. She bent down to his level, and saw a vixen and her cubs playing in a clearing. The moonlight caught the red fur and amber eyes as the animals rolled on the ground.

'It's the first time she's let them out to play,' he whispered.

She had to coax him away from the animals to talk about the Thorn family. It was like chatting to a small child and nothing in his attitude led her to believe he meant Anna Thorn any harm, or that he'd dumped a mutilated cat on their doorstep. She left him writing notes in a grubby little book and made her way to the Thorn house.

ELEVEN

Feral creatures watch.
Rus in urbe, wild and free.
Parallel worlds here.

His name is Mick O'Brien. He's been unemployed and is well pleased to get the gardening job. The Head Parkie asked him to check out night-time urban fox movements, which is why he's in the park after hours. Yes, he'd hung around our house, but he meant no harm. Anna's a friend who shares his interest in animals. He knows nothing about the mutilated cat. He loves animals. He never knew Susan Bradley. He's been in Ireland seeing family. He recognises that he has frightened the lady with the red hair and the black clothes, and promises not to do it again. Obviously, as a park gardener he might have to work near our house a lot – probably every day, but he's sure the nice officer understands there's not much he can do if it's required in the course of his duties.

Studying urban fox movements?

Please.

He's the only urban fox I see round here, and if he

thinks he's going to sink his teeth into my little chicken he can think again.

WPC Black – whose name, believe it or not, is Penny – is sure Mick O'Brien isn't dangerous. I say, waspishly, that he obviously has her stamp of approval, but she doesn't register the joke. She says he has a legitimate reason for being in the park near our house, and that therefore there's nothing the police can do. She promises, however, to keep an eye out for him, and also to recheck the police computer now she has a name.

I wish I had her confidence. The bad feeling's strong again tonight. Why did you die, Rob? You should be here to protect your family, not lurking in an urn, reduced to a handful of ash. I'm so angry with you. Why didn't you look before you crossed that road? Too bloody arrogant, that's why. You always assumed everything would stop for you, even speeding cars. Miscalculation, Rob. Thanks a bunch, sweetheart.

After Penny Black leaves, I creep into Rob's room in the dark and peer out. A man leans against the chestnut tree near the gate. He's smiling. The smug smile of someone who thinks he's pulled a fast one.

Well, Squirrel Man, you may have convinced Anna and the police that you didn't dump that cat on my doorstep, but I've got your number. One step out of line and I'll be on your back like a ton of nutty slack.

I ring round my immediate neighbours and explain the situation. I'm gratified at the violence of their reaction. I always thought we were a peaceable bunch here in Albert Road. Apparently not. Everyone's outraged that the police should allow such a man to hang around outside my house, ogling my daughter, and they vow to monitor Mick O'Brien twenty-four seven. One wrong move on his part and the entire population of Albert Road might form a posse and string him up from one of the faux Victorian lamp posts. Singing Vic's mother, Marge – who came down from Liverpool twenty years ago to keep house for Vic till he found a wife, and is still here, living in hope – is particularly indignant.

'It's the bloody Micks. They're all the same – dirty little gyppos. If I see the mucky sod so much as blink in Anna's direction, I'll have 'im with my popgun.'

For a split second I feel sorry for Squirrel Man. Singing Vic's mum conducts an ongoing war of attrition against the local squirrels who persist in launching commando raids on her bulbs. She's an ace shot. I wouldn't fancy his chances if she sets her sights on him.

Vic himself was adamant that at the first sign of trouble we were to call him.

'I'd do anything to protect that girl. I love her like she's one of my own.'

Steady on, Vic. You don't have any of your own. Is that guilt driving your protestations? If you're so keen on protecting my child, what about coughing up the money you owe, to give her an easier life?

Guy the Groper was surprisingly bellicose for one so chilled.

'I'll have a word with my mate Barry. He knows some seriously unpleasant people, Barry.'

With friends like these . . .

I feel better after my phone calls. Danny, Dwaine and Delroy appear and I bring them up-to-date. Danny's really annoying. Everything about his attitude implies that I'm making a drama out of a crisis. Freed from the constraints of Westminster School, he's grown his hair over the summer and wears it in shoulder-length braids.

It suits him and he knows it. I've noticed when I see him in school nowadays that he's always surrounded by at least three or four girls, all competing for his attention.

As it seems I am now.

He lounges against the dresser looking at me with his father's eyes, and smirking as I rail against O'Brien. I want to shake him. Mick O'Brien's not a problem. He's just a sad git. Ignore him and he'll go away. As for the one-eyed cat, maybe someone thought we'd give it a good home. No problem. No sweat. For a moment, I'm reminded of my conversation with O'Brien himself. There's the same bizarre mis-connection. He opens his mouth and I know what he's going to say.

'Danny, if you tell me to chill, I'll throttle you.'

'Cool. Come on, guys. Show-time.'

I was a little cheered to hear Dwaine say, as they walked away, 'Your mum's right, man. I wouldn't want no looney tunes slobberin' after my sister.'

Dwaine's sister, as it happens, is Crystal. I'm sure she's fully capable of looking after herself when faced with the Mick O'Briens of this world. But Anna?

Anna is in her room, engrossed in homework.

'You've been at it for hours. It's bedtime. What are you doing?' I pick up her book, but she snatches it away.

'Leave it.'

'Pardon me for showing an interest.'

'It's an English essay for tomorrow, so can I get on with it?'

'You shouldn't spend two and a half hours on a Year Nine English essay. That's an A-Level workload. I'll see Jess. It's too much.'

'NO!!' Anna's eyes blaze. 'Don't you DARE complain to Jess.'

I'm shocked by this sudden ferocity.

'I won't say a word. But it's not fair to overload you like this. It's not the first night you've spent hours more than you should on homework. I thought it was independent schools that overworked students, not comprehensives.'

'I'm new. All my courses are different. I've loads of catching up to do. I've got pages and pages of notes to copy up for all my subjects. Just leave me alone.'

I couldn't face telling her about The Return of Squirrel Man. Like Scarlett O'Hara, I thought – tomorrow is another day.

Anna stared at the blank sheet of paper in front of her. One down, two to go. Her eyes prickled with tiredness. It was so tempting to lie down on her bed and drift off into blissful sleep. She focused on a sepia photograph on the wall, of an Edwardian woman wearing a huge hat swathed in feathers. The flinty eyes and strong jaw belied the frivolity of the feathers. It was her great-grandmother, a formidable woman who'd left school aged ten to work in a cotton mill. Rosa had told Anna many stories about Nana Bates, including her legendary ability to produce the perfect adage for any situation life might throw up. Anna remembered the favourite.

'There's more than one way to skin a cat,' she muttered, staring at the photograph. Her great-granny stared back.

'Needs must when the devil drives,' she agreed.

After the rehearsal Danny walked Dwaine and Delroy to the end of the road. Instead of peeling off towards the estate, Dwaine turned towards Kilburn.

'Where you going?' said Delroy.

'Ask no questions, you'll be told no lies,' said Dwaine, and loped off into the darkness.

Danny and Delroy avoided looking at each other. Something was happening that neither of them wanted to acknowledge.

'Night, bro,' said Delroy. 'Great session tonight.'

'Yeah,' said Danny. 'Laters.'

As he walked home he wondered what to do. He didn't want anything to endanger the group. It was the only good thing to happen in this pissy year. It could be the future. It could be everything.

TWELVE

Magpie. *Corvidae. Pica pica.* A bird universally condemned for spying on garden birds in order to destroy and pillage their nests.

The following morning O'Brien is planting bulbs next to the railings. He gives me a cheery wave with his trowel and I fume all the way to school. I'm early today. Leo wants to see me.

Marion, Leo's secretary, is waiting for me. She's rake-thin and has the pop-eyed stare caused by an over-active thyroid. Much of her hair has fallen out, giving her the look of a balding turkey. Everyone knows that working for Leo has caused this galloping alopecia, but Marion insists it's a virus. She would die for Leo. She follows him from school to school leaving a trail of disgruntled, demoted secretaries in her wake. Leo calls her his PA. He thinks it sounds more cutting-edge. Jess says she's in love with him.

'If he asked her to eat his fucking shit she would.'

According to Jess, Leo's brooding good looks and invalid wife are a double whammy to a certain type of woman. The Needys, she calls them. Women whose men are dead, divorced or disaffected. His soulful eyes, chiselled profile and melodious voice draw them in while the invalid wife gives him tragic-hero status and keeps him safely unavailable.

Jess claims Leo has surrounded himself with these women. She says that as old staff leave they are replaced by highly competent, emotionally-damaged women who are putty in his long pale hands. All except her.

I told her about my summons.

'He wants something,' she says immediately. 'Guard your weak spots. He'll home in on them like a fucking heat-seeking missile. Don't say yes to anything until you've checked with me.'

Sometimes I get tired of Jess's rantings about Leo. I wish she'd allow me to make up my own mind.

'He'll see you now,' says Marion, and I climb the spiral staircase to the Observatory. The Head is looking at London through a huge telescope mounted on a brass swivel stand.

'Earth hath not anything to show more fair . . .' He gestures vaguely, encompassing the capital. 'Come.'

He shows me how to adjust the focus and I'm amazed by its powerful lens. To the north I can see the hills of Hampstead and to the east the shabby shops of Kilburn disgorge their even shabbier customers. Kilburn never disappoints: it remains the steadfast rock of threadbare grimness it's always been. Nearer home, Guy the Groper is outside his house, handing something to a small fat man, and further down the road Singing Vic is on his mobile, gesticulating operatically. In the park Jules, Jacques et Georges are having one of their Gallic rows. These three came over with the French Resistance in 1940 and never left. They fell for a woman who ran a cake shop on Willesden High Road. Eventually she tired of doing everything as a foursome, particularly as she didn't speak French, so she married a jeweller and moved to Penge. The Free French, as they're known, were devastated and took a vow of celibacy. They opened the first French bistro in North London, and have been here ever since, arguing viciously with each other about anything and everything, particularly pétanque or boules, which is their obsession since retirement.

I become conscious that Leo's well within the eighteen inches of my personal exclusion zone. He smells of peppermint and Penhaligon aftershave. It's a heady mixture for quarter past eight in the morning. I start to feel a bit giddy.

'It's a great city to send our kids into,' he muses, and I feel his warm breath on my neck, 'but do we prepare them properly? Sometimes I feel it's like sending lambs to the slaughter . . .'

He smiles and says with self-mocking pathos: 'It's a lonely job, steering the good ship *Churchill* through the storm-tossed seas of teacher shortages, inadequate funding and constant new government initiatives.'

The combination of his close physical presence and his appeal for my sympathy is having its effect. He smells so nice. So masculine. A recently published study claims that women are turned on by men who smell like their fathers. I know my grumpy, bigoted Lancashire dad wouldn't be seen dead wearing aftershave – 'poof's perfume', he used to call it – and all I ever remember him smelling of was Woodbines and sweat. But Leo's pheromones must be putting out something, for I'm well on track to join The Needys and succumb to what Jess calls 'his dodgy charisma'. Then, through the telescope,

I see my daughter walking to school. She's talking to someone. No prizes for guessing who. I return to reality.

'You wanted to see me?' I ask.

'Are you happy with us, Rosa?' Compassion flows from his navy-blue eyes. 'It can't be easy, after what's happened to you this year . . .'

I mumble something inarticulate. Leo touches me gently on the arm.

'I know what it's like, you know, bearing the burden of caring alone.' His eyes slide towards a photograph in a silver frame placed prominently on his desk. It's the invalid wife. Jess's face flashes across my retina. I suppress a hysterical giggle, and I know I'm safe. No more Ms Needy.

'I'm fine, Leo,' I say. 'Did you want something specific? Only I've some paperwork I was hoping to finish before school starts.'

He's good at reading people. With a smile, and a shrug, he forges on to the meat of the matter. He wants a Christmas show. He knows I'm on a supply contract and therefore under no obligation, but he's appealing to my better nature . . . the deprived inner-city children and how they'd benefit, blah blah . . . the great good fortune for the school having a professional actress on the staff, blah blah . . .

He's good. I can see why TV companies love him. Jess says the thing about Leo is that he's a thesp. There's not necessarily a word of sincerity spoken, but the performance is so compelling nobody notices. Except her.

Well, I'm a thesp too. It doesn't mean I'm not sincere when I say things. Just that the saying is rather emphatic. Jess is too hard on the man. I tell him I'll think about it.

He bounds ahead and opens the door.

'If there's anything that you ever need to talk about, my door is always open.' He smiles. 'I'm a very good listener.'

'I'll remember that, Leo,' I say, and run off to find Jess before school starts.

Rosa Thorn's wonderful hair shimmered off down the staircase. Leo watched until she was out of sight. What a woman. A strong, vibrant woman. A woman to share things with. Things he couldn't tell another living soul. If only his longterm plans could include someone like her. Well, why not? Why should she not become close to him? Then he remembered her best friend. How could he ensure Mackenzie didn't poison Rosa's mind against him?

He was so preoccupied that Marion had to remind him about Assembly. His theme that morning was 'Thou shalt not covet'. He smiled. He coveted Rosa Thorn. He coveted her very badly indeed.

THIRTEEN

One is for sorrow
Wrapped round the heart like a vice
Two is for fierce joy.

I'd forgotten that today is Year Nine Drugs Awareness Day, and so it's wonderful to discover that I'm off timetable, accompanying 9Y through various talks and workshops. This might give me the mental space to think about how to tackle Squirrel Man.

But any supervision of children is incompatible with thinking. By the end of the morning, I've broken up three fights, persuaded the first speaker, a former heroin addict, not to relapse after half an hour with 9Y has driven her to think that being stoned is an infinitely better option than living in a world full of children like Ryan Potter and his friends, and returned a social worker's briefcase having found Shireen Jackson trying to stuff the contents down the toilet. I'm completely frazzled as I shepherd 9Y into the hall for their pep-talk from the police.

I'm surprised to see Tom Brice on the platform. He has a look on his face that says don't mess with me. 9Y immediately quieten down. How does he do that? I feel a twinge of envy. He spots me and winks. I think I've imagined it until the small boy on my left says, 'He winked at you, miss.'

'Nonsense, Ahmed,' I say. 'It's a trick of the light.'

I feel disproportionately pleased.

The man gives a storming performance. Without talking down to the kids, he presents a devastating case against drug use, peppered with stories of overdose tragedies, families torn apart, young lives in ruins, all from his experience as a police officer. He seems genuinely upset by the things he's encountered. This large policeman, all six foot four of him, speaking of the death of a young girl after her first Ecstasy tablet reduces the room of restless adolescents to silence. They're riveted, and so am I.

Afterwards, I congratulate him.

'You've missed your calling. Maybe you could come and give me some tips on how to be an effective teacher.'

His habitual mocking expression slips and he flashes me a wry smile.

'The little buggers scare me stiff. I used to work at Consort Park before I joined AMIT. This is a left-over date. I was hoping to get out of it but my old guv'nor was a bit stuck, so I said I'd do it.'

He asks about Squirrel Man. I tell him about the mangled cat, and Squirrel Man's new horticultural career path.

'Do you know Penny Black?' I ask.

'Yeah. She's a good officer.'

'Says she can't do anything. Still, at least we've got a name.'

'Oh?'

'Mick O'Brien.'

'Rings a bell. Dunno why, but it'll come to me. If it's something you need to know I'll call you.'

'Thanks.'

Then there's one of those silences that happen when people have run out of conversation. Except I get the feeling it's just me who's finished. Brice fiddles with his tie as if there's something he wants to say.

Whatever it is, he can't quite spit it out, so after a few more awkward seconds I say, 'I'd better be off – things to do, kids to kill et cetera. Well done again for your talk. It was great.'

I'm heading towards the canteen when he catches up with me. He looks embarrassed. He wants a favour – I can see it in his eyes. I also see that he hates asking.

'You said you were going to rent out a room. Is it still available? I'm looking for somewhere quite urgently.'

This stops me in my tracks.

'I've just bought a flat and it's being done up so I can't live in it for a couple of months. I'm on a friend's sofa at the moment, but I don't want to outstay my welcome. I need somewhere a bit more settled and your house would be ideal – not too far from my office in Hendon and near all my old mates at Consort Park.'

I'm someone who has to go at her own pace. I don't like being hassled; I have to feel in control. So although I'd planned to put the advert on the staffroom noticeboard today, I say, with the card burning a hole in my bag, 'Sorry, I've offered it to a cousin.'

He looks devastated and I nearly change my mind. But I don't. It's nothing personal. It's just that I really am not ready. It's taken this to make me realise it.

Knowing the devious way my mind works, I suspect that I would accidentally-on-purpose have forgotten to put up my notice today anyway. For several days, probably. Until I was just that bit more reconciled to having a stranger living in my house. Using my bathroom. Cooking meals in my kitchen. Seeing me looking repulsive in the mornings.

'Sorry,' I say again, more firmly.

His extraordinary blue eyes meet mine. I blush. He's a detective. Trained to recognise liars.

'Fair enough,' he says. 'Here's my card. If your cousin drops out, give me a bell.'

'Of course,' I say, effusive now the danger's past. 'She's had a bad time recently. I couldn't very well say no to her. Such a pity. It would have been really great to have you as a lodger.'

Never apologise. Never explain. Rosa, you've told a whopper and now you're expanding it into a full-length novel. No need for complicated elaboration. Brice cuts across my babbling.

'Where's the Media Resources office?'

'I'll show you.'

'Just point me in the right direction.' He can't wait to get away. He's obviously fed up. I've rarely seen anyone disappear so fast.

After school I see him in the playground, surrounded by admiring Year Nine girls. Anna's new friends are part of his fan club, batting their eyelids, wiggling their bottoms, talking in overloud voices, and blatantly attention-seeking.

Not Anna. She stands apart, hunched and mute. I walk over and hug her.

'Cheer up. It might never happen.'

She pushes me away. 'With you around it happens all the time.'

'What?'

'Don't touch me,' she hisses. 'Not here.'

'Anna . . .'

'Go away!'

She's shouting. The group around the Inspector stop twittering and start staring. Brice has forgiven me – the teasing look is back in his eyes.

'Hello again, Mrs Thorn. Is this your daughter? Hi.'

Anna scowls at him, marches across the playground and out of the gate. The fan club sniggers.

Witnessing your children's bad manners is peculiarly humiliating. In front of him, of all people – the man to whom I'd told a giant porky only hours before. I mumble an apology and follow Anna.

'How could you be so rude? You disgraced both of us.'

'It's bad enough you teach at Churchill without you slobbering all over me in front of everyone. Stay away from me at school.'

'I give up. Don't come crawling to me for a bit of TLC when you next feel the need, because I shan't be there.'

'Fine.'

We've reached Albert Road. I can't be in the same house as my daughter right now. The thought of her brooding in her corner and me fuming in mine is too much. I should persevere, persuade her to tell me what's really the matter. But I can't do it. I'm at the end of my own particular rope. Not mother enough today. I want Rob. Badly. Anna was Daddy's girl. He'd be able to deal with her now. I can't.

I walk over to Kilburn for some retail therapy. I can't afford to buy anything interesting, so I go to one of the Everything-for-Under-a-Pound shops on the High Road. I buy cleaning materials and a new colander. I'm paying at the checkout when someone taps me on the shoulder. It's Charlene Johnson – Dwaine and Crystal's mother, clutching six packs of Christmas cards at 75p for a dozen. I didn't think she knew who I was.

'Good value here,' she says.

'Sure is. Fifty pan scrubs for a pound.'

Charlene laughs. 'You planning on doing lots of cooking, girl?'

'If there's a world pan-scrub shortage, you'll be laughing on the other side of your face.'

'I just want to say I'm real glad Dwaine's taken up with your boy. Danny have this calming influence on him.'

Is this the moment to bring up my suspicions about Dwaine's little habits? I think not. I need to know Charlene a bit more before dumping that one on her. However, a little fishing expedition wouldn't harm.

'Has he always been so . . . high-spirited?'

Charlene laughs. 'High-spirited! That a good one.' Then she sighs. 'When he was little he was always full of ideas – tings to do, games an' such-like, but since his dad been gone it different. He never still . . . always talk talk. I say, "Dwaine, shut up boy, you givin' me a headache." That's why I'm so glad he friends with Danny. The music ting give him a focus.'

'Well, Danny's life's a million times better since he palled up with Dwaine and Delroy.'

'It's so kind of you to let them rehearse at your place.'

'No problem. I don't hear them. They're in a shed at the bottom of the garden.'

'So what the music like? Are they going to make a fortune and keep us in our old age?'

'Don't hold your breath.'

We smile at each other.

'And I'm very grateful to your Crystal. She's really taken Anna under her wing. I worried so much about her making new friends at Churchill. Actually, she's such a moody cow at the moment, I wouldn't want to be her friend.' The moment the words are out I feel incredibly disloyal. 'I don't mean it,' I say hastily. 'She's lovely normally, but with my husband's death, and a new school, it's all a bit much. That's why it's so great that she's got Crystal.'

'Pleased to hear it. Lordy, is that the time? I gotta rush. Nice to talk to you. Don't clean the bottom right out of your pans with all them scrubs, girl.'

I watch her zoom off into Woolworth's. Do I smell or something? It's the second time this afternoon someone's rushed from my side at the speed of light.

Back home, Anna's nowhere to be seen. Danny and the boys are in the shed. I know this from the indescribable noise drifting up the garden. Did I really tell Charlene I couldn't hear it? I notice a light on in Singing Vic's shed. Has he taken to gardening in the dark? Maybe it's a way of escaping from his mother. Then I see a figure slip out of the shed and drift down the garden towards the railway line. Not Vic – too thin. Someone's nicking their garden implements. I'm about to phone next door when Vic emerges from the shed. I move away from the window in case he thinks I'm spying on him. Curiouser and curiouser. Still, what Singing Vic does in his spare time is no business of mine. Except, perhaps, for his poker habit.

I'm cooking supper when the bell rings. When I open the door, no one's there. I step outside to check.

No one.

Then something wet hits my cheek. I look up. Suspended from the beam in the porch, steaming in the chilly autumn air, are two plump magpies whose black, white and blue feathers gleam as they catch the light from the hall. Their hot, fresh blood drips down onto the step.

Neither of them has a head.

I am not going to scream. I close the front door and pick up my bag from the hall floor. My hand is shaking so much that, at first, I can't undo the clasp. Gagging, I find a tissue and scrub the magpie's blood off my face. Then I rummage further, till my hand closes on a small business card. I go to the phone.

'Inspector Brice? It's Rosa Thorn. My cousin's had a change of plan. She's not coming. When can you move in?'

FOURTEEN

Tom Brice arrives the following day with two suitcases, a laptop and a CD player. He says if all goes well with his flat he'll only be here for a couple of months, but I don't care. I just want another adult body around – particularly a big strong male one who happens to be a policeman. I didn't sleep much last night, my head aches and I feel pressured by events into asking Brice to share my house, so my greeting is less than effusive.

'Is that it?'

'Most of my stuff's in storage.'

I take him up to his room. I'm proud of what I've created: white walls and blinds, stripped pine floor and cool blue furnishings. Minimal but comfortable. The ideal bachelor pad. He obviously thinks so too. He surveys his new home, and a smile spreads across his usually watchful face. Happiness suits him.

'Brilliant.' He catches my eye and his expression changes to concern. 'I don't want to get in your way, so say if I do anything that pisses you off. I work very odd hours, so I'm in and out – sometimes I'm away for days on end. I won't be a nuisance – you'll hardly know I'm here.'

Ashamed of my grudging welcome, I force my lips into a welcoming smile.

'I'll show you the bathroom.'

In spite of my misgivings, Tom Brice is the perfect lodger. He cleans up after himself in the kitchen and bathroom. He staggers his meals so they don't coincide with ours. I tell him he can watch our TV, but he stays in his own room playing music. I get the impression he reads a lot. His only request is do I mind him installing another phone line, and whether he can fit a lock on his door at his own expense, since some of his work is highly confidential? His way of saying, 'Keep out of my room.' I don't care. It'll be a selling-point for the next lodger.

The children are the only flies in the ointment. On the odd occasion that Tom coincides with the whole family, he tries to be nice, offering to help Danny restring his guitar, volunteering to de-flea the one-eyed cat, but they're barely civil to him. Even easygoing Danny responds in monosyllables when Tom attempts conversation, and Anna leaves the room if he appears. I'm ashamed of both of them. One morning I try to explain.

'They're still raw after Rob's death. They didn't want a lodger – particularly one living in his studio.'

'It's not a problem.'

'It is for me. I could throttle them.'

Tom is heading for the front door. 'If you do,' he says drily, 'I'll have to arrest you. Don't worry. It doesn't bother me.'

'I'm their mother. It's my job to worry if they're badly behaved.'

He heads off down the path. I follow. I wish he'd stand still. I feel like some irritating insect buzzing round his head. Any minute now he'll swat me.

'I just don't want you to feel unwelcome.'

'I don't.'

'You've been very good about not intruding. I really appreciate it.' Why won't he listen? It's as I feared: lodger equals stress. I can't handle it. He'll have to go.

Then I realise he's come to a halt. He leans on the gate, staring at me. Now I've finally got his attention I feel uncomfortable. He has an intensity that disconcerts me. When most people make eye-contact, their gaze flitters back and forth, engaging and disengaging. This man really looks. I feel as if my inner workings are exposed for him to examine. After a silence which goes on for a beat too long, he speaks. His voice is gentle.

'The kids don't mean to be rude. They'll come round eventually. I'm a big boy. I can handle a brush-off from two grieving children.'

I feel a complete heel. I wanted someone who wouldn't get in our hair, and he's exactly that. It's irrational for me to be irritated because he's exactly what I wanted him to be. He's never been anything but considerate and accommodating. However, I still can't hack the tension when he's around the children. Then my brain, as if by magic, delivers the solution.

'We're going about this the wrong way. Maybe keeping your distance isn't so good. The more they see you, the quicker they'll get used to you being around. Familiarity . . .'

'Breeds contempt?'

'I didn't mean . . .'

'I know.' He's laughing at me.

'I just think it might be better if you join in, instead of keeping your distance. If you can bear it.'

What am I saying? I wanted him to be Roger the Invisible Lodger, who emerges to pay his rent and disappears the rest of the time. Which is more or less what he does. So why am I now asking him to dive into family life and be everybody's favourite uncle?

Tom looks down at me. Again I get the uncomfortable feeling he can read me like the proverbial book.

'Let things happen at their own pace. It'll all work out . . .'

'Yes, but—'

'Must dash. See you.'

I feel like a silly child dismissed by the Headmaster. What an infuriating man. Thinks he calls all the shots. When he's said his piece, that's it. Off he goes. No thought for whether I've finished or not. Completely wrapped up in his own concerns. No wonder the kids don't like him. He's as rude as they are, but he's an adult so there's no excuse. Well, sod him. I don't care whether he feels excluded. From now on, he's on his own.

It isn't even as if he's shown any concern about Squirrel Man or the dead magpies. I thought he might have a word with O'Brien, who's turning our corner of the park into a horticultural paradise in his eagerness to stake out the house. But he seems to have no interest in the matter. Obviously a Murder Squad detective's too grand to chase stalkers. He leaves all that to the likes of Penny Black. So having my own pet policeman on the premises is worse than useless.

Penny came to examine the magpie corpses on the night they were left. She didn't have a clue what to do.

Said she'd never come across anything like it before, and took a perverse pleasure in her own floundering.

'Forensics'll have a butcher's,' she said, 'but there won't be any prints. Not on feathers.'

'Talk to O'Brien,' I begged. 'It's no coincidence that he starts stalking my daughter and then we get these incidents with animals.'

'I don't see as how it'll do much good – not without any evidence. He's hardly going to confess. Anyway, I can't see him doing a thing like this. He's dead keen on wildlife, from what I've seen.'

Why not start a Mick O'Brien Fan Club, Penny?

'Is there anyone else who might have a grudge against you or your family?'

I was about to say no, when Singing Vic's IOU came to mind. I pushed it to one side. Vic's very fond of our family. He's a friend. He was the last person to tend Rob before he died. And he was devastated.

Not so devastated that he coughed up his gambling debts. Or even acknowledged them.

But why would he start persecuting us? It doesn't make sense.

Unless he wants us to move. Get out of his hair so he doesn't have the guilt of knowing he's cheating a widow and two orphans every time he sees us.

I dismissed these ridiculous thoughts. This was my good neighbour of twenty years.

'No one has a grudge against us. Talk to other people who live in the street. Someone might have seen him.'

'Not with it being so dark. Ever think of having a porch-light installed?'

I hoped Rob was listening.

Penny's like Eeyore. She has the same streak of dull

pessimism. She's from Lancashire like my mother and has a similar doomladen take on life. It really gets to me, but I have to be nice in order to persuade her that O'Brien's dangerous. As a consequence, I waste ages serving her tea and listening to her gloomy tales of life and crimes in Consort Park nick. If she spends as much time with every member of the public who seeks her help, her clear-up rate must be abysmal. I mentioned my new lodger who was due to arrive the following morning.

'Tom Brice? Fancy.'

'Do you know him?'

'Yeah.'

'What's he like?'

'All right.'

'What's the goss, then?'

'One of those fast-track buggers. Think they're cleverer than the rest of us. Made quite a name for himself at Consort. Clear-up rate was the best in the nick. Super was really hacked off when he went to AMIT.'

'How old is he?'

'Don't be fooled by the baby blues – look past them and you'll see the crows' feet. At least forty.'

'No family?'

'Married – but it went pear-shaped recently. Always game for a laugh – good team-player. Can't say what makes him tick though.'

Talking about him had an odd effect on Penny Black. She became gruff monosyllabic – completely different from her previous verbosity – and soon after, she left, complete with two dead magpies. She either hates his guts, or has a crush on him. Whatever it is, it's affected her attitude to me, because she still sounded weird and unfriendly the next day when she phoned to say she'd talked to O'Brien and he'd denied all knowledge of the magpies.

'Surprise surprise,' I said.

I haven't seen Penny since. Which is good, because it means I've had no reason to call her. O'Brien's still around all day, sweeping up the carpet of red and gold leaves which cover Consort Park in November. My stomach doesn't lurch any more when I see him. I've stopped imagining he's going to abduct Anna every time I catch a glimpse. But I don't feel any better. In spite of having a policeman in the house, I still have a feeling of dread that's nothing to do with Rob's death, or my job. I've told Anna she's not to talk to O'Brien any more – that there's no room for negotiation here – and, to my astonishment, she's accepted this. I've seen her walk past him without so much as a glance.

I've also seen his face as he stares at her retreating back.

Penny scowled at her mountain of paperwork. How many trees did it take to process a criminal? And how many woman hours? She'd been with the Met seven years, but sometimes it felt like twenty-seven. She'd transferred from Chorley in pursuit of an insurance salesman from Croydon who turned out to be married, and somehow she never got round to going home. Thanks to his perfidy, she took a dim view of the South, reinforced by the relentless procession of robbings, rapings and killings with which she had to deal. Each one represented another example of London decadence. Penny felt steeped in vice, marinated in murder, a Northern crusader against Southern sin. In the previous week alone, she'd rescued an abandoned, lice-ridden four year old from a coal bunker, witnessed the sordid death of an addict down a sleazy alleyway, and comforted a woman who'd been gang-raped.

So she had no patience with Rosa bloody Thorn. People like her, with her education, her posh house and her striking looks expected everyone to come running the first time anything nasty spoiled their perfect lives. They treated the police as their own personal bodyguards. Therefore Penny wasn't about to launch a major investigation into the poor Irish bugger who'd taken a shine to Miss Spoiled Brat – particularly since Thorn had Brice's size twelves under her kitchen table. Penny hated Brice. She still burned with shame whenever she remembered the time she had asked him out for a drink. He'd turned her down. Later, she'd seen him in the pub with the lads. They were all sniggering and she just knew it was about her. She wondered how to use the information that he was Rosa Thorn's lodger. Officer in charge of Bradley case living with woman employed at victim's former school. Bit close to the line. The Super would undoubtedly be interested, even though Brice was no longer on his patch. For the moment though, she'd wait and see. She picked up her report on the dead magpies, and transferred it to the bottom of the pile.

FIFTEEN

Silence at daybreak
Then the morning comes with clear
Singing of the birds.

Tom Brice did listen.

He now joins us in the kitchen occasionally, cooking his meal as we eat. He's good at blending in, catching the mood of the day, and it never feels like he's crowding us. He doesn't say much, but what he does say is usually worth hearing. He has a fund of stories about the villains of North-West London, and he's totally unconcerned when Anna and I have one of our frequent shouting matches. I caught him and Danny exchanging wry glances the other day as I tried to persuade Anna not to spend hours on her homework and she shrieked at me to get off her back.

'Mums usually tell their children to do more homework, not less,' he said.

'Exactly,' snapped Anna. 'Thank you, Tom.'

I'm torn between relief that they're responding more positively to him, and irritation at his mockery. I'm also wary. Do I need him all over my house and my life, peddling his opinions? Now he's jumped out of his lodger compartment, will he jump back in if I want him to?

Still, it's good to have the occasional adult conversation over a cup of coffee after the kids have disappeared. He's easy to talk to. He invites confidences and his comments are usually spot on. And he teases me a lot in his dry way. Like Rob.

One of the things I miss most is the teasing.

However, there's still a reserve about him – a sense of things held back. One day, stung by a minimal, tongue-in-cheek response to a rather good school story of mine about Karen, Sharon and the chewing gum on my chair, I ask him why he's so quiet.

'Am I?'

'You never use ten words if one'll do.'

'Is that so?'

'And you nearly always answer a question with a question.'

'Do I?'

'There you go.'

'My job, I suppose. We're trained to listen and look – to absent our own personalities from the equation. Be a blank slate. If we let our egos get in the way, we miss things.'

'But something in you is obviously attracted to a job that needs those skills.'

'Probably being an only child. I spent a lot of time when I was young on my own, or listening to the adults – working out how they ticked. I hated it when the spotlight fell on me.'

'Then how come you're so good at public speaking? That talk on drugs was amazing.'

He smiles – the smile that, coming after one of his minimal comments, always seems like a special bonus, a gift.

'When I'm talking to large groups, I'm hiding behind my policeman persona, so I can natter on without a problem.'

'Like me. As an actor.'

He smiles again. Like the sun coming out on a grey day. 'I don't see you hiding behind any persona.'

Is this a compliment or an insult?

'What do you mean?'

'With you, what you see is what you get.'

I don't like this. I prefer to be thought of as someone with hidden depths. Tom's laughing at me.

'You don't have a clue what's in my head, Tom Brice. If you did, you'd have a big shock.'

'Oh yeah?' he says.

As November trickles drably towards December, I come to look forward, more than I care to admit, to these evening chats. My fears that Tom will mount a fullscale invasion of our family life are unfounded, and I find myself wishing for more of his company, not less. He's not at home much. Sometimes we don't see him for days. He doesn't talk about what he does, but I know that being a Murder Squad detective he has to deal with the worst. I've resisted adding him to my list of people to worry about when they're late. Just as well, since sometimes he doesn't come back at all.

The children have finally accepted his presence. They know he's not trying to supplant Rob, and since he doesn't respond to their rudeness they've concluded that there's no point in continuing it. They're no longer hostile, and his laidback attitude makes it hard for them to maintain their distance. Danny has to be watched, though. He's particularly sensitive to his position as man of the house. Last week Tom fixed a shelf that had broken months ago. Danny was furious.

'Why didn't you ask me to do that?'

'I did. Three times.'

'You should have asked again. It's my job, not his.'

'He offered. It's no big deal.'

But it was to Danny.

Anna's much better with Tom, mainly due to the delicacy of his dealings with her. She asks him the odd question about homework, and occasionally she's even enquired about his day.

These instances are few and far between, however, for Anna's alienation from everything and everyone except Crystal, Athy and Laxmi continues unabated. Which is why I was thrilled when Charlene told me the other day how well Crystal's doing academically since she befriended Anna.

'When you said they were friends I was a bit worried. Crystal she a good girl at heart, but she can be a bit high-spirited, and I was hoping she don't lead Anna into bad ways. Now The Lord has answered my prayers and it look like it your girl doing the leading, and making my Crystal think about she schoolin' for a change.'

I'm pleased Anna's influencing someone for the good, even if we at home are not getting the benefit of this saintly figure. Today she asks me for twenty pounds.

'What for?'

'A new school bag.'

'I just bought you a new school bag.'

'It's lost.'

'When?'

'I put it down on a wall and forgot about it. When I walked back it was gone.'

'Anna!'

'I'm really sorry, Mum. Can I have the cash?'

'No. I haven't got twenty pounds to spare, and even if I had, I'm not prepared to stump up all that money because of your carelessness. Use your old bag.'

'It's cack.'

'I never understood why you needed a new one in the first place.'

'Forget it. I'll use a bin bag.'

Off she goes again. Up to Fortress Anna. I feel like Scrooge, but it's the truth: one, I can't afford it and two, I don't think it's right to reward her scattiness with twenty crisp ones.

I hate having no money. I've forgotten how to be poor.

When Rob and I started out we didn't have two pennies to rub together, but somehow we managed and it was fun improvising. Now it's different. I've lost the saving habit since Rob started selling his work for a decent amount. At first I carried on budgeting in my frugal Northern way, but after Rob lost his temper when I bought a bargain music system, I stopped worrying and started enjoying our good fortune. Now I've forgotten the delights of improvising to make ends meet.

And there's no Rob.

I'm bawling into my coffee when Tom appears. He looks alarmed, as men do when faced with women's tears. But he doesn't disappear. Instead he subjects me to the Brice scrutiny – the one criminals must hate when they're trying to hide their dastardly deeds.

'What's up?'

I'm not going to tell him that I can't afford a new school bag for Anna, so I just say, 'You know – things.'

'What things?'

'Do you have children?'

'No.'

'Sorry. None of my business.'

'I wanted kids. My ex-wife didn't.'

So. He does have an ex-wife. How ex? Divorced or separated? Not that I care either way.

'Why not?'

'You don't want to know.'

In other words, Tom doesn't want to tell me. Fair enough. Except that sometimes I wish this was a more reciprocal relationship, where we confided in each other equally.

Relationship? He's the lodger! The only relationship we have is financial.

'Parenthood's not all it's cracked up to be. You're well out of it.'

'You don't mean that.' He's laughing at me again. Infuriating man.

'I do. No, I don't. Except a little bit. Anna's impossible. She used to be such an easy child . . .'

'She's had a lot to deal with.'

'I've had a lot to deal with too, and I'm fed up.'

I'm sobbing again. I can't believe I've let my guard down. Particularly to him. He hovers awkwardly. Though he's a good listener, he's not brilliant with tears. He obviously missed out on the bit of his training that taught him how to deal with weeping women.

'Anna's very lucky to have you as a mum.'

'Try telling her that.'

'Maybe I will.'

'No!' I'm shouting. Cool it, Rosa. 'She's only just begun to accept you. If you start lecturing, we'll be back to square one.'

He's going to abandon me to my misery. I wouldn't blame him. Who needs this after a hard day catching crooks?

But he sits down, eyes kind. 'Come on – get it off your chest.'

I end up telling him about the bag and Anna's weird behaviour. I confess how frightened I still am about Mick O'Brien and the animals on the doorstep. I tell him I'm worried that the band seems to be taking up too much of Danny's time, and I end up sharing my money troubles.

I'm ashamed of my earlier uncharitable thoughts. So what if he doesn't want to open up about his private life? Marriage break-ups are hell. It's probably too painful. I'll just enjoy the fact that he's a bloody good listener. I'm feeling better already.

Then he spoils it. 'Let me give you more rent.'

He thinks I'm fishing for a rent rise. How humiliating.

'You pay enough. I wouldn't dream of charging more. We can get by. I just have to economise. And so must Anna.'

'Well, if you change your mind, just say.'

Our intimacy is over. I wipe the kitchen table. Tom fiddles around in the fridge. Eventually he says, 'Gotta go. Anna will sort herself out. Kids always do.'

And away he goes.

You know nothing, Tom Brice. When you've brought up kids of your own, then perhaps you can tell me what teenagers do and don't do.

What is it about this man? One minute he's Mr Perfect, and the next I want to thump him. I'm appalled at my inconsistency.

Then I think, Hey, why add his behaviour to the list of things that bug you at the moment?

He's only the lodger.

SIXTEEN

Grey Squirrel: *Sciurus carolinensis*. Loud squeals, flicking tails and grinding molars indicate a fear of predators.

The next day, I wake up determined to get a grip. I'll sort out Anna and force her to tell me what's wrong, I'll tackle Danny about Dwaine and drugs and I'll find out more about Mick O'Brien. On the financial front, I'll go and see two people I've been avoiding since Rob's death. One of them is Rob's art dealer, Larry L'Estrange, and the other is Boo Hardy, my agent.

Larry discovered Rob a year before he died. He saw a painting in the house of a friend. Rob was teaching at Chelsea School of Art and beginning to think he'd end his days as one of those sad sacks who teach because they can't cut the mustard as artists. You see them in the pubs around the London art schools, faces bloated by booze, pontificating to eager students about the demise of real art, while hinting that their own work is too controversial for the corrupt, cowardly, money-grubbing major dealers to take on, and too profound for the shallow, fashion-crazed critics to understand. Rob hadn't reached that stage, but his faith in his talent was slowly being eroded by the lack of recognition, and I'd noticed the odd remark creeping into his conversation about the racist establishment's neglectful attitude towards black artists. Then along came Larry and took him on immediately.

Larry's gallery in Vigo Street in the West End is cutting edge. If L'Estrange backs an artist, critical coverage is a given. Collectors will buy. And so it was with Rob. Overnight he became the name on everybody's lips, and his first show sold out. The popular press cottoned on to the fact that he only painted doors, and this led to the usual 'Is it Art?' coverage in the tabloids and on TV that always follows anything that isn't photographically accurate, paintings of beautiful views, or lifelike portraits of someone's auntie or the Queen. Rob was invited onto news programmes and talkshows to debate with the usual crew of reactionary opportunists who always crawl out of the woodwork to defend the status quo and earn themselves a few bob at the same time, and everyone in the country seemed to have a view on whether his paintings were great art or a huge con-trick. The furore settled down, but by then Rob had a committed following of serious critics and collectors who all believed him to be one of the most exciting artists around. There'd been whispers about the Turner Prize shortlist. But posthumous entries are not allowed.

Larry's keen to do a memorial retrospective, and has been asking for months to see the studio. Prices were low in Rob's first show since he was comparatively unknown. The memorial show is Larry's opportunity to recoup his investment and make a killing. He wants it to be the opening exhibition in his spanking new gallery in Hoxton.

I haven't dared tell him that I couldn't enter the studio without having a panic attack, and that I didn't want anyone else to, either. Larry's very persuasive and would have pushed me before I was ready. Well, I'm ready now. I want my husband's work to shine one last time for the world.

There's only one other problem: Rob's art is all I have left of him.

I can't sell it.

And selling is what Larry does.

If he mounts a show, he'll want to make pots of money. I need to see if there's a solution to the problem – something to make us both happy. I called him first thing, and he'll see me later today. I feel somewhat out of my depth here, since negotiating about Rob's work was not part of my previous job description.

Before I put on the slap for my first appointment, with Boo, I go to the shed to have a quick look at Rob's work so I'll know what I'm talking about when I see Larry. The November day is grey and dank. Over the fence, Singing Vic is staring at a clump of Michaelmas daisies. I feel odd whenever I see him now. Maybe he's noticed, for lately when I've bumped into him he's more subdued – less his normal ebullient self.

'Nasty morning,' I say.

'Winter's here,' he says. 'These are the last of the flowers.'

We stand awkwardly.

'I've finished shifting Rob's stuff to the shed,' I tell him. 'I'm meeting his dealer today.'

'Oh?'

'Yeah. It's been quite a mission sorting out his studio. There was all sorts of old gunk in there.'

'Oh.'

I feel my heart thumping slightly behind my ribs.

'I found that dirty old pack of cards you three used for your poker games. Do you want it – as a memento?'

Is it the cold air bringing the blood to his cheeks? There's an unfamiliar tone in his voice.

'I don't need objects to remember Rob. He's here in my head.'

I shiver and it's not the grey day making me cold.

'Just thought I'd ask. Have a good day.'

I hurry into the shed, feeling Vic's eyes boring into my back. When I'm inside I look through the window and see that he's walking towards his back door.

It's chilly in the studio. Rob never got round to installing heating. A slight mist has drifted in with me and within seconds I feel the cold seeping into my bones. The paintings are stacked against the walls and there are also hundreds of drawings and sketches in portfolios and plan-chests. A sob unexpectedly tears itself from my throat. All that remains of my vibrant Rob lies here, alone and neglected at the end of the garden in the winter gloom. A surge of pity for my poor dead husband floods through me.

For a while, I'm lost in grief. But when I return to reality, I wonder how I managed to shift this colossal amount of stuff in less than a day. I didn't look at anything when I moved it. I couldn't – I still can't. I'll have to force myself to do this. The work, more than photographs, videos or letters, is the essence of Rob. It's what he was. What made him tick. When I look at his paintings, it's as if he's showing me his soul.

Rob was born in Port of Spain, Trinidad, to a mother who didn't want him and a father who didn't know. His mother showed him no love and no care. He was the family scapegoat, treated like a dog, left to run wild on the dazzling tropical beaches. When he was nine his grandmother, Miss Pearl, came out from England to visit and was appalled at the loveless life of the neglected little boy. She took him back to England with her and for two years Rob was happy, living a Caribbean village life in Brixton, alternately being scolded and spoiled rotten by Miss Pearl. Then one day he came home from school to find the front door of his terraced house closed. This was unheard of at that time in that place, where his grandmother and her friends ruled the street from their chairs on the front doorsteps of their houses and where they spent their days gossiping and feuding. Rob let himself into the house, which was dark and silent. It stank of last night's stale food instead of the mouthwatering aroma of ackee and saltfish that he was expecting. His grandmother's bedroom door was closed too, but when Rob opened it he saw her, lying on the floor beside the great brass bed she'd shipped over from Trinidad. Rob had never seen a dead person before, but he knew, even before he touched her, that she was gone. And when he knelt down to stroke her cheek, calling her name in spite of his awful knowledge, the icy feel of her skin made him scream so loudly that the neighbours came running.

After the funeral, the Social Services wrote to his mother in Port of Spain, but receiving no reply, they packed off the little boy, still numb with grief and shock, to the local children's home. This was a place of unparalleled viciousness and depravity, which many years later was the central feature of a major police investigation. By that time, however, Rob was long gone, having been dragged through a series of institutions and foster homes until he reached the age of sixteen when he was left to fend for himself. He would have gone under, had it not been for the unprofessional and compassionate actions of his art teacher at school who, finding him one night kipping down next to the pottery kiln, took him home to live with her. The Head Teacher berated her for getting too involved, but it made no difference. She already knew Rob had an extraordinary talent, and so she encouraged and cajoled him into art school. Even though she didn't live long enough to see his success, she was always adamant that the world would one day applaud the orphan boy from Brixton.

It wasn't until he was in his mid-twenties that the doors theme surfaced in Rob's work and then took over. I know what all those closed doors were. It didn't take a Brain of Britain to see where they were coming from, and why they wouldn't go away and leave him free to pursue other ideas.

It's no use. I still can't bring myself to look at the work. Larry will have to be content with numbers, not descriptions. However, I think I can tolerate the idea of him coming to look for himself now, so the trip to the bottom of the garden hasn't been wasted.

I'm about to leave when I spot something on the floor – an empty Rizla packet. My heart sinks. They've been smoking in here. After all I said to Danny about the paintings. Also – smoking what? I become aware of the distinctive sweet smell of cannabis. I take a closer look around the room. There are traces of white powder on the window-sill. Dope and coke. Great.

Steady, Rosa. It could be flour. Or icing sugar.

Like Danny's involved in secret baking sessions?

I don't think so.

I'll kill him.

No, I won't. I'll trust in his good sense. My son wouldn't be snorting class A substances in my garden shed.

No way.

As I walk through the park to the tube I convince myself that the powder's harmless. There's a perfectly simple explanation which will make perfectly simple sense.

I see Greg, one of the gardeners. He's been around Consort Park since forever, and has seen our family grow from the tiny tots who used to ask him where to find the best conkers, to the lanky teenagers they are now. I ask him about Mick O'Brien.

Greg snorts. 'Useless bag o' shite. No qualifications, no experience. He's rubbish. Don't know a trowel from a pair of long-handled loppers.'

'Why did he get the job?'

'Fucking positive discrimination, that's why. Pardon my French. He's not right in the head so he fits our "people with disabilities" quota. And they've docked my hours to fit him in.'

'Not right in the head?'

Greg becomes vague. 'Oh, you know. A fag short of a packet.'

'Like how?'

'Some sort of breakdown. I've seen him taking pills. I reckon it's them whatdyacallem – Blu-Tak.'

'Prozac?'

'That's it. Someone said his mum died a while ago and that's what turned him funny.'

'Funny?'

'I seen him talking to hisself many a time. Once I was coming out my mate's house at three in the morning and I seen his lordship sitting in a puddle in the rain singing his head off. Crap Irish rubbish. I says, "You all right, mate?" He looks at me like I'm Ian bleedin' Paisley and belts off down the road. Didn't know me from Adam. I said, "You know me all right, matey. I'm the one whose bleedin' job you fucked up." Pardon my French. But he didn't stop.'

I tell Greg about our dealings with O'Brien.

'If it were my daughter I know what I'd do,' he says.

'What?'

'I'd get someone to sort him out.'

Greg and Guy the Groper obviously have a similar outlook on how to solve life's little problems. I ask him to keep an eye on O'Brien, and also to tell me if he hears anything about him that we should know. Then I make a quick exit from the park before he embarks on one of his long and convoluted tales about how the Head Parkie picks on him.

SEVENTEEN

In earth's brown belly
Vulpine claws tear soft new flesh
Bloodlust cries for more.

Central London is humming and I love it – the noise, the grime, the pollution, everything. By the time I return home I'll have had enough, but for now this is just what I need. In Regent Street workmen on cranes are putting up the Christmas lights, and there's a festive urgency to the shoppers jostling up and down the crowded streets.

My agent's office is in Soho, in Poland Street. Boo is more theatrical than any actor. She wears outrageously patterned kaftans, lots of chunky jewellery, and her hair is strangely blonde for someone of fifty-five, with a couple of artistically placed chestnut streaks at the front.

'My angel! Let me *look* at you. Naughty girl, leaving it so long. I thought you'd forgotten all about us.'

She sweeps me over to a sofa piled high with exotic cushions. I remember the last time I was here. Rob was still alive and Boo was mouthing coffee commercial castings that never materialised.

'So . . .' Boo holds my hand and stares with soulful concern into my eyes. 'Tell me how you *really* are. Has it all been too horrible, my darling? I'd have taken to my bed and *never* got up again.'

Boo's sympathy is genuine. It's just vastly overdone. After all, it's not as if I'm one of her major clients or her best friend. She hasn't even been that good at finding me work over the years, and since her initial bout of mega-wailing over Rob's death I haven't heard a squeak. Boo lives in the moment. She means things at the time, but out of sight is out of mind, and once the object of her sympathy leaves, so does Boo's urge to help.

That's why I'm not exactly bowled over by my wonderful welcome. On the other hand I do need work, so I try to match her vivacity and enthusiasm.

'I'm great, Boo. Really good. The kids are coping well, and it's fantastic to see you again. I've missed you so much.' I summon up all my acting skills to make this sound convincing.

I succeed. Boo clasps me to her vast breasts and says, with a catch in her throat, 'I've missed you too, my darling.'

When I surface, she is fixing me with a look of deeply insincere sincerity.

'So, my treasure, what can I do for you?'

What do you think, Boo? I'm an actor. You're my agent. Take a wild guess.

'I'm ready to go back to work. I'm doing a bit of supply teaching, but I really want to get back into the business.'

'Of course you do, my darling.'

Boo adopts her thinking pose: two fingers on the

temples and eyes raised heavenward. This is a prelude for her to tell me that things are very slack at present.

'Things are very slack at present, but . . . (here she gives a gallant little smile and pats me on the knee) . . . leave it to me, darling. I'll come up with something.'

I'm so relieved that she still wants to help me find work.

'Though it won't be easy, in the circumstances . . .'

'What circumstances?'

'This teaching job. How will it affect your ability to go to castings? Also, what about the children if you land a job in regional rep or on location?'

She has a point. But I'm not going to tell her that.

'The teaching's temporary. And very flexible.' (Lie number one.) 'And I have arrangements in place for the kids if I have to travel.' (Lie number two.)

I don't say that rep is, of course, totally out of the question. I can't go off for weeks at a time, leaving the kids and the teaching to fend for themselves. Likewise any Hollywood blockbuster crying out for my services.

Boo's still pensive. 'Then there's the other teensy snag.' Her eyes roam around the contours of my face.

'Snag?'

'Well, my darling, not to put too fine a point on it, your age.'

'My age?'

Boo's benign aura slips momentarily and I see the shark beneath the skin.

'Don't be naïve, darling. You know any actress over thirty-five's not that saleable, and unless I'm mistaken, you're coming up for the big four-o.'

So. Finished at thirty-nine. Doomed to fall into that

black hole for ageing actresses from which there's no return.

'Are you saying forget it?'

Boo's eyes widen. 'My darling! *Pas du tout*. Merely warning you that things won't be easy. But I've always had the greatest respect for your talent. I'll soon be able to find you something absolutely *delicious*.'

Suddenly, she executes an elaborate pantomime of catching sight of her watch and screaming. It's Oscar-winning.

'See what you've done, darling? I've been so thrilled to have this wonderful little chat that I completely forgot I'm lunching at The Ivy with Dame Judi.'

I'm hustled out of the office and into the street. Boo, throwing on a vast crimson cloak, is seamlessly segueing into her farewell patter.

'As soon as I hear of anything, *anything* at all, I'll give you a bell. Wonderful to see you again. Best love to the infants.'

She grabs me, delivers two enormous air kisses and is away down Poland Street, leaving me speechless beside her office door.

Any calls from Boo will be few and far between. I was always an also-ran on her books, and now, with the added complications, she's hardly going to be pulling out all the stops on my behalf. Still, maybe I'm misjudging her. I hear Rob's voice saying, 'Don't be defeatist, girl. If she doesn't call you, you call her. Ten times a day if that's what it takes.'

That's what he said when I embarked on my acting career when both children had started school. I wasn't hungry enough for it then, so I didn't. But now . . .

I make my way to Vigo Street through Soho. Most

of the sleazy bars and clubs have gone, and the streets throng with affluent young gays and media types from the film production offices scattered around the area. There are still a few sex parlours left, though. I notice one with a particularly lurid neon sign advertising its delights. Two men stand outside, deep in conversation. One's a stereotypical bouncer, beefy and bullet-headed. The other's tall, fair and wears a flash leather jacket. As I walk past, he turns.

It's Tom Brice. He looks straight at me. I'm about to say hello when he shakes his head imperceptibly.

Well, well. What a place to spot the lodger. That's one for the anecdotes. I wonder if he'll mention it? And if he doesn't, should I?

It's none of my business.

When I arrive at L'Estrange Gallery, Larry L'Estrange glides forward to greet me.

'We're so pleased you could come.'

Larry always refers to himself in the plural. No one knows why. His eyes, the colour of sea-drenched pebbles, pop out slightly from his deathly pale, ultra-smooth moon face. As always he's immaculate, tailored by Savile Row, and as I follow him through into his exquisitely minimal office, I catch a very faint whiff of expensive cologne and an even fainter whiff of brandy. In his elaborately understated way, he's as theatrical as Boo.

Here, unlike Poland Street, the positions are reversed. Larry wants something from me.

We talk about Rob. I give Larry an estimate of the number of works, and I even find myself confessing that I can't look at them, and I don't want to sell them. It's shockingly easy to talk to Larry. He's perfected listening to a fine art. In a competition he'd even beat Tom Brice.

When Larry listens, people open up: they tell all. It's impossible not to. He's the most focused person I've ever met. All the richest collectors sooner or later find their way to Vigo Street. And once they've found Larry, he's their man. He's one of the most powerful movers in the London art world, and I'm very lucky that he's Rob's dealer.

He's wonderful. He says there's no need for me to look through the work: he and his staff will do that. And with regard to selling, we can have a show where nothing's for sale. I ask what's in it for him. I see him wince. Larry doesn't like direct questions. But he rallies and says with a self-mocking smile, 'The kudos.' He says that later, when I do feel able to part with some of the work, there'll be a queue of people who have already fallen in love with the paintings, ready to buy.

He makes it sound so simple. As I leave the gallery, having arranged for Larry to come and view at my convenience, I feel a burden's been lifted. Rob's work won't languish unseen. I've taken the first step to make sure of it.

It's mid-afternoon. The short winter day's already over. I'd planned to do some shopping but I'm too tired. The effort of dealing with Boo and Larry has left me drained. I'm ready to return to Consort Park.

As I rattle home on the tube, I hear the sing-song robot woman who tells me where I am before each stop. Some voice-over actress, I suppose. I wonder fleetingly how people break into the lucrative voice-over market. Then I glance through to the next carriage and see Dwaine. He's slumped in his seat, and his eyes are glassy. When we arrive at our stop, as I debate whether to rush through and shake him, he comes out of his daze and staggers off the train. I follow him into the street.

'Hello, Dwaine.'

He ignores me, and crosses the road towards the estate.

'Leave it,' I tell myself. But my feet refuse to turn homewards. Surely this is the ideal time to find out exactly what's going on with Dwaine, and what is Danny's involvement.

Dwaine's moving quite fast. If I'm going to catch him I'd better put on a spurt. I step out into the road. There's a squealing of brakes and I see a red van hurtling towards me. I've done it now. My poor children – both parents killed by speeding cars.

The van is inches away when a pair of strong hands seize me. Then I'm sitting on the pavement surrounded by people asking whether I'm OK, and there's an irate van driver telling me exactly what he'd like to do with stupid bitches who career in front of him without looking. I say I'm fine and ask the group of concerned faces which one of them saved me.

But none of them had.

Then a woman says that it was a young man with long dark hair, who'd slipped away as the crowd began to gather.

Surely not.

I get to my feet, apologise profusely to the van driver, brush myself down, and after reassuring my well-wishers that I'm all right, I turn towards home.

A young man with long dark hair . . .

EIGHTEEN

From the beast's belly
Emerges that which sets free
The flower of youth.

When I arrive home there's an old lady on my doorstep. The snow-white hair is pinned into a perfect chignon, the make-up's a masterpiece of understatement, and the coat has 'couturier' written all over it. I estimate she's in her early seventies, but she has the carriage and posture of a woman half her age.

'Mrs Thorn?'

'Yes?'

'I believe my son, Thomas Brice, lodges here.'

'Yes.'

'He said he'd meet me off the train at Paddington Station – I've come from Cheltenham, you see – but he didn't appear. So I telephoned his flat, and the builders directed me here.'

'You're Tom's mother?'

'Perhaps you know where I might find him?'

I nearly said, 'The last time I saw him he was talking to a thug outside a strip club in Soho.'

I park her in the sitting room.

'What a lovely room,' she says insincerely.

'Would you like a cup of tea?'

'How kind. Do you have Lapsang?'

'Just bog-standard breakfast.'

She smiles bravely. 'Thank you, my dear. That would be delightful.'

I've always had a thing about people calling me dear.

I make the tea and find a few biscuits that the children have missed in their daily trawl of the cupboard. I wash a cup, saucer, and the teapot, and despise myself for bothering. I should give her the Bagpuss mug like any other visitor. But somehow I can't.

I carry my tray of tinkling china to the sitting room. God help me, I've even unearthed a tray-cloth.

'Custard cream?'

She gives an almost imperceptible little shudder. 'The cup of tea will be quite sufficient.'

Can this woman really be Tom's mother? She's so . . . not to put too fine a point on it, posh. It's occurred to me that Tom's a bit middle-class for a policeman, but she's coming on like Queen Victoria. Tom's pronunciation is RP sloping into Estuary. Hers is comedy duchess. She says 'orf' and 'hev' instead of 'have', for God's sake. Her eyes are Tom's, only where his are soft and fuzzy round the edges hers are glass chips, hard and bright.

'Don't let me detain you, my dear. I know how difficult a landlady's life is. There's a little woman in Cheltenham, runs up the odd frock for me, she takes in lodgers – poor thing's permanently exhausted, so thin and pale and worn . . .' She looks me up and down.

She's starting to seriously piss me off.

'I'm not a professional landlady, just renting my spare room to your son on a temporary basis. As a favour. Make yourself at home, Mrs Brice. I'm sure Tom will be back soon.'

As I turn to leave, a long, liver-spotted claw detains me.

'My dear, did I offend you? If so, I'm deeply sorry. Please forgive me. I know what a port in a storm your sweet little house is to Tommy.'

How can she make an apology sound like an insult?

'Help yourself to more tea when you're ready.'

I phone Tom. 'Remember someone you were supposed to meet this afternoon?'

'What?'

'Someone old and fragile with beautiful white hair and a liking for exotic teas?'

He groaned. 'My mother.'

'She's here now in my "sweet little house".'

'I'm on my way.'

'Make it quick.'

Within fifteen minutes he's greeting his aged parent. After a few moments he comes to the kitchen.

'She does this kind of thing.'

'Sweet.'

'She gets lonely . . . Listen, thanks for earlier.'

'What?'

'In Soho. It's an undercover thing. We're doing a surveillance on this guy who bumped off his business partner. We know he did it – we just need the proof. If you'd blown my cover, that would've been three months' work up the spout.'

I feel quite excited to be the saviour of a police undercover job.

'No problem,' I say, in a suitably nonchalant way.

Tom returns to his mother and I prepare supper. The sitting-room door's open. I'm not listening, but occasionally I can't help hearing the odd phrase.

'Think about Uncle Harry's offer . . . police nonsense . . . so embarrassing for me at the club.'

Tom's speaking very softly, so I don't hear his side of this intriguing conversation until finally he says, 'Leave it, Ma.'

Then there's a lull. I'm tossing a salad when it starts to get interesting again.

'What right does she have to sit in that beautiful house in Hampstead, when you're pigging it down here in this dowdy little hole.'

Dowdy little hole? Pigging it? Now I am officially eavesdropping. I sneak out of the kitchen and hover in the hall, dusting the mirror.

'Never had any time for her . . . neurotic little bitch . . . didn't appreciate . . . no support . . . if you'd done as I asked . . . wouldn't even speak to me when I telephoned . . . called me a jumped-up *parvenue* . . . thinks she can get away with treating us . . .'

If I squint, I can see through the partly-open door. Tom has his back to me. His shoulders sag. He makes no attempt to stop his mother. I'd be inclined to give her a left hook, but he's showing remarkable restraint. Must be his police training. Or long experience.

'And this place simply won't do. Are you involved with this Thorn woman?'

'She's renting me a room. It's convenient – near my work. When the flat's finished, I'll be out of here double quick, don't you worry.'

'Promise?'

'Promise. Satisfied?'

'I'll have to be. It's not what I'd wish, but of course you never think of my feelings. This whole thing has been very difficult for me.'

Without being aware of it, I'm now in full view of the sitting room.

Mrs Brice sees me. Our eyes lock. A small smile twists the cupid's bow of her thin damson lips.

'Well, Tommy, I'd hate to think of you becoming involved with Mrs Thorn. She's not our sort at all.'

'No.'

No?

'That dyed red hair and those shabby clothes. Quite the little ex-hippy, and a bit sneaky, too. Not at all suitable.'

I'm enraged and humiliated and I've never in my life used hair-dye.

'Ma, this is just a place to stay. Rosa Thorn's not my type. Come on, I'll take you out to dinner, and then put you on the train.'

Heart thundering in my chest, I retreat into the kitchen. Moments later, Tom calls out.

'I'm taking my mother to dinner, Rosa.'

I'm full of hatred beneath my smile.

'Goodbye, Mrs Brice. Tom's very lucky to have such a caring mother. It can't be easy, travelling at your age. My grandmother always said that once you hit your late eighties, it's better to stay put.'

Mrs Brice's marble eyes glitter. I hear a short intake of breath from Tom.

'I'm seventy-four, dear.' She looks pointedly round the hall. 'Such a sweet little house. So unspoiled.'

Tom gives me a long-suffering look as he ushers her out. I don't respond.

Why am I not his type? Not that I'd want to be. Not in a million years.

Guy Gropius smoked a cigarette on his porch, waiting for Nikos to arrive. He heard Rosa's door open and watched a tall bloke emerge from her house, a little old lady on his arm.

Rosa's lodger.

The Great Detective.

What a bummer. Just as things were going so well. Nik was starting to put a fair bit of business his way, and the last thing he needed was a plod as a neighbour. He heard the sound of an engine – Nik's clapped-out van. Fuck! It was going to coincide with the policeman's painful perambulations down the street. He strolled towards the edge of the pavement, and as Nik drew level, caught his eye. Nik, though no Stephen Hawking, was no fool either, and roared away. Guy seethed. Nik wouldn't return tonight – not if he thought there was the slightest whiff of trouble. Which meant that all the promises he'd made to people would be worth nothing, along with his reputation as Mr Reliable. It wouldn't do. A policeman for a neighbour was bad news. Things had to change.

NINETEEN

From the dead grey husk
Sweetness, blossoming, comes forth
And rouses the blood.

At school this morning, I'm accosted by Primrose Pepper, the Deputy Head at Churchill Towers. This is unusual. Communications from her are usually by Post-it note.

'Leo's told me about your offer to do a Christmas play. Could you give the details to Max in Media Resources, so he can start thinking posters and promotion? December the sixteenth would be a good evening, and we can do a performance to our feeder primary schools the same morning – good for recruitment. So wonderful having a play directed by a professional actress.'

If Primrose mentions once more that I'm an actress, I may commit murder. Every time I run into her she makes some bright reference to it. Jess says she's a thwarted thesp who, in her youth, was turned down by all the major drama schools so went into teaching instead. Apparently she's green with envy over anyone who's within shouting distance of the business.

Disaster! I'd completely forgotten Leo's request. There's no way I can produce a show by 16 December. That's not much more than a month away. Who do they think I am? Trevor Nunn?

I find Jess. She's in the English office, marking Year Eleven *Romeo and Juliet* coursework and cursing.

'I never agreed to it,' I complain. 'Why's he told Primmy Post-it-note it's a done deal?'

'He's a cunning wanker. That's how he operates. You could always tell him where to shove it . . .'

'But?'

'How do you know there's a "but"?'

'I know you.'

'You don't want to get into his bad books. You may need more supply work when this job's over. If you're on Ratshit's black-list he'll never ask you back.'

'You can talk! It's your life's work to insert yourself up his nose as often as possible.'

'That's different. I'm on a permanent contract. Besides, I've got stuff on him that he wouldn't like to see the light of day.'

'Such as?'

'Don't ask. This school's very convenient for you. It's virtually at the end of your road. It'd be a pity to blow it.'

'I can't produce a full-length play in a month.'

Jess wears chunky rings. When she's thinking, she fiddles with them. She's rubbing a large rock of amethyst as we speak.

'You're right. Even if you and the little sods were all off timetable from now until the sixteenth, it wouldn't be long enough.' Then she exclaims, 'I've got it!' And carries on twiddling.

'Are you going to tell me or do I have to pick it up telepathically?'

'How are you on musicals?'

'Pretty good. But if it's impossible to do a play in a month . . .'

'Not a whole musical – a couple of set-piece numbers, like the Clam Bake scene from *Carousel*, or something from *Annie*. Everyone fucking loves *Annie* for some bizarre reason. You could direct and Singing Vic could coach them in the songs.'

I don't mention that I'm not Vic's favourite person at the moment. I haven't told Jess about the IOU. I'll tell her when I've decided what to do about it.

'I could do that, but it's hardly a whole evening's entertainment.'

'We make it a Christmas variety show. There are loads of kids who love devising their own dance numbers – usually bump and grind, verging on the pornographic, but Ratshit wouldn't know that till it was too late. He never bothers himself with visits to rehearsals. My eager-beaver Year Sevens have written some brilliant poetry this term – rap stuff. There's bound to be a couple of instrumentalists we could persuade to perform – saxophone, piano – sexy instruments, no violins. And there's a girl in the Sixth Form who fancies herself as Judy Garland. Hey – you could persuade Danny and his mates to give the band its first outing. Genius or fucking what?'

Jess is beaming. 'Sorted then?'

It sounds good to me.

'Will he go for a show instead of a play?'

'He'll go for it. He's got a Prospective Parents' Evening coming up, and he needs to convince them that we do shitloads of extra-curricular stuff. Concert, play, show – he won't give a toss so long as he can blag about something.'

'Jess, I owe you bigtime.'

'You bet your fucking life you do, sunshine. Now – dish the latest dirt on the Met's Finest.'

Jess, ex-Greenham Common, rabidly anti-authority, is at her most satirical when it comes to my new-found connections with the police force. She keeps angling for an invitation to meet Tom, but I don't trust her. She'll say something acid about police corruption, or start grunting like a pig when he comes into the room. So far I've managed to keep them apart.

Though why I should be so careful to spare Tom Brice's sensitive soul is beyond me. Or is it that I don't think he'd take to Jess? And is it important anyway that the two of them get on?

'He has the mother of all mothers,' I say, and relate my meeting with Mrs B.

I can't quite face telling Jess about my Keyhole Kate impersonation. Not because she disapproves of eavesdropping: she has no scruples about listening in to anyone's conversation about anything. Her view is that if it's spoken within hearing distance, it's fair game. It's more that my pride won't let me relay the various disparaging remarks made about me by both Tom and his precious Mama.

Instead, I do an impersonation of La Brice and her cut-glass accent.

'Jessica Mackenzie's Rule Number One: Never date a Man with a Mother,' she says.

'Lucky I'm not dating him then. He's my lodger, that's all. I don't even know if I like him.'

'Why not?'

'I'm not sure.' I can't tell her that I don't like him because he told his mother I wasn't his type. 'He can be a laugh – sometimes. And he's been very sensitive about not getting in the way at home. And he's very good with the kids, but . . .'

'But what?'

'I don't know. One minute he seems concerned and involved, the next he's out of the door and away. I can't get a handle on him.'

Jess is looking quizzically at me.

'What?' I ask.

'Sounds to me like you're spending fuckloads of time trying.'

'For God's sake, Jessie. I'm not remotely interested in Tom Brice. You seem to forget it's only a few months since Rob died.'

Jess looks upset and has the grace to apologise. The bell goes for lessons, so I leave her and go to tackle 8C.

After school I spend ages scribbling out audition notices for the show, and then finally make my way to the Old Building to see Leo. For once Marion's not on guard in her office, so I climb the winding stairs to the Observatory. The door's closed, and from inside I can hear Leo's melodious voice punctuated by bursts of eager laughter. I knock.

'Enter.'

He's surrounded by girls. Fat girls, thin girls, girls as ugly as sin, girls as pretty as pictures. They're sitting in chairs, on the floor, leaning on window-sills, perched on chair-arms. They stare in hostile unison as I stand in the doorway.

'Ah, Ms Thorn . . .'

'I'll come back tomorrow, if it's more convenient?'

'No no. We were just finishing.'

I hear a few petulant 'Oh, sir!'s' before Leo claps his hands and says breezily, 'Off you go, girls. Next week we'll look at the diminishing role of the manual worker in a post-industrial economy. Away with you now! Don't keep the boyfriends waiting.'

As the last reluctant girl files out, flashing him a radiant smile as she passes, Leo closes the door with a flourish.

'My Sixth Form political discussion group,' he says. 'Such a bright bunch. Nothing like the challenge of stimulating fresh young minds, is there?'

'Are there no boys in need of stimulation?'

Leo smiles. 'It would seem not,' he says. 'Girls are so much more intellectually precocious, don't you find?'

Intellect isn't the only way seventeen-year-old girls are precocious. The atmosphere in the room when I entered had a fevered intensity. Bees around a honey-pot.

'Sit down. What can I do for you?' he says, patting the chair next to him. Long legs elegantly crossed, he lounges in a magisterial wingchair. It gives him an air of scholarly authority.

What can he do for *me*?

I present the idea of a Christmas variety show. As I flounder through the concept, his dark eyes are so intently focused on mine that I almost feel myself going into a trance. Finally I finish. There's a silence.

'What do you think?'

He shakes himself, as if returning from a far-off place. 'Great idea. Brilliant. Go ahead. You have my full permission.'

As if *I'd* pleaded with him to do a show – not the other way round.

I'm furious. Having pushed me into volunteering to organise a major school event, he now behaves as if it's a mere speck on his consciousness. Nothing special. Not important. Not compared with his inner musings.

'If you aren't that bothered,' I snap, 'I'd much rather you said so right now. It's a lot of work, and as you pointed out when you first mentioned it, I'm only on a supply contract.'

I'm doing just what Jess advised me against: being a stroppy cow.

Leo looks bewildered. 'I'm so sorry,' he says. 'I've upset you. That's the last thing I want. I'm thrilled you'll do a show for us. I know it won't be easy with such a short timescale, and I'm well aware that on your contract you're not obliged to do anything at all. I'm very grateful that you're willing to take it on . . . No, it's just that you remind me of someone who's very special to me.'

Leo rakes his hand through his luxuriant waves. He's over fifty and yet there's not one grey hair to be seen. Is it my imagination or are his eyes moist?

'My wife.' His voice is not quite steady. 'You may have heard. She's not well.'

Normally I'm the first to fall for a sob story, but somehow Leo's sick wife isn't pressing the right buttons.

'What's wrong with her?' I hear myself saying, far too bluntly. What are you doing, Rosa?

Leo gestures sadly. 'Oh, you know . . .'

'Cancer?'

'Something like that,' he says. 'You're so like her, Rosa. How she used to be. So full of life.' He shields his face with his hand.

'I'd better go,' I say, and get up. But he catches my arm.

'Stay and keep me company. Just for a bit. I've something to show you.'

He presses a button on the remote control that's never far from his fingers. The lights go out. I'm alone with him in a pitch-black room.

But then, the electric blinds go up, and instead of making for the door, I move to the window, transfixed.

Below us, London sparkles through the darkness of the winter evening. To the east, Canary Wharf and the tall towers of the City, St Paul's Cathedral in their midst. Then, more centrally, the Millennium Wheel, the Houses of Parliament, the Telecom Tower and the Victorian bulk of Westminster Cathedral. Dotted all around us, the lights twinkle and shine. Magic. The first time he showed me the view, it was daytime and I was distracted by the sight of Anna talking to Mick O'Brien. By night, the scene is mindblowing. I came to London as a student and never left. It's my city and I love it. I love its dirt and its diversity and the fact that I never really reach the end of it – there's always something more to discover. And there it is laid out below me, a glittering vat of seething life. I feel godlike. I could plunge my hand into the crazy melting pot and pull out a million stories.

For a moment I forget about Leo until, like the first time, I become aware that he's right behind me. Almost touching. I tell myself not to give in to wild imaginings. Being a widow, a woman without a man, is making me think I'm fair game for anything in trousers. How sad is that? I can't ask him to move away. I'd sound prim and stupid. So I say nothing and as I move around the glass dome, he follows me, always slightly too close. It occurs to me that he and I are probably alone in the building. Marion's gone and so have all the other administrative staff. What should I do if he lunges? I spot the microphone belonging to his precious PA system, and the wild thought goes through my head that I could grab it and call for help – in the hope that any diligent teachers still working in the other buildings might come to my rescue. Or, if push came to shove, I could hit him over the head with it. It's next to his telescope. I stroll over to it, trying to appear casual and relaxed. Leo follows close behind.

'The telescope really comes into its own at night,' I say.

Leo's arm snakes over my shoulder. Does it brush against my breast, or am I imagining it? He gives the telescope a loving stroke. I feel queasy. Am I overreacting and reading sinister intentions into perfectly harmless actions? Am I becoming like the middle-aged woman in the old Dick Emery sketch who reads sex into everything? Should I just thump him on the shoulder and say: 'Oh, you are *awful*,' and stride off down the stairs?

'It's a very powerful instrument . . . When things get me down I come and sit up here and look at the stars and the city. I've only one regret: that I can't share it all with my wife.'

The line trips easily off the tongue. Has he used it before? Maybe to vulnerable, ageing female teachers looking for happiness before it's too late? Or gullible adolescents, flattered by the attention of an older man who's not only their charismatic Head Teacher, but also a TV celeb? Or am I just being melodramatic?

He talks for a while longer. He covers loneliness, fear of death and existential angst. I gradually edge myself towards the door. If he's making a pass, he's taking his time. I'm almost there when the penny drops. This man isn't stupid. He won't go any further unless I give him a signal. He's far too canny to risk his reputation. Apart from standing too close, he hasn't actually done anything. He won't unless I give him the green light. I start to breathe more easily.

'I must go: I promised my daughter I'd take her late-night shopping.'

Leo's gaze locks with mine. Then he flicks on the lights.

'You mustn't keep her waiting,' he says. 'I've enjoyed our little chat, and I'm very much looking forward to your show.'

His hand shoots up and grabs my hair. I can't help it, I flinch. He smiles.

'Cobweb,' he says. 'Can't have you going home with that wonderful hair covered in spiders' webs.'

I take the Observatory stairs two at a time. I can't wait to get away from Churchill Towers tonight. Then I remember I've left my bag in the Drama Studio.

Alfred Churchill's building is connected to the rest of the site by a cloister. When Churchill Towers was turned into a school in the 1960s, the new buildings were thrown up very quickly and, over the next thirty years, fell down rather more slowly. Or rather, subsided. When the main Expressive Arts Block was only held upright by steel girders clamped onto the outside of the building, the Council finally agreed to build us another one. And last July, before I arrived at Churchill, a state-of-the-art complex of Drama, Music and Art Studios was opened by the Mayor of Brent, with much municipal back-slapping. After this, money ran out, and the old building still awaits demolition.

I run along the cloister. The new complex, lights blazing, is on my left at the end, while on my right, the poor old abandoned building lurks shabbily in the darkness, padlocked and barred, awaiting the day when it will become rubble and dust. I've never been along here after dark on my own. The deserted block, sinister and secretive, gives me the creeps, and I'm glad to reach the well-lit Drama Studio. I grab my bag. Churchill has its fair share of pilferers, so I'm relieved to find my purse still untouched inside it. I turn off the lights and walk back. Now everything's in darkness it's difficult to see where I'm going. Someone's broken the lights at either end of the cloister, so I only have moonlight to guide me.

Suddenly there's a crash. From the abandoned building. It must be some animal. Both staff and pupils are strictly forbidden to go there for safety reasons, and the place is very securely barred and locked off. I continue walking. Then I hear faint voices, and from somewhere in the crumbling hulk, I'm sure I see the flicker of a torch. I wait for what seems like five centuries. But there's nothing else, and I'm left wondering whether I imagined the whole thing. I don't know what to do. If someone is in there, they're up to no good, and won't appreciate being discovered. So I'm not about to make my presence felt. However, if it's kids messing around, then they're in danger. The building's very unstable. The only person in authority who is definitely on-site is Leo, and wild horses wouldn't drag me back up to his eyrie.

In the end, I do the obvious thing. I go to the site

manager's office. In my day they were called caretakers. Nowadays the role's much grander and they are site managers with degrees in urban planning. But Fred Borrage is of the old school. Very definitely a caretaker, with all the bad-tempered, morose and grudging qualities that have distinguished caretakers from time immemorial. To my surprise he's talking to Guy the Groper.

'What are you doing here?' I ask.

Guy smiles lazily, lounging against the wall. 'Just shooting the breeze with my old pal Fred.'

I can't say I admire Guy's taste in friends.

I tell Fred my tale. He blows his bulbous purple nose on a filthy handkerchief and grunts, 'There ain't nobody can get into that building. I inspect it personally every day.'

'I'd be grateful if you could check it out.'

'I did me rounds earlier. It was as quiet as the grave.'

'Well, I heard something, and I saw a light. If a student's broken in, it could be dangerous.'

'Listen, miss, why don't you do your job, and let me do mine. If I say that building's secure, it's secure.'

His reputation for idleness is legendary, but I persist. 'I really think you need to have a look.'

'I know you ladies and your imaginations . . .'

Guy intervenes. 'Wouldn't do any harm to check it out, Fred. Set her mind at rest.' He winks at Borrage – two solid blokes faced with an hysterical female.

I assert myself. 'If anyone has an accident, it won't look good, Fred. Particularly if I let slip that I reported a disturbance to you.'

'All right! Anything for a quiet life.' He pushes past me, muttering under his breath. I start to follow, but he turns on me. 'Leave it to me, miss.' And he stomps off, still grumbling to himself.

Guy grins. 'Lazy bastard.' He shows no sign of moving. 'See you, Rosa.'

'Bye then.' I say it frostily. He needn't think I'll forget that wink in a hurry.

When I arrive home, the boys are in the kitchen, foraging. I tell them about the show and ask if they'd like to perform. Underneath their obligatory cool, they're jubilant.

'You'll have to give yourselves a name, of course.'

Delroy laughs. 'Hasn't Dan told you? We've got one already.'

'And?' I can tell they're nervous. Wondering whether I'll like it.

'3D,' says Dwaine.

'3D?'

'Danny, Dwaine and Delroy.'

'Brilliant,' I say. 'Who wants some cauliflower cheese?'

Leo Ratchett called his wife.

'I'll be a bit late, sweetheart. Mountains of paperwork . . . Love you.'

He arranged himself comfortably in his chair, and focused the telescope. The stars seemed extra clear tonight. He thought about infinity and the futility of desire. After a while he swung the telescope down and round, and readjusted it. Unlike the heavens, Consort Park was dark and mysterious. No clarity there. Just night creatures going about their business. For a while he watched a vixen carrying something furry and viscous in her powerful jaws, before finally sliding the telescope round to what he'd always suspected would be its final destination: Rosa Thorn's house. There was a light burning in a first-floor window. Her bedroom, perhaps?

TWENTY

On warm dark damp nights
Slimy amphibians hunt.
Slugs and snails beware.

Weekend blues. Mick O'Brien traps me in the corner-shop. I realise he's following me as soon as I leave the house. I see him throw down his rake and run out of the park after me. He's so close as I walk up the road that I can hear his ragged breathing. I tell myself not to panic. I'm taller than him, and I could easily throw him to the ground. He follows me into the shop. I groan inwardly when I see it's Old Mr Pindoria behind the counter, and not his son, Young Mr Pindoria who, though permanently depressed, is much fitter and stronger and hasn't had recent heart-bypass surgery. I grab some bread, trying to keep an eye on O'Brien without looking at him.

He's blocking the doorway. In order to leave I will have to ask him to move. I pick up a tin of beans and catch his eye. He smiles. His smile is crazily beautiful, and if I could obliterate it with my beans I would.

'Why don't you leave us alone?' I feel my temper

rising. I've had it with nutters and lechers snuffling around me and my family.

'Baked beans,' says O'Brien. 'A complete meal and no animals harmed in the making.'

'You're blocking the doorway.'

'Sure and I didn't know you'd finished, did I? You haven't paid yet.' He makes no attempt to move. I'm trapped. I feel in my pocket for my mobile. I've left it at home.

I turn to Old Mr Pindoria. 'Phone the police. This man is preventing me from leaving your shop.'

Mr Pindoria looks shifty. He mutters something.

'Sorry?'

Mr Pindoria speaks out of the side of his mouth in a stage whisper that must be audible as far away as Swiss Cottage.

'I said, I don't phone police. I know this man. He is mental. I don't want trouble.'

Great. I'm stuck here indefinitely between a nutcase and a terrified pensioner with a dicky heart.

'In that case, can I use your phone?'

Reluctantly, the old man hands it over. I don't call the police. I call Danny. He arrives in less than two minutes. O'Brien's still blocking the doorway. He doesn't see Danny come up behind him. Danny yanks him back by his long black hair. My cool son is incandescent. He flattens O'Brien up against the shop window and bellows into his face.

'What are you doing to my mother, you piece of bogshite? Fuck off and leave my family alone, or I'll smash your fucking head in.'

The 'bogshite' bit particularly surprises me. I didn't think Danny had a prejudiced bone in his body. He's always the first one to pounce on me if I say anything that could remotely be considered politically incorrect.

O'Brien's gasping for breath. Danny's arm is across his windpipe. It strikes me that the last thing we need is Danny up on an assault charge.

'Let go, Dan.'

I have to repeat this several times before he finally eases his grip, and even then he still eyeballs O'Brien who, once he can breathe, rapidly recovers his composure and is actually smiling the smile again. Danny's eyes, usually soft-focus treacle, have metamorphosed into adamantine flashes of coal-black fury.

'What is it with you, man? Why are you hanging around us all the time?'

Danny's making the mistake of trying to hold a rational conversation with O'Brien.

'Save your breath,' I say. 'Let's go home.'

But he persists. 'Why are you doing this? Does it turn you on or something, sniffing around schoolgirls and harassing women?'

O'Brien's seraphic smile is still firmly in place.

'Are you deaf, Irish boy? I'm asking you a question.'

With one quick movement, O'Brien slips under Danny's arm.

'Give Anna my love, will ye?' he says to me. 'And tell her to watch out.'

And then he's away. I pay for my bread and beans, my hands trembling. What does he mean, 'Tell Anna to watch out'?

As we leave, Old Mr Pindoria puts the *Closed* sign up. After our little visit, he obviously feels the need for a siesta. I must pop back later and see if he's OK. When we reach the corner, O'Brien's closing our gate behind him. He waves and saunters off into the park. Danny and I break into a run. When we enter the house everything seems normal, but there's a postcard lying on the mat addressed to Anna. On one side is a heart, coloured in red biro with an arrow and the words *Ana* and *Mik*. Printed in the corner in small letters it says 'Natural History Museum'. There is a scrawled message, also in red biro. *After spornin froggs ushally stay in the watter until the wheather get worma.* I turn it over. Staring up at me is a picture of two copulating frogs.

Danny is outraged.

'Scuzzy little wanker!' He puts his arm round me. 'Don't worry, Mum. I'll deal with the pervert. He won't mess this family around any more – I'll see to that.'

Then I make my mistake. 'I'll show it to Tom. See what he thinks.'

The animation vanishes from Danny's face. He drops his arm and walks away.

'Danny! What's the matter?'

'Nothing. Do what you like.'

I wish time had a rewind button. I've really hurt his feelings. I've just seen for myself the protective fury my desperate SOS call aroused in him, and I imagine what it must be like to be him. Part-child, part-man, struggling with his new role as the only son of a widowed mother. Dealing with my grief and Anna's, and putting his own on the back burner to protect us from his sorrow. I realise how much the laidback, easy-come-easy-go front which he's displayed since Rob's death has been an attempt to shield me from the power of his grief. He hasn't wanted to burden me and I, in my despair, have bought into his apparent ability to cope, because it's been easier than probing beneath the veneer. This morning, I call on his help and protection as a man. What a torrent of love and rage that call released. I asked him, in effect, to take his father's place. And that's exactly what he did. He sent O'Brien packing and brought me home. He dealt with it. And what's my response? Before I've even thanked him, I'm talking about calling on the services of a real man. I've well and truly humiliated my son. Congratulations, Rosa.

'Dan. Let me make you a drink.'

'No, thanks. The lads are coming in a minute.'

'They're not here yet. Talk to me. Please.'

Reluctantly he returns.

'I don't know what I would have done if you hadn't rescued me,' I said. 'I was very scared. You reminded me so much of your dad, you know. I remember once years ago, some drunk in a bar started coming on to me, and your dad kicked him into the street and nearly got himself arrested. You're so, so like him.'

Danny looks slightly mollified. 'I should have smashed his face in.'

'No. What you did was perfect. He's had to face the fact that we aren't just two defenceless females in the house. It'll make him think. Maybe he'll decide it's not worth it.'

I'm good. I nearly convince myself that what I say is true. And Danny's definitely starting to thaw out.

'I think there's some law about sending obscene publications through the post that the police could use against O'Brien,' I go on. 'And since Tom's on the spot it'd save calling Penny Black. You know how long she'll hang around, and I've got so much to do today.'

Danny laughs. My repair job's coming along nicely.

'But if you think it's better to call Penny, then that's what I'll do. I'll be guided by you.'

I can almost hear his bruised ego healing over.

'You're right. She'll want to waste my time as well as yours, and I've got a band practice. Tell Tom. It'll be much quicker.'

I give him a hug. 'You know, you were so fierce, I thought Old Mr Pindoria was going to have another heart attack. I even felt a bit sorry for O'Brien. I hope you're never that cross with me.'

Danny knows I'm joking, but he likes it nonetheless.

'Any time you're worried about O'Brien, or anything else for that matter, you tell me. I'm here for you. Whenever. Wherever. Whatever.'

I'm choked. My little boy isn't little any more. As we stand by the cooker clutching each other, I'm also aware that even at five feet ten I'm now dwarfed by him and I can feel hard male muscle under his sweatshirt where once there was soft baby flesh.

'I promise,' I say.

After that we wind down to our more usual prosaic level of communication. Things are chugging along nicely. Maybe now's the time to bring up my suspicions about Dwaine. Danny and I don't get much chance for quiet chats.

'There is one thing I've been a bit concerned about,' I say.

Danny looks pleased that I'm consulting him so soon after his offer to share my worries. He's hardly ecstatic, however, when I tell him what's bothering me.

'You're not worrying about whether Dwaine's taking drugs,' he says. 'It's whether I am.'

Down the toilet goes my bridge-building. Why do I

never know when to leave well alone? Why do my children always see straight through me? Another minefield stretches ahead into infinity and beyond.

'Lots of people your age in your situation would be tempted. As a way of escaping reality . . . You've had a lot on your plate this year. And I did find the Rizla paper and that white powder in the studio.'

My words hang in the air.

'Don't you trust me?'

'Of course.'

'Well then.'

He hasn't denied it. And he hasn't explained the stuff in the shed. Oh God. I can't ask again. I'm such a coward. I'll focus on Dwaine instead.

'Danny, I like Dwaine and I like his mum, and I don't want to see him ruining his life. You must have noticed that he's really spaced out a lot of the time.'

'That's just Dwaine. It's an act. He thinks it makes him look cool.'

I tell him about the tube, and how Dwaine didn't even seem to recognise me.

'I expect he had stuff on his mind.'

'It wasn't like that.'

'What do you want me to do about it?'

'Does he confide in you?'

'If he does, by definition it would be confidential so I wouldn't tell you anyway.'

This conversation's worse than useless. It's just fuelling my neurotic imaginings. A picture of Danny snorting coke in the school toilets slaps itself unbidden onto my internal big screen, complete with Surround Sound.

'Well, if Dwaine's serious about the group, not to

mention his college prospects, being off his face isn't the way to succeed.'

I don't know what Danny's reply would have been, for at that moment Anna ambles into the room. Like a heatseeking missile she homes in on O'Brien's postcard.

'It's from Mick,' she says.

'Probably the same Mick who trapped Mum in the cornershop half an hour ago.' Danny gives Anna chapter and verse, finishing off with, 'He's weird and that's one weird postcard. Stay away from him.'

Anna turns on him. 'You're my brother, not my father. Don't tell me what to do.'

'I'm not telling you what to do—'

'You are. You just said stay away from him.'

'For fuck's sake, we're only trying to protect you. This bloke's looney tunes.'

'Danny, don't swear. He's right, Anna. Mick O'Brien's very odd, and I've forbidden you to speak to him. I hope you've remembered that.'

'What happened to democracy in this family? I thought we discussed things and then came to a collective decision. That's how it used to be, when Dad was around. Now you boss me about and give me no say at all. You don't care about my feelings. It's like living in Stalinist Russia.'

'You're not to have anything to do with him. I mean it.'

'I heard you the first time.' She moves towards the door.

'Leave the card here, please.'

'Why?'

'I want to show it to the police.'

'The *police*? Why?'

'It's not a suitable postcard for a man to send to a young girl.'

'Why not?'

'Fucking frogs? Do me a favour.'

'Shut up, Danny. It's none of your business.'

'If I see that pervent anywhere near you, it *will* be my business.'

'It's a nature-study card of things in nature doing natural things, and you're both pathetic, dirty-minded idiots.' She rips the card into tiny little pieces and throws them up into the air. 'Try showing *that* to the police.'

Then she storms out of the kitchen, shouting, 'I'm going out!'

'Where?'

'To Crystal's.'

Danny and I wince as the front door slams shut. I'm surprised the glass panel doesn't shatter. We gather up the torn pieces of card. A moment later, Tom appears.

'What's up with Anna?' he asks. 'I saw her running up the road as if the hounds of hell were after her.'

I tell him. He says the postcard wouldn't count as an obscene publication anyway. Not since it's issued by the Natural History Museum.

'Should I have a word? Warn this man O'Brien off again?' he says.

Here's where I have to be diplomatic. 'What do you think, Dan?'

I can see he's not thrilled, but common sense prevails.

'Yeah. OK.' And then, grudgingly, 'Thanks.'

After that I offer Tom some lunch. But he refuses.

'I'm in the middle of a tricky case. Gang of young thugs have beaten up a ninety-two-year-old woman. She died this morning, so it's murder. I need some names and so far nobody's been willing to talk, but this afternoon I'm going to see someone who might just do the business. I left the address in my other coat. That's why I popped back. See ya later, folks.'

Is this man never off duty? He has that gleam in his eye that I've come to recognise: his bloodhound gleam. Detecting gives him a real buzz.

On balance it's better he's out of the way – in case Danny's feathers get accidentally ruffled again by me inadvertently asking him for advice, or for his opinion, or for anything else that makes my son feel insecure.

After lunch, Dwaine and Delroy appear and I'm extra specially nice to Dwaine, so that Danny doesn't think I'm treating him like a street-corner junkie.

Being Director-General of the UN would be a breeze after living with my children.

In the afternoon I feel restless. Anna's out, so is Tom, and the boys are breaking the sound barrier in the shed. No one needs me and there's nothing I want to do. Eventually I make a momentous decision.

I'll have a proper walk round the park.

I'm going to confront my ridiculous fears and try to make my feelings about our lovely park change back to what they once were. When Rob and I wanted to talk privately, without being interrupted by the children, we always used to go to the park. We had some of our best conversations out there, looping round in a figure of eight, through the woodland walk, past the bandstand and the tennis courts and into the flower garden, before ending up on a bench next to Prince Albert. How stupid to deprive myself of something so pleasant because it reminds me of things that are gone.

Be honest, Rosa.

Because I'm frightened of how it makes me feel.

Because I somehow feel the park's out to get me.

It's all in the mind.

I overcame my fear of Rob's old studio. Now it's time to tackle the park. What's the point of living opposite a beautiful place if you never use it?

It crosses my mind that Mick O'Brien might accost me again, but I don't care. I stride purposefully across the road.

It's not good. But it could be worse.

In spite of the cold, I'm sweating, and every step is a struggle. I start off by pretending to myself that I'm doing one of my usual quick trips through on my way to somewhere else. Then I realise that's counter-productive. I must face up to what I'm doing. Where I am. Which is walking round the football field and the winter-bare flower gardens, just for the sake of it.

Just for pleasure.

To take the air.

No stress.

Once I'm near Prince Albert and the top gate, I breathe more easily. I stop flinching at shadows and imagining malevolent squirrels are on the attack. I even manage to wave at Jules and Georges and wonder at the absence of Jacques without reading anything sinister into it.

It's not easy, but I think I'm winning. I've nearly completed my circuit when I spot Singing Vic. He's sitting on a bench in deep conversation with someone – I can't see who. I see the person rise, as if to go, and then Vic pulling him or her back down. It looks like some kind of argument.

Maybe it's another gambling crony to whom he owes money, I think sourly as I make my way home.

Anna doesn't return until nine. At eight o'clock when I am staring out of the window for the umpteenth time, wondering if she's OK, I see Tom talking to Mick O'Brien. Whatever he's saying has completely eradicated O'Brien's infuriating smile. When Tom comes in a moment later, I call out to him, but he merely shouts a greeting and rushes straight up to his room. A change of clothes later, he emerges, looking very flash in his leather jacket.

'Can't stop – things to do, people to nick,' he carols as he strides past the kitchen on his way out.

As he reached the gate, Tom looked back at the house and smiled with pleasure. Through the curtains a warm glow was visible and the whole place looked so inviting and cosy that he was almost tempted to forget about his evening's work and go back inside. He'd open a bottle of wine which he and Rosa could drink whilst watching some trashy TV. Eventually Anna would return and then Danny, and they'd all chat about everything and nothing until it was time for bed. A real home. A real family. Something he'd never experienced. Not like this. His mother's massive ego allowed for only one main player in their family saga, and when he looked back over his life with Flick, all he could see was arctic permafrost, or electric storms. Two people inhabiting the same space, but worlds apart. Spinning in their own lonely orbit, occasionally colliding with devastating results. No peace. No tranquillity. No real love. Not like the Thorn household where, in spite of all their troubles and their family squabbles, the love shone through, bright and steady.

He'd thought he didn't need this. That it was better to keep himself to himself. His marriage to Flick had proved that. But now he found his defences crumbling. He wanted to warm himself in this brightness for a while longer. When he'd called at his new flat earlier he'd had a shock. The builders were nearly finished. He'd panicked and impulsively told them he needed a complete new bathroom. That would keep them busy for another few weeks.

As he passed Vic Verdi's house, he saw a figure sitting on the front wall. Vic himself. On his mobile.

'Evening,' he said, wanting to spread his good mood around. Vic acknowledged him with a minimal gesture, and carried on talking. His tone was urgent and intense.

Tom grinned. Takes one to know one, he thought. Anyone who'd spent a lifetime dealing with Eunice Brice understood immediately why a man with a perfectly good home and a working landline would choose to spend a dank November evening making phone calls on the pavement outside his house.

Vic Verdi glared at the retreating back of Rosa's policeman. What gave him the right to be so cheerful? At the moment, Vic hated happiness. Until recently, happiness had been his best friend, his constant companion. He and happiness had hung out together – best mates. Vic took happiness's company for granted.

Not any more. For happiness had slung his hook. Vanished into the wide blue yonder. Disappeared without trace. Rosa said her policeman was a detective. Maybe if Vic asked nicely, he would detect where happiness had taken himself, and send him back, tail between his legs, to Vic.

Or then again, maybe not. The last thing he needed was the law snooping around.

Why had Rosa said that thing about the pack of cards? What did she know? She was a very forthright person, Vic told himself. If she knew, she'd have said something.

Maybe she was waiting. For the right moment.

The sword of Damocles glittered over Vic's head, driving him almost to distraction.

If she knew about the cards, what else did she know? And if she told anyone, then it would all come out. Not just the cards thing, but all of it. And he couldn't bear that. Not yet. Maybe not ever.

How could he keep his secrets?

He couldn't. But one thing he did know.

Rosa Thorn must not be allowed to spoil things.

TWENTY-ONE

Common frog. *Rana temporaria.* In the summer months, frogs lurk under tall plants, and only come out on damp, clement evenings for the purpose of hunting small insects.

I never used to mind Monday mornings. When I was just an actor and a mother, Mondays were like any other day – some good, some bad. But now one of my stints at Churchill Towers is on a Monday, I have a whole different attitude. Since Rob died, my sleep patterns have been odd at the best of times. I tend to wake in the night for no reason, and nearly every day I surface at 5.30 and that's the end of any pretence at slumber. I just lie in my bed feeling bleak. And on Mondays, I also have the ghastly sinking sensation that marks a session at the chalkface.

This dank November Monday is particularly grim. Everyone in the house slouches around, avoiding each other and snarling. I've been up since five, cleaning the house, and I'm trying hard not to play the martyr, as I see my newly spotless kitchen surfaces being desecrated by spilled milk, tea rings and bits of cereal. I used to be a household slut, careless and sloppy. I preferred places to look cosy and lived-in, not clinically spick and span. In past months I've suffered a sea change. Nowadays dirt is The Enemy in Our Midst, to be rooted out and destroyed, and a crooked picture sends me into paroxysms of discomfort until it's straight. It doesn't take Sigmund Freud to work out why a fully paid-up member of the Filth Packet Association has suddenly metamorphosed into Mistress Houseproud. But we all, including me, find this new manifestation quite difficult to take.

I'm too busy scrubbing a coffee-stain off a kitchen chair cushion, therefore, to fully register the fact that Anna is carrying a new school bag. By the time it clicks and I ask myself where the bag has come from, she's left.

Danny is uncharacteristically grim this morning. He was out late last night. I try not to interrogate him, or to examine his pupils too closely, but remind him of the rule on being home by ten on school nights. He sucks his teeth and stomps off after Anna.

When Tom appears I'm looking forward to some adult conversation, but he gulps down a cup of coffee in three seconds flat and tells me he'll be away for a couple of days.

'Oh.' I must sound a bit put out, for he sits down opposite me.

'Are you OK?'

The last thing I want is for him to think I care one way or the other whether he's here or not.

'Fine,' I say. 'Just a bit early-morningish. Not my best time of day. I usually feel like Medusa the Gorgon till at least ten thirty and five cups of strong coffee.'

He smiles. He has a dimple on his left cheek. It's

nice. I've chosen the wrong image to convey my grouchiness, for I know my hair, which I haven't yet brushed, does indeed resemble Medusa's nest of serpents.

'Don't say it,' I snap.

'Say what?'

'Say that I look like Medusa as well as feeling like her.'

He bursts out laughing. 'You look fine to me.'

Why does that lift my spirits?

Not for long. He's on his feet again, washing his coffee mug, pulling on his coat while telling me his plans. His informant in the granny-killing has decamped without leaving a forwarding address. Tom has it on good authority that he's somewhere in Brighton, so he's going there to track him down with the help of the local CID.

'Hope you catch him,' I say to his retreating back.

I ignore the feeling inside which tells me that I'm a bit upset that he's going away and, moreover, can't wait to be out of my house, and pretend it's a natural unease at the thought of once more being alone with the children without a man around, and with O'Brien digging for Britain over in the park. I convince myself that this is the case, and having wiped down the oven and folded the dishcloths, I can no longer put off the evil moment. I set off for work.

Before school starts I see Fred Borrage talking to Fax Max near the derelict building.

'Morning, Fred. Was anyone in there last Friday?'

'Course they wasn't, miss. Must of bin your imagination.'

Fax Max sniggers. 'Bet you've got quite an imagination an' all, Rosa.' He licks his full red lips. They glisten. I notice he's holding a flashy camera.

'Going creative, are we, Max?' I ask.

'What?'

'Taking Fred's photo. Gritty urban shots?'

'What? No . . . Leo wants some snaps of the building before it's demolished – for the archives.'

'I'll leave you to it then.'

Once I'm well away from them, I hear the low rumble of voices as they resume their conversation. Max looked uncomfortable there for a moment. Wonder why? I'll ask Guy the Groper what he knows about those two. Not that I see much of him nowadays. If I didn't know better, I'd think he was avoiding me. After doing up Rob's room he'd got into the habit of popping in every now and again for a coffee. All that's stopped in the last month.

Both my neighbours seem to have crossed me off their Christmas list.

A Maths teacher at Churchill, a bitter woman whose husband died fifteen years ago, said that sooner or later, all widows are dropped by their married friends. The wives fear their husbands might stray when confronted by the ever-available presence of the merry widow. But this theory, whose truth I've yet to prove with regard to my married friends who've all treated me well, in spite of my being so unsociable since Rob's death, cannot apply when it comes to Singing Vic and Guy the Groper, neither of whom have wives.

Guy's having a lot of visitors at the moment, and for once they're not lovestruck women. This lot are male and they come under cover of darkness. Nor are they the sort you'd take home to Mother. One evening as I went to dump some rubbish in the bin out the front, Guy was on his doorstep talking with a couple of really shifty characters. For want of anything better to say, I asked jokily whether he was having a party and could we all come, but he laughed in the way people do when they don't want to chat, and whizzed his seedy pals into the house.

Whizzing isn't a verb normally associated with Guy, whose leisurely take on life is legendary. Maybe it's the widow thing. Maybe he's scared I have a plan to be the next Mrs Groper.

He should be so lucky.

I don't think about Guy for long. I'm too busy. As well as my normal classes, which include the dreaded 9P who locked me in the staff loo last week, I'm auditioning for the Christmas Show. I'm amazed at how many kids want to take part. By the end of the afternoon I've whittled it down to eight acts including Crystal, Athy and friends who perform a storming dance routine to a hip-hop number. I'm disappointed but not surprised that Anna doesn't audition. As a small child she loved dancing, but now she's self-conscious. It would take a miracle to coax her onto a stage. And with the director being her mother, I doubt even a very large bribe would be sufficient to bring her anywhere near the Drama Studio.

I find the relationship between Anna and her new friends puzzling. Jess is right: they're not her type. They're too loud, too brash, too in-your-face. At Godolphin, Anna's best friend was a tiny Chinese girl called Lin whose father was a diplomat. Her return to China shortly after Rob died was another blow for Anna: the girls had been friends since primary school. Lin had exquisite manners, a mischievous sense of humour, and she loved what she called 'little chats'. She and Anna, unlike many of their contemporaries, had not yet entered full-blown adolescence, and were still happiest doing little-girl things. I've an image of them last Christmas, Anna's fuzzy blonde curls next to Lin's shiny black bob. Anna gave Lin a cuddly toy dog, and Lin gave Anna a writing set – paper, a bottle of black ink, and special Chinese calligraphy brushes. Little-girls' presents. Anna's a one-best-friend girl, and she wept for days after Lin left.

She doesn't fit in any way with the streetwise Crystal and Athy. I don't know about Laxmi. I've yet to hear her utter more than one or two words, so I can't tell what she's really like. I think she's a camp-follower. I suspect that if Crystal told Laxmi to jump off a tall building she'd be up there without a parachute before you could say kamikaze.

Laxmi comes to watch Athy and Crystal audition. I ask her why she isn't in their group. Crystal answers for her.

'Laxmi don't dance, miss.'

Laxmi giggles. Then Athy sticks her oar in.

'All she can do is that boring Indian stuff. She does it on Saturdays with her cack Indian mates. Got the saris and little bells and everything.'

I feel slightly betwixt and between with Anna's friends. Not quite a mum, and not quite a teacher. But I can't let this pass.

'Don't rubbish other people's culture, Athy. And if you want to be in this show you'll have to watch your language.'

Athy looks ashamed. 'Sorry, miss. Only joking. Sorry, Lax. Your dancing's really cool.'

'Laxmi, is it true? Do you do proper Indian dancing?'

The girl blushes and nods.

'I'd love to have one of your dances in the show. Who do you dance with?'

'Dimple, Vandna and Kalpna.'

'Bring them to see me tomorrow and show me what you can do.'

Laxmi's huge dark eyes betray her excitement, but she pretends she doesn't care one way or the other. She nods in what she considers is a suitably nonchalant way.

'If you like, miss.'

As they're leaving after the auditions, I hear Athy say: 'Let's find Anna and persuade her to audition. She'd be cool.'

'Yeah,' says Crystal, 'but she says she don't want to be in the show.'

'We'll just have to persuade her then.'

You'll be lucky, I think to myself. But I'm touched that her friends are so anxious for Anna to take part.

As I walk along the cloister, I glance towards the derelict building. Tonight there's no disturbance from behind the shuttered windows. The place is empty. Dead. There's a poignancy about it. Like a discarded lover, once the centre of someone's universe, it lies in the darkness, unkempt and uncared for, brooding hopelessly over its past. No use to anyone. I shiver. The November night is damp and chilly. I'll wear my heavy winter coat tomorrow.

At the gate I glance back. Lights blaze in the Observatory and I see Leo peering through his telescope. It's trained in my direction. As I watch him watching me, he flicks his remote and the lights go off. I turn back to the street and collide with Mary the Hologram. She's carrying a 1950s standard lamp with a fringed shade in maroon and beige.

'Sacred heart, you gave me a shock, Rosa. What are you doing lurking around in the night, frightening folks out of their wits?'

'I could say the same for you.'

'Haven't I just been making old Mrs Bains comfortable for the evening. Not that I get any thanks for it. That woman would try the patience of The Lord God and all His angels. Look at this lamp, would ye? The ould dear was chucking it out. What a waste. 'Tis a lovely thing, real quality.'

Mary works for the Council as a home help, which is one of the reasons she knows so much about what's going on in the neighbourhood. Her network of old folk with time on their hands is more effective than the CIA and MI5 rolled into one, and the products of her scavenging skills could refurbish Buckingham Palace.

'I'll give it to Marge. She'd maybe get a few quid for it on her stall.'

Singing Vic's mother Marge runs a bric-à-brac stall on Camden Market at the weekends. Thanks to Mary, much of the discarded rubbish of Consort Park finds its way onto this stall, with small commissions for her as part of the deal.

Now she bends towards me. 'Do ye know what's up with himself at the present?'

'Himself?'

'Victor. His ma's real worried about him.'

Oh yes? 'Worried about what, Mary?'

'Apparently he's out all hours, coming and going as he pleases with no thought whatsoever for poor Marge. And he won't be spoken to – he's developed a powerful temper all of a sudden – and him always so pleasant.'

'Oh dear.'

'And . . .' here she becomes even more conspiratorial, 'she says he might be In Debt. He's been selling some of their stuff. He thinks she hasn't noticed, but she has.'

Well, well.

'Have ye noticed anything? Has he said anything to you, what with you being next door and all?'

The trick with Mary is to keep your own counsel. She's a wonderful fount of gossip, but in order not to become part of it, you learn to listen but never to speak, however harmless your words may seem to you.

'I'm out at work a lot nowadays. I hardly ever see him.'

Mary's eager face falls. Then she rallies, and clutches my arm, eyes big and earnest. 'You want to watch that O'Brien fella, the one that's sniffing around your Anna.'

Tell me something I don't know, Mary. 'Why?'

'I know someone who was friends with his poor mother.'

'And?'

Mary leaned even closer. 'Apparently he used to wallop her something awful, poor soul.'

I knew it. I've seen the violence in those beautiful eyes. The violence that belies the soft Irish lilt and the ubiquitous smile.

'Are ye all right, Rosa? You look a mite peaky.'

'I'm fine. Are you sure that's what this woman said?'

Mary's outraged that anyone should question the quality of her information.

'As God is my witness, Rosa, the man is dreadful bad news. Didn't Mrs Hogan see the bruises with her own eyes! And since the ma died he's not been right in the head. Mrs Hogan says it's the guilt.'

She clutches my arm. 'There's talk that she didn't die of a heart attack, though that's what it says on the death certificate.'

'What do you mean? Are you saying he killed her?'

Mary clamps her lips tight shut. Then she says, 'As you well know, I'm not one to gossip. All I'm saying is, if it were my daughter I'd be very careful. Now if you'll excuse me, Rosa, I have to be at Mr Williams's before six o'clock or he'll wet his pants.'

She stalks off, clutching the lamp like a Roman centurion.

I know how Mary operates – I've heard it before. She takes one tiny bit of unsubstantiated gossip and embroiders it until even the protagonists of her tall tales wouldn't recognise themselves. I don't necessarily believe what she says. After all, in spite of his activities, it was O'Brien who saved me from certain death by red van. I keep remembering this – clutching onto it for comfort when my suspicions about him spring up again. It doesn't square with the notion of him as a deranged stalker with nothing but evil in his heart.

I'm so preoccupied with my festering thoughts that I'm not looking where I'm going, and on the corner of George Street I cannonade straight into two figures. It's Guy and a plump little man. I recognise him as the most frequent visitor among his new friends.

'Sorry!'

The man scowls. 'See you, Guy.' Then he jumps into a van and drives away.

'I didn't hurt him that much, did I?'

Guy laughs. 'He was just off anyway. How's life then, Rose?'

'You never told me you knew Fred Borrage,' I said.

'Didn't I? There you go . . .'

Sometimes Guy's old hippy insouciance irritates me.

'I hope he's not a close friend,' I say. 'I think he's a nasty old windbag.'

'He's OK. You just have to know how to get on his right side.'

'And you do, I suppose.'

He shrugs. I change the subject before my irritation gets the better of me. 'Have you seen Vic lately?'

'No, why?'

'I just wondered if he's OK. He seems a bit quiet.'

'Vic – quiet! That'll be a first. Actually, I don't have much to do with him any more, not since Rob . . . To be honest, Rose, we were never that close. We used to meet round at yours for the odd game of cards, but it was Rob who'd organise that. Do you think something's up with him?'

I'm unwilling to continue. The mention of card games puts me off. I don't want to start a conversation that may lead to me having to take action that I'm not ready for yet.

'Forget it. Just me being daft.'

We chat for a little longer about everything and nothing. Eventually I go home. The first thing I notice is Anna's new school bag on the hall floor. It bears the logo of the latest cool designer label, and I know it hasn't come cheap.

She's watching TV.

'Where'd you get the bag?'.

'Should I move into the interrogation cell now or later?'

'Ha ha. Where did you get the money to buy a highly expensive designer bag?'

'Are you saying I nicked it?'

'Of course not.'

'Well then.'

'Well then what?'

'Mind your own business.'

'Don't you speak to me like that. I want to know.'

'Tough.'

'That's it! Go to your room.'

'Suits me.'

She brushes past me defiantly. Clever girl. By provoking me into banishing her she's brought to a halt all questions about the bag.

Apart from her birthday cash, Anna has only a few pounds saved from her pocket-money – certainly not enough to buy this particular item. I look at it, hoping that maybe it'll yield a clue. But it just lies there looking smugly expensive.

What I don't want to consider is the possibility that the bag is a gift. A gift from an admirer.

Anna had thought a new bag with the right credentials might make her feel better. Of course it didn't. Nothing would. How could it? She might just as well have used her old bag from last year and not gone through all those hoops to obtain another. Dad always said 'things' didn't make you happy. Well, it was true . . . Except for some things. She was certain that those things might do the trick. If she got it right, did it properly . . . but with everything as it was, it sometimes seemed too difficult. She felt a creeping sense of helplessness. She didn't have what it took. Didn't have it in her. She wished she could hibernate until the spring, like the small frog she'd found hidden under the shed in the garden. She pulled the duvet over her head and imagined she was in a small dark warm space smelling of wood and grass where no one could find her.

TWENTY-TWO

I can't sleep tonight. I thrash around in bed indulging in one gloriously extravagant worry-fest.

Then I start worrying about my worrying.

In an attempt to wear myself out, I take a walk around the sleeping house. The moon is full and the night clear, so I don't need lights. Anna's sleeping with her duvet thrown back, in spite of the winter chill. She still sucks her thumb when she's asleep. It makes her look much younger than she is. Her dressing-table's devoid of the clutter that used to cover its surface. It's now home to the shrine that I discovered in Rob's old studio. In the middle, the urn and the photograph, and on either side the tapering church candles smelling faintly of beeswax. I stare at the black jar. I try to associate it with Rob. I think to myself, That's Rob in there. Rob.

I used to run my fingers through his curls. Now I could open the lid and run my fingers through his ashes.

Same thing.

Rob.

Isn't it?

As I look at the urn, I'm hit by a certainty. The Rob I loved would not want to be housed in such an ornament. He'd be utterly offended by the cheap imitation Greek vase, and his restless spirit, not to mention his tendency to claustrophobia, would go mad confined to that jar for all eternity. I make a vow that sometime soon, Anna, Danny and I will set him free. I'll talk to them about where and when. I cover Anna with the duvet and continue my perambulations.

I pass Tom's room and am suddenly overwhelmed by raging nosiness. I can't bear the thought of a space in my house forbidden to me.

Since he's been living here, he hasn't once invited me into his room – not even as a courtesy to see what he's done with it. At the same time, he's made pretty free with my kitchen. Oh yes, he's made himself at home in there, all right. In a frenzy of indignation, I bend down and peer through the keyhole. I can see very little. Just a plain wooden desk by the window with a phone, fax, laptop and printer. There's also a photo, but I can't see who's in it. Ex-wife? Mother? I sense that the rest of the room is very empty. A minimal space. Our Tom travels light. No excess clutter in his life. That includes people. He hasn't invited one friend back for coffee or a meal in all the weeks he's been here. I try the handle. It's locked. I could, if I wanted, lever the door open with one of Rob's chisels. Tonight would be a good time – while he's away. Then I could hire a locksmith to mend the door tomorrow before he comes back. He'd never know.

The grandfather clock on the landing strikes three and brings me to my senses. I'm behaving like a nosy landlady in a sitcom. Of course Tom hasn't got much stuff. It's in storage waiting for when his flat's finished. And he works such long and irregular hours that he doesn't have time to bring friends back. Or maybe he does and I just haven't been around.

Maybe it's not his friends he's keeping away from me and the house, but me and the house he's keeping away from his friends. Maybe he doesn't think me fit company for them, or my house a good enough venue. Maybe he's ashamed of us. That would fit in with what he said when his mother was here.

Anyway, locksmiths cost a fortune and I couldn't care less about Tom Brice or his room. As long as he pays his rent on time, that's all that bothers me. He can keep fifty dancing girls in there as far as I'm concerned.

In Danny's room, I trip over his guitar. He's left it lying in the doorway. Typical. He turns over and murmurs, 'Wass up?'

'Nothing,' I say. 'Go back to sleep.'

My final port of call is the kitchen, where I make myself a mug of hot milk in the hope that it'll send me to sleep. It does the trick. I climb back into bed and drop off immediately.

Then I'm sitting bolt upright. Something's woken me.

The house is completely still. Nothing stirs, and yet . . . The air around me feels wrong. I'm paralysed. I can't move. I listen to the fierce thudding of my heart – but it's not my heart I'm hearing. It's something else. And it's the something else that's not right.

Our upstairs landing is never completely silent. There's always the grandfather clock. I inherited it from my Great-aunt Alice and it keeps perfect time. It sits in the centre of our home, the beat of its swinging pendulum underscoring all we do. I know its rhythm so well that I no longer register it.

Except tonight.

The rhythm's wrong. It's lopsided. Unequal. And it jangles. Like it does when someone knocks against it. Danny or Anna must have gone to the loo and blundered into it.

They don't pass the clock to get to the loo.

Danny and Anna. I must go to them. Because if they didn't bump the clock, then who did?

I command my fear-frozen body to move, and eventually it obeys. I grab one of my stiletto heels from the shoe-rack and creep out of my room. I can hear the first birdsong. On the landing the pendulum still ticks unevenly. I look along the corridor. Steely light is pushing back the night shadows but there are still pools of darkness hanging in the air. Danny's door is closed.

Wasn't it open when I made my earlier visit?

I tiptoe down the landing clutching my weapon. I'm shaking. In spite of my fear, I know that if anyone has harmed my boy, I will kill them. I turn the handle and open his door.

He lies on his back snoring gently. Thank God. I'm about to leave him to sleep when I see his guitar. It's propped up by the far side of his bed. The same guitar that I tripped over earlier.

Except then it was blocking the doorway.

Danny must have woken at some point and moved it. Mustn't he?

I go to Anna's room. She too sleeps peacefully, duvet flung off again. I inspect her room. Nothing seems to have changed. But then I notice something.

Rob's photo is face down on Anna's dressing-table.

It must have fallen over. Mustn't it?

Someone's broken into my house.

Maybe they're still here.

I curse the fact that we don't have an upstairs phone. Rob couldn't stand the ringing when he was working. I meant to rectify this when I became a defenceless widow lady, but never got round to it. The nearest phone is in the kitchen. I'm too scared to go downstairs. I stand quivering and dithering on the landing for what seems like a millennium. My ears strain to hear any strange sounds. I will myself to move, but my feet remain rooted to the spot.

Then an electric current of terror surges through me. Something has touched my leg.

I force myself to look down. It's the one-eyed cat.

My heart is thumping so intensely I think it will burst, but at least I've been jolted out of my paralysis. I follow the cat downstairs, aware of every creak. The sitting-room door's open. I do a quick check. Nobody is there, but I spot all sorts of little alterations. The photos are at a slightly different angle, the coffee-table is nearer the armchair, the curtain folds are disturbed. In the kitchen it's the same. Fruit bowl at the wrong end of the table. Chair cushions changed round. Egg-timer on the window-sill instead of the shelf. Someone's spent a long time in my house, scrutinising every object.

How did he gain entry? I check all the doors and windows. In the bathroom is a tiny open window high up over the bath. If this was his way in, he must have been very slight. But if he didn't come that way, how else did he get in? He must have had a key. Apart from the family and Tom, who else has keys? Have any gone missing? I check the spare ones. They're still all there.

I try to remember which of the neighbours have emergency keys. Several – but none of them would have the remotest interest in wandering round my house in the dead of night.

This is weird. This is horrible. But I mustn't panic. I have to be strong, and protect the children. I've checked everywhere now. Whoever it was has gone. He must have climbed out of the bathroom window, knocking against the clock on his way along the landing. The thought calms me.

I wake Anna and Danny, then phone the police. I hope Penny Black comes. She'll understand why I'm so spooked – she knows the background. I'm in luck. I feel weak with relief at the sight of her sturdy body through the stained-glass panel on the front door. She's with a male colleague. I take them round the house, showing them all the objects that have been moved. Penny asks if anything's been stolen. I have to say no. I catch sight of her studiously blank face, and I feel foolish, as if I'm making it all up. I'm glad the children are able to confirm what I'm saying. She takes me to one side.

'Is Inspector Brice here?' Do I detect an extra note of curiosity in her voice?

'No. He's out of town.'

I ask her whether she thinks Mick O'Brien is responsible. She gives an almost imperceptible sigh. A 'here-we-go-again' type of noise. She tells me he has no previous form for housebreaking – or anything else. She then says they've other calls to make, and that the Scene of Crime officer will be in touch. I was wrong about Penny understanding. I don't think she likes me any more. Her offhand attitude is more than simple lack of interest. I wonder what I've done to deserve it. I ask whether this man has to rape and kill my daughter before she takes him seriously. I see from her face that she thinks I'm hysterical. She probably suspects I've organised it all myself as an attention-seeking device. She assures me that Mick O'Brien will have her best attention but that without proof . . .

After the police have gone, the three of us sit silently round the kitchen table nursing cups of strong tea. A short film runs through my mind on a repeating loop: *Ravenlocks and the Three Thorns.* The Thorn family sleep while a hooded figure, with long dark hair and an earring, moves around their home, poking and prying. He examines the posters on Danny's wall. He sniffs the perfume on my dressing-table. He tries out our sofa, then moving through to the kitchen helps himself to food from the fridge. And the climax of my film is when I see him staring down at my daughter as she sleeps, duvet thrown back, honey limbs exposed.

Anna listened to Rosa rabbiting on to Penny Black about intruders. She was embarrassed. Her mother sounded so middle-class and shrill. It was pointless calling the cops. She knew who'd visited her room in the night. It was obvious. It was a message. From him. To say he loved her. To say he was watching over her. In spite of everything. But she couldn't tell anyone that. No one would believe her. They'd think she was mad.

TWENTY-THREE

Earth-covered white bone,
Separated from the rest.
A lonely remnant.

Dawn breaks, and we're still in the kitchen, unable to take ourselves back to bed. Then Anna stands up.

'I'm going down the garden.'

This is code for 'I'm going to sit with my dead pets.'

Our garden's very long, and at the far end, by the railway line, hidden from the house by a willow-cane fence, is the Pet Cemetery. Each animal has a wooden headstone containing the animal's name and dates and an appropriate motto or motif, all carved by Rob. The Cemetery contains a couple of cats, several hamsters, a guinea pig, some mice and a pair of gerbils. And the most recent addition is the squirrel which brought Mick O'Brien into our lives. Its wooden cross is more makeshift than its fellows since there's no Rob to carve it. I never understood why he colluded so wholeheartedly with Anna's wishes on the subject of dead animals. I felt he was encouraging her to be morbid. He just laughed at me.

'In the midst of life we are in death,' I remember him intoning. 'She's learning that nothing's for ever. It's a good thing to know.'

Little did he realise that all the dead things were merely a rehearsal for the Big One: his very own demise. Now Anna truly knows that nothing is for ever. I suppose her attachment to Rob's urn is another expression of her graveyard preoccupations. Rob's fractured early life explains his understanding of her need to keep close the things she loves. But the superstitious, irrational part of me wonders whether, on some level, he knew he wouldn't be around for too long, and was preparing her.

When Anna wants to think she often takes herself off to the Pet Cemetery, so Danny and I are unsurprised at her announcement, even though we both agree that no one in their right mind would choose to sit on a wet bench in the dank winter dawn surrounded by animal graves.

Then we hear her scream.

In the silence of early morning the scream goes on and on, the shrill notes of shock modulating into a keening wail. Danny and I fall over each other in our rush towards the end of the garden.

I shall never forget what lies behind the willow fence.

Anna is surrounded by desecration. The crosses have been ripped out. They lie splintered and scattered, their jagged edges pointing at the sky. The graves are torn open, revealing the pitiful skeletal remains of their little occupants. The squirrel is the nastiest. It's in an advanced state of decomposition and alive with maggots. Whoever did this was in a frenzy. This is no silly prank. It smacks of malevolent, galloping insanity.

Danny and I drag Anna back to the house. The lights

come on next door and as we approach the kitchen, Vic's back door is flung open.

'Vic? Is that you?' It's Vic's mother, sounding panicked.

'No, Marge. It's us,' I call out. 'Nothing to worry about.' The last thing I need is Marge muscling in with helpful suggestions.

My nerves are so on edge that when our door opens, I think it's O'Brien come to gloat. But it's Tom.

'You're supposed to be in Brighton,' I say.

'Found my man and brought him back to London. He's sitting in a cell waiting for me. I thought I'd catch a bit of shut-eye before interviewing him. What's up?'

Danny fills him in while I put Anna to bed. She's inconsolable. I'm filled with impotent rage. I don't know how to make her feel better. All I can do is hold her tight. Eventually she cries herself to sleep. I can't bring myself to go back downstairs. While I'm up here, in this cocoon of sorrow, I don't have to act.

Anna's room is at the back of the house and I can see the Pet Cemetery through her window. I watch as Tom speaks to Penny Black and colleague, who are back with us sooner than they thought. There's a lot of talking and gesticulating, mainly on Tom's part. Penny looks furtive and a bit ashamed. Eventually they return to the house with Danny, and I hear him saying goodbye. Tom's alone in the garden. He has his back to me, looking into the Pet Cemetery. He stands there for a long time. Eventually he turns, an unreadable expression on his face. I leave Anna to her sleep and go down to the kitchen. He's standing by the table.

'How is she?'

'Asleep.' I'm drained dry. I don't even have the energy to sit down.

'Rosa.'

'What?'

'I'm so sorry I wasn't here for you.' His voice is intense.

Through the layers of fatigue, I feel irritated. 'Why should you be?'

He takes me by the shoulders. 'I won't let anything else happen to any of you.' He's talking as if he has some kind of obligation to us.

I summon the last of my strength. 'You're not responsible for me or my family. Tonight's been horrible, but we'll cope. We've come through worse. It's great having you here, but as a lodger – not our private security guard. Our safety's not your problem.'

Tom says nothing. He's still gripping my shoulders.

'I need your rent money, not your protection.'

My words finally penetrate. He removes his hands. They drop heavily to his sides, and hang, helpless.

'You don't get it, do you?' he says. 'I want to look after you.'

A thin beam of early morning winter sun filters through the window, irradiating his face. My stomach does a little flip.

What's going on here? Whatever it is, I can't deal with it now. And I certainly can't deal with the unmistakable frisson of longing that suddenly shoots through my body.

It's the wrong time for this.

'I must get some sleep,' I say. 'I'll talk to you later.'

I go up to my bed and plunge into a dreamless sleep which lasts for hours. When I finally surface, I find Danny and Anna huddled together on the sofa watching daytime TV under a duvet. There's no sign of Tom.

* * *

Danny watched the images flicker away on the TV, knowing that if anyone asked him to fill them in about the programme, he wouldn't be able to do it. His mind was too preoccupied with what had happened in the night. Everyone seemed convinced the Irish git was responsible, but Danny knew better. What he didn't know was how to put things right.

TWENTY-FOUR

Penny Black calls me the next day. The address Mick O'Brien gave the Head Parkie doesn't exist and he hasn't been into work for two days. Penny says a description's been circulated, and if seen he'll be picked up at once. She also assures me that this time there'll definitely be police keeping an eye on the house. She's more attentive than usual. I wonder what Tom said to her.

Anna's taken to her bed and refuses to get up. I'll give it another day and then call the doctor. She won't eat, and that worries me. She's like me and Rob and Danny: tall and skinny but with a huge appetite. A friend once dubbed us The Disappearing Thorns and said watching the four of us walking down the street was like watching animated Giacomettis. Anna has no excess fat stored for times of famine. If she doesn't eat, she'll fade away.

Danny's been magnificent. Late yesterday afternoon while Anna and I were still asleep, he went down to the Pet Cemetery, and reburied all the animals including the revolting squirrel. He gathered up all the bits of broken crosses, and has painstakingly glued them back together. This morning he took me down there, and as I stood on the newly raked gravel, I cried.

Danny's eager face clouded over. 'Hey Mum, I thought it'd make you feel better.'

'I do feel better,' I howled. 'You're a miracle-worker, Danny Thorn.'

But we couldn't persuade Anna to come and look.

'It's spoiled,' she said, and turned her face to the wall.

Danny's disappointment got the better of him. 'Thanks a lot,' he said. 'I wish I hadn't wasted my precious time.'

Then he stormed out. I know he didn't go to school because I phoned in yesterday, and warned them that all three of us would be absent for a couple of days. We need to recover from the shock, and Churchill Towers isn't exactly The Priory. I called Delroy after school, but he wasn't in. Likewise Dwaine. Charlene said she hadn't a clue where he was. Why do I hope that he and Danny aren't together?

I haven't seen Tom and I'm glad. I need to sort out in my mind what's happening here, and how I feel. Every time I rerun that sentence 'I want to look after you', my mind skitters off into another place. If I try to picture his face, all I can see is Anna on her knees surrounded by desecration, or Danny snorting white powder in a seedy public toilet. So it's just as well Tom's made himself scarce. I haven't room in my head for him, too.

Larry L'Estrange chooses this morning to ask if he can come and look at Rob's paintings, with a view to moving them to the gallery ready for the show. He says he has an unexpected 'window' in his exhibition programme and he could mount a show as early as summer next year. In view of what's happened, maybe the sooner Rob's work is away from here, the better. I tell him that today's good. Since my mind's refusing to focus on anything else in a productive way, today would, in fact, be more than good. It would be excellent.

When I go down to check the studio in preparation for Larry's arrival I hear Singing Vic's voice. In his shed. Another voice speaks so quietly I can't hear what's being said. Not that I'm listening, you understand. Vic's tone is urgent.

'You've got to give me more time. It's not easy. There are so many things to consider . . .'

There's an incomprehensible muttering from the other person and then Vic – louder now, more emphatic.

'That's not true. I've told you I'll do it, and I will.'

His shed door opens and I skip into the studio double quick. Vic's cross enough with me as it is. If he caught me eavesdropping he'd never speak to me again. I hear footsteps scrunching off towards the railway line, but I don't dare peek out of the window in case I'm spotted.

Larry arrives two hours later, resplendent in astrakhan overcoat and fedora. His face gleams pale and translucent in the chilly studio. He has to be one of the undead. He's accompanied by Julian, his personal assistant, a young anorexic in his late twenties whose extreme boniness and death-filled orbs have spawned a worrying trend in gallery administration circles. Art-world gossip has it that Larry and Julian are an item, but I don't think so. I've visited Larry's Belgravia mansion and know how devoted he is to his rich, reclusive wife who put up the seed money for the new gallery. Julian's attachment is plain old-fashioned hero-worship, and Larry's acceptance of it, blatant opportunism.

Julian's gimlet eye sweeps across the studio, taking in a couple of damp patches, 3D's musical paraphernalia, and some mouldering plates and cups left over from late-night band rehearsals. He executes an elaborate shudder and hisses, *sotto voce* to Larry: 'The work's rotting away!'

Julian's absence of tact rivals my own.

'It's not,' I start to say defensively, but Larry forestalls me. He lays a restraining hand, sheathed in a glove of softest kid, on Julian's arm.

'We're here to make sure the work is exhibited for all the world to see, and I know Rosa will agree that the L'Estrange Gallery would make the best possible venue for poor Rob.'

I mutter a reluctant assent and leave them to it. I go indoors and prepare a pot of special Japanese tea called 'Mu' that Larry takes with him everywhere. I'm sure Larry's quirks are on the increase. Today it's not just the tea he's brought: it's also a porcelain pot and two matching cups, all exquisitely packed in a lacquered box lined with shot-silk in deepest magenta. I concentrate hard on my preparations. Knowing my present run of luck, I'll probably drop the whole lot on the floor. Then Larry, in a fit of pique, will abandon Rob and his reputation, and I'll end up showing the work in some cosy Hampstead gallery of which no one's ever heard.

I realise that I must want this exhibition if I'm starting to worry about it.

When I take their tea down to the studio, I find them in ecstasy. Or rather, Julian's doing the exclaiming while Larry's flicking a thin tongue backwards and forwards over his lips and dabbing his forehead repeatedly with a snow-white hankie. The tongue-flicking thing is notorious in the art world. It's a sign that Larry's interested. The more flicks, the more interest. He badly wants to get his kid gloves on Rob's work. I'm not surprised. Remembering back to before Rob died, when I could look at the paintings without great shafts of pain streaking through my body, I'd thought it his best stuff ever.

Rob's very first door painting was inspired by his memory of finding Miss Pearl dead. He told me that he'd known something was wrong as soon as he entered the house, and when he saw her closed bedroom door, he looked at it for a very long time before he could open it. He said the image of the door became burned into his memory. One day, at a low point in his life when he thought his work would never be recognised, and that he'd be stuck teaching for ever, his mind once more threw up Miss Pearl's door. On impulse, he started to reproduce it in paint. Just the door, nothing else. He had a compulsion to paint every detail – to get it absolutely right. Like a kind of exorcism. It was a large canvas, nearly three metres high. The image of the door entirely filled its surface. Rob meticulously reproduced the grain of the wood, and all the little blemishes that he remembered were on it, including his own childish initials in the bottom left-hand corner. The initials were special. He'd carved them secretly when he first came from Trinidad. It was one sleepless night, he told me, when he woke up and felt he didn't exist: a nowhere boy. The initials proved to him that he was alive.

The exorcism worked, and Rob found himself more and more preoccupied with the symbolism of doors in his life. He stopped wanting to paint anything else. Doors took over. However, the series he was working on at the time of his death was different: something his fans and collectors would find difficult to believe.

These doors were open.

Not a lot. Only slightly. But open they were, and through the crack, intriguing shapes and forms could be glimpsed, tantalisingly out of focus.

Larry is beside himself with dealer's delight. But being Larry, and cute as a cartload of monkeys, he feigns casual.

'A significant departure, we feel. Robin Thorn painting open doors! Well, well.'

'Of course,' trills Larry's alter ego, 'it might not be what the collectors want. These people are like sheep – anything different from the norm and they panic.'

'I'm sure our collectors will recognise the irreplaceable quality of these particular paintings,' murmurs Larry. 'But Julian does have a point, Rosa. In our experience, people have to be smoothed and soothed into accepting work that's different from an artist's previous *oeuvre*. It may be a wise move to pop everything over to the gallery *tout de suite*, and then we could prepare the ground with some of our more open-minded clientèle.'

I let him stew.

'Of course,' he continues, 'it's entirely your decision. Obviously it would be much easier for us if the canvases were at the gallery . . .'

Julian's hopping up and down in a frenzy of barely controlled greed. He's about to barge in with one of his clangers, but Larry motions him to keep silent.

'The crucial factor is the timing, Rosa. *Carpe diem*, as they say. Robin Thorn was one of this country's most promising artists, but Mistress Public's a fickle jade. At present, his tragic death is still fresh in her mind, and hence, tasteless though it seems, his work is very much flavour of the month. However, it could be a different story if we leave things for another year or so. It's a harsh world out there. We do so understand how much you want to keep Rob's work to yourself. But you have his children to consider, and perhaps, if we may be bold enough to say it, you owe it to them to seize the moment.'

Larry has gone too far.

How dare he lecture me on what's best for my family! I try to control myself but it's useless. Rob always said I find it impossible to hide my feelings.

'I'm not stupid, Larry, and I won't be patronised by you or your sidekick. If you think that's the way to get what you want, you're totally off-beam. You might as well get lost right now.'

The fact that he's absolutely right doesn't make it any easier to bear. I told myself, before he and his one-man entourage arrived, that I wouldn't allow his unctuous manner to get to me. And here I am, falling at the first fence. Julian's skeletal features are a study in fastidious offence, and Larry's an even whiter shade of pale. There's a long pause. We all stare at the dirty floor of the studio.

Eventually Larry coughs delicately.

'We're mortified. If we've offended you, however unintentionally, please accept our deepest apologies. Put it down to our very sincere concern for you and your family, and our inordinate respect for your husband's genius.'

Julian gives a strangulated squawk. I've dared to challenge his idol, so I'm now dead meat as far as he's concerned. His face is contorted with the effort of emulating

Larry's tolerant forbearance. I don't mind. All I care is that I haven't blown Rob's reputation by alienating the most powerful man in the art world. He wants the work enough to swallow my rudeness. That's all that matters. I attempt vulnerable mode.

'I'm sorry, Larry. You didn't deserve that. You're giving me the very best care and advice, and I know how happy that would make Rob. He had such respect for you. It's just that I'm still a bit raw . . .'

Larry oozes compassion. 'My dear girl. Enough said. It's forgotten. Let's all be the best of friends again.'

There's another lull. Julian's mentally measuring canvases. Larry's waiting for me.

Waiting for me to hand over Rob's last canvases.

I open my mouth, but for a split second no words come. My voice has gone into hiding. Then I hear myself.

'It would be wonderful to do the show next summer. And of course you must take the work to the gallery. As soon as possible.'

Julian's gasp of triumph reverberates around the wooden walls. Larry, lizard tongue flicking, extends his gloved hand.

'We're deeply honoured that you should trust us with this so, so precious cargo. I give you my solemn promise that we will mount a memorial show to demonstrate to the entire world what a prodigious talent we've lost.'

He inclines his face towards mine, and I catch a whiff of peppermint beneath the smell of Japanese tea, and beneath that something else, foul and rotting.

'We will make such a show that *le monde entier* will beat a path to our humble door to sing the praises of the great Robin Thorn.'

After the high drama come the mundane details; arrangements about the work being collected and taken to the gallery. Now I've made my decision, I feel empty. Larry and Julian have also had enough. They can't wait to see the back of me. Larry's driver appears as if by magic, and I wave as they glide off down Albert Road in Larry's sleek silver Mercedes. We're all smiling hard. We've all got what we wanted. I can't keep my eyes open. I crash out for at least three hours.

When I wake up, Danny's home.

He's particularly evasive when I ask where he's been.

'Around' is the best he can come up with.

Larry L'Estrange sank back into the expensive leather seat of his expensive car.

'Make the arrangements to extricate those paintings sooner than soon,' he murmured. 'I'm getting one of my feelings.'

'Oh Lord, Larry. The last time that happened, we lost the Baron Hubler Collection to the Wentworth Gallery.'

'Exactly so, dear boy. Exactly so. And this time it's much stronger. Robin Thorn's work should not stay where it is for a second more than is absolutely necessary. See to it, Julian.'

TWENTY-FIVE

I've had to force my personal problems off the agenda for the last month in an effort to get the Churchill Towers Christmas Extravaganza up and running. I'd no idea how difficult it would be to organise teenagers into something that could pass as a semblance of entertainment. Rehearsals have been a nightmare. My own two set-pieces from *Annie* and *Oklahoma!* seemed jinxed from the word go. Singing Vic, who promised to help with the songs, doesn't turn up to rehearsals half the time, and when he does come he's so low energy that the children get bored and don't listen. I asked him once if anything was the matter. He told me to mind my own business and stormed into Dave Alessi's office to talk about next term's peripatetic teachers' timetable. Four days ago, the boy playing Curly in *Oklahoma!* fell off his micro-scooter and broke his leg in three places, so he's singing and dancing in plaster from ankle to thigh. And we're on our third Annie. Annie Number One's parents took her on a bargain pre-Christmas ski trip. Annie Number Two caught a bad dose of chicken-pox, and Annie Number Three is a nightmare creature, blackmailed into taking part by Jess who has some serious dirt on her. She's categorically refusing to wear the Annie wig, because she says she ain't no mingin' ginge. Since the show opens tonight, I think we may have a problem.

Added to this, Jess's Year Seven rap poetry final version is so full of disgusting epithets that the school will hit the tabloid headlines and be closed down if anyone outside Churchill gets wind of it. When Jess told them to tone things down, she was accused of stifling freedom of expression. The precocious little swines said that Jess was a foul-mouthed hypocrite, and suggested they could have a word with their parents about her own linguistic foibles. A compromise was eventually reached, but only by allowing several very dicey words to remain. I'm hoping they say them so quickly that parents won't realise what they are. Crystal and Athy had such a violent disagreement with the other members of their dance group after one rehearsal, that blows were exchanged. Parents came to complain and ended up having their own fight which threatened to spill out onto the streets of South Kilburn and cause a riot. This has now been resolved, or rather, is simmering on the back burner, and I have to ensure that Crystal's mum, Charlene, and Athy's dad aren't sitting anywhere near Rachel's parents and Melina's stepdad tonight when they come to see the show. The only item that's perfect is Laxmi's Indian dance. She and her friends have practised every lunch hour, provided themselves with the most exquisite saris, and look completely gorgeous when they perform.

And what of 3D?

They've refused to come to any rehearsals in school, including the dress rehearsal which we've just finished.

I don't think they've been doing much practice in the studio, either. Danny says everything's under control, but I know something's wrong. By the time I arrive home from rehearsals every day, Danny's already gone. He says he's round at Dwaine's, but when I phoned Charlene she hadn't seen Danny for weeks. She also sounded sick with worry. Dwaine's not arriving home till three in the morning, won't tell her where he's been, and is bright-eyed and hyperactive for the rest of the night, falling asleep round five and having to be kicked out of bed by Charlene every day for school.

'He running wild, that boy. I tell him I am his mother and he must do what I say, but he just laugh at me. He have no respect. I can't do nothing with him Rosa. And it affecting Crystal too. A couple of times I've caught her creeping in late when I thought she fast asleep in she room. She only fourteen years old. I don't know what to do. Can you have a word wit' them? You a teacher. They'll respect what you say.'

In your dreams, Charlene. I can't talk to Dwaine because I never see him nowadays, and I'm loath to do anything to upset the applecart for Anna by giving Crystal the benefit of my wisdom. The friendship is very important to her. She goes off to Crystal's every Saturday and any day Crystal isn't rehearsing. She wouldn't thank me for laying a heavy number on her friend. She's still very wobbly after the Pet Cemetery incident. I don't want to make her worse. Thank God the show will be over tomorrow, and I can get my head around how to spend our first Christmas without Rob.

It's nearly showtime and I've got butterflies. Jess arrived half an hour ago and opened a bottle of Chardonnay, which she keeps trying to pour down my throat. I feel as nervous as if I were performing myself. In a sense I am: Leo's muttering about extending my supply contract into the summer term, but I get the impression this is conditional on my producing a good evening for him, his governors and the Mayor of Brent. Ever since our encounter in the Observatory he's treated me with sad-eyed regret. I reckon he'd like to see the back of me. But Drama teachers are hard to come by, so with any luck my job's safe for a while yet.

If I produce a good show.

The performers are arriving. The atmosphere in the dressing-room has that familiar edge of hysteria. The drama queens in the show are in full flood, with panic-stricken squeals over lost costumes, boastful exaggerations about the hundreds of relatives out front, and the odd bout of tears over nothing in particular and everything in general. I realise that none of 3D has arrived. And neither has their equipment. I phone home.

No reply.

Anna's supposed to be coming with Danny. Yesterday she said she wouldn't come at all, but for once I stopped pussy-footing round her.

'I've worked my butt off organising this show. The group's doing their debut gig. Your best friends are performing. Don't you care about any of us?'

Anna said nothing.

'You're going to stay here stewing in your own miserable juice, are you?'

She shrugged. 'If it's such a big deal I suppose I'll come,' she finally said.

I fixed Danny with my beadiest eye. 'I won't be home before the show. Bring Anna up with you, OK?'

Danny knew better than to say no. So where are they both?

Time's wingèd chariot hurtles towards half past seven. The audience is starting to fill the hall. The noise level's rising: that unmistakable sound of meeting and greeting, excitement and anticipation that sets the actor's veins buzzing.

I now know it's the same for directors.

I peep through the curtains and see Leo ushering his party of dignitaries into their seats. They're all flushed from the fine wine he's been serving them in the Observatory, courtesy of the school budget. Leo's entertainment allowance is a legend in the Borough.

I also see Melina's mum brush past Charlene with a disdainful glance, and even through the ambient noise I hear the sound of Charlene sucking her teeth.

What I don't see is Anna.

I call Danny on his mobile. It's switched off. The stage-manager, a pimply Sixth Former called Perry, says it's 7.30 and time to start. I tell him to wait another few minutes and go out into the street to see if there's any sign of 3D and Anna.

Nothing.

Time passes. The audience is getting restless and so is Leo. He's aiming meaningful glances towards the curtains while chatting manically to the Mayor of Brent. Jess appears.

'We'll have to start without them. They're on last, so let's cross our fucking fingers and hope they arrive by the interval.'

She's right. I take a breath, give Perry the signal and sneak out front to watch.

After all the *Sturm and Drang* of the past month, the

show is a triumph. What is it about children that makes them able to pull the rabbit out of the hat on the day, having demonstrated the commitment and intelligence of lesser life-forms all the way through rehearsals? Annie, resplendent in the wig which she finally agreed to wear two minutes before curtain up, gives a virtuoso performance of moppet pathos, and the audience melts into a puddle of gooey sentiment as she sings 'The sun'll come out tomorrow' with all the little orphans grouped around her, gazing pitifully heavenwards. Laxmi and the Indian girls are mesmerising as they weave their graceful spell back and forth across the stage. A would-be Madonna and an aspiring violinist nicely sandwich a Year Eight boy who beguiles us all with card-tricks that don't always work, and the first half closes with Crystal's group. Their dance routine is a complex concoction of hip grinding and pelvic thrusting that wouldn't look out of place in a lap dancing club. It's saved from obscenity – just – by the sheer *joie de vivre* the girls bring to it. When I'm able to psych myself up to look at Leo and his dignitaries, I'm very relieved to see the Mayor's face. He looks like it's his birthday and Christmas rolled into one. After the dance it's the interval. I notice the warring parents of the dance group congratulating each other on their respective daughters' performances. As I walk past them, Athy, eyes shining, stops me.

'Miss, this is my dad, Nikos. Dad, this is Ms Thorn who directed the show. She's Anna's mum, too.'

It's the man who hangs out with Guy the Groper.

'Hello,' I say. 'We've already met – outside Guy Gropius's house. I nearly knocked you down.'

He doesn't think this is as funny as I do, and can hardly stretch his surly little mouth into a smile.

'Wasn't Athy wonderful?' I say, and his face softens.

'You betcha,' he says, and I hear the Greek accent under the Cockney.

When I reach the dressing-room, 3D has arrived.

'Where've you been?' I shriek. 'And where's Anna?'

'Hi, Mum. Nice to see you, too. Anna's gone to find her seat. We borrowed Stuart's dad's van to bring the gear, and it broke down halfway up Albert Road.'

There's a strange expression on his face.

'Guess who fixed it?'

'I don't have time for guessing games.'

'O'Brien. I went indoors for a screwdriver, and when I came back, there he was. Delroy said he knew straight away what was wrong, and it only took him a couple of minutes to fix. He'd finished by the time I arrived. I wanted to ask him about the Pet Cemetery stuff, but he took off.'

I can't process this information. Not now. 'Thank God someone helped you, even if it was him. Now get that stuff on stage.'

The boys hardly get their equipment in place before the end of the interval. Singing Vic is a tower of strength. He and Dave Alessi lift the heavy speakers like they're taking part in a competition for the world's strongest man. Vic's his old self tonight – loud, ebullient, singing snatches from *The Barber of Seville* as he hauls equipment around. He and Dave have evolved a music-hall patter which has the kids in fits of laughter, and helps calm their jitters. Maybe it's the proximity to an audience, even in a backstage capacity, that's turned him from Mr Misery into Mr Funny.

Then it's the second half, which is quite short: *Oklahoma!*, the rap poetry, a saxophone solo, and finally 3D.

I must now be the most nervous person in the hall. Not about my show, but about 3D. What if they're crap? What if everybody laughs at them? I haven't a clue about the music. I've only heard odd snatches drifting up from the studio. I sit through Curly's triumph as he receives a standing ovation for his all-singing, all-dancing plaster-cast performance. I'm distantly relieved that the rap poets have sussed that if they swear in front of their proud parents, it won't be just the school who get it in the neck, and have therefore toned down their stuff to something even their grannies could live with. When I hear the mournful wailing of the saxophone, I think as I always do, what a sexy instrument it is. And inside I'm quivering and quaking, waiting for 3D.

When they slouch onto the stage, smouldering and arrogant, the whole audience erupts into whoops, cheers and the booing sound that I've learned means approbation, not condemnation, from today's youth.

Hang on, I think. They haven't done anything yet.

Their ecstatic reception gives them the boost they need. They launch into their set with a raw, gut-crunching energy that even an ageing mother finds electrifying. The songs, lyrical yet wild, have a strong melodic line, with a bass beat to die for, and the fusion of styles produces a genuinely original sound. As well as playing guitar, Danny is lead singer. I have to keep reminding myself that this is my baby up there, for the naked power and magnetism of his performance has turned him into a formidable stranger. Of course it's easy to see that this is a group-in-progress – occasionally the insecure schoolboys can be seen peeping through the insolent rock idols. But everyone in the audience knows they're in the presence of something special.

When the set finishes, the place goes into orbit – clapping, stamping, cheering, whooping. The boys do three encores before Leo calls a halt. He delivers a virtuoso thank you to everyone, and Jess and I are pushed on stage to receive flowers, wine and a peck on the cheek. I have to hand it to him: he gives a good speech. I suppose this ability to be sincere yet fluent in off-the-cuff situations is what's helped turn him into Britain's most sought-after Talking Head.

I'm suffused with post-show euphoria. I drag Anna up from the audience and take her backstage. Even she is fizzing with excitement and has lost her air of tragedy. Her beaming face reminds me of what she used to be like, and I realise how much she's changed.

I'll think about that tomorrow.

When we reach the dressing-room, we can't get anywhere near Danny. He and the other Ds are being mobbed by most of the female population of the school, and I don't just mean students. Quite a few of the female teachers are trying to muscle in, too. I find Jess. We've bought goodies for a cast party, to be held in the Drama Studio and so, having enlisted the help of some overexcited orphans, farmers and cowboys, we set off along the cloister.

But our path is blocked by Fred Borrage.

'A superb show. Congratulations,' he booms. 'May I ask where you're going with them boxes and bottles?'

'Fucking cast party, Fred,' carols Jess. I try to ignore the sniggers of the cast. Jess's language never fails to amuse. 'You can come if you like.'

'I don't think so, miss,' says Fred. His body swells with the virtuous self-importance of one who has bad news to impart. 'The Head has informed me that there are to be no post-concert revels on school property.'

We're flabbergasted.

'What?'

'But we promised the children!'

'I can't help that. Rules is rules.'

Jess thrusts her face close to Fred's. The orphans, farmers, cowboys and I regard her apprehensively. We all know Jess on the rampage.

'What rules, you fucking pompous old fart?'

Fred bristles. The rest of us cower.

'There's no call for that,' he says.

'Since when have we not been allowed after-show parties at this pissy school, Fred Borrage?'

'Since now. Please vacate the site. I have to secure it for the night.'

'We'll see about that. You lot, don't fucking move.'

Jess storms off. The children and I have a staring match with Fred Borrage. He wins.

Five minutes later Jess returns, seething.

'Bastard's bolted with the Mayor. I asked Dave Alessi since he's the Head of Creative Arts, but he says it's beyond his remit. What a wuss.'

Fred smirks. 'Glad we've cleared that one up, miss,' he says, jangling his keys. 'Now, if you don't mind . . . Mrs Borrage has already made my bedtime cocoa and she gets very agitated if I don't drink it while it's hot.'

We trail disconsolately towards the dressing-room. What a way to end our triumph. I can't bear the disappointment on the children's faces.

I make a decision.

'We'll have the party at my house, since it's so near the school.'

The children all cheer. Jess looks apprehensive.

'You do know what you're saying? There are some

fucking raving kids at this school – present company excluded – no respect for property or anything else.'

I suddenly, really, want my death-struck house to come to life again. I want it to be full of people laughing and drinking and enjoying themselves.

'I'm sure,' I say. 'Kids, tell the rest of the cast and get your parents' permission. They're welcome, too. Let's get the show on the road.'

Fred Borrage watched the last reveller leave the grounds. He grunted. Good riddance. Who did those bitches think they were, ordering him around in his own buildings? Having the brass nerve to imagine they could hold a function without squaring it with him first. Churchill Towers was his manor. He decided what was what. Teachers, Head Teachers, they all came and went, but he was the nerve centre, the beating heart, the one who kept it all from falling apart. They might imagine they ruled the roost – that was fine by him during school hours. He let them, poor deluded sods. But at all other times the place belonged to him. He decided what went down. No one else. His dream and firm belief was that when he retired, they'd put up a brass plaque to commemorate him. He'd passed many satisfying moments picturing the wording. His favourite read something like In Remembrance of Fred Borrage, the Spirit of Churchill Towers School. *Thinking of the plaque calmed him down, as did thoughts of his retirement which, if everything went to plan, would turn out to be considerably more cushy than he'd ever imagined. He padlocked the main gate and retreated to his office where he picked up the phone and dialled a number.*

'Coast's clear,' he said. 'Spread the word.'

TWENTY-SIX

Fox. *Vulpes vulpes.* Foxes within the same collective, albeit solitary during the hunt for food, enjoy communal activity at night, during which they may emit a strange, barking cry.

The procession down the hill from Churchill Towers draws stares from the few people out and about on this cold December evening. There's a carnival atmosphere as we walk along carrying our party goodies. In many windows Christmas trees twinkle out, their coloured lights adding to the festivity. We don't have a tree this year. We didn't have the heart for it, and the decorations remain in the loft. The house, when we reach it, is dark and unwelcoming, and as I fumble for my keys I can feel the general jollity wavering.

So I fling open the door, shouting, 'Merry Christmas! Welcome to the most brilliant performers in the world! Come party!'

I rush around switching on all the lights to make things look more cheerful. Danny and Anna take on my mood, and for the first time in months we're united as we work to put all our guests at ease.

Jess deals with booze for the adults and I fill bowls with nuts and crisps. Danny and Anna give the kids Coke and lemonade. I wish I'd thought of having the party here earlier, then I could have done it properly. But in my heart I know that I would have shrieked with horror had anyone suggested the idea. I thrust away the thought that it's inappropriate to party when Rob's been dead less than a year. Rob was the original party boy. He loved telling us tales of carnival in Trinidad when he was a boy, and any excuse for a celebration he'd be there, in Caribbean mode, larger than life, making things hum.

Danny's put on some music, and people are starting to thaw out. Someone's dad starts to dance, accompanied by the embarrassed wails of their offspring. Jess hands me a glass of wine and a vol-au-vent.

'Eat, drink and be merry,' she roars. 'For tomorrow we die!' Then she realises what she's said. 'Oh shit, Rosa! What a fucking tactless cow. I'm really sorry.'

But I'm feeling good tonight. Jess's blunder just makes me laugh.

'Darling Jess,' I shout over the noise, 'you're absolutely right. Life's a bitch and then you die, so let's get hammered.'

The evening wears on. Various neighbours come and join in. Jules, Georges et Jacques arrive with cognac and an accordion, and Singing Vic brings his mum. Marge clutches a bottle of advocaat.

'It's the only thing that sits well on my stomach, and I knew you wouldn't have any – no one ever does. I don't understand why, it's a cracking good tipple. Do you want some?'

Vic is boring Curly's mother to death with tales of

his tour of Poland and Bulgaria with ENO in 1987. Guy the Groper lounges in a corner chatting to Athy's dad. Annie Three's become so attached to her wig that she won't be parted from it. And Mary the Hologram's in the kitchen supervising the food and giving advice to anyone who seems to need it – and quite a few who don't.

Lots of people are dancing now. Jess is gyrating round the floor with Dave Alessi. She's forgiven him for his cowardice in the face of Fred Borrage. They're very loud and theatrical and take up more than their fair share of floor space. Some of my pupils look a little unsteady, in a way that would suggest lemonade isn't the only thing they're consuming. The sad old house is being reclaimed by merriment. People sit on the stairs, huddle on landings, congregate in the bedrooms. For the first time since Rob died I feel pleasure pumping through my body. In spite of everything, there's life after death.

I'm drinking too much and I don't care. I must talk to my children – tell them I love them. I see Danny, in a corner surrounded by girls. Move over, darlings – I'm his mother.

'Danny Boy! You were bloody fantastic. One day you'll be a superstar. You won't forget your old mum when you're earning your fat millions, will you?'

'You're drunk.' He's laughing at me.

'I'm serious. You were amazing, and I love you very much.'

I'm choked by the pathos of what I am about to say. I clutch hold of Danny and look into his eyes – Rob's eyes – to ensure he knows how very serious I am.

'Your dad would have been bloody proud of you tonight . . . bloody proud. You're so like him . . .'

I'm crying. Danny's arm is round me.

'Hey, Mum,' he whispers.

He takes me to the kitchen, where Mary makes me a strong coffee which I don't drink. I don't want to be sober. I go in search of my daughter. She's with Laxmi, who's teaching her an Indian dance. The contrast between tall, honey-coloured Anna and tiny dark Laxmi as they both wave their arms in graceful curves through the air strikes me as unbelievably funny and I start to laugh. I laugh till my stomach aches. I can't seem to stop. All the laughter which I thought died with Rob is bubbling out of me in a torrent. It didn't die after all. Just hid away for a while.

Laxmi grins. 'Miss, you're pissed.'

'Yiss! Miss iss pissed.' I'm so witty.

Anna steers me into the hall.

'I love you Anna, my little one.'

'I know.'

'Do you? Do you really? Do you really know how much I love you?'

'Course I do.'

'You've a funny way of showing it. You're such a grumpy baby nowadays. Do you love me, Anna? Do you love your mummy?'

'You need a lie down.'

I feel a gust of cold air. The front door's opened. It's Tom. After a hard day catching criminals, he's probably looking forward to a quiet night in. Think again, Tom.

'It's our pet piggy,' I chortle. 'Come and party, Tom. Have a drink.'

I sway forward. He catches me, and I'm crushed up against him. I smell fresh air mixed with tangy citrus aftershave. Nice male body. Nice male smells. Nice. Very nice.

Then everything accelerates round me, and strong arms help me up the stairs to my bedroom. I'm dimly aware of Dwaine and some girl leaping off my bed, straightening their clothes. After that, everything goes hazy. I dream of an *Oklahoma!* cowboy playing sax in front of the Taj Mahal, and the dream repeats itself interminably.

When I wake, it's three in the morning. I can hear the party continuing downstairs. I'm surprisingly sober. What I want more than anything, is a glass of water. I stagger onto the landing, but I feel a bit unsteady, so I sit on the stairs. From here I can see both the sitting room and kitchen. The music's slow and intimate now. Some couples still dance, clinging together like they're the last people on the planet. Curly's draped over Annie, his tongue down her throat. Mary the Hologram and Singing Vic's mum are huddled in a corner, sharing the dregs of the advocaat. Mary's chattering away, but Marge is only half-listening. She's trying to introduce Curly's big sister to Singing Vic. Vic, deep in conversation with Dave Alessi, ignores her. Meanwhile the Groper's trying to snare Melina's mum. He's attempted the lopsided smile, the intimate stare, the appreciative remark. All for nothing. She's fixated on Delroy. He, sweet boy, doesn't realise and is telling her about his mum's hysterectomy. Tom's trapped by Crystal and Athy, who are in fourteen-year-old flirting overdrive. He looks tired. His face is a study of contained patience. Jess's son Lozz bumps into him, spilling wine over his suit. He shouts at the boy. Lozz is sixteen but has a mental age of five. He hates being told off and breaks into loud wailing. I rise to comfort him, but Jess gets there first. She says something to Tom, who looks ashamed. He apologises to Lozz, patting him awkwardly. He sees me staring. I drop my gaze. I don't want to talk to him now. As Lozz moves away with Jess, Athy crosses to Singing Vic and whispers something in his ear before going through to the back garden. After a couple of minutes he follows. What's going on? I hear Crystal's raucous laugh. She's still monopolising Tom. I wonder whether to rescue him. Then I think of Lozz and decide he can extricate himself.

In the kitchen, Danny's talking to Dwaine. He's angry about something. Dwaine storms into the sitting room. He grabs Crystal and drags her to the front door. She's cursing and swearing, but when she sees me, she grins.

'Great party, miss. Laters.'

Ms Perfect Thorn, thought Crystal. Thinks her daughter's too good for me. I've seen how she looks at me. Thinks I'm common. And she thinks I'm too thick to notice that's what she's thinking. Imagines she knows everything. Well, miss, you don't know nothing. Nothing at all.

Vic Green watched Athy Petros go back into Rosa's house. He'd only come across her during rehearsals for the show so he didn't know her well, but she had seemed like a nice girl. Someone whose word you could trust. He couldn't believe what she'd just said. It wasn't possible. Not now, when things were starting to turn the corner. What to do? It needed a lot of thought – not something he felt capable of right now. In the kitchen he could see his mother looking for someone. Undoubtedly him. Athy spoke to her and pointed to the garden. He heard a scurrying on the ground near his foot, and caught a glimpse of a hedgehog weaving in and out of the winter foliage. He wished he were as well defended as the prickly little creature. Then nothing would matter.

TWENTY-SEVEN

Baiting and waiting
Is best done from inside out
Until the trap springs.

We're all a bit the worse for wear the following day, but it's Saturday, term's nearly over, and something's happened. Although nursing a colossal hangover, I feel better than I have for months. I find myself thinking of Rob, but in a good way. The children feel it too. We spend the weekend reminiscing, laughing and crying together. Anna's no longer so grim, and Danny's stayed in two nights running which must be a record. Tom's kept out of our way. Maybe he realises we need time together alone. Or maybe it's just work. He didn't come back at all last night. I'm glad. I'm still avoiding him since his outburst the other week. I dimly remember his arms around me at the party. It felt good. But that was the alcohol talking. If he does have feelings for me, last night, when everyone was pretty uninhibited, would have been a good time to declare himself. But if anything, he seemed to be avoiding me. As I entered a room, he would invariably exit. What to make of that?

On Monday, school's buzzing. 3D are the school pin-ups, and I've been approached more times than I care to recall by small girls, and not so small girls, asking me to procure Danny's autograph. I bump into him at lunchtime. I say I'm applying for the post of his Press Secretary. He's not amused.

'Have you seen Dwaine?' he demands.

'No. Why?'

'Doesn't matter.' He's not as happy as a newly crowned pop idol should be. Why not?

In the cloister I see Leo staring at the derelict building.

'Great show, Rosa,' he says. 'Pop into Marion's office later – she has your contract for next term.'

Mission accomplished! The Thorn finances stagger on.

'Cheers, Leo,' I say. 'Merry Christmas. I hope you and your wife have a really good holiday.'

His face darkens. 'She's not too good at the moment, I'm afraid. It'll be a quiet Christmas for us.'

'I'm so sorry. I hope she's better soon.'

Leo gestures towards the building. 'Good news. The contractors are finally demolishing this excrescence. Early in the New Year.'

Suddenly he strides over to the barbed-wire fence which surrounds the building and disentangles something: a pair of scanty panties.

'Revolting! Nothing to do with your show, I hope. Get rid of them, Rosa.'

He thrusts them into my hand and hurries away. *Touché*, Rosa. Serves you right for mentioning the wife. I find a bin and drop them in. I'm not even going to contemplate why a pair of frilly knickers is kicking around the grounds.

When I arrive home, there's a message from Boo.

'Rosa, darling. Are you free for a casting on Wednesday? Nothing too taxing. They want a frumpy housewife for a bleach commercial. It's perfect for you. Let me know soonest. Ciao.'

I delete the frumpy housewife bit from my memory bank and tell myself not to hold it against Boo. She's doing her best to find me work. Of course she is. And I am free on Wednesday because we break up tomorrow. Could it be that Lady Luck is my new best friend? When Anna arrives home she's thrilled, and we spend a happy hour planning my frumpy outfit.

I can't stop looking at my daughter. She's her old self again – funny, kind, mischievous. The party has definitely snapped her out of her misery. I give her a big cuddle. She doesn't shrug me off.

'Is it too late to buy a Christmas tree?'

Anna beams. 'Can we?'

'I reckon Dad would want us to have one.'

She hugs me back – so hard I can't breathe.

'He would. He loved Christmas. Let's buy it now and surprise Danny.'

So we buy a tree. Not our usual giant, but we both think it's perfect.

When we're dragging it into the house, Tom appears. I'm embarrassed. The last time I saw him, I fell into his arms, three sheets to the wind. And there's still the question of his little outburst the other week.

But he's his normal self.

'Want me to fix the tree in its stand?'

He hauls the tree upright and lowers it into the stand. I'm very aware of his strength as I see the knotted muscles on his arm take the strain of the heavy trunk. Anna's watching him closely too. Suddenly she blurts out, 'Would you help us decorate it? We want to surprise Danny.'

Tom gives me a questioning look. He's sensitive enough to acknowledge that I might not want him participating in such an intimate family ritual. I like that.

'Another pair of hands would be great,' I say. 'Dan could arrive at any moment and catch us in the act.'

'OK,' he says, and smiles down at me. I feel hot. Must be the effort of lugging the tree indoors.

We bring the bags of baubles down from the loft, and Anna explains the significance of each one to Tom.

'This is the Father Christmas that Danny made at infant school. These glass icicles smelled of cat pee when we first bought them. Dad kept our cat outdoors for days till we tracked down the stink. Those wooden carvings are Norwegian – the little rocking horse is my favourite. And this is our angel for the top of the tree. Daddy made it. It's me.'

The angel has Anna's five-year-old face and her cloud of curls. Rob spent days modelling it and I'll never forget Anna's joy when he fixed it in place.

Tom receives each of these disclosures seriously, examining the objects and making the odd appreciative comment before hanging them on the fragrant green branches. What a strange man he is, so caring and sensitive one minute, hardly able to spare us the time of day the next. Without thinking I break into a song. Then I see Tom looking at me quizzically.

I'm singing 'A policeman's lot is not a happy one'.

'I was thinking it must be tough being a police officer,' I explain hastily. 'You deal with things the rest of us only experience on the TV. Somehow that song came to mind . . .'

When Tom smiles, little lines crinkle up on either side of his eyes. 'Your mum's not exactly subtle, is she?' he says to Anna.

'An open book,' Anna agrees disloyally. 'She can't hide what she's thinking, however hard she tries. It's quite useful really.'

I throw a glittery bauble at her. She laughs and ducks and it hits Tom.

'Watch it, madam, or I'll have to arrest you for assaulting a police officer. What did you say about finishing this before Danny gets back?'

Soon the tree is ready. It shimmers in the corner of the sitting room, filling the house with the pungent odour of fresh pine.

Christmas has come.

Danny arrives. He makes all the right noises, and echoes Anna's excitement. But there are dark smudges under his eyes, highlighting the strain I see flickering away in them.

Later, I corner him in the kitchen. 'What's up?'

'Nothing.'

Before I can stop myself, out it comes. 'It's Dwaine, isn't it? It's drugs.'

'Just leave it, Mum,' he says in a carefully controlled voice. Then he walks out of the house down to the studio. Moments later I hear his guitar, clashing and discordant.

I return to the sitting room.

'What do you know about Dwaine?' I ask Anna, feeling guilty that I'm asking one child to snitch on the other.

'Nothing,' she says.

'Surely you see him at Crystal's? What's he like?'

Anna looks furtive. I know that what she says will either be a lie, or a rearrangement of the truth.

'He's usually out,' she says. 'And when he isn't, he stays in his room. He's not interested in us.'

'I thought you got on really well.'

'We do. I just don't see that much of him.'

'Have you noticed how spaced out he is lately?'

'No.' She isn't about to tell me about Dwaine, Danny, drugs or anything else.

I give up and turn to Tom. 'What are your Christmas plans?'

'I'm on duty,' he says.

'All through Christmas and Boxing Day? That's awful.'

'It's usually pretty quiet. Even villains take time out to celebrate the festive season. I'm not really a Christmas junkie, anyway.'

'Will they let you off to eat Christmas dinner? You could have it with us,' says Anna.

From being hated intruder, Tom's become favourite uncle.

But do I want a stranger at the table on Christmas Day? Especially this particular Christmas Day. Especially this particular stranger. For he is still a stranger, whichever way you look at it. OK, he's good company when he's not obsessing over his latest crime. And he makes me laugh. But I'm confused about him at the moment. And Christmas is such an intimate time.

Anna and Tom are looking at me.

'You're very welcome, Tom, if you can swing it.'

He smiles. The kind of smile that implies he knows

exactly what's going through my head. Maybe Anna's right and I am an open book, my inner thoughts on permanent view for all the world to see. Or maybe just him . . .

'I'm sure I can slip away for a couple of hours. Thanks, Rosa.'

I'll kill Anna.

Later I say to her, 'Next time you invite a guest for Christmas, check with me first.'

She looks so hurt that I quickly follow it up with, 'Not that it wasn't a very kind idea. We can't have our lodger celebrating Christmas on his own.'

I'm relieved to see her face clear. Anything not to have her back to her pre-show misery.

Danny doesn't come in for supper. He must have slipped away without my noticing. At two in the morning I'm still awake, worrying. As I tweak the bedroom curtains in another fruitless scan of the road, I spot Singing Vic, half-hidden by the hedge outside his house.

He's snogging for Britain.

I can't see who he's with, but I wish him luck. If he's got a new girlfriend, maybe he'll revert to his usual cheerful self, and also deal with his gambling debts.

An hour later I hear Danny come in.

Forget the policeman's lot – it's a mother's lot that's not a happy one.

Anna had the idea as they decorated the tree. Tom would make the perfect Dad substitute for Christmas. Not in any real sense, of course. More a clockwork, Dad-shaped cut-out. He was the same height as Dad, more or less, and he also had a good sense of humour, like Dad. So if she blurred her eyes, it didn't make any difference that

Dad was black and Tom was white, she could imagine it was Dad standing by the tree, or carving the turkey. She didn't care that her mother was pissed off – she'd just have to put up with it. Anna still hadn't forgiven her for destroying Dad's studio. Rosa owed her, and Tom Brice filling the Dad-sized hole on Christmas Day was the price she would have to pay.

Playing a few riffs was usually enough to mellow him out – take him into that world of sound and sensation where nothing mattered but his fingers moving up and down the strings. Not today. He'd tried to be cool about the tree – say the right things, but then Mum had started with her questions. Just what he didn't need. He had to work out what to do. Every day the burden grew heavier. Even 3D's blazing success at the concert hadn't changed anything. Life used to be simple – his role clear-cut. But now other people were involved. He'd always believed in loyalty. People had to know they could trust you to do the right thing. Dad always said that. But what if the right thing was different for different people, what advice would Dad give then? Danny knew what Rob would say. And he couldn't go along with it. Not yet.

His guitar wasn't working its usual magic. He locked up the shed, and looked towards the house. The kitchen window made a bright square of light in the blackness. He saw Mum, Anna and Tom talking and laughing, and longed to join them. He shivered. Time to go, or he'd freeze into a column of self-pity, and they'd find him in the morning, rigid and stiff, eyes rolling heavenward in an attitude of martyred suffering. No. It was time to resume his task. To walk the walk, talk the talk. And the rest. Perhaps tonight it would all become clear.

He slipped down the side entrance. He couldn't risk going back into the house. If he did, he'd weaken. He'd never do what he'd sworn to do.

Near the front gate he heard voices. Angry voices. A van was parked outside the Groper's house. Beside it were two people arguing violently: Athy Petros and her father.

The last thing Danny wanted was to be seen, so he lurked in the shadows until Athy ran off down George Street and her father stormed up to Guy the Groper's door. As soon as Guy motioned Petros in, Danny legged it to Kilburn as fast as he could.

TWENTY-EIGHT

Soft smothering rage,
Twisting the heart with such pain.
Suffocating love.

The last morning of term passes in a flurry: no teaching, lots of cards and presents exchanged, and promises to meet for a drink in the holidays which everyone knows no one will get round to doing. And then, Leo's End of Term Assembly. These are legendary for their unendurable tedium. Everybody has to attend. Even Fred Borrage and the canteen staff.

The Christmas Assembly is the worst.

Leo's resplendent in cap and gown – a rare sight at a comprehensive school. Fax Max has rigged special lighting. It plays over his fine bone structure and adds depth to his navy-blue eyes which sweep the room like powerful searchlights. It's his big moment. Rumour has it he starts preparing straight after Hallowe'en. Jess has warned me, but I'm still not prepared for the full onslaught.

Firstly, anyone who has achieved anything during the term is thanked: sporting prowess, academic success,

First Aid badges, music exams – you name it, Leo thanks them. In triplicate. They all have to shake not only his hand but also those of the Deputies. This takes a long time. Next he bids farewell to the leaving staff. Churchill Towers has a high turnover, so this takes even longer, since the merits of each person have to be enumerated in detail and embellished with amusing little anecdotes. Then there is a thank you to those who've raised money for charity in the school's name, coupled with a homily on how good it is to give, and then there's a list of all school functions that have taken place during the term with a blow-by-blow account of each event, followed by a round of applause. This bit includes my show, but by this time I'm comatose. Jess nudges me into consciousness so I can look modestly pleased when my name is mentioned. By now, the kids have reached the end. It's taking the combined authority of all the teachers to restrain them. Leo rambles on, oblivious. And it's not over yet. All that has passed is a mere preamble, a warm-up for Leo's Christmas Address to the School. His theme is 'Forgiveness' and by the time he's teased out every conceivable relevance of this quality to Churchill Towers, I swear that any leanings towards forgiveness I may once have harboured towards Leonard Ratchett have vanished into the Christmas night.

For by now it is night. Leo's address has taken so long that darkness has fallen upon the face of the earth.

Finally we are allowed to go. Or rather, the children are. We staff have to man our posts, allocated by Marion, to make sure that every student has not only left the building, but also the grounds, and the immediate neighbourhood. If it were possible, I think he'd like them all to leave the country, the world and the cosmos. Now his speech is over, he's lost interest in them. In all of us.

Eventually not a single child can be seen. We're free. When I'm collecting my stuff I bump into Athy emerging from Dave Alessi's office.

'Merry Christmas, miss,' she says.

'You should be off-site, Athy.'

''S'all right, miss, Mr Alessi knows all about it. Bye.'

I realise she's clutching a bunch of mistletoe in her hand. Poor Dave.

I put my head around his door to say goodbye and check he's survived ordeal by Athy, but he's on the phone. He gives a distracted wave. I know when I'm not wanted, so I grab my things and head out. It's the holidays! I feel the same euphoria I used to as a child.

I go home and co-ordinate my frumpy outfit. The casting's first thing tomorrow morning. Anna's playing carols on the piano and Danny's singing along. It's easy to pretend it's just a normal Christmas, with Rob putting some last-minute touches to his latest painting, up in the studio.

As I pass Tom's room on my way down to join in the fun, his phone rings. The answer machine picks up, and I hear the silvery tones of Eunice Brice. Her cut-glass accent slices through the airwaves. I can't help overhearing.

'It's ridiculous that you're working over Christmas. I've always said the police force is a barbaric institution. Now I don't want you to worry about me. The angina's playing up a little, but I'm sure the new pills will deal with that. My leg means I can't venture out, but the Council's sending round a little man with meals for the whole festive period. Isn't that wonderful? They come in foil cases and I heat them up when I'm hungry. Not that I'll be hungry – not with my stomach. But it's comforting to know they're there. Mrs Allardyce next door may pop in, although she's very busy with her family. She's going to Lance on Christmas Eve, Shirley on Christmas Day, and then Barbara's taking her for a little break in a country hotel until the New Year. They asked why I was spending Christmas alone and I pointed out that somebody has to guard our streets and hold back the tide of filth. Did I mention that Lance has been made Managing Director of Lyall's? Such a dull boy he was, too . . . Oh, before I forget – I've sent a card to Felicity. Just because you and she persist in this divorce silliness I don't see why I shouldn't remain friends. Is her father holding the usual Christmas shindig at The Manor House? Only I haven't received my invitation . . .'

At this point the answer phone cuts off. Even machines can only stand short bursts of Mrs B. Merry Christmas, Tom.

After this, I'm not too surprised when he says to me next morning: 'Change of plan. I'm not on duty over Christmas after all, so I guess I ought to spend it with my mother. She's not too well and it's a bit much for her, being alone at this time of year. Hope it doesn't mess you up too much?'

What Mrs B wants, Mrs B gets. I'm glad it's not me spending Christmas with her. I bet the fair Felicity regards the absence of Mrs B as one of the perks of life as the ex-Mrs B Junior. I wonder how many favours Tom had to call in to swing that. His face is a mixture of embarrassment and something else. Disappointment? No – stronger than that. Yearning? Don't be melodramatic, Rosa. He's sampled your cooking already. Your offer of Christmas dinner isn't that irresistible. I don't look too closely at my own pang of disappointment.

''Course not. Your mum needs you. When are you off?'

'Christmas Eve, coming back the day after Boxing Day.'

'Christmas in the country. Nice.' Any more clichés, Rosa?

Tom's staring round the festive kitchen, decked out with sprigs of holly and Christmas candles. His gaze finally settles on a spot above my head. I look up. I'm standing below a bunch of mistletoe. I want to die.

'I'd rather be here,' he says, eyes meeting mine.

A deep blush makes its way from my neck up my face.

'No, you wouldn't.' I try to regain my composure. 'It's hell here on Christmas Day. Everybody moaning about their presents, and squabbling over the extra washing-up. You're much better off in Cheltenham.' What is it with me? One minute I'm wishing he'd open up a bit more, then when he does, I'm running away as fast as my skinny legs can carry me.

'Thanks for inviting me. I really appreciate it.'

'No problem,' I trill. 'Although Anna will be gutted you're not here. She'd set her heart on it for some reason.' I stop short, realising how rude that sounds. 'Sorry . . . That came out all wrong.'

He laughs. 'It's OK.'

'I didn't mean it like that.' This conversation's going from bad to worse. He must think I'm a complete idiot. But he's still laughing.

'I'll forgive you if you promise I can join in the family hell when I get back.'

He glances up. Is he looking at the mistletoe again? Maybe he thinks I'm deliberately standing underneath it. I quickly move over to the sink, grab a cloth and wipe down the draining-board.

'You'll be very welcome,' I say, as graciously as I can.

Silence falls. Finally he says, 'Better be off then. See you later.'

He goes up to his room. Done his duty by the landlady for the day, I think acidly, and then wonder at the workings of my jaundiced mind.

A minute later he's back.

'Good luck with the casting.'

Then he's gone, leaving me in what my mother used to describe as a bit of tizzy. He always manages to wrong-foot me. It's infuriating. All the way to my casting I feel infuriated.

When I arrive at Golden Square, I realise how long I've been away from the business. There are a dozen other actresses crammed together in a tiny waiting area, not one of them frumpy. They all look a million dollars. I forgot the rule – always dress to kill whatever your agent tells you. Several of the dazzling specimens glance at me and smirk. I'm not surprised: when I see myself in a mirror, I don't just look frumpy, I look demented. I go to the Ladies to glam up, but it's too late. My name's being called.

The interview is short. The director of the commercial takes one cursory glance, his face registers the word 'nutter', and less than a minute later I'm out on the pavement. So much for kick-starting my brilliant career. I call Boo on my mobile.

'Not to worry, darling. Something else will come up. Besides, they haven't called me yet. You might be wrong.'

'Trust me, Boo, don't break open the champagne.'

I'm passing the club where I saw Tom Brice. There's no one outside today, but to my astonishment a familiar figure is slipping into Bertie's next door. It's Dwaine. Or Dwaine's double. I must be seeing things. I follow him into the bar. He has his back to me, and is talking to a seedy, bald man with a pockmarked face and threatening expression. Then he turns round. I duck behind the doorpost. It *is* Dwaine.

What's a seventeen year old from Consort Park doing in a sleazy bar in Soho?

And what should I do about it?

Dwaine Johnson indulged himself in a momentary flashback. He experienced once more the euphoria of standing on the stage at Churchill Towers, keyboard magic under his fingers, and the audience whooping and roaring to the beat. It was so real he could smell his own sweat sizzling under the fierce stage lights.

With an effort he dragged himself back to reality. He stared at his reflection in the mirrored panel running along one side of the bar.

'You're fucked, bro,' he said. 'You're completely fucked.'

TWENTY-NINE

Liquid amber and
Rose quartz wrapped in silver shroud
Can't save topaz soul.

Christmas Day is quiet. It's both better and worse than we feared. We're used to having just us since Rob's grandmother is dead, and my father cut me off for marrying 'a darkie', and I haven't seen him for twenty years. My mother, who's always done what my father tells her, and has therefore never seen her grandchildren, nevertheless always sends a secret parcel which we call 'The Package from The North'. It's full of inappropriate presents. This year it's an Enid Blyton novel for Anna and a box of simple board games for Danny. Her gift to me is a bottle of Coty L'Aimant, which I made the mistake of saying I liked back in 1982. She sends it every year. Rob never received anything, so no change there.

I did inform my parents about his death. My mother wrote a short letter of condolence relaying a message from my father saying that since circumstances were now different, he was prepared to let bygones be bygones, and I was welcome to visit them at any time. Provided

I came alone. I haven't told the children about this letter. It's better that I keep the hurt to myself on this one. It doesn't need sharing around.

The other thing I keep to myself today is the parcel I found on the doorstep this morning. It's addressed to Anna, and I recognise the childish scrawl from the frog postcard. So I open it. Inside, wrapped in tissue paper, is a rose quartz pendant on a silver chain. Anna would love it, but I'm not letting her suspect it even exists. I hide it and then secretly phone the police. Being Christmas Day, there's a skeleton staff at the station. No one's heard about Mick O'Brien and his antics. After a frustrating few minutes trying to explain the significance and background of the pendant, I slam down the phone.

My present from Anna and Danny is a beautiful scarlet velour dressing-gown. I can see it becoming my comfort blanket, and indeed over the next few days it hardly leaves my back. We don't go out, except for a trip to Hampstead Heath on Boxing Day. It's enough just to be together. I don't tell Danny about seeing Dwaine in Soho, and I make sure my searching eyes, which see Mick O'Brien behind every tree, are shielded from the children.

When Tom returns from Cheltenham we're all pleased to see him, even though his presence breaks our dreamlike isolation. We teach him some of our Christmas games, and his presence gives us licence to have fun without feeling guilty: he's our guest, we must entertain him. I tell him about the pendant, and he says he'll phone Consort nick to make sure the extra patrols are still passing the house. I'm alarmed at the relief I feel now he's back. I tell myself it's not him, or the fact that he's male, but that he's a policeman.

He's at his best over this Christmas period. He makes huge efforts to entertain Danny and Anna, and to help around the house. He's funny and affectionate, and thanks to him, something happens that I wouldn't have believed possible: our first Christmas without Rob is not only bearable, but positively enjoyable.

He and I get into the habit of having a glass of wine after supper. I've always been a nosy person. It's an occupational hazard for an actor. I like digging around in people's lives. I think I'm very discreet. Danny says not. He says I'm as subtle as a ten-ton truck. For some reason which I don't examine too closely, I find myself very curious about Tom's history. I test the water with the odd question and once I'm sure he isn't going to bite my head off, I pump him.

I tell myself that my curiosity is no different than my usual prying interest in anyone and everyone, but if I'm honest, I feel far more interested in Tom's past than, say, the childhood antics of Singing Vic – whose mother, given half the chance, will spend hours fondly recounting every golden moment.

Tom's an only child. His father was an estate agent whose firm dealt with land and property sales of country houses around Gloucestershire and the Marches. A pillar of local society, he was active in Rotary, and a major mover and shaker for the County Show. His business dealings brought him into constant contact with the local bigwigs, and he was often invited on shoots and other county activities, along with Mrs B, who revelled in the social cachet. Somewhere along the line the two of them lost the plot, and forgot they were basically in trade. They bought a vast Georgian mansion outside Cheltenham, with several acres, a barn and some stables, and spent all their time and money convincing themselves and everyone else that they were Very Grand Indeed. The expense of keeping up with the gentry eventually bankrupted the firm. On the day the receivers were called in, Tom's father shot himself in his medieval timbered barn, with his spanking new Purdey shotgun.

Tom, aged seven, found the body.

After this revelation, he sits forward, looking into the fire, rubbing his hands together. His face is pinched and tight. I have to prevent myself from putting my arms around him.

'I've never said this to anyone before, but it wasn't the sight of Dad with half his head blown off that got to me. It was Blondie.'

'Blondie?'

'Dad's dog – a retriever. Before he topped himself, he shot the dog. I'll never forget the sight of her, lying there in a puddle of blood. She had beautiful golden fur, and it was stained deep red. I touched it and I remember being surprised at the stickiness, and how dark it was.'

He looks intently at me. 'Are you sure it's OK, telling you this stuff? It's not very festive.' He sounds so sad. 'After the funeral I was sent away to prep school. It'd been on the cards anyway, but my mother was in no fit state to look after anyone so they took me early.'

I've always been adamantly opposed to the idea of boarding school, particularly for very young children. I say this to Tom.

'You get used to it,' he says. 'You have to. Otherwise you go under.'

'How do you survive?'

'By growing a shell. You don't let anybody in, and you only let selected parts of yourself out. The tough parts.'

Light dawns. The way he alternates between friendliness and distance – the thing that's been irritating me so much – now makes sense.

'I always say that my years at boarding school have given me a useful insight into the old lag mentality. In a way I spent years in prison too, just like them.'

'It sounds grim.'

Tom smiles. 'Yes and no. My defence was humour. I found I had a gift for mockery. I could send people up – pupils or teachers – and make everyone laugh. I was very good at it.'

I know all about his mockery, having been on the receiving end of it more than once. But, in my case, I realise, his teasing has always been benign, even though it has the capacity to completely infuriate me.

'Once the bullies realised I could home in on their weak spots and destroy their credibility, they left me alone. I gravitated towards other disaffected yobbos, and we spent most of our time satirising the absurdity of it all and being hated by the staff who thought we had an irresponsible attitude towards authority. They were right too.'

'I don't know how you stood it. I'd have gone crazy.'

'Depends on the alternative. Life at home was pretty difficult. We had to sell the house to pay the debts, and my mother was forced to buy this tiny bungalow on an ex-council estate. Not her cup of tea at all, if you can imagine.'

I could imagine. Only too well.

'She loathed that place,' said Tom. 'I wasn't allowed to bring any friends home from school, because she was so ashamed of living there. And if anyone asked, I had to tell them that I lived in a cottage in the country near Cheltenham.'

'Is she still there?'

'When I left home, she sold up and found a small flat in the centre of Cheltenham, which suits her perfectly. She calls it her *pied-à-terre*.'

Tom says this with his tongue firmly in his cheek. Could it be that one day we might be able to laugh together about La Brice? Until now I've had the impression that jokes about his mother are a no-go area. He's very protective. Hearing the family history, I understand why, but it doesn't stop me thinking she's a nightmare. She sent me a Christmas card. I was touched, until I read the message: *To Mrs Thorn. I wish you and your family a pleasant Christmas. Thank you for providing such an excellent service in your lodging-house for my son. I would not hesitate to recommend your establishment to anyone in need of a decent little place to stay in London. With very best wishes, Eunice Brice.*

Her behaviour over Tom's marriage is another example of her giant ego. Felicity Gordon, the only daughter of Sir John Gordon of The Manor House, Hawesbury, meets Tom at university. They're attracted to each other but the relationship's pretty lightweight. Then Felicity gets pregnant. Both Felicity and Tom are in favour of a termination. Tom makes the mistake of telling his mother. Mrs B is wetting her knickers over the fact that Tom's landed the landed gentry, and seizes the pregnancy as an opportunity to permanently attach herself to the nobs. She persuades Tom and Felicity to have the baby, and pushes Sir John into paying for a society wedding at The Manor House with a big marquee in the grounds and all the trimmings. It's her apotheosis. She's never been happier.

So Tom and Felicity live unhappily ever after. Felicity miscarries soon after the wedding, and the couple realise they've nothing in common at all. A divorce would be the sensible thing, but Mrs B throws a fit every time Tom brings up the subject, and he can't bear to heap even more sorrow on her tragic head. So the marriage jogs on, with Tom and Felicity leading separate lives. Finally, this summer, Felicity meets a Colonel in the Guards, and suggests divorce. Tom's happy for her and makes no objection. But La Brice refuses to believe her sojourn in county circles is at an end, and is behaving as though it's a temporary blip on the marital screen.

'But your marriage really is over?'

'Couldn't be more over if it tried,' he says.

There is a silence between us which goes on for a beat too long.

'Flick and I were a total mismatch. She wanted to go to hunt balls and ride a lot . . .'

'And you?'

'I wanted to be a policeman.'

'What did she think of that?'

'It was the only area where she and my mother agreed. Ma pretends she and Flick are friends, but they've always detested each other. Ma thinks she's a lady, but Flick's the real McCoy. She despises Mum for trying to be something she isn't. The only thing they've both been united over is my career. They both hate me being a copper.'

'You're not my idea of a typical policeman.'

'So what's a typical policeman?' His eyes sparkle with mischief.

'Oh, you know . . .'

'What? Size twelve boots and saying *hello hello hello* every time I come into the room?'

'You know what I mean. What made you so set on the idea, particularly since you must have known what a fuss your mother would make?'

Tom shrugs. 'I dunno. It was what I always wanted – right from early on.'

'Come on, Tom Brice, you're holding out on me. You do know why. You just don't want to say.'

'If you're so certain, you tell me.' He sighs and leans back in his chair, eyes focused on the far wall. I can't tell whether my questions have finally proved too much and he's clammed up, or whether he's trying to decide if he'll let me in.

'What made *you* want to act?' he says finally.

A nifty piece of deflection, but I'll go along with it. Particularly as he looks as if he really wants to know the answer.

I think about it, obsessively rolling a chocolate wrapper between my fingers.

'See?' he says. 'It's not so easy. People's motivations aren't always clear cut. You can't really tell me, can you?'

Not true, Tom. I can – but do I want to? Then I realise I'm doing what he's doing. I'm as wary of disclosure as he is. When did I become so mistrustful of people?

'I didn't become an actor. It's what I am – I had no choice. It's the only thing I feel right doing. It's not that I'm particularly brilliant at it. And it's not that I'm on the fame trail. It's just the thing I do better than anything else. And when I'm working on something, I feel at home – in the right place – where I should be. Which, incidentally, is not in school. At the moment it's killing me, having to teach instead of acting.'

Where did that come from? I've said too much. To my own ears I sound melodramatic. Over the top and down the other side. He probably thinks I'm the worst kind of poseur. Oh well – tough. What do I care anyway?

'I've had my go,' I say. 'Your turn now.'

'I didn't realise this was a game.' He smiles, but his voice has a slight edge. The interrogator doesn't like being interrogated. Our cosy fireside chat's taking on a different complexion. Too serious by half. Not what I want.

'I was just interested. I'm a nosy cow. Forget it.' I rise and start to collect coffee cups and glasses, but he stops me.

'Please. I'm not used to explaining myself, that's all.'

'You don't have to explain yourself. I'm your landlady, not your shrink.'

But he's made his decision. I'm going to hear what he has to say whether I like it or not.

'I used to read a lot of crime novels at school – nothing much else to do. I always admired the detectives. I wanted to be like them. To fit the pieces together.'

'Why?'

He looks into the fire, scowling. Then he shrugs. 'To solve the mystery,' he says.

'What mystery?'

'I dunno. Life, death, the universe . . .' He laughs and motions dismissively with his hand, as if surrendering something. 'There was all that crazy curiosity I felt as a child, about my dad's death,' he says slowly. 'At the time no one told me the truth. To spare me, I suppose. So I didn't understand. Why did my dad choose to leave us like that? Where had he gone? Why did he shoot the dog? And all that blood – all that spilled red stuff – what was that all about? I remember asking questions and being fobbed off without answers. I'd try to trick people into giving the game away – revealing the truth. But no one ever did. Not until I grew up. Then my mother told me: he died because he couldn't bear the disgrace of failure. But by that time I was addicted to mystery. I saw it in everything: underneath the bland surface, the dark things festering. The logical career for me was to become a detective. Why not earn my living by doing what came as naturally to me as breathing?'

'So your work's a kind of perpetual re-enactment? Making sure that you always know the root cause of things?' I feel pompous as I say this, and have to suppress the cod German analyst who's threatening to take over my vocal cords.

Tom leans back, relaxed all of a sudden, and shoots me a smile in which affection is mixed with . . . with what?

'Yeah, that's right. That's just what it's about. Making known the unknown. Answering all the questions.'

At that moment, Anna comes in to watch TV, so nothing else is said. But I feel from then on a subtle change in our relationship. We've shared something, and an intimacy exists that wasn't there before.

Do I want it?

The film on the TV was about a girl who cuts herself. She can't take the pressure of feuding parents and their high expectations for her. It's all OK at the end, though. The parents discover her unconscious in the bathroom with slit wrists, and realise what their behaviour's done. The shock brings them back together, and the whole family move to another town and start again.

Afterwards Anna went upstairs. In the bathroom, she searched through the cabinet until she found what she was looking for: a packet of Danny's razor blades. She removed one and replaced the rest. In her bedroom she examined the small sliver of steel. So tiny yet so lethal. She ran the top of her finger lightly over the cutting edge. A thin crimson slit appeared, followed by a stinging pain which made Anna wince. But with the pain came a welcome feeling. Release. Like pulling the cork from a bottle of champagne. She sucked her finger, wiped the blade with a tissue, and then hid it at the bottom of her bedside table. It felt good knowing it was there. Like an insurance policy.

THIRTY

As January approaches Anna starts to look sad again and Danny's permanently out of it.

On the morning of New Year's Eve, Crystal and Athy appear. Crystal's wearing a fake-fur coat in deepest magenta. Athy wears no coat, just a skimpy pink sequinned Lycra top that exposes most of her goose-pimply breasts.

'Happy New Year, miss. Is Anna in?'

I call Anna, but there's no reply. 'She must have popped out.'

'Shit! Whoops, sorry, miss. We want to invite her to this New Year's Eve party.'

'Tell her to call us.'

They teeter back down the path in their ridiculously high heels. Athy spots Singing Vic staring out of his window.

'I didn't know Mr Verdi lived next door to you, miss.' She nudges Crystal, and together they shriek, 'Hi, Mr Verdi! Happy New Year!'

Singing Vic moves out of view. The girls are overcome by fits of giggles.

'Bye, miss,' they chorus, and totter off down the road cackling.

I'm in the kitchen when Anna reappears. 'You just missed Crystal and Athy,' I say.

'I met them.'

'Did they say about the party?'

'Yeah.'

'Are you going?'

'I'd rather stay here with you and Jess and Lozz.'

'Most girls your age are begging their parents to let them go to New Year parties.'

'I don't know most of Crystal and Athy's mates. It'll be horrible.'

'Why?'

'Stupid kids thinking it's cool to drink shedloads of alcohol and take drugs.'

Suddenly, the party loses its appeal. Drugs? Oh God. Probably supplied by Crystal's loving brother. And as she says, there'll definitely be booze. What if she gets drunk, passes out and chokes on her own vomit? Worrying about Danny's relationship with illegal substances is quite enough to cope with – he's out late every night at the moment. I don't want to be a party pooper – it is Christmas, after all – so I try not to interrogate. Meanwhile I watch his face for signs of substance abuse. Anna's right to stay in. Fourteen's far too young for all-night parties, even if it is New Year.

And it's a significant New Year for me. In two days' time, I leave my thirties behind for ever. I thought it would be a huge turning-point, but Rob's death has made my life turn such a big corner already, that being forty pales into insignificance. I leave Anna devising games for Lozz, and go upstairs. I stare at my face in the mirror. This is me at forty. I can adjust the mirror for the best view, turning three-quarters profile, chin up. Hair – chestnut red, shoulder-length, thick, wavy, almost no grey. Eyes – amber, still startling and sparkling. Best feature. Cheekbones – bony. Mouth – wide and plump with only a couple of vertical bleeding lines above top lip. Chin – too pointy and succumbing to flab. Skin – pale, but holding up. In candlelight I'd pass for thirty-five. Maybe. I swivel the mirror and stare downwards. Horror! My flesh hangs down off the bone like rotting pork. It undulates as I move, slopping from side to side. I look like a waxwork, melting and distorting in a fire. Forget the face, Rosa. Focus instead on festive frocks.

At five o'clock I go next door. Marge has invited me round for a New Year tipple with her and Vic. A staggeringly pale woman of around thirty, in a long black dress and fingerless net gloves, is sitting on Marge's overstuffed sofa, clutching a glass of sherry.

'Rosa, meet Artemis,' Marge says. 'She runs the stall next to mine at the Lock.'

'What do you sell on your stall?' I ask.

'Crystals and candles.' Her voice is thin and reedy, like a small child's.

Vic appears. Scowling.

'Give everyone a refill, will you, love,' says Marge, putting on some music. '*The Messiah*,' she explains to Artemis. 'Victor's the tenor soloist. Lovely, isn't it?'

The penny drops. Marge is on one of her matchmaking crusades. Over the years she's striven valiantly to find a wife for Vic. As time has passed, her choices have become more and more bizarre. Witness Artemis.

But it's blindingly obvious that no sexual chemistry

is being generated here. Vic pours her sherry with supreme indifference, and she's only interested in picking bits of black fluff off her dress. Marge, who isn't looking her usual chipper self today, has subsided into a heap after her abortive attempts to showcase Vic's vocal brilliance. Conversation has vanished into a Bermuda Triangle of desperation.

Rosa to the rescue.

'Athy Petros and Crystal Johnson have a big crush on you, Vic, judging by their behaviour this morning.'

'Stupid little tarts,' he mutters, and leaves the room.

'He's exhausted at the moment – auditions,' Marge says to Artemis, as I pitch in with, 'End of year fatigue – we're all shattered.'

After another half-hour of excruciating non-conversation, I make my excuses. As I leave, Marge is asking Vic to give Artemis a lift home, and Vic's claiming that his battery's flat.

At home, Jess and Lozz arrive with champagne and chocolates. Around eleven o'clock it starts to snow: London snow that will probably be gone by morning. But for now it settles, white and quiet over everything. Lozz is ecstatic. He and Anna build a tiny snow woman in the front garden. They drag us out to admire.

'She's guarding you,' Lozz says. 'From the nasty man.'

'What nasty man? You haven't seen anyone hanging around, have you?'

Anna groans. 'Give it a rest, Mum,' she says. 'Mick O'Brien's gone.'

She doesn't know about the pendant.

The others go inside. I linger for a moment, enjoying the muffled, snow-filled silence. The sky's clear now, and I can see the stars. One shines extra brightly. Probably a satellite – or maybe . . .

'Happy New Year, Rob.'

And a Happy New Year to me, thought Danny as he relived his evening, ducking and diving around the shabby side streets of Kilburn, trying to blend into the background. Trying not to be noticed by the seedy sinister figures who drifted back and forth, muttering their hidden messages to each other, conducting their furtive exchanges. Danny wondered, not for the first time, what the fuck he was doing, and marvelled how far he'd come since his privileged lounging around the cobbled alleyways and courtyards of Westminster School, with its groups and huddles of fresh-faced schoolboys. But the answer always came back the same: once upon a time, when he was looking the other way, he'd lost the most important person in his life. And that changed your perspective on everything. That made it imperative to keep the vows you made, and see things through. However difficult.

THIRTY-ONE

Soft velvet comfort
Hiding the Queen's cold dead heart
From all except one.

It's 2 January and I'm forty. I don't feel any different. Partly because I'm preoccupied with the blue velvet cloak that appeared on the snow woman yesterday morning. The cloak was child-size, and fitted well over the fast diminishing white lady. With the hood draped over her blonde wig, she looked like a blue version of the psychotic red dwarf in the movie *Don't Look Now*. A note was pinned to it.

Hapy New Yeer Ana. Bee carful.

I removed the cloak and the note before Anna saw them. Since the desecration of her Pet Cemetery, Anna's no longer such a fan of Mick O'Brien. I don't want her frightened again. Tom says he'll take the note to Consort police station to check the handwriting against any samples they might get from O'Brien.

Back to square one.

But I won't let it ruin my birthday. I've always loved birthdays and forty, unpalatable though it is, is no exception. Anna, Danny, Jess and Lozz spend the entire day spoiling me. We have a birthday lunch at my favourite Italian restaurant in Portobello Road, followed by a walk on Hampstead Heath. We look down on London from Parliament Hill and exclaim over the white cityscape sparkling below us. Anna and Danny help Lozz fly the kite they gave him for Christmas. Then it's home for presents and birthday tea, including a strange-tasting cake which I pretend I didn't know Anna was baking yesterday. Then Jess and Lozz go home. Before bed Anna and Danny give me extra large hugs.

I'm staring into the fire, thinking about birthdays past and present, when the doorbell rings. At this time of night? After my experiences with the magpies and the cat, I don't want to answer it. Then I tell myself not to be such a wuss. I won't be intimidated in my own home. Nevertheless, I put the chain on before opening up.

I'm glad I did.

It's Mick O'Brien.

I'm about to slam the door in his face when I see what he's holding, cradling it like a baby.

The one-eyed cat. Its breathing is fast and irregular.

'A car nearly hit her. She's had a shock.' He tries to hand the animal over, but she mews piteously and snuggles into his arms. He strokes her, making soothing noises. 'Poor little thing,' he says. 'She's trembling.'

'Are you certain she wasn't hit?'

'Oh yes. I saw it all. The car missed her by a foot or two. She's so lovely and white that she was camouflaged by the snow. He didn't see her.'

I watch him through the crack in the door. Is this the monster I've feared all these weeks? Is this man capable of inflicting sadistic injuries on the animal he's now so lovingly tending? Could he really have left the decapitated magpies on my doorstep and ripped up the Pet Cemetery? The worm of doubt that's been eating away inside me ever since his knight-errant routine outside Consort Park Station now takes over my whole abdominal cavity, chomping away at my mistrust of Mick O'Brien.

He's smiling: a beautiful smile, with no hint of the craziness I've seen before.

'She's feeling better. Listen.' The cat is purring. A soft purr which builds to a crescendo.

I unchain the door and hold out my arms. He gently passes over the animal.

'Thanks,' I say, and he shuffles shyly from foot to foot.

'You seem to make a habit of saving me and mine from being flattened by cars,' I say. 'It *was* you outside the station the other week?'

He looks embarrassed.

'I'm very grateful. If it weren't for you, my children might be orphans.' I make a decision. 'About Anna,' I say.

'Anna's my friend. I love Anna.'

I've been here before. Maybe this time I'll get through.

'I love Anna too, but I have to protect her. You're too old to be her friend. You must let her get on with her own life. With people her own age. You mustn't follow her around.'

'Anna's my friend.'

Same old story. The flame of sympathy is guttering. But before it goes out there's something I need to ask.

'It was also you who left that note on the snow woman, wasn't it?'

He shuffles about, head down, mute.

'I'm not going to shout at you. I just need to know one thing: why did you tell Anna to be careful?'

His head jerks up. I can't fathom his expression. I try again.

'Why did you tell her to be careful?'

He's chewing his lip, thinking about it, when there's the sound of footsteps coming closer down the empty street. He leaps into Guy the Groper's garden and melts into the shadows.

The footsteps stop.

O'Brien's panic is contagious. My heart's hammering like a pneumatic drill.

'Waiting for me, Rosa? I'm touched.' Singing Vic's tone is jokey, and beer fumes roll over the wall towards me in great waves. All the surliness has disappeared. He's his old self. But he's drunk. So it doesn't count.

'The cat was mewing to get in,' I say. To my astonishment, I don't mention O'Brien, lurking only a few feet away from us.

What's this? Surely I'm not protecting the man who's been stalking my daughter for three months? The man I've begged the police to arrest?

I must be.

My fear of him as a pervert and a sadist seems to have evaporated. I'm left with an impression of a damaged, inadequate man who wouldn't harm a fly. Besides, I owe him my life.

I'm aware of him cowering in Guy's garden. I should tell Vic what's happened, but my mouth refuses to say the words. I think of the terror in those beautiful eyes and even though I don't know the reason for it, I feel in my guts that for the moment I don't want to tell anyone about his visit.

I could use this late-night intimate moment with a drunken Vic to ask about the IOU – *in vino veritas* as they say – but the longer we dally on the doorstep, the more likely it is that O'Brien will give himself away. I say good night to Vic and carry the cat into the house. I check her over for damage. She's unharmed, so I put her in her basket. I should go to bed, but I feel strangely wound up and weepy. It's my birthday. I want Rob. I'm desperate for him. I have a sudden crazy notion that if I want him enough, he'll come to me. What a present that would be: my husband back from the dead, wrapped in gaudy paper and tied with bright ribbons.

I'm so deep into my fantasy that I don't hear the door open, and I jump as the voice of Tom Brice crashes into my consciousness.

'May I join you?'

I'm pissed off with him, truth be told. This morning he dashed out without even wishing me Happy Birthday. So I have to struggle with myself not to be distant. He probably didn't know it was my birthday. And even if he did, he's only the lodger, as his mother made abundantly clear in her Christmas card. It's none of his business that I'm celebrating one of life's major moments today.

I find it an effort to sound welcoming. 'Grab a brandy and sit down.'

But he doesn't. Instead, from behind his back, he produces a parcel. His expression is a mixture of shyness and excitement.

'Happy Birthday,' he says. 'I didn't want to muscle

in on the family celebrations, so I thought I'd wait till now.'

I'm mortified. Far from being uncaring, he's held back because he's sensitive and perceptive and tactful. He knew if he'd given me something earlier I'd have felt obliged to include him in the day. And he knew how awkward that would be with Jess and Lozz.

'Aren't you going to open it?'

There are parcels which are just parcels, and parcels which make the heart quicken with greedy excitement. This is one of the latter. The wrapping paper is a soft cream handmade parchment printed with exotic pale blue elephants. When I take hold of it, the parcel flops and rustles in my hand as parcels do when they contain something delicate and diaphanous. I tear off the paper.

Inside, wrapped in layers of cream-coloured tissue, is a ravishing dress. A dress to die for. It's emerald green – not garish emerald, but clear and pure, made with two very fine layers of material, devoré velvet over silk. And it's the kind of shape that insinuates itself around the wearer, becoming part of her. It's gorgeous. I'm speechless.

'If you don't like it, I can take it back.'

Eventually I find my voice. 'It's beautiful. I have to try it on. Right now.'

I rush upstairs and tear off my clothes. Perhaps it won't fit. Perhaps it'll look ghastly. Now I'm forty, I don't want to be mutton dressed as lamb. But it does fit. It clings in the right places and swirls in all the others. And the best thing is the colour, which enhances both my hair and my eyes. Since Rob died, I've dressed mainly in black. Not to signal mourning, like a Victorian widow, but rather as an emotional response. Black was how I felt. What I wanted to be. Now, in this glowing green, I look – if I say so myself – pretty hot for a wrinklie. I'm about to show Tom when I'm overcome by a wave of inhibition. This is not what our relationship is about: me modelling dresses for his approval. But I can't just stay here, and he'll think it odd if I don't let him see it. So down I go.

'What do you think?' I give him a self-conscious twirl.

He doesn't say anything. He just stares. And stares. A prickle of discomfort runs up my back.

'Surely I don't look that bad?'

He continues to stare. His eyes are more brilliantly blue than ever and he seems even taller. He fills the room. I'm drawn into his intense gaze. I can't look away. Time goes into slow-mo. Finally, he speaks.

'You are so beautiful.'

And he takes me in his arms and kisses me.

No one's kissed me since Rob died. I haven't wanted anyone to kiss me since Rob died. I've been content to be untouchable in my wilderness of pain. But this kiss . . . this kiss . . .

It lasts for a long, long time and I'm shaking at the end of it.

Tom's whispering to me, his breath warm on my cheek. 'Will you come to bed with me?'

There's only one answer to his question. I nod. I can't speak. He takes my hand and leads me upstairs to my bedroom. For a moment the spell breaks.

'Not in Rob's bed.'

We go to Tom's room. Rob's old studio. But there's nothing of my husband in here now. It's bare, minimal, cold. The blinds are up and the moon shines in. The whiteness of the snow outside blends into the room and becomes part of it. The only sign of habitation is the laptop open on the desk and a few scattered papers beside it. The spareness of the room inflames me. It reflects what I'm drawn to in this man. In spite of his sense of fun, there's a coolness in him. A reserve. A holding back. There are depths to Tom Brice that I haven't even started to plumb.

He's anything but cool now. He burns. I feel the heat he's generating. Eyes never leaving my face, he removes my beautiful dress, then everything else, and then he kisses me again. All over. Then it's my turn. I slowly and gently remove his clothes till we're both naked, pressed against each other, white-hot in the cold room in the moonlight. Then we lie down on the bed and nothing is cold any more.

The night is endless. We don't sleep. We don't talk. We just love each other through the long, dark hours. By the time a wintry dawn breaks I know every centimetre of his white flesh, so different from Rob's. And he has brought me such pleasure that I'm beyond thought.

At six o'clock I rise. Still no words. No need for words. He watches me, unsmiling, intense. We kiss again. A goodbye kiss. I leave Tom's room, praying that my children don't see me. I hang my dress in the wardrobe and climb into bed, where I fall into a dreamless sleep.

Anna wakes me at midday.

'Rise and shine, lazybones. We'll have to ban your birthday next year. Too much excitement for someone of your age. We're going skating at Queensway. Wanna come?'

'Too sleepy. I'll meet you there this afternoon and we can do the sales in Oxford Street.'

'Are you OK?'

'I'm great. Really great. Thanks again for my wonderful birthday. I love you both to bits. Go skate.'

After Anna and Danny leave, I get up. The house is silent. I knock on Tom's door. No reply. I make a sandwich and go back to bed. My body feels sated – heavy with sexual contentment. But my mind? That's something else. Rob dead less than a year, and I've slept with another man. The Merry Widow. Do I feel consumed with guilt, or alive with possibilities? I don't know.

What I do know is that when I survey the blasted landscape of my inner life, I see almost imperceptible green shoots sprouting from the crevices of barren rock.

I try to think about Tom, but his essence eludes me. After our extraordinary night I can't get any distance on him. I still feel his body melding so closely with mine that we seem indivisible. I'm not a moonstruck teenager, so I know this is hormones, not heart, and will pass, but when it does, what will I be left with? A bloke who's passing through and fancies a casual shag with his landlady – or something more? And do I want it?

I want something, that's for sure. I try to snatch at the shifting shades of Tom but find instead that I'm ramming slap bang up against my own psyche. I realise that although bad and inexplicable things have really occurred over the past two months, my response to them has bordered on the irrational. The reason for this is my profound sense of being cast adrift into the unknown with no markers. But today, for the first time since Rob's death, I feel I could be putting into harbour.

Putting into harbour?

Please.

Tom Brice is not my Port in a Storm. I will not cling to him like a piece of flotsam tossed from the wreckage of my life.

Even if I wanted to, he isn't the sheltering type.

He's an attractive, clever, moody bastard with enough baggage of his own to sink my little ship. He gives what he wants to give of himself, and keeps the rest well hidden from any prying gaze. But don't we all do that to some extent? I don't need anything more from him. His presence in the house has helped me feel safer than when we were alone. His company over Christmas made an unbearable time bearable, and having sex with him has brought part of me back to life. All these things are sufficient in themselves without wasting any more time analysing what's happened and trying to predict what may or may not happen in the future.

I am tired of thinking. I shower, put on some warm clothes and go to meet my children.

Tom spent the day in the AMIT office in Hendon. One of the best parts of his job was his freedom to range around, following his nose, sniffing out miscreants, nosing into the dark corners of people's lives and generally being unrestricted in his movements. He couldn't have stuck a job that kept him in one room every day, looking at the same four walls and the same people.

But after last night he needed the stability of the busy office around him. He did genuinely have paperwork to catch up on, and boring though it was, he felt it might ground him.

He badly needed to be grounded.

As the morning wore on, the image of Rosa interposed

itself more and more between his eyes and the reports on his desk. Her white body in the moonlight, the way she clung to him, her perfume seeping into his senses so strongly that he could almost smell it now, wafting through the grimy office.

He hadn't expected to be so overwhelmed. He didn't know what to do with the strength of his feelings. He wanted to indulge them and at the same time cast them off. He felt confused, and that was an emotion with which he was not familiar. He was usually so decisive. He needed time to sort out in his own mind what to do next. He suspected Rosa needed time too. He knew how big a deal it was for her to sleep with him. He smiled wryly. Here he was, wondering what his next step might be, whereas in reality it was her call. In the cold light of day she might be appalled at what she'd done. She might want nothing further to do with him. She might even ask him to leave. Tom's stomach flipped. But it could happen. Her husband might be dead, but in her own mind Rosa was still very much married. Whatever his plans, whatever hopes he had, in the end he was at her mercy.

One thing was clear: the children mustn't know. They weren't yet ready to replace Rob Thorn, and Anna was in a very fragile state. He didn't want to be the one to upset her equilibrium.

For the moment it was between him and Rosa.

THIRTY-TWO

Tom's been out a lot since our midnight encounter. I don't know whether I'm glad or sorry. When we do coincide, the presence of Danny or Anna prevents us from talking. But I'm intensely aware of him, like a magnetic forcefield dragging me into his orbit. We brush past each other in corridors, accidentally touch fingers at the kitchen sink, are excessively polite over use of the cooker, and on each occasion I make physical contact I feel faint with lust. If our eyes meet I have to look away in case I betray myself to the children. I'm not ready to tell them what's happening. Anyway, what *is* happening? One swallow doesn't make a summer, and one night of lust doesn't make a relationship. Most evenings he's at work, but on two nights when he's at home I wait for him to come to me, forgetting I've forbidden him my bedroom. Another night I wait till Anna and Danny are asleep and then go to his room. But he isn't there, and I'm consumed with disappointment and frustration.

Tomorrow we return to Churchill Towers. Deep gloom pervades the house. I want to act, not teach. The strength and willpower required to extract decent drama or even elementary courtesy from dippy teenagers is beyond me. The only thing to be said in favour of teaching is that maybe it'll take my mind off Tom. Why doesn't Boo find me something? I frequently utter the cry familiar to all unsuccessful actors: 'I'm gonna change my agent.'

But it's not entirely Boo's fault. To find work you have to be in there pitching, and I'm not. I'm mouldering away at Churchill Towers. I can't afford to focus on acting. I need the regular money from teaching, and that's the grim reality.

My financial worries have forced me to deal with something I've been putting off for weeks. This morning I had a showdown with Singing Vic. I spent ages summoning up the courage to confront him. Finally I marched round and rang his bell.

When he answered, he looked even more dishevelled than usual.

'Can I have a word?'

He knew this was more than a neighbourly chat.

'Come in.'

The house was strangely silent. Usually Marge is bustling around cleaning, baking, singing music-hall songs and shouting things to Vic that he can't possibly hear, from various far-flung outposts of the building. But today there was a neglected, dead feel to the place.

He took me up to the music room – a place forbidden to his mother on pain of death.

'How's Marge?' I asked. 'She looked a bit tired on New Year's Eve.'

'Fine. Bad cold, that's all. She's having a day in bed today, as a matter of fact. Get her back up to scratch. What can I do for you?'

Now the moment had come I was speechless. Friends and family always say how tactless I am, and I was terrified of expressing the problem in an unacceptable way and putting my foot in it.

Vic's face was hard. He seemed very different from the shambling, affable neighbour I'd known for so many years. He knew what I was going to say.

My lips couldn't form the right words. After five million years staring at the metronome on his piano, I gave up and handed him the note I'd found in Rob's box.

I watched his face change from grey to pink to puce. He started trembling. I was horrified. I'd precipitated a breakdown – over stupid money. Then I realised that what I saw in his face wasn't nervous disintegration, but rage. So strong that I involuntarily stepped back.

'You think I owe you money?' he spat. 'Or rather, you think I owed Rob money, and that when he died I kept schtumm. And now you want your pound of flesh.' He looked at me with deep contempt. I wanted to run home and cry, but I made myself hold still.

'What's it about, Vic?'

'If you need to ask, after all these years of what I thought was friendship, then I don't need to answer. Piss off, you money-grubbing bitch.' He screwed up the note and threw it at me. I turned and ran.

What had I done? Instead of believing that Rob and his friends only played for matchsticks, I'd more or less accused Vic of stealing from widows and orphans. But then I realised something.

I still didn't have an explanation. Instead of clearing things up, Vic had thrown a tantrum, and his bullying contempt had driven me away. And, what was worse – I no longer had the IOU. In my mind's eye I saw it lying in a crumpled ball on Vic's floor.

Maybe when he'd calmed down, he'd stop hating me and realise that I did have a right to know what the note meant. Then again – maybe not. Maybe the anger was a strategy to frighten and humiliate me into leaving well alone.

Then I thought of something else.

Vic's house. So cold and dead. I had a flashback: me running out of the music room. Something wasn't right. But what?

I've been over and over it all day, and finally, I've got it.

Marge.

Vic said Marge was spending the day in bed, but when I passed her bedroom, it was empty, the bed neatly made. No sign of Marge.

Where was Vic's mother? What had happened to her since New Year's Eve?

Vic watched Rosa Thorn as she fled back to her house. His head ached. He moved away from the window to the piano. Maybe a few scales would clarify things. The sound of his own voice, rich and powerful, was usually enough to calm him.

Not this time.

He laid his head on the cool keys. Their discordant response echoed his state of mind. Why did she have to find that IOU? It added yet another dimension to the disaster area masquerading as his life.

He must act, now the house was empty. He set to work in his mother's room. It was important that he missed nothing. It took a while, but finally he was finished.

Time to go. He went into the music room for his jacket, and glanced through the window. Emerging from the park were Crystal Johnson and Athy Petros. He groaned. Would nothing go right? He shrank behind the curtain. After a few minutes he risked looking out again. They'd disappeared, and he was finally able to leave the house.

THIRTY-THREE

Snagged in vicious trap
Waiting helpless for hunter
Frantic gazelle pants.

I must find out about Marge. She may be a bit of a bore, but I'm very fond of her. I want to be sure she's OK. But top of my list tonight is tackling Anna. The week since my birthday has been a downward spiral as far as the children are concerned. Danny's mysteriously out and about again, and Anna's mood has plummeted.

It has to be school.

This time I won't let it go. I'm determined to discover what it is about Churchill that makes her so miserable.

She's lying on her bed.

'Anna, I want to know what's up, and don't say "nothing" because that's not true and we both know it. I'm not leaving this room till you tell me. Even if I have to sit here all night.'

Anna stares at the ceiling. I've said my piece. She knows I won't budge.

I wait. And wait. Then her face contorts. She's trying

not to cry, but she can't stop herself. Tears roll down her cheeks, and her hand is gripping the duvet so hard that the knuckles are bone-white.

I put my arms around her.

Eventually the dam bursts and Anna cries like I've never heard her cry. She sobs and howls and holds onto me as if her existence depended on it. I'm crying too: her tears are too much for one person to shed. I stroke her and rock her and kiss her until finally she quietens. We lie there silent for a while. Then she gets up. She pulls a battered old leather suitcase from the top of her cupboard – the one Rob used when he came to live with Miss Pearl. Anna keeps her private things in this suitcase. I know because she told me, not because I've ever looked in it, though God knows I've been sorely tempted in the last few months.

The first thing she shows me is her supposedly stolen school bag, which she fishes out of a bin liner. I know why she's kept it wrapped up: there's a disgusting smell coming off it.

Urine.

It's slashed in several places, and scrawled over it in red felt tip are the words *AnnaRexic Bitch Hoe Die Dirty Pussy Stikinsect*. The obscenity lies there on the bed, but before I can speak Anna produces other things: notes threatening to cut her and beat her up, calling her a mongrel slag and other choice epithets. Two of the notes mention me: *Dont tell yore cow mum or she betr not go down anny dark alys* and *Yor mum smels of dirty fiish lik yew*. The final item is Anna's PE shirt. It's stained and slashed like the bag. The stains are yellow and they stink.

The grotesque things squat on the bed. I stare at

them. They stare back up at me. Then rage kicks in, and I want to kill the monsters who have done this to my child. She watches me fearfully, trying to gauge my reaction.

'What's been going on, Anna?'

She tells of the whispering campaign that began the moment she arrived at Churchill: remarks about her posh voice, her height, her weight, her blonde Afro hair and light-honey skin, girls calling her a freak skeleton bitch and worse. She tells of the sneering and teeth-sucking whenever she answers questions in class – cleverly done so that no teacher spots it. She tells of the jostling, pinching and scratching in corridors and the torment in the shower after PE, when they make remarks about her skinniness and hide her clothes. She tells me of the obscene notes stuck onto her back in class – swiftly removed if a teacher comes near. And some days, the whole class is orchestrated in a campaign to ignore her. Anyone who disobeys the bullies is threatened with the same treatment.

Anna hasn't eaten school lunch for a whole term, because every day her dinner money's stolen. When she takes a packed lunch, that's snatched and she's told to bring money the following day or else. And then the final humiliation: she's been coerced into doing homework for them, faking their handwriting and spelling, but using her brains and ideas to get them good marks. At first she refused, but they cornered her in the Science Block one lunchtime and used a lighted cigarette on her stomach, hidden away near the groin where no one would see it. She shows me two ugly little red burnmarks.

Now I know why she spent so long on her homework every night.

'You said you were really happy with the school – your new friends – everything. You were so convincing I was completely taken in. I feel terrible. I should have known.'

'I thought it would stop. And I didn't want to worry you – I know how hard things have been for you. I didn't want to add to your problems. Also they were horrible about you being a teacher, and I thought things would get even worse if I told. I thought no one would ever speak to me again. So I tried to deal with it myself.'

She hasn't named names. She's just referred to 'these girls'.

'Who are they?'

Silence.

'Why didn't your friends stand up for you? Where were Athy and Crystal and Laxmi when all this was going on?'

The expression on her face is unreadable. No, it isn't. It's shame. Suddenly, I know everything.

'It's them, isn't it? It's Crystal and Athy and Laxmi!'

Finally she speaks. 'Not Laxmi. She didn't do any of the worst things. She's just weak, and she kind of hero-worships Crystal.'

I'm bewildered. 'I thought Crystal and Athy were your friends.'

'They never were. You saw them frog-marching me home that day and jumped to the wrong conclusion. I didn't say anything because I needed you to think I had friends. I didn't want you to have a sad loner for a daughter, so I invited them in. They went along with it because they liked the idea that I couldn't escape them – they could even come into my house. On New

Year's Eve when they came, I was here. I hid until they'd gone, and then pretended I'd been to the shop.'

I look at her sad little face and I can't bear it. I'll find Crystal and Athy and rip their throats out.

'I am so, so sorry. How could I be so dense?'

It's Anna's turn to comfort me. 'It's not your fault. They're very cunning, and I didn't want you to suspect anything. When you thought I had mates, you stopped worrying so much about me.'

'But I didn't! I knew something was wrong, I just didn't try hard enough to find out what because you were so difficult to talk to. Does Danny know?'

'No. Dwaine is Crystal's brother. I didn't want to cause trouble. Danny'd hit the roof if he knew. It'd be the end of 3D, and he loves that band. It's helped him more than anything since Dad died. I couldn't destroy that.'

My poor little girl: protecting everyone except herself. And she's right about Danny. He's inherited his father's hatred of injustice and my tendency to fly off the handle. A lethal mix.

'I'll figure out the best way of telling him. He has to know. Listen, I'm sorry I was so mean about your bag. You must've been desperate to take money off Mick O'Brien.'

For the first time Anna laughs. 'It wasn't him. It was Tom.'

'What?'

'He found me crying after our row about the bag, and got it out of me that I'd been bullied. I said it was minor, new girl stuff, and made him promise not to tell you. I said it'd be much worse at school if you were breathing down my neck all the time to make sure I was OK.'

I don't know whether to be furious with Tom for not telling me, or pleased that he honoured his promise to Anna and kept quiet.

'Be cool. He only did what he thought was best.'

I won't delve into the intricacies of Tom Brice's actions right now, so I tell Anna I'm well cool. My daughter's eyes are filling up again. She wants to say more, but she can't bring herself to speak.

I prompt her. 'A problem shared is a problem halved, as my granny used to say.' Then I wait. The silence in the room intensifies. Finally, very slowly, she rolls up her sleeves.

Her arms are criss-crossed in cuts. Some are tiny. Some are long gashes. Some are old scars. Some are red and freshly scabbed.

'They did this?' I barely trust myself to speak.

I know the answer before it comes.

'I did it to myself.'

I'm overwhelmed by horror, pity and guilt. To mutilate herself like this, she must be so much more unhappy than I ever imagined. I've failed her completely. I've selfishly cocooned myself in grief and let her problems become a minor sideshow. I knew she was unhappy and I allowed it to continue without making any real effort to find out what was upsetting her.

Anna's waiting for a response. I mustn't say the wrong thing. Her arms repel me, yet it feels like my own flesh has been torn into. I reach out my hands and notice they're wet as my tears spill down on to them. Forty-year-old hands, and they look newly minted beside Anna's ravaged forearms.

In the end it's simple: she's my baby. I kiss every one of her scars. I can't make them disappear, but I can try to eradicate the wounds festering inside her head. It's not the time to interrogate her, to find out what made her choose this route to ease her pain. For now it's enough to let her know that she's loved no matter what.

'I can't go back there, Mum. If they find out I've told, they'll kill me. And they know where I live. I'll never be safe.'

'Listen to me. I will personally make sure that those little shits get exactly what they deserve, and I promise that they will never, ever bother you again.'

'I can't go back. Please don't make me.'

'Tomorrow you'll stay here while I sort things out. After that, we'll play it by ear. Those girls will be permanently excluded. And that's just for starters. I'll see Leo first thing.'

'Are you ashamed of me for being so unpopular?'

My poor little girl.

'Anna, I couldn't be less ashamed – and more proud of you – if I tried. You've been incredibly strong, dealing with this on your own, on top of Dad's death. Most people would have cracked up.'

'But there must be something wrong with me for them to treat me like that.'

'No way.'

'Then why?'

'Probably good old-fashioned jealousy. You're pretty and clever. That's enough for some people. They have the problem, not you.'

'There are lots of people prettier and cleverer than me, and they don't get bullied.'

'Who knows how their putrid little minds work. It's probably some tiny thing they decided they didn't like, and then it escalated.'

Anna digests this. 'There's a boy in my class that all the girls fancy. He sat next to me on my first day and helped me find my way round. Athy thinks he's really fit. She kind of goes out with him sometimes, too.'

'There you are! Open and shut. Female jealousy over an alpha male.'

'But why did everyone go along with it?'

'Because as long as Crystal and Athy have their victim, they're not picking on anyone else. And no one's brave enough to defend you, in case they get dumped on, too.'

Anna's thinking this through.

'Right – suppertime. Afterwards we can snuggle up with a film and then you can go to sleep without a care in the world.'

Anna smiles. 'I do love you, Mum,' she says.

Later, when she's asleep, I brood at the kitchen table. It's not as simple as I made out to my daughter. She's right. What's to stop two expelled and disaffected little bitches from perpetrating all sorts of mayhem? I'm tempted to phone Charlene and tell her about her daughter, but common sense prevails. I'll do this strictly by the book.

I hear the front door slam. It's Tom. For the first time since my birthday, I don't feel faint when he comes into the room. My concern for Anna dwarfs everything else. He senses this, for he's his old matter-of-fact self as he sits down. The current's switched off.

'What's up?'

'How do you know anything's up?'

'I'm a detective. I always know when something's up.' His face is concerned and all at once I'm tired of dealing with everything on my own.

I tell him about Anna.

He's horrified. More than horrified. He paces up and down the room, his mouth a grim slit, his eyes marble-hard. He blames himself for believing that the bullying was minor.

'Some detective! I should have been able to see the truth.'

'I'm her mother, and I didn't.'

Tom wonders whether there's grounds for a criminal prosecution, in view of the cigarette burns. We come to no conclusions, except that he agrees it would be foolish of me to storm round to Charlene's. It feels good to share the burden. I realise how lonely I've felt, being a single parent all these months. As I calm down, my body starts to feel its inevitable pull towards Tom. His hand lies inert on the table, the fingers long, slim and strong. The memory of those fingers on my body suddenly hits me. I want to reach out and stroke them, but Tom's speaking.

'I'm still on duty. There's been a breakthrough in my wheelie-bin case. We're going for an arrest. I've just dashed back for some stuff. I'd better go, or the Super'll have my guts for garters. Will you be OK?'

I nod, swallowing my disappointment. He stands up. Then he bends over, takes my face in both hands and gently kisses me. The kiss is long and lingering and I am lost. Then he goes, leaving me quivering slightly over the kitchen table.

When Danny comes in, I tell him about Anna. I can see the muscles in his jaw clenching and unclenching. He says what Tom and I have said before him.

'I should have noticed. I could have stopped it.'

'No, you couldn't. Anna went out of her way to hide

it from us. And she didn't want to ruin things between you and Dwaine.'

He isn't really appeased by this. From our experiences with Mick O'Brien, I know what he's thinking: as the man of the family he's failed to protect his women.

'Don't blame yourself. It's true we've both been absorbed in our own stuff, but I also know Anna worked very hard to make sure we didn't find out.'

'Fuck Dwaine. Why can't he keep his sister in order?'

'It's not Dwaine's fault, either. Anna's very anxious it doesn't interfere between you and him. You're not to do anything. I'll sort it. Athy and Crystal are the ones to blame. And I'm going to make damn sure they pay.'

The news about Anna was a complication he could well do without, thought Danny. His mind churned like a cement-mixer with a faulty on-off switch. He couldn't stop the thoughts going round and round. He wanted to sleep, but his bio-rhythms were shot to pieces and he lay wide-eyed staring at a stain on the ceiling. When would it all end? How would it all end?

Tom waited until The Apple Bough restaurant closed before moving in. It was easier once the public was out of the equation. He had a couple of officers with him, Billy James and Jack Shaw, so it shouldn't have been a problem, but Jose Garcia, the young waiter they'd come to arrest, tried to escape by chucking chairs at them. Then he grabbed a hot frying-pan and threatened to burn anyone who came near him. For a while it was a stand-off, then Billy James moved slightly. Garcia swung towards him, catching his arm on the hot range. He yelped, and dropped the pan. Tom rushed forward, but the boy didn't intend to go quietly. The officers had their work cut out holding him down long enough to put the cuffs on. At one point someone's elbow jabbed into Tom's eye. He was filled with the white-hot rage of intense pain. The image of the girls who'd hurt Anna swam up in front of him, and for a split second he thought it was one of them he was struggling with. He was overcome by the desire to do some serious damage. He banged the slight body up and down against the tiled floor.

He was brought to his senses by Jack. 'Steady on, Guv. Cuffs are on.'

His vision cleared and he saw Garcia's frightened face staring up at him.

'Jose Garcia, you're under arrest,' he said. It wasn't until the end of the caution that he felt himself back under control.

THIRTY-FOUR

Although it's only half seven, Leo's already in. So's Marion. She tries to stop me going up.

'Could you make an appointment for later? He's frightfully busy this morning. The BBC have arrived to interview him about the Government's new business initiative proposals for schools. He can't be disturbed.'

'The BBC will have to wait.' I take the stairs two at a time, Marion twittering behind me.

Leo's admiring himself in the full-length mirror he keeps in the corner.

'I'm so sorry, Leo. I tried to stop her, but—'

Leo's no fool. He recognises intransigence when he sees it.

'It's all right, Marion. Tell the producer I won't be long. And make sure no one else interrupts. Sit down, Rosa.' He sees the bin bag I'm clutching. 'Come to collect my rubbish?'

'No. I've come to show you *your* rubbish.'

I tip the contents on the floor and explain their significance. I tell him about Anna's hellish term, and ask him what he's going to do about it. I say I want Crystal and Athy permanently excluded, and that Anna must be able to come to school without fear of reprisal. He listens, intently.

'This is appalling. I can't believe nobody picked up on it. There'll have to be a through investigation, obviously.'

'So you'll get rid of them?'

Leo's eyes burn. 'I won't tolerate bullying. I wrote a pamphlet about it once for the DES – *Freedom to Learn: A Child's Charter*. You may have read it?'

'No.'

'Churchill's classroom code of conduct clearly states that each student has the right to learn, free from fear or intimidation.'

'I want your word that you'll get rid of these girls.'

Leo sighs and bites his lip. 'Would that it were so simple.'

'What do you mean?'

'There are complicated procedures to go through before we can permanently exclude a student.'

'You can send them home on a temporary exclusion, though.'

'Yes.'

'Good. Then you can set in motion your complicated procedures to get rid of them altogether.'

Leo shifts uneasily in his chair. 'Rosa, I'm sure you'd be the first to acknowledge that a good school is a democracy.'

'So?'

'There are two sides to every question. What you've told me is very shocking, but it's only half the story. I must hear Athy and Crystal's version.'

'Are you saying Anna's lying?'

'Absolutely not. But it's my duty to get the overview.'

'Overview?'

'Until I've interviewed them, I won't know what's behind their behaviour. But from experience, I can take a good guess. And while not in any way condoning them, my theory might go some way towards explaining their behaviour.'

'I'm not interested in explanations, I just want them out.'

But Leo's going to tell me his theory anyway.

'A bright girl fresh from an independent school comes to a rough-and-ready comprehensive. This school's very different from Godolphin. She may, without meaning to, put people's backs up.'

'What?'

'Sometimes the self-confident veneer of public-school children can be mistaken for arrogance. Our youngsters from the estates can be confused by the Annas of this world. And that confusion can lead them to behave inappropriately.'

I can't believe I'm hearing this. Is Leo implying that poor, persecuted Anna has alienated the entire school with her high-falutin' airs and graces?

'Inappropriate? They slashed her possessions, pissed on them, subjected her to abuse and extortion and physically attacked her. And you're insinuating that it's her fault because she doesn't have the right accent?'

'Merely proposing an explanation. As I said, it's my job to hear both sides.'

I try to get my mind around the notion that Leo somehow considers Anna has brought disaster on her own head. He's gearing up for a further nugget of pedagogic wisdom.

'In my experience, it's best if all parties meet together and air their grievances. Conciliation, that's the key.'

Is he really suggesting I expose Anna to a meeting with her tormentors so they can all make friends? *Please.* I open my mouth to tell him what I think of his stinking proposal, but he hasn't finished.

'Another thing. As Head Teacher I've all sorts of things to take into account. I have to deliver the greatest good for the greatest number.'

He's rubbing his chin now and looking uncomfortable. 'We're all one big, happy family here at Churchill. Support staff as well as students and teachers.'

What's he getting at?

'I'm thinking about Charlene. She'll be devastated if Crystal's permanently excluded. Mrs Johnson has been with us in the canteen for years. Has it running like clockwork. One of the mainstays of the school. If Crystal goes, she'll probably go too. I dread to think how we would manage . . .'

Below, I hear the frightfully well-spoken tones of the BBC producer, talking to Marion. My time with Leo is about to be terminated.

'OK, Leo, if that's the way you want it. On my way out I think I'll have a word with that nice producer downstairs. I'm sure the story of how my daughter acquired cigarette burns on her stomach from two of your students would be far more interesting to the BBC than your views on the schools business initiative. Particularly the bit about you refusing to exclude them. And today the Beeb, tomorrow the tabloids – "Britain's Pet Head Colludes with School Bullies". Sounds good.'

I mean it, too. I'll tell the whole world how Ratshit runs his poxy school. I rise to leave.

'Stop! I do know how devastating it must have been for Anna. If you think it would be bad for her to meet with Crystal and Athy, then so be it. You're right – temporary exclusion's the first step. I tell you what, I'll see both girls before registration, even if . . .' here he paused for maximum effect '. . . even if I have to cut short my TV interview. I'll fill out a temporary exclusion order, and we'll take it from there.'

I let him sweat. I hear the film crew coming upstairs, nattering about ambient sound.

'I dunno, Leo. I'm so angry about what's happened. It'd make me feel really good to see those girls shamed on national TV.'

'No, no, no. No need for that. Really, there isn't. We can mop up our own mess. No need to involve others. No need to turn it into a massive issue.'

'It *is* a massive issue. A school with a culture of bullying deserves to be exposed.' I turn to go.

'The reputation of the school will be ruined.'

'Yours too.'

'Please, Rosa.'

'You'll send them packing?'

'Yes.'

'And you'll make sure the temporary exclusion becomes permanent?'

'Yes.'

'I don't want Anna to have any contact with them *whatsoever* – is that clear?'

'Absolutely. We don't want to see her suffer any more heartache. And we'll put together a package to integrate her back into her class.' As he talks, his eyes flick down the stairs towards the advancing media.

'OK, Leo. We have a deal.'

Until this morning, in spite of all Jess's comments and my discomfort on my two previous occasions in the Observatory, I've given Leo Ratchett the benefit of the doubt. But now I've only one thing to say – and I quote my friend, Jess.

What a wanker.

Throughout the morning, as I try to focus on my teaching, I wonder if Leo's kept his word. At lunchtime I discover he hasn't. But it's not his fault.

Athy and Crystal haven't come to school. And nobody knows why, or where they could be.

The next day they're still absent. Charlene's not at school either. Apparently she and Nikos Petros haven't seen the girls since early Sunday evening.

By the following day it's official: Athy and Crystal have vanished.

Fred Borrage put down the phone and scowled. Fax Max's assistant claimed that once again Max wasn't in the office. Somehow he was always elsewhere whenever Fred rang, ever since yesterday when news of those little tarts' disappearance had come out. If he didn't know better, he'd swear Max was trying to avoid him.

It wouldn't do. It wouldn't do at all. Things were getting out of hand.

He adjusted his security monitors so he could see everyone entering and leaving the Media Resources office, and sat down to wait. Eventually his patience was rewarded. A furtive figure slipped out and along the corridor towards the Gents.

'Gotcha!'

With an agility surprising in one so large, Fred leaped out of his seat, and within one minute was lurking, his face a dangerous shade of puce, his breath coming in jagged bursts, outside the staff loos when Fax Max emerged.

'A word, Max,' said Fred.

A thin film of sweat appeared on Max's pasty brow. Fred steered him into an empty classroom.

THIRTY-FIVE

The disappearance of a child: every parent's nightmare. Much as I loathe Crystal and Athy, my heart goes out to Charlene and Dwaine, and Nikos Petros, all of whom are waiting for news that never arrives.

It's an age-old story of teenage deception. On Sunday evening, Athy told her dad she was staying with Crystal, and Crystal told Charlene she was staying with Athy. So it wasn't until Monday, when both girls were summoned to Leo's office, that their absence was discovered.

The police think the girls have done a bunk for a couple of days, like thousands of other teenage runaways. But Charlene and Nikos Petros know different. For one thing, neither of the girls had any major disagreements with their parents, and secondly, they've taken nothing with them. Not a toothbrush, not a spare pair of knickers, nothing. Athy hasn't even taken her coat. Crystal, who never goes anywhere without a sackful of slap, has left it all, down to the last lipstick. And Athy, who wears contact lenses, but always carries her glasses, has left those behind as well. The parents are adamant:

the girls have not gone anywhere voluntarily. They've been abducted.

The school's in a ferment. The police have been asking questions. Did anyone see them on Sunday night? Was anything unusual happening in their lives? But no one knows anything. I ask Tom what he thinks.

'Have they been abducted?'

'If you want my personal opinion, no. Those girls are toe-rags. I reckon they went clubbing, met some blokes who offered them a trip to the seaside or something, and off they trotted, not giving a toss about their parents. In a couple of days they'll turn up like bad pennies.'

'But they haven't taken anything.'

'They wouldn't take the risk of going home for stuff in case their parents collared them.'

I want to believe him, but the next day the girls still haven't turned up, and I'm beginning to have a very bad feeling.

This morning, Anna braved her class. They've been given a serious talk by their Head of Year, and warned that if anything else happens, whoever's responsible will be out on their ear. Janie, their tutor, says they're all deeply ashamed about their role in Anna's misery, and she doesn't think Anna will have any more problems, particularly as the main perpetrators have gone. More stories have emerged about Crystal and Athy's reign of terror. Anna hasn't been the only one suffering. Amongst other things, the two girls were extorting dinner-money from new Year Sevens, and blackmailing a boy they thought was gay. Janie gives a wry smile. 'You haven't done away with them in a fit of parental rage, have you, Rosa?'

'When Anna told me what they'd done, I think if either of them had been in the room I might well have sent them flying through the window. They're despicable little shits, but I hope they're OK, if only so that when they come back I can wring their necks.'

Janie looks uncomfortable. 'I'm really sorry about everything. I can't believe none of us spotted it.'

'Easier said than done. They were very clever, and Anna was so terrified she colluded. Seeing them walking around the school with her, all smiles, anyone would have thought they were best buddies.'

'It's kind of you to be so forgiving. But I still feel terrible. Anna was a new girl in my class. I should have picked up on her misery. Life's so hectic here that we stumble from one thing to another without getting the chance to talk to any of the students most of the time. Unless someone's actually having hysterics or throwing desks round the room, or completely catatonic, it's hard to see when someone's not happy.'

She stopped.

'Excuses excuses. Her pastoral care's my responsibility. Crystal and Athy, too. I knew they were loud and in-your-face, but they were always as nice as pie to me, and I fell for it. I saw what they wanted me to see. It's not just the way they treated Anna. They were terrorising half of Year Seven as well. Why didn't anybody tell on them? Not one child came forward. The students obviously don't trust us. Something's gone badly wrong with this school. There's a subculture of intimidation and bullying, and we're not dealing with it.'

'It starts at the top,' I put in. 'Leo's a coward who likes to pretend everything's going well. As long as the surface seems smooth, to hell with what's going on underneath. He's all presentation and no content.'

I told her about his disinclination to act until I threatened him with prime-time TV exposure. She wasn't surprised.

'The man only cares about one thing – The Brilliant Career of Leonard Ratchett.'

So . . . Jess isn't the only one who isn't a fully paid-up member of The Leo Ratchett Fan Club.

After I leave Janie, I lurk around Anna's classroom until break. I watch them file out. Anna looks fine, thank God, but it's not her I'm after. And I don't want her to spot me, either. It's Laxmi I'm gunning for. I wait until Anna's out of sight, and then pounce.

'Laxmi?'

The girl jumps like a frightened ferret, eyes scanning the corridor for the nearest exit.

I shepherd her into an empty classroom. Before I can say anything, she starts to babble.

'I'm really, really sorry, miss. I didn't want to be mean to Anna. I really like her.'

'You could have kidded me, Laxmi.'

'I know. I really hate myself.'

'So why did you go along with it?'

'I dunno. Crystal's so . . . I dunno. It's like, really hard not to do what she says.'

'Did you make Anna do your homework?'

Laxmi flushed. 'Just once, miss. A bit of French. I hated it. I felt a real cheat.'

'Why didn't you tell someone what was going on?'

'Athy said she'd hurt me.'

'Your parents would be appalled if they knew.'

Laxmi nods.

'I don't think you'll do this again, will you?'

She gazes at me, big-eyed. 'No, miss. I promise.'

'Will you do something for me?'

'Yeah. Anything. You were so nice to me in the show. It like, made me feel even worse about Anna.'

'Will you keep an eye on Anna, and make sure she's OK?'

Laxmi was incredulous. 'Like, hang out with her?'

'Yes.'

'You'd trust me to be Anna's friend – after all I did?'

'I don't want to force you into anything you don't want to do.'

'No, no. I really like Anna. She's great. I'll take really good care of her.'

'Maybe you shouldn't mention this conversation to Anna.'

Laxmi gives a knowing smile. 'You got it, miss.'

I hope I've done the right thing. I dread to think what Anna will say if she finds out about my meddling. I cross my fingers and pray Laxmi's not a blabbermouth.

As I reach the Drama Studio, Singing Vic emerges from Dave Alessi's office. I wish he didn't teach here. I can't bear the thought of bumping into him all the time. I remember my worries about Marge, which have been on the back-burner since Anna's revelations. The last thing I want to do is talk to Vic, but I must make sure Marge is OK.

When he sees me his face turns to stone.

'Hi, Vic. Is Marge feeling better?'

'She's fine.'

'May I pop in and see her sometime?'

He shoves his face into mine. 'Stay away from us. All right?' Then he strides away without a second glance.

I'm stunned by his ferocity. I'd thought he'd have calmed down, perhaps acknowledged that I've a valid reason to ask about the IOU. His anger's excessive.

Unless it's a deliberate ploy to keep me at a distance. From Marge as well as him.

Someone's calling me. It's Charlene and she looks dreadful. She's normally immaculate, clothes just so, hair scraped back into a severe French pleat, not a strand out of place. Today it's loose, wild curls swirling round her face which is free of its usual layer of make-up, and she looks like she's slept in her clothes. But it's the eyes that tell the story. Eyes that stare into the pit of hell.

'I thought you were at home.' My stomach lurches. 'It isn't bad news?'

'I came in to see you.'

'Me?'

'I've been told what my girl did to Anna.'

'Oh.'

'I'm so sorry. So ashamed. All night I ask God what I done that she hurt her friend in this way, and I promise Him that when she come home I will punish her until she repent her sins.'

What do I say to this woman whose child has nearly broken mine? What does she expect me to say?

'It stupid, I know, but I felt that if I could apologise to you, then somehow Crystal will be found safe.'

Not so much a genuine apology then. More like desperate self-interest. Do penance for Crystal's sins and maybe all will be well.

I chide myself for my cynicism. The woman's in torment. I want to say that it doesn't matter – but I can't, because it does. I can't give her absolution. Not yet.

Maybe not ever. We stand in the corridor, both of us helpless.

'She not a bad girl. Not really.'

I mumble something incomprehensible, even to myself.

'That Athy. She something else. She a real piece of work. I tell Crystal many times to find another friend.'

Athy's dad would probably say the same about Crystal. It's hard to face up to the fact that your child's a monster. Easier to blame someone else's.

'Leave that for now,' I say wearily. 'You need to concentrate your efforts on being strong for Dwaine. How's he coping?'

The pleading intensity in her eyes dwindles and dies.

'He like a madman. He out looking for she all the time, night and day. I don't think he slept at all since Sunday.' She's so miserable. 'If anything has happened to my little girl . . .'

'She's very tough. I can't see her letting anyone take advantage.'

The image of Crystal's toughness, with all its implications, hangs in the air between us.

'Please forgive her. Please, Rosa.'

I have to make her feel better. How would I feel if it were Anna missing? Looking into her face, criss-crossed with pain, I know what I must do. My mouth is dry as I force the words out.

'OK.'

It's almost the truth. I certainly don't want Crystal to have come to serious harm. Maybe that will do for now. Charlene's eyes devour mine. Eventually she looks away. Her body sags, as if the effort of squeezing forgiveness out of me has exhausted the last of her strength.

'Thank you so much,' she whispers.

'Go home. Get some sleep. When you wake up she'll probably be back.'

'She might be home already. She'll wonder where I am.'

'Yes.'

'Now you've forgiven her it'll be all right. I'll remember you and your family in my prayers.' Charlene embraces me awkwardly, then trails off towards the main doors.

I wish I believed my own words. The foreboding that's consumed me on and off for the last couple of months is back with a vengeance. The girls' disappearance fuses in my mind with Susan Bradley's death, the autumn of dead and mutilated animals, men lurking and spying, neighbours becoming strangers, and most of all the pervasive, shifting atmosphere of unease hanging over our lives like dirty smog.

Penny Black, questioning people about the missing girls, watched Rosa Thorn talking to Charlene Johnson. Such a fuss about nothing. The streets of North London were teeming with addicts and pushers, gunmen and pimps, and she had to waste time on two teenagers who'd skived off on a jaunt. Penny had joined the Force to catch criminals, not babysit spoiled schoolgirls. She wouldn't be surprised if it was Thorn behind the big to-do being made over these girls' disappearance. She'd asked Penny whether the police would consider a TV appeal. Melodramatic or what? What business was it of hers anyway? Not content with wasting hours of police time yelping about supposed stalkers interfering with her own precious daughter, she was now squawking about other people's children.

What a poser, thought Penny, watching Rosa embrace Charlene Johnson. Women like that think they've got everyone else just where they want them, even down to having their personal policeman lodging with them . . . Well, she'd had enough. Maybe she'd ask for a transfer to somewhere where she'd be dealing with proper crime.

THIRTY-SIX

After school, I think I see Mick O'Brien lurking behind the chestnut tree opposite our house. I run into the park, but he's gone – if he was ever there in the first place. An old woman is feeding squirrels.

'Did you just see a man behind that tree?'

She backs away. I must seem deranged.

'What are you doing, Mum?' For the first time Anna's come home from Churchill Towers looking cheerful.

'I thought I saw someone I knew,' I say carelessly.

Anna isn't fooled. 'Mum, he's gone.'

'It's just that with those girls missing . . .'

The colour drains from her face. 'You don't think he's got anything to do with that?'

I silently curse my big mouth. Why am I saying things I don't even believe myself, making Anna anxious when she seems happy for the first time in months?

'No, of course not. I think the little cows have gone partying, like Tom says. They'll have a shock when they come back and find they've been expelled. How was your day?'

For once, Anna's keen to tell me. It's been brilliant.

Everyone in her class has apologised. All the girls want to be her friend, but Laxmi's the most attentive and helpful. A boy has asked her out to the cinema, and a girl called Louise has invited her to a birthday party. Oh, and Laxmi has asked her round for supper.

'I'd feel great if Crystal and Athy weren't missing,' she ends.

'Thought you'd be glad to see the back of them.'

'I am, but . . .'

'What?'

'It's just . . . last term I wished they were dead so many times . . .'

'I'm not surprised.'

'Don't you see? I wished them gone, and now they are.'

From whatever dark place they're skulking in, Crystal and Athy are still extending their long tentacles and pulling her down.

'Watch my lips,' I tell her. 'It's not *your* fault those little shits have disappeared. It's nothing – *but nothing* – to do with you. Now stop blaming yourself and start enjoying things. This term will be great – if you let it.'

Never one to miss an opportunity, Anna capitalises on my wish for her to have a good term by securing my permission to go to Laxmi's even though it's a school night.

'It would be rude to her mum if I refused,' she says.

Laxmi's fulfilling her promise. It's worth relaxing the homework regime for one night.

'Just this once.'

Later I find Danny. 'How's Dwaine?' I ask.

'How do you think?'

'Only asking.'

'His sister's gone. He's worried.'

'Does he have any theories?'

'No. He says she used to hang out with him and Delroy till Athy came on the scene but he hasn't a clue what she does nowadays.'

'I thought Athy had always been around?'

'Only since last spring. She was living with her mum in Walthamstow, but she died, and Athy moved in with her dad. Dwaine says Crystal changed when she made friends with Athy.'

'How?'

'He says she's really rude to their mum, and Charlene's very upset because she won't go to church any more. She's also started wearing tarty clothes and make-up behind her mum's back. He's tried to talk to her but she won't listen.'

'Has he told Charlene what's going on?'

'He's not a grass.'

'It's a lot for him to cope with. Especially if he has his own problems.'

Danny could ask me what I mean by this. But he doesn't.

'It's not Dwaine's fault Crystal's in trouble. Listen, Mum, I gotta get ready now. I'm going out in a minute.'

Out again. Never saying where or what. I've had it with secrets in this family. I make a decision. I'm going to follow him and see what he's up to.

'OK,' I say. 'I'm just popping round to Vic's.'

I put on my black anorak, pulling the hood up, and leave the house. I lurk behind the pyracantha, feeling stupid. Vic's house is dark, which is unusual. Marge loves light. Even when she's out, she always leaves all the lights on. I'm tempted to ring their bell, to make sure she's OK, but then Danny emerges. He walks quickly. I follow at a distance. I have to almost run to keep up. I'm terrified he'll turn round and see me, but he doesn't.

He goes into Consort Park Station. I pray that a train's waiting and I don't have to hang round the station being furtive. I'm full of admiration for private detectives who do this all the time. I didn't realise it was so difficult to remain invisible. A train arrives and Danny leaps down the stairs two at a time. I follow, hoping I don't trip and fall at his feet. We both make it. I sit in the next carriage but I can still see him. He has his headphones on, and I know he'll be listening to loud garage music. I spend the journey worrying about him developing tinnitus and wondering where we're going.

At Piccadilly Circus Danny gets up. For one moment I think he's seen me, but he's just clocking some blonde bimbo nearby. Then he's away, weaving through the early evening commuters towards the Shaftesbury Avenue exit. I follow, terrified of losing him.

The pavements of Piccadilly are packed, and it's very difficult to keep up. His dark head bobs in front of me up Shaftesbury Avenue, past the bad portrait painters fleecing the tourists, past the stalls selling London tat, past the shop selling repellent slices of rubbery pizza, up past the fire station, and through to Soho. Suddenly I know exactly where he's going. It's no surprise when I see him enter Bertie's, the bar I watched Dwaine visit after my disastrous casting.

The pub's crowded, so it's easy for me to mingle unseen. Danny's talking to someone. It's Dwaine. Actually, talking's the wrong word. Ranting would be a better way of putting it. He uses his arms a lot when he speaks. Rob used to say I'd be struck dumb if anyone ever chopped off my arms. Danny's the same. He stands there gesticulating, talking urgently. Dwaine shakes his head. Then he starts to shout back. Whatever he's saying is enough for Danny. He shrugs and turns away. He's coming towards me so I dive into the Ladies. When I emerge he's gone. But Dwaine's still here, talking to someone else. I can't see who because he has his back to me, but every now and again I catch a glimpse. He's small and stocky and there's something familiar about him. I see him slip something to Dwaine: a small package. Then Dwaine heads for the door and I have to hide again. When I next emerge, the man, too, has gone.

As I make my way home I try to put a face to him, but the image eludes me. I know this man. His name's on the tip of my tongue.

I see a familiar van parked outside Guy the Groper's house. Two men stand beside it, deep in conversation. One is Guy. The other is Nikos Petros – Guy's late-night associate. The man whose daughter terrorised mine. The man whose daughter has been missing for more than two days.

Our eyes meet. His are inscrutable. No sign of shame for his daughter's behaviour or anxiety over her absence.

'Mr Petros. Any news on Athy?'

'No.'

I can tell he and Guy are anxious for me to be gone, so I oblige.

Petros is obviously not allowing his worries over his daughter's disappearance to affect his business plans.

THIRTY-SEVEN

The world holds its breath.
The hunter becomes the prey
And learns of last things.

As I potter round the kitchen this morning, I wonder whether to confront Danny about his trip to Soho. But then I'd have to reveal my spying exploits. Maybe I should just talk to Charlene. Dwaine's clearly mixed up in something murky. But poor Charlene has enough on her plate with her disappearing daughter.

Tom comes down for breakfast. Since our nocturnal encounter, for whatever reason, we're still stepping round each other in a delicate dance of avoidance. Today we talk brightly about the weather and the latest cinema releases. After a couple of minutes, however, I realise that although I'm not too keen to chat with Tom the Lover, I'm longing to tell Tom the Detective about my amateur sleuthing.

What will he think of a woman who spies on her own son?

Do I care?

But I'm worried sick about Danny and what he might

be getting into. I dither around opening and closing cupboard doors, washing cups, scrubbing surfaces.

'You've washed that cup five times. What's up? Do you want to chuck me out after what happened between us? I'll understand if you do.'

I erupt into laughter at the absurdity of the idea. It hits me how strongly I don't want him to go anywhere.

'It's nothing to do with you.'

I'm startled by the overwhelming relief that floods his face. And equally startled by my reaction to it: I want to run away at top speed.

The only way to cope is to switch off – concentrate on Danny. I tell Tom about my spying. He has a way of listening that makes you feel that what you say is really important. And far from being shocked at me following my son, he seems to find it quite funny, God knows why. But then he gets serious.

'I know that bar. It's not somewhere Danny should be. Do you want me to have a word?'

'He'll go ape shit – particularly if it comes from you. I'll do a bit more probing – see if he'll open up. Not that there's much chance of that. Those days vanished when his voice broke.'

Tom is looking shifty.

'Your turn now. What's on your mind?'

He shrugs.

'Spit it out.'

'Young Dwaine's been mentioned at Consort nick. I was there when his name came up. Nothing major, but I gather he's mixing with a few of the local bad lads.'

I don't believe this! 'How long have you known?' I demand.

'Not long.'

'You know how worried I've been about Danny, yet you don't tell me that Dwaine's mixing with criminals?'

'I'm telling you now. And they're not criminals, just a bit wild.'

'What kind of wild?'

'Oh, you know . . .'

I wait for him to say the word 'drugs', but he doesn't. Should I? Now's the chance to mention the white powder. But I can't bring myself to betray the boy to the police.

Tom's stopped talking.

'You're not going to say, are you? So what do you think I should do?'

'Dwaine might not be the best person for Danny to hang out with.'

'The whole family's clearly a disaster area.' I scowl at Tom.

He takes my hand and kisses it. 'Don't be cross with me.'

I feel, as they say, conflicted. It's tempting to pretend that nothing serious happened on my birthday, but the touch of his hand is doing unimaginable things to my insides. And I can hear Anna coming downstairs.

'Promise you'll say if you hear anything else about my children's unsuitable friends. If it turns out they're all mass murderers, I'd like to know.'

His smile tells me all sorts of things about him and me, and I find it very hard to appear unflustered when Anna appears.

Later at Churchill, as I walk to the Drama Studio, I'm concentrating so hard on my earlier conversation with Tom that I bump into Leo.

'Sorry.' The Head is gazing at the old building. 'Today's the day, Rosa. It's finally happening.'

I become aware of a loud rumbling. Two diggers, a lorry carrying a wrecking ball, and three yellow trucks, trundle across the playing-field.

'The demolition?'

'Yes indeed,' he says. 'At last we'll be rid of all this dereliction.'

For once I agree with him. With the old building gone, I'll have a wonderful view from my Drama Studio. Not as good as the Observatory, but pretty special.

'There'll be a lot of noise and dirt for the next few days, but it'll be worth it.'

He's right about the noise and dirt. I spend the morning bellowing at my classes over the hollow boom of wrecking balls smashing into walls, and the thunderous roar of collapsing masonry. I'm wondering whether to introduce sessions on the art of mime when suddenly there's silence. A profound silence. My class is so stunned by the hush that it falls quiet too. Then I hear a voice.

'Call the police!'

We all rush to the window. Outside, the workmen huddle round something. The foreman's on his mobile. Another man's running towards my studio, the nearest building to the demolition site.

'What's going on, miss?' My pupils have a touching faith in my telepathic powers.

The man sees me and gestures urgently. I tell my students to behave themselves, on pain of death, and go outside. The man's shaking.

'You'd better come over here, love.'

The men part to let me through.

I stare at a heap of old clothes. Then I see an arm. And a leg. And a face. It's streaked with blood and dirt. It's utterly still.

It's the face of a child.

My legs buckle. One of the men steadies me.

It's Crystal. She's been crushed by falling bricks. They cover most of her body. One of the men is gently removing them. Her closed eyelids are smeared with violet eye-shadow, which gleams garishly from her lifeless face. I've seen that face in my mind so many times since Anna told me of her persecution, wanting to smash my fist into its nastiness. Now I just wish it would move, speak. I touch her cheek.

Her skin's cold. But not as cold as Rob's when I went to say goodbye to him in the hospital mortuary. His flesh was tomb-cold. This is different. Not the skin of a dead person.

'She's alive!' I'm shouting. 'Call an ambulance!'

I feel for a pulse. Nothing. I try again. Nothing. And then . . . the faintest little flutter. She *is* alive. I call her name but there's no response. I try desperately to remember the First Aid drill for unconscious victims. A, B, C. Airway, Breathing, Circulation. I've established C already: she has a pulse. I tilt the head back to clear the airway and look at her chest. Yes, it's moving up and down. Just. What's next? The recovery position. But ought we to move her? What if her back's broken by the weight of all those bricks? Better leave it for the paramedics.

When the bricks have been cleared off her body, there's a collective intake of breath.

Crystal's hands and feet are bound.

Someone imprisoned her in the abandoned building, and left her there to be buried.

The spell is broken by the wail of a siren. The ambulance has arrived.

Fred Borrage stared at the security monitors, his eyes fixed on one particular screen: the one showing the old building. A purple vein pulsed on his right temple. Apart from the vein, everything else about him was motionless.

He'd been making a cup of Ovaltine for elevenses when, glancing idly at the monitors, he'd noticed a commotion taking place. When he saw which monitor, he forgot all about his Ovaltine and sat down in front of the screens. He watched as the girl's body was uncovered. He saw the horror on the builders' faces. He became aware of Rosa Thorn running across from the Drama Studio. He heard the ambulance in the distance.

The phone rang. He jerked back into life.

It was Ratchett.

'Borrage. How could this have happened?'

THIRTY-EIGHT

There's no sign of Athy, and Crystal's in a coma. Doctors are unsure whether she'll ever regain consciousness, so she's unable to clear up what's happened to her friend. At the hospital she's under police guard while Charlene keeps vigil at her bedside. Danny asks whether Dwaine can come to us. The police have called for a media blackout on the story, in case coverage damages the chance of Athy's safe return, but even so there are people looking like journalists hanging round Charlene's block of flats. So I say he can stay, in spite of Tom's little bombshell about Dwaine the Delinquent.

In the event, Dwaine is more focused than he's been for months. The dreadful thing that's happened to Crystal has wakened him from his self-destructive slumber. He's no longer out of it. He's very much in the here and now and suddenly seems older than his seventeen years.

There's a glint in his eye which worries me.

I've tried to talk to him, but like Danny and Anna he's a world expert on deflecting adult interrogation. I study him when he doesn't know I'm watching. He's deciding on a plan of action. I just hope whatever it is doesn't involve Danny.

The police question all Crystal and Athy's friends and acquaintances to try and find out who would harm them. Quite a few, judging by what's come out recently, and my family could well be first in the queue of suspects. Maybe I'll capitalise on having a lodger who's a police officer, but I don't know what the form is. Is it *de rigueur* for me to ask if he knows how things are going? Or is it like doctor-patient confidentiality, and an embarrassment for him if I ask questions? I decide I couldn't give a damn. He's a big boy. If he thinks I'm being too nosy, he'll tell me.

'Are there any suspects?'

'Dunno.'

'Can't you find out?'

'It's Consort's case. It'll only come to AMIT if Crystal or Athy dies. I've heard they've got one lead, but I don't know any more.'

'Is it connected to Susan Bradley?'

'She topped herself. It's official.'

'Since when?'

'Since the inquest returned a suicide verdict. I meant to tell you.'

'Thanks a bunch. You know how worried I was.'

'Sorry. It slipped my mind. It was in the local rag though.'

'I don't read it.'

'Didn't anyone say anything at school?'

'I'm not in every day, so sometimes I miss out on the gossip.'

Tom's looking really guilty. I relent.

'Relax. I know how easy it is to forget stuff. I've been

like that myself lately what with the show, and the children . . . and other things.'

'What other things might they be, Mrs Thorn?'

The way he looks at me makes the pit of my stomach ache. I ignore it and try to appear sensible.

'What's this other lead?' I ask.

'They want to interview Mick O'Brien.'

'What! They said he's harmless.'

'What's happened to Crystal changes everything. His behaviour towards Anna has put him slap bang in the frame. Unfortunately they can't find him. He's disappeared off the face of North London.'

I can't believe that after all my ups and downs with O'Brien, just when I'd decided he wouldn't hurt a fly, the police should produce him as their number one suspect. They're wrong. Setting aside my initial fears about O'Brien, which I now realise were self-generated, I normally trust my own judgement. The man tenderly cradling the one-eyed cat on my doorstep would be incapable of leaving Crystal to be crushed by a falling building.

'You don't suppose Anna would know where to find him?' Tom asks.

'Why should she?'

'Until the graveyard thing, she liked him. It was you who kept telling him to bugger off,' he reminds me.

True. 'She hasn't a clue where he lives,' I say.

'How do you know? She doesn't tell you everything.'

'I'd take bets on her not knowing.'

'Ask her.'

'You're the detective.'

'Not my case.'

'I don't want to stir all that up again, have her looking

over her shoulder all the time for Mick O'Brien – particularly as an attempted murderer.'

'Someone from the enquiry's bound to come and ask.'

'I can't see O'Brien as a killer.'

'You've changed your tune,' Tom says mildly. 'At one time you thought he was the devil incarnate.'

I've dug myself into a hole here. I can't give reasons for my change of heart because I never told Tom about O'Brien's late-night visit, and it would make me sound devious and underhand to tell him now.

I fall back on the fluffy woman number.

'Oh,' I say airily, 'I just have a feeling about him. You know, female intuition.'

'Yeah?' He smiles. 'Female intuition: a powerful force.'

His eyes lock with mine and time slows down. Why do my conversations with him take such unpredictable turns? I thought we were talking about Mick O'Brien.

'What does your intuition tell you about me?' he murmurs.

I look at the contours of his face, the crinkles round his eyes, the blond hair flopping forward. All of it becoming so familiar, so much part of my world.

Too much part of my world. I'm not ready for whatever it is he might want from me.

'My intuition tells me you're about to be late for work.'

The warmth disappears from Tom's eyes. 'Ask Anna about O'Brien. Better you than one of Consort's finest.'

When he's gone, I think about what he's said. I remember all the times I thought Anna was at Crystal's house. She obviously wasn't. Wild horses wouldn't have dragged her there. So where was she? With Mick O'Brien? With a man the police suspect of attacking children and leaving them for dead? I feel sick. Maybe I was wrong about him. How arrogant to trust my stupid intuitions! He's a total stranger. That's the truth.

When she comes in, fresh from an evening at the cinema with Laxmi, she's so much her old self that I can't face asking her directly if she knows where O'Brien lives. Instead I say, 'Last term when you used to say you were round at Crystal's, where were you really?'

Anna reddens. 'At the library.'

'What's wrong with that?'

'I didn't want you to think I was a sad weirdo with no friends, who spent her free time alone in libraries. Also, I thought you wouldn't spot all the extra homework if I did it away from the house.'

I'm sure she's telling the truth. I get no sense of deceit. Mind you, there wasn't on the original occasions, was there? But this time I'd swear she's not lying.

I can't ask her outright where O'Brien lives. It will look as if I haven't believed that she's stopped talking to him. And I don't want her lying awake tonight, rehashing the events of the past few months.

In the event it's me, not Anna, who has insomnia. I can't get Crystal's face out of my head. Every time I close my eyes it's there, empty and lifeless, devoid of the faux-innocent smile I know so well. Eventually I fall into a fitful doze, but then I'm wide awake again, eyes staring into the night depths of my bedroom. Have I had a nightmare? If so, I've no memory of it. Was that an engine roaring down the road? I can't be sure. The glow from the streetlamp casts an eerie light, turning objects and furniture a yellowish colour. My arm on the duvet looks otherworldly and detached from the rest of me. Somewhere in the park I hear the unearthly bark of a fox. Inside the house, all is quiet. Not a creak, not a rustle. Nothing to explain why I've jerked so convulsively into wakefulness. Or why I'm sweating and shaking. I listen to the ticking of the grandfather clock, trying to get a grip.

Maybe someone's broken in again. I must check the children. I don't want to turn any lights on, so I feel my way along the walls. I open Anna's door and can just make out her sleeping form under the bedclothes. She's fine. I check Danny and Dwaine. Two mounds on two bunk-beds. All is as it should be. I wish Tom were here and not on duty. I badly need the sound of another human voice. I make myself a glass of hot milk and take it to the sitting room.

The dread's back. When will I shake it?

I pick up a photo of Rob and look at his familiar, lovable features. His brown eyes stare back at me enigmatically. It hits me in the gut: I've slept with another man. What do you think of that, Rob? Do you forgive me? Is there anything to forgive? Is it adultery now you're dead? If not, why do I feel so bad? Would you have done the same in my place? How would I react, if you'd slept with some woman less than a year after my death? Is this the reason I've woken so strangely in the night? Rob, is this your way of saying you're devastated by my betrayal?

I realise I've started to ask my questions out loud. I'm on the way to becoming a basket case. I kiss the photo, return it to its place and go up to my bedroom. I'm calmer now. It must have been a bad dream, instantly forgotten on waking. I go to the window, drawn towards the park. Tonight it's mysterious, velvety, impenetrable in the darkness beyond the street lamps. I'm glad I've started to beat the anxiety attacks associated with it. I want my old park back again – the park that Rob and I chose to live beside, all those years ago.

Out of the corner of my eye I see something to my left, up the road against the railings. Something white. I don't want to look directly at it. Why not? It's probably a sheet of newspaper. I have an overwhelming impulse to go back to bed and pull the duvet over my head. After all, nothing's happening, is it? Nobody's stealing cars. Nobody's fighting in the street. If I hadn't woken up I wouldn't be standing here at my window, and I wouldn't have seen anything. In the morning, the paper would've blown away and I'd be none the wiser and a great deal more alert to face the day. I try to go back to bed, but my feet stay fixed to the floor as I turn to look at what's caught on the railings.

It's four in the morning and the street wears its middle-of-the-night deserted look, as if no one will ever again walk along it in the sunshine. The cars, coated in frost, gleam emptily under the skeletal winter trees. I notice that someone's given Singing Vic's Renault a bit of a bash. I observe all this quite dispassionately with one bit of my brain, while the rest is witless with horror.

The arms of the figure are outstretched like Christ on the Cross. They're tied to the railings with white rags, fluttering in the night breeze. The feet sprawl over the pavement, giving the creature the boneless gait of a giant ragdoll. The face, unrecognisable from here, is twisted into a grotesque, Grand Guignol mask of fear. The hair's thick, dark and shoulder-length. As I register this I think, Danny, and my legs turn to jelly until I remember I've just seen him sleeping. Something is fixed onto the head. Some kind of head-dress. The body's very thin and I can't make out whether it's male or female. A large dog fox is prowling around the feet, licking something on the pavement.

In a daze, not even stopping to clothe myself against the cold, I run downstairs, out of the house and into the street. The fox, something glistening dangling from its jaws, sees me and slips into the park. I order my feet to walk, every step a triumph against terror. When I'm close enough to see details, I stop and vomit. Then I force myself to look properly. Not at the face. Not yet. I start at ground level. Guts spill onto the pavement from the stomach, which has been torn open. The thighs are criss-crossed with vicious knife slashes. Above the gaping belly, the most pitiful sight: the budding breasts of a young girl, and thrusting up between them, the iron railing on which she's impaled. Her head's almost severed from the neck, which explains its strange lolling angle. It's time to look at the face, although by now I know who it is. She's plastered in make-up, inexpertly applied and hideously garish. The lips are a crimson gash, incongruously echoing the slash across her slit throat. The cheeks are deeply rouged, the eyes framed by lashes coated in spidery black mascara, and the lids are heavy with layers of bright blue shadow. Her thick black hair stirs in the wind, momentarily masking the terror in her dead eyes, and I see that the thing on her head is a crown of woven twigs. Rose branches. The vicious thorns gleam as they catch the light from the street lamp.

From behind me I hear a sob. Dwaine, tears rolling down his cheeks, has his arm round Anna, who is shaking uncontrollably. Danny crosses the road to join us. We stand, motionless, for what seems like hours, until finally I say: 'Go inside and phone the police.'

Dwaine and Anna, moving like automatons, head towards the house.

'Go on, Danny.'

'Aren't you coming?'

'She shouldn't be left by herself.'

'Then we'll keep watch together.'

The two of us stay with Athy until the police arrive.

Anna knew what she must do before the police came. She ran up to her bedroom and went straight to the bottom drawer of her desk. She scrabbled around under books and paper and pulled something out. It sat in the palm of her hand, a tiny Plasticine doll. The eyes, two turquoise sequins, twinkled up at her. It had long dark hair and was dressed in a beautifully stitched bright pink mini-dress with an A embroidered on the front. Stuck into its throat was a long dressmaker's pin with a coloured glass tip. Anna removed the pin, the dress and the sequins. Then, closing her fingers round the doll, she squeezed hard, rolling the Plasticine into a ball. She threw it into her wastebasket on top of the dress which she had ripped into fragments.

His mother was a stubborn woman, thought Danny, when he finally persuaded her to come back inside and leave Athy to the police. She was shivering, and suffering from the effects of shock. Her eyes were glassy and she seemed dazed and disoriented. He sent her to have a hot shower, and went to find Dwaine. But it was too late. A nosy-looking fed was already asking lots of questions. Danny tried to catch Dwaine's eye, but Dwaine wouldn't look. Danny felt sick. This wasn't happening. Images of the body on the railings kept thrusting themselves into his field of vision. It was easier to say 'the body'. Much easier than using her name. Made it less real somehow. Danny felt that the last thing he needed at the moment was reality. He wanted to know whether Rosa realised he hadn't come from his bed to see Athy's body. But surely she would have said something. He cursed himself for falling asleep outside the club earlier that night, and ballsing up everything he'd set out to do. Tonight of all nights. He checked in on Anna, who was curled up on her bed, wide awake and staring. He tried to talk to her, but received only monosyllabic replies. Eventually he went back downstairs to wait for the inevitable questions from the police. He hoped his answers would satisfy them.

THIRTY-NINE

The rest of the night has the unreal quality of a nightmare. A false dawn appears with the advent of the police arc-lights, shedding a harsh metallic glow across the street and the park. A tent is erected over Athy's body to shield her from the prying residents of Albert Road, who have left their warm beds in response to the sirens. Police tape cordons off a large area. Some officers do a fingertip search of the ground, both on Albert Road and in the park, while others go from door to door asking questions. Inside the tent, the shadows of the forensic team can be seen going about their grisly tasks. Finally, well after true break of day, a mortuary van appears and Athy is taken away. The tent, the tape and the police remain. Early morning commuters are diverted past, their eyes sharp with curiosity. I keep reminding myself that this isn't a film set, and that nothing in my wildest revenge fantasies could remotely come close to the reality of what's actually happened to Athy Petros. I'm still shivery. My face and hands feel cold and clammy. I don't think I'll ever feel normal again. At some point Tom appears. AMIT's taking over from the local police, and Tom's in charge since he knows a bit about Churchill after his enquiries on the Susan Bradley case. His face is concerned.

'Are you OK? How are the kids? I couldn't believe it when I got the call from Consort nick.'

I want to cry. But if I start, I'll never stop, and Tom has a job to do. I can't foist a weeping woman routine onto him. I tell him that we're coping. I give him a resumé of what's happened. I try to sound matter-of-fact. I must be fairly convincing, because he relaxes a little. The doorbell rings again, and I see the outline of a police uniform. I go to answer, but Tom pulls me back.

'Don't mention to anyone that I live here. I really want this case. If they find out I'm your lodger they'll have to take me off it. Police rules.'

It's Penny Black. The one police officer who definitely knows Tom's my lodger. She's here to talk about victim support. I wonder whether to ask her to keep her mouth shut about Tom, but I sense she's not my biggest fan. In fact, she hasn't been the same since I mentioned that he was moving in. If I speak to her it might make things worse. Ostrichlike, I tell myself that perhaps she won't remember Tom lives here.

Marion rings. Leo's been informed of the tragedy by the police and has closed school for the day, partly as a mark of respect, and partly to protect the students from the media hordes who are already besieging Churchill Towers. They're also swarming all over Consort Park. Our bit of street and the area of park near to us is within the cordon, so thankfully no one's been able to get to us yet, but it's only a matter of time. Anna, Danny and I are trapped. Dwaine left before the press arrived. He refused to stay. I tried, ineffectually, to stop him, but I was still in shock. I phoned Charlene, then remembered she'd be at the hospital. Maybe that's where he's gone – to reassure himself that Crystal's still alive. I decided that I had enough to think about without adding Dwaine and his movements to my list. Besides, he doesn't have to be here. Someone took our statements earlier, and said we're free to go about our business.

As if. We're stuck here for the foreseeable future, until the press swoop off to another story. We switch on the TV. The story's made the local news. Girl's body found in Consort Park. That's all. Tom's told me that the Police Press Office will keep a lid on the gruesome details for as long as they can.

It's a bad dream. I keep expecting to wake up, but I never do.

Whoever left Crystal to die is probably the same person who murdered Athy. Why didn't he kill Crystal too? Maybe that was his plan. Maybe he'd hidden her in the old building to finish her off some other time, but hadn't reckoned with the demolition.

Anna sits huddled on the sofa clutching the remote, channel surfing for news programmes, listening to the basic facts regurgitated again and again. I make her switch off, but five minutes later she's hunkered down in front of the screen again, her eyes over-large in her pinched face.

I know what she's thinking.

It's what she felt when she heard about Crystal, magnified to the power of ten. I imagine how it must appear to her – scarcely out of childhood with all its myths and superstitions. Two girls turn her life into a living hell.

For months on end she hates them with a passion – wishes them dead. Then, suddenly, one of them is dead, and the other as good as. How is she to deal with what she sees as a force in herself so powerful that she only has to think murderous thoughts for them to be made manifest? I try to talk to her, but she doesn't respond. The more I try, the more she snaps at me. It's counter-productive. She'll talk when she's ready.

Danny's method of coping is, as usual, to be strong and ultra-competent. He's striving hard to be Mr Normal. As if finding a mutilated body happens every day. He made us all a cooked breakfast, which no one ate, and now he's tidying up, whisking briskly round with a duster in a totally uncharacteristic way, and asking whether I need him to do a supermarket run.

But I see how often he gravitates towards the window to gaze down at the tent, and I notice that his nails are bitten and bleeding.

My poor, poor children. So young and vulnerable in the grey morning light. Most people go through their whole lives without witnessing the kind of horror they saw last night. How do I help them get through it? How do *I* get through it? I keep having flashbacks – Athy's dead face, her guts on the ground. The police asked whether we wanted their doctor to prescribe something for shock, but we all said no. I think we feel we need our wits about us. Penny said Victim Support was available, but we refused. We need to be left alone. Anyway, all the support in the world won't eradicate the image of that horror on the railings.

At about ten o'clock Tom reappears, ostentatiously ringing the doorbell to prove that he doesn't live here.

He produces a transparent wallet containing a gold hoop earring, with a cross of minute seed pearls dangling down from it.

'Recognise this?'

Anna gasps. 'It's Mick O'Brien's.'

'We found it next to the body.'

Anna bursts into tears and rushes upstairs. Tom watches her with calculation.

'Did you ask her if she has his address?' he raps out.

'I was going to, but then all this happened . . .'

'Come on, no time like the present.'

Enough is enough.

'Tom, she's had a huge shock. I won't let you upset her even more.'

'The earring caused a pretty violent reaction, didn't it?'

'What do you expect? The man's been stalking her and now you're implying he killed Athy.'

'She'll have to put up with lots more questions, however bad she's feeling. This is a murder enquiry, not the Teddy Bears' Picnic.'

I know Tom's in full Sherlock mode, but I don't like it. I try to make excuses for him. He's tracking a dangerous killer. There's no time for niceties. But still . . .

I must look pissed off because suddenly his face softens. He crosses the room and before I know it, his arms are wrapped around me.

And I see Danny's incredulous face behind him.

I want to tell Tom to stop, but I'm powerless to change what's happening. He's talking gently, stroking my hair.

'I'm sorry, I wasn't thinking. There's no hurry. We've other leads to work on. Don't worry, Rosa. I don't want you to worry about anything.'

My son, witness to this touching scene, doesn't look happy. And who can blame him? All of a sudden, Roger the Lodger is Roger the Todger. This is not how I planned to tell my children about my new relationship – if that's what it is. I catch Danny's eye and he looks away. I can't read the expression on his face. Embarrassment? Disgust? Or a combination of the two, with a dash of fury added in for good measure?

Tom's still talking. 'Back to the fray. I'll come home at lunchtime if I can.'

Danny sucks his teeth.

Tom, seemingly unaware of my seething son, kisses me.

'Take it easy for the rest of the day. I'll ask my questions later. I promise I'll be nice.'

As he's leaving, I'm overcome by . . . what? I don't know.

'Tom . . .'

He turns. His face is becoming so familiar to me.

'Nothing. Take care.'

He blows me a kiss, clapping Danny on the shoulder as he passes.

There's a long, loaded silence and then Danny speaks. His voice is clipped and hard.

'What's going on?'

I take a deep breath. 'What does it look like?'

That wasn't the right response.

'It looks like you're fucking the fuzz.'

'Don't be crude.'

'I'm not the crude one here.'

'Danny!'

'Tell me you aren't fucking him then?'

Another silence.

'How long's my father been dead?'

'You know how long.'

'But you obviously don't, so I'll remind you. This time last January Dad was alive. A year later you're screwing someone else.'

There's nothing so violently aggressive as self-righteous youth.

'I didn't plan it. It just happened. These things do.'

Beneath the anger, Danny hurts. I can feel his pain as if it were my own. Maybe it is. I touch his arm, but he jerks away.

'When were you planning to tell us your dirty little secret?'

'It's early days. There's nothing to tell.'

'No?'

'Well . . . not much.'

'So you haven't fucked him?'

My silence tells him everything.

'Do you do it when we're asleep? Does he screw you in my dad's bed?'

'Stop it.' I don't know what will happen between me and Tom, but this is definitely not the way I wanted my children to find out. 'Leave it – before you say something you regret. Now's not the time for family rows.'

He eyes me with contempt. Then he's gone. I look out of the window. He's pushing his way through the journalists and rubbernecks, ignoring their attempts to question him.

Anna appears. 'What's up with Danny?'

'He's cross with me.'

'Why?'

It's very tempting to lie, but she'll find out soon enough. Better she hears my version. I tell her.

She laughs.

'What's so funny?'

'I don't believe you,' she says. 'You wouldn't do that to Dad. And certainly not with *him*.'

That went well.

'I thought you liked Tom. You got on really well over Christmas. And he was very kind, lending you that money for your school bag.'

Anna shrugs her shoulders. 'He's a fed. Anyway, it's so naff – having it away with the lodger. I just don't believe you'd do such a disgusting thing.'

'But Anna . . .'

'I'm having a shower, then I'm off to Laxmi's.'

Well, Rosa, it's all going splendidly.

Maybe they'll come round to the idea of Tom Brice. Maybe they won't. Maybe the whole thing will fizzle out. The only certainty is that Anna and Danny will always associate finding out about their mother's lover with death and destruction. Great. Start saving for the therapy now.

Vic had watched the comings and goings closely, from the beginning. The police would knock on his door sooner or later, and he tried to prepare himself. Around tennish he saw Rosa's lodger leave her house, closely followed by Danny and, a little later, Anna. He wondered whether that meant Rosa was alone. He thought not. The police would still be there.

Not to worry.

He peered down Albert Road. No sign of what he most wanted to see, although it was difficult with all the people hanging about. He noticed that already the ubiquitous sign of national tragedy had put in an appearance: several bunches of flowers lay on the pavement by the police tape. Athy Petros was on her way to sainthood.

Not.

If only they knew.

He looked through the bare trees in the park, to the winter sky above. It was a lovely day. Nature couldn't give a damn about the ugly tragedy played out beneath its bright, clear sky. Vic found himself humming Beethoven's 'Ode to Joy', the notes rumbling involuntarily from his barrel chest like a great geyser.

The piercing ring of the doorbell interrupted his song. He ran downstairs three at a time. A familiar figure was outlined behind the glass. He threw open the door. At last. The day he thought would never come had arrived.

FORTY

Now Anna and Danny have gone, it's horribly quiet.

I wonder whether their reaction to me and Tom is one way of dealing with the violence they witnessed last night. Their precipitate flight from the house is perhaps fuelled as much by the knowledge that their mother has taken the lodger as a lover as it is by the need to escape the image of Athy's butchered body.

They have the right idea – running away. I want to escape too, but I can't go for a walk – too many journalists. Maybe I should go shopping – that's Marge's chief remedy for stress. But shopping seems disrespectful somehow.

Marge.

I still don't know what's happened to her. It's none of my business. There must be a simple explanation for why she wasn't in bed, as Vic claimed, when I paid my call the other day. I need to confront Vic again like I need a dose of radiation, but the questionmark over Marge's welfare niggles and nags, refusing to go away. I attempt to clarify what it is that bothers me. Although Marge's incessant attentions sometimes drive Vic to distraction, he's always seemed completely devoted to her. So why am I so worried?

I know why: it's Vic himself.

He's different: morose, introverted and, in his dealings with me, downright aggressive. The man who threw me out of his house the other day is quite capable of committing an act of violence. What if Marge tried his patience once too often? Maybe it was her shameless promotion of the lovely Artemis on New Year's Eve.

The only way to dispel my fears – expose them as the product of my fevered imagination – is to see Marge. It will also distract me from the horrors of last night, and the children's reaction to my thing with Tom.

Without taking time to talk myself out of it, I march round to Vic's. I'm about to ring the bell, when I hear talking in the hallway. Through the Victorian stained-glass panel I dimly make out two figures. The voices are low and confiding.

Then the figures move together in what is quite clearly an intimate embrace.

Not a good moment to pay a house call.

I'm confused. I'm not abandoning Marge but I need to think. In my haste to escape I knock over three full milk bottles. As I'm picking them up the door's flung open.

Dave Alessi hovers in the background. Dave Alessi? Looking very uncomfortable.

In front of me is Vic, who stares stonily down as I scrabble about on the step.

'If you want to borrow milk you only have to ask,' he says coldly.

All at once I snap. On top of the night's events, Vic's nastiness is the last straw.

'Shut up, Vic! I want to see Marge. Whatever your quarrel with me, she and I have always got on well, and if she's ill I want to make sure there's nothing I can do for her.'

'There is nothing you can do for my mother. Nothing at all.'

'I'd prefer to hear it from her.'

'You can't.'

'Why?'

'She's gone to stay with her sister in Liverpool.'

'I thought you said she was ill.'

'She is.'

'What's the matter with her? She looked fine on New Year's Eve. Just a bit tired.'

'Bad dose of 'flu.'

Yeah, right. How could she go to Liverpool with bad 'flu? When I last had it I couldn't travel from my bed to the bathroom, let alone halfway across the country.

'What's the number? I'll give her a ring.'

'My aunt's not on the phone. Is that all? I'm very busy.'

I look at Dave Alessi. I'll bet you are.

I don't know what else to do.

'When you next speak to Marge, give her my love.'

Vic nods curtly.

'Thanks,' I say. 'Bye, Dave. See you at school tomorrow.'

My last sight as Vic closes the door is Dave's sickly grin as he acknowledges my farewell. I walk up my path and see Guy. He's peering across the road at the police who are still milling about.

'I wonder when they'll get round to me,' he says. 'I suppose they've talked to you already?'

'Yes. But Tom says they'll be back.'

'Do they have any leads?'

'Anna's stalker's top of the list.'

'Really?'

'But they can't find him. He's disappeared.'

'Right. I dare say there are other things they're following up too?'

'Probably.'

'Are they very nosy – like on the TV when they ask all about your business, whether or not it's relevant?'

'They'll want to know where you were last night and if you saw anything.'

'I'll be no help. Didn't see a thing. Slept like a top.'

'Have you spoken to Athy's dad?'

Guy looks at me sharply. 'No.'

'He's a friend of yours, isn't he?'

'Oh,' says Guy. 'Yeah. Right. Actually I don't know him that well. He puts a bit of business my way sometimes, that's all. I've tried to get through but his mobile's switched off. Poor bloke. Terrible business. Is that my phone? See you, Rose.' He dives back into his house.

I didn't hear his phone ringing, but I've other things to think about. Singing Vic and Dave Alessi: Love's Young Dream. Dave's no surprise. I hadn't really thought about his sexuality, but although I don't know him that well, it figures.

But Vic?

Vic's always come over as a man's man – down to the pub for a few beers with the lads, rowdy rugger songs when he's pissed, the clothes sense of an overweight scarecrow – that kind of thing. Lots of girlfriends, but never anyone special.

It all fits into place. I've often wondered why he never married. He's not badlooking in a shambling, bearlike way. And until the last few weeks, when I've seen a different side to him, he's always struck me as an affable and gentle man. Someone whom many women would find a real turn-on.

Why did it never occur to me that he might be gay?

It's Vic. He's done a brilliant job of hiding his true self behind his macho, laddish façade. He's fooled us all. But why? Nowadays only Cabinet ministers try to conceal their sexuality, and even that taboo's breaking down. Why has Vic gone to such lengths to live a lie? I know the answer even as I ask the question.

Marge.

When Marge descended on Vic from Liverpool twenty years ago, her heaviest item of luggage was her sackful of reactionary Northern prejudices. Wogs, Gippos, Frogs, Spics, Wops, Kikes, Krauts and, more reviled than all the rest put together, nancy-boy poofters, all receive the constant benefit of her vivid Scouse invective. I made a decision years ago that, in the name of neighbourly relations, I had to turn a deaf ear to Marge's frequent outbursts of politically incorrect bile and focus on her genuinely kind heart and other good qualities. I'm ashamed to say I've taken the coward's path of non-resistance.

So, quite clearly, has Vic.

But now Dave Alessi is in his house. With an overnight bag.

And Marge has disappeared.

Guy had a moral dilemma. Not something he was used to. Normally, things were crystal clear. His modus vivendi *was 'All gain, no pain'.*

The right course of action was what was right for Guy

Gropius. But this time it was different. The right course of action would quite possibly land him in big trouble. Correction – would quite definitely *land him in very big trouble.*

On the other hand, even he, with his comfortably elastic moral code, could see that keeping silent was wrong.

FORTY-ONE

Later in the day, Leo Ratchett phones. 'Are you alone, Rosa?'

'Apart from the world's press.'

'There's something I need to talk to you about.'

I don't want him in my house. 'Can't it wait till tomorrow at school?'

'It's something best discussed away from school. It's about Danny.'

My heart bangs in my chest. 'You'd better come round.' What does he want to tell me about Danny that's too sensitive to be talked of in school?

It's not long before he's ringing the bell.

'Lots of police activity out there,' he says.

I take him into the kitchen.

'What a pretty room. Very Clarice Cliff.'

'So what's this about Danny?'

Now his moment of revelation has arrived, Leo looks strangely unwilling to begin.

'He's an extremely intelligent young man. It must have been hard for him after your husband's death, moving to a school like Churchill. Very different from Westminster . . .'

'Is there a problem with his work?'

'God, no. All his teachers think he's the bee's knees. You must know that.'

'So?'

'This is difficult . . .'

'If Danny's in trouble, I need to know.'

'It's not that straightforward.'

I haven't been having the best of times in the last few hours. The thought of Leo pussyfooting at my kitchen table for even one more minute is too much.

'Leo, if you've something to say then say it. If not, you'd better go. I'm expecting the police.'

'The thing is, you might take what I'm going to say in the wrong way . . .'

'Just tell me.'

He clears his throat. 'As an amateur astronomer, I often spend the night in the Observatory. To tell you the truth, the Observatory's the main reason I went for this Headship. It binds me to the place in spite of other offers – and there have been a couple over the years.'

'And?'

He realises I don't want to hear more details from his CV.

'Here's where it might sound a bit . . . well, not quite . . .'

'Go on.'

'It's not just the stars I look at. I love studying the urban wildlife, particularly down in the park. The telescope's very powerful. I can see all sorts of things – foxes mating, owls killing prey – all sorts.'

'And is the wildlife the only thing you look at?'

Leo drops his gaze.

'You spy on us all, don't you? You sit in your little eyrie and watch us living our lives.'

'I knew that's what you'd think.'

'Our very own Neighbourhood Watch.'

'You won't be so dismissive when I tell you what I saw last night.'

'You were spying last night?'

'I couldn't sleep so I went to the Observatory. It wasn't a good night for stars so I thought I'd see what was going on in the park. Someone had told me wild deer come there at night – escapees from other London herds. They hide in the bushes by the railway during the day . . .'

'Skip the nature notes.'

'I saw you come out of your house and find Athy Petros.'

'You must have felt you'd won the Peeping Tom Lottery. A mutilated body *and* a woman in her nightie. I expect you thought you'd died and gone to heaven. Where does Danny fit into all this?'

'You weren't the only person out and about . . .'

'I should think you saw most of the neighbourhood, not to mention half the police force of Kilburn before the night was out.'

'That was later. I was tracking a big dog fox when I saw the body on the railings. There was a young man with long dark hair bending over it, who ran off when he heard your front door open.'

His eyes radiate compassion. 'It was Danny.'

The inside of my mouth has dried up. Danny was in bed. I checked. I conjure an image of the bunk-beds and the two mounds beneath the duvets.

I didn't actually see their faces.

'I'm so sorry, Rosa.'

'Have you told the police?'

'If I had, Danny would be under lock and key by now.' He places his hand over mine. It feels dry and cool against my fingers. 'There'll be an explanation,' his voice is hypnotically reassuring, 'and I'm sure Danny will tell you what it is. But the fact that he was roaming around out there in the middle of the night, for whatever reason, suggests to me he has some issues that need dealing with.'

'Like what?'

'Maybe he's not coping with his dad's death as well as you think.' Leo's voice is gentle. 'You're obviously a wonderful mother, but . . .'

'But?'

'That's just it – you're a mother. Not a father. There are things that with the best will in the world, you can't do for Danny. He needs a man's hand.'

Tell me something I don't know.

'What do you suggest I do? Advertise?'

'I've become very fond of you, Rosa. I'd hate to see you and your family suffer any more than you already have. I'd like to help. Not just as Danny's Head Teacher, but in a more personal way. As a close friend of the family. As *more* than a close friend . . .'

I can't stand my hand being trapped under his for a moment longer. I jerk it away. Leo quickens up, anxious for me to hear the rest of his pitch.

'I'm a loyal person. I don't tell tales. The reason he was out there last night – whatever's troubling him – would be much better sorted out without police involvement, by the two of us, in a loving and supportive environment.'

I can't believe what I'm hearing.

'Let me see if I've got this right. Basically you're

saying that if I agree to screw you, you won't tell the police you saw Danny bending over Athy's body.'

He winces. 'You've a very crude way of putting things, Rosa. I suppose that's part of the reason I'm so attracted to you.'

'Leo Ratchett, you are something else.'

He thinks this is a compliment and smiles.

'What about your wife?'

'There's been nothing physical between us for years. She knows I love her, and that I would never leave her, but she also realises I need something she can't give. She's happy when I am happy.'

At this moment the front door slams and I hear Tom's voice. 'Rosa?'

'Kitchen,' I say.

Leo's eyes widen. 'Is that Inspector Brice?' he whispers.

'He's in charge of the case.'

This isn't part of Leo's game-plan, but he rallies nonetheless. His eyes, as they flick from me to the door, hold an unmistakable challenge. I hope he hasn't noticed that Tom has a key to my house. I needn't worry. He's still preoccupied by his proposal.

'So what do you think, Rosa?'

Then Tom comes in.

I'm shaking. I hope it doesn't show.

'Inspector Brice, Leo has some important evidence for you.' I see the colour leave Leo's face.

Tom's eyes go from me to Leo. 'What's that, Mr Ratchett?'

Leo looks at me. I stare back. Eventually he shrugs.

'I saw Danny bending over Athy Petros's body, a few minutes before Rosa discovered it.'

There's a long silence.

'You must have been very relieved to find you were mistaken.'

Leo's eyebrows shoot up so high they nearly fly off the top of his face. 'Mistaken?'

'When Mrs Thorn told you she'd checked Danny before leaving the house, and that he was fast asleep.'

Leo's face betrays nothing, but he grips the edge of the table so hard that his knuckles turn white.

Tom looks at me. 'Haven't you told him?'

'I was about to when you arrived. Are you all right, Leo? You're very pale.'

Leo manages a sick smile. 'I'm fine. What a relief. I've been beside myself at the thought that one of our brightest students – and the son of a member of staff – might be involved in this awful business.'

Tom assesses the Head Teacher with a hard, speculative gaze. He knows there's more going on here than Leo cares to acknowledge.

'However, what you say you saw corroborates the presence at the scene of our chief suspect, who also has shoulder-length dark hair.'

Leo's recovering fast. 'Do I know him?' he asks.

'I'm not at liberty to say, sir.' Tom assumes his pompous plod voice. 'But I'd like you to make a formal statement at some point.'

'Whenever you like.'

'I'll see you later today then. Let me show you out.'

After Leo's scurried off, I tell Tom the full story. He's furious. He paces round the kitchen like a demented bear.

'Spying on people! Ogling you through his telescope! Imagining you'd sleep with him! I'll arrest him for attempting to pervert the course of justice, the filthy little shit.'

'Forget it, Tom. He's not worth stressing over.'

'Bastard! When you think about it, we've only got his word that he saw what he saw through a telescope. He could have been down here, on the spot – not half a mile up the road with his eye glued to a long tube.'

'Are you saying he could be involved?'

'Put it this way, he's just added himself to my list of suspects.'

I'm not one of Leo's biggest fans – particularly after his latest performance – but can I see him as a psychotic killer?

'That telescope is very powerful. I've looked through it myself.'

Tom grunts. 'Doesn't prove that's how he knows so much about last night. His efforts to show concern are completely bogus. He couldn't give a shit that one of his students has been slaughtered, and another's in a coma. I'm going to do a thorough background check on Chummy as soon as possible.'

A bit of me is inordinately pleased that Tom's had such a violent reaction to Leo's assault on my virtue.

Another bit can't wait to tackle Danny about suspiciously immobile humps under blankets. My son isn't a murderer, but if he was out and about last night, I want to know why.

FORTY-TWO

I don't have a chance to tackle Danny about last night's nocturnal activities, because tonight, he's giving a repeat performance. When he hasn't arrived home by four in the morning, I realise he isn't going to. Dwaine's still out too. They must be together. Is this good or bad? I'm dizzy with fatigue but I can't sleep. Danny's out there somewhere with a crazy killer on the loose. I haven't slept since I found Athy's body. I think I'll never sleep again. Danny must really hate me. He teases me about my worry-wart tendencies, but usually gives some sort of indication of when he'll be home. Not tonight. Tonight he wants to punish me.

Who can blame him?

To take my mind off Danny, I focus on me and Tom. I try to put things into perspective. I've only slept with him once, but it's like we've been intimate for ever. What is it that draws me to him? I think back to when we first met. There was something about him, right from the word go – the gentle mockery, the contained strength, the sympathy and understanding underneath the cool exterior. But I hate the way he blows hot and cold – one minute loving and concerned – the next, absorbed in his work and out of the door. And I hate his mother. I need a woman like her in my life like I need genital herpes. If Tom and I become a serious item, she'll be slap bang in my face. She phones him all the time. I hear the voice through his door. The genie of the answer phone – a malevolent presence lurking in his room even though she's really in Cheltenham. A leech, ready to suck his lifeblood if he lets her.

Rob and I never had in-law problems. His were dead and mine might as well have been. For one absurd moment, I desperately want to ask his advice on my new relationship. If that's what it is. I want to ask my very best friend, my dead love.

What would Rob really think of me and Tom? I've put off asking this question, because I know the answer. Rob once said that if anything ever happened to him, he'd want me to find someone else and be happy. But I know he'd hate it. When Miss Pearl died, Rob lost everything. There wasn't one person in the whole world he could call his own. Until me. We weren't much more than children when we met. I filled all the voids in his lonely life, took the place of all the absences, became mother, father, sister, brother, lover and best friend. And when my parents cast me off, he did the same for me. Aged nineteen, we plugged the empty holes in the fabric of our existence with each other. An unhealthy symbiosis, according to some. But it worked for us. Our marriage was inviolate. I'm not saying we didn't row or have problems. I'm not saying there weren't difficult times when we didn't even like each other much. But there was never a moment when either of us thought of calling it a day.

I make myself imagine – really imagine – Rob seeing me with Tom. I conjure him wraithlike outside the window of his old studio, looking at Tom and me together. I rerun everything, down to the smallest detail, and I watch Rob watching us. My body burns with a mixture of shame and something else I won't admit to at first.

It's desire.

To my horror, I realise that it's giving me an erotic charge, thinking of Rob seeing me with another man.

But then I force myself to really focus on his face. His beloved face with its high cheekbones, full mouth and dark, dark eyes. It's the eyes I see most clearly. They glitter with anguish and loss. And a complete knowledge of me, inside and out, that no one else on earth will ever have.

All desire drains away, leaving a limitless well of sorrow. The night with Tom fades to nothing alongside the weight of my whole life with Rob, and all the things we were to each other.

I'm not ready for another lover. I can't leave my old one behind.

Not yet.

Maybe not ever.

I relive our last night together. Not the lovemaking, although that was good, but afterwards, with the glow from the streetlights falling on his dark skin, giving it the appearance of burnished mahogany. I see our limbs intertwined, the white and the black, damp with sweat. I remember his musky smell. I feel him stroking my belly and winding my hair round his fingers and across his face. I remember our innocent, desultory chat about our lives: his latest painting, the possibility of a small part in a TV soap for me. And our children. We talked of them and their little ways and our little worries: should we let Danny go to his first rock festival – should Anna be allowed to give up her piano lessons.

Idle, intimate talk after good love.

All that love. Me and Rob and the children. Woven inextricably together in our rumpled bed in the night.

We didn't know that the Angel of Death in his Ford Mondeo hovered above us, chatting on his mobile.

Waiting to destroy.

Tom is special. But he's not Rob.

I'm finally starting to feel sleepy. Making my way upstairs I glance out of the landing window into the back garden, and experience for the second time in twenty-four hours a surge of adrenalin. Someone is in the shed. I can see the flickering of a candle, and figures moving to and fro.

Do I go down and confront them? Or do I wake Tom? No contest, Rosa.

I'm on my way to Tom's room when I remember he's out. I turn off the landing light and peer through the window again. I watch the shed for a few minutes. Then go to my bed, ready at last to sleep. There are no intruders.

It's Danny in the shed. And Dwaine. I glimpsed them through the window.

Danny can't face being in the same house as me and Tom, so instead of joining the rest of London's young homeless and sleeping in a doorway, he's very sensibly taken himself off to the shed for the night. It'll be a good punishment for me. I'll be imagining all sorts of bad things happening to him. Serve me right for screwing the lodger.

And Dwaine's keeping him company.

Good on you, Danny. I won't let on I know you're there. Stay at the end of the garden as long as you like. I'll make sure there's plenty of food in the fridge for you to nick when I'm not around, and when you're ready you'll come inside and we'll talk.

I'm asleep before my head even hits the pillow, and when I wake, with a start, it's morning. For a moment I'm twenty years old, in my student digs, and I panic because I have to kick Rob out before the landlady discovers him.

Chance would be a fine thing.

Someone's ringing the doorbell. I stagger downstairs, still partly inhabiting my dreamworld.

It's Guy the Groper. Guy prides himself on his cool. Things which send the rest of us into a major tizzy leave Guy scarcely breaking sweat. I'm surprised, therefore, to see how rough he looks. Like someone who's actually bothered about something.

'Is your pet policeman at home?'

'Do you want to speak to him?'

'Maybe. I need to talk to you first.'

'You'll have to put up with me getting ready for work.'

He helps himself to coffee whilst I shower and dress. Finally I'm ready to listen.

'What's up?'

Guy shifts in his seat uneasily. 'If I tell you something, will you keep it to yourself?'

I'm not a priest, or a doctor. Guy isn't a close friend. He's a neighbour.

'It depends what it is.'

'I won't tell you stuff you don't need to know.'

Stuff I don't need to know?

'Sounds dodgy. Maybe you'd better talk to someone else.'

'It has to be you.'

'Why?'

'Because I want to ask about Brice. Is he the sort of copper that'd turn a blind eye to something minor if he thought it could lead him to something bigger?'

'What's going on?'

He's about to launch in when Anna appears. She sees her mother breakfasting with yet another man who isn't her father, and walks out again, taking herself off to school on an empty stomach.

Guy hardly registers either her appearance or her abrupt departure.

'It's to do with Athy's dad.'

Do I want to hear what's coming next?

'We've worked together a lot, recently – a little business venture . . .'

'And?'

'And I've seen a fair bit of his kid, too.'

I'm definitely starting to feel bad about this.

'Athy used to come with us in his van sometimes. Nikos said he didn't want her left alone at nights.'

'And?'

'They had this very volatile relationship.'

'In what way?'

'He went a bundle on the heavy Greek father routine. He thought she should make like the Virgin Mary. He couldn't hack her waltzing around looking like a cheap hooker. He once told me he ripped all her clothes up and locked her in the house for three days until she promised to wear stuff he'd chosen.'

'Are you saying you think he harmed her?'

'I never saw him lay a finger on her, but he was always saying it was his right and duty to beat her black and blue, if necessary.'

'You're joking.'

'Since she disappeared he's been weird. And not in the way you'd expect. Very subdued – won't talk about it. Insists on working, like nothing's happened.'

'Maybe it's his way of coping.'

'The night she died we'd been doing a bit of business. When we got back to my house round midnight we had some gear to stash.'

Too much information, Guy. I don't need to know about your dodgy doings.

'We unloaded most of it, then he said he'd do the rest. I came out just as he was finishing. He said the van was empty, but I saw something covered over, behind the back seat. He said he had things to do, but later I saw the van outside still, and him like a bloody waxwork at the wheel.' Guy grinds to a halt.

'What are you saying?'

'Something's not right. I should tell the police, but I don't want them nosing about in my business. Will Brice nobble me if I split on Nikos?'

'If you don't tell him, I will. Your little schemes don't matter a damn compared to what's happened to Athy. And Crystal. The person who did this is a dangerous lunatic. If it's Petros, he should be arrested. Pronto.' I hand him the phone. 'Here.'

Guy realises he doesn't have a choice. He phones Tom and arranges to meet.

'You've done the right thing.'

He gives a rueful smile. 'Will you come and see me in Wormwood Scrubs, Rose?'

At the school gates a couple of Constables are on duty, but the media have all but disappeared. Athy is yesterday's news. The world moves on. There are several bunches of flowers left against the wall with sorrowful notes addressed to Athy. One card says *God has another little angel in heaven tonight.* I feel sorry for God. There'll be trouble in Paradise if Athy's in residence.

I make my way through groups of worried parents who've escorted their children to school – something that doesn't usually happen. Even the occasional Sixth Former can be seen slipping furtively out of a parental car. My own children are not with me. Danny presumably waited till I left the house before vacating his shed for the day, and Anna was gone the moment she saw Guy the Groper slumped over our breakfast-table.

Inside school, things are far from normal. The usual crowds of chattering students, giggling and pushing their way towards their classrooms, have been replaced by subdued boys and girls sometimes muttering quietly to each other, but often silent, pacing the corridors wrapped in their own thoughts.

Leo holds a special assembly where he articulates everyone's shock and sorrow about Athy's death, coming as it does, hard on the heels of Crystal's accident. He implores any student who knows anything that might shed light on what has happened to come forward immediately, warns that no one must speak to the press, and concludes by saying that the thoughts and prayers of our whole community are with the families of the two girls. I want to pelt him with rotten eggs. This is the man who, in order to get his leg over, was ready to conceal the identity of the boy he suspected of murdering Athy. I have to stop myself hissing and booing as he pontificates to the packed hall.

I say as much to Jess.

'He's a fucking disgrace,' she agrees. 'We should shop him to the governors. Get rid of him.'

'In your dreams. They like the TV thing too much.'

'Yeah. And that committee's full of middle-aged, middle-class housewives with too much fucking time on their hands. Literally. He's had every single one of them, you know. They all think he's Superman and Jesus Christ rolled into one.'

Once upon a time I'd have thought this was one of Jess's slanderous exaggerations. Now I'm not so sure. Nothing about Leo Ratchett's behaviour would surprise me.

We walk up to the Media Resources office: Jess needs to collect something from Fax Max. But the door's locked. A note pinned to the door says he's away. Jess is enraged.

'I asked for these fucking things two days ago. Yesterday I came to school specially to pick them up. He's not teaching staff so he should've been here, but he wasn't. And he's still away. Fucking skiver. I'll kill him.'

Primmy Post-it-note hovers into view, wincing as Jess's invective bounces off the walls.

'Is anything wrong, Jess?'

'Fucking Fax Max. I was relying on those photo displays for my A-level group. Now I've precisely ten minutes to prepare something else.'

'Actually we're a little concerned about Max. His wife says he hasn't been home for two days. She's desperately worried.'

'I'm amazed he has a wife, let alone one who'd worry about him. Oily little shite.'

'This is strictly between ourselves,' Primmy warns us. 'We don't want to make people more edgy than they are already.'

'Have you told the police?'

'I've had a word with Mr Brice. He's sending someone round to interview Max's wife.'

She bustles off and Jess clutches my arm melodramatically.

'It's him! Aaargh!'

'What?'

'Him wot did the murder.'

'What?' I laugh in spite of myself.

'Think about it. He's always mooching around outside the girls' changing-rooms with his fucking tongue hanging out. Maybe Athy's belly stud overwhelmed him and he killed her in a fit of slavering lust.'

'Jess!'

'All right – I'm heartless, I know. You look so awful I just wanted to cheer you up.'

'Go teach, Jess. You're as bad as Tom. He's put Leo on his list of potential killers.'

'Now there's a thought.'

On my way to the Drama Studio, I pass the demolished building. The forensic team are still examining the rubble. I recall the day I saw Max standing there, talking to Fred Borrage. Why were they inside the fence? It was out of bounds, even to staff, because of its instability. Did Leo really ask Max to take photos of the building?

I wonder about the unlikely friendship between Max and Borrage. Borrage is often to be found eating his sandwiches in the Media Resources office at lunchtime, and I've seen them driving off together in Max's car on more than one occasion. Is it simply a case of the two most unlikeable people in the school palling up together for support?

Borrage is universally hated by the students. He always appears when they least want him. He's omnipresent. No secret card-game in the gym changing-room, no furtive fag behind the bushes on the playing-field escapes his gimlet eye. His hobby is catching people in the act – staff as well as students. As a consequence he's shunned by all.

Max, by contrast, has wormed his way in everywhere. Not with the staff, who see past his fawning attempts at friendship, but with the kids, who for some reason have accepted him as one of their own. I've lost count of the number of times I've seen him at the centre of a group of laughing students. Adolescents aren't famous for their acceptance of oddballs, and they're ultra-quick to spot the staff who try to be one of the lads. So what makes Max so popular?

Another image springs to mind: Max chatting to Athy and Crystal.

More than once.

Quite often.

I then remember something that stops me in my tracks: Dwaine in the Soho bar, handing something to a man whose backview seemed familiar. A man who, try as I might, I could not identify even though I was convinced I knew him.

Fax Max.

That's who it was.

I think.

* * *

Fred Borrage's face streamed with sweat as he strove to complete his task. The boiler-room was more than hot. It was how Fred imagined hell would be: a roaring inferno – the flames competing with his conscience for the privilege of searing his mind into oblivion. He blessed the inadequate school funding which meant the boiler still worked on solid fuel rather than gas or oil. He didn't know how he would have managed otherwise. Every few minutes he dialled Max's mobile, becoming angrier and angrier with each message that told him the thing was switched off. If Max thought he was dumping Fred in it, then he had another think coming.

Nobody messed with Fred Borrage.

FORTY-THREE

At lunchtime I go to my office to be alone. I thought it would be good for me to be working today – that it would take my mind off things. But after a morning's teaching I'm completely strung out and on the point of tears. The children are disturbed and overexcited, and instead of calming them down I've added to the general hysteria by behaving like Mrs Hitler. I can't hack it. Maybe I should go home. I notice a Post-it note stuck to my mark register. I'm about to read it when I hear a voice in the next-door office. Our new, flash Performing Arts complex has one major flaw about which we are currently in dispute with the architects: the soundproofing is total crap. In the old building, decrepit though it was, apparently you could perform the 1812 Overture without anyone being any the wiser. In the new building, by contrast, a halfway decent pair of ears can pick up the gist of the quietest conversation.

Dave Alessi is talking on the phone. In spite of all my efforts to tune out, my attention is caught.

'We don't know that she told her . . . Most likely not – I can't see her wanting to . . . She'd have said something to you when . . . Calm down, for Christ's sake . . . You say nothing. You've got to be strong, for both of us. We haven't come this far to trip up now.'

At this point I hear his door open, and the voice becomes fainter as he moves off down the corridor. He's using his mobile and not the school phone. I wonder why. Who's he talking to?

Three guesses.

What he's talking about is another matter. I'm going over the conversation when my eye takes in what's written on the Post-it note I'm clutching. All thoughts of Dave and his beloved are swept from my head.

Rosa – Leo has informed me that Joanna, our permanent Drama teacher, is returning from maternity leave after half-term, so sadly we will have to terminate your contract as from 20 Feb. Marion.

I'm being given the push. Can this day get any worse? Joanna was supposed to be wedded to hearth, home and new baby till Easter at the earliest. Or so I'd been told.

This is Leo's revenge. The little weasel. I'm going to give him a very large piece of my mind.

Fuming, I leave the office and crash straight into Tom. 'What are you doing here?' I snap.

'Came to take Ratchett's statement. Thought I'd say hello. What's up?'

I burst into tears.

I seem to have spent a disproportionate part of my life recently, being comforted by Tom. He says all the right things and we end up laughing immoderately – at Leo, the cowardly lion, who always makes Marion do his dirty work. It's hard to remember my decision to chuck him while tucked so snugly into his chest.

Eventually I extricate myself.

'What if someone comes in and finds The Great Detective and The Supply Teacher having a snog? Leo would jump for joy and fire me on the spot.'

'I bet he can't terminate your contract in the middle of a term. Call your union.'

'I don't belong to a teaching union.'

'That's a bit daft, isn't it?'

'Equity's my union. I'm an actor, not a teacher.'

Suddenly Tom executes one of his instant transformations from personal to professional. I'm talking to a different man.

'Listen, Rosa, I've checked the police computer, Social Services – all the agencies I can think of, and there's no record of O'Brien. I really do need you to find out if Anna knows where he lives. I have asked her myself. She says she hasn't a clue, but I get the feeling she's not being honest. She might open up to you, though.'

I'd said it had to be me who talked to Anna about O'Brien. And I don't like him calling my daughter dishonest.

'She won't tell me if she hasn't told you,' I object. 'It's a point of honour with my children to let me know as little as possible about their lives. I'm drip-fed information on a need-to-know basis.'

'This is a murder enquiry. Anna could be concealing information that would lead us to a killer.'

Who the hell does he think he is, talking to me in that tone?

'I told you about Mick O'Brien months ago. You wouldn't take me seriously. Now you've decided he's a maniac, and suddenly we're all expected to jump to your tune.'

I'm devastated that Mick O'Brien is back as the big baddie in our lives. I'd so wanted to think of him as mad, not bad. And I don't necessarily think that he's guilty. There are probably lots of people who wished Athy Petros dead, and as far as I know, O'Brien never even met her. I don't like the idea of him being made a scapegoat.

'For Christ's sake, Rosa, listen . . .'

'No, *you* listen. I will ask Anna about him, but I'll do it in my own way in my own time. And if you want my opinion, which you obviously don't since you've already made up your mind, I reckon there's something very fishy going on in this school.'

Tom becomes very still. His eyes lock on to mine. No intimacy there now. Just calculation.

'That's a large claim, Rosa.'

'For a start, there's Max's disappearance. I've been remembering things about him.'

'Go on.'

'He and Fred Borrage the caretaker were always hanging round that building where Crystal was found. There were noises in there one night. Fred swore everything was fenced off and no one could get in, but I know what I heard. Then there's something Jess said this morning – about Max always chatting up the girls, making jokes, offering them sweets, giving them jobs to do, generally being there . . .'

I nearly tell him about my probable sighting of Max and Dwaine in the Soho bar, but something holds me back. I don't want to tell a policeman, even one I've slept with, about my fear that Danny's involved with drugs. Especially after what Tom's said about Dwaine. So I bring up the other new development.

'Have you talked to Guy Gropius?'

'Yes. Petros is at the station now, waiting to be interviewed.'

'He couldn't kill his own daughter, whatever Guy says.'

'Most homicides are from within the family.'

'When I saw them together at the Christmas show, I got the impression he was devoted to her.'

'You think Max is a better bet?'

'I think there's a lot of murky stuff going on round here. You're the detective. So detect.' As I say this I remember finding Guy in Borrage's office. This is becoming ridiculous. Suddenly the whole world's a suspect.

I forge on. 'All I know is, I'm suddenly getting very bad vibes about Churchill Towers. But hey, maybe that's sour grapes since I've just been told to sling my hook. Whaddaya think, Poirot?'

Tom's eyes have changed again. 'I like it when you're cross,' he says.

I am not hot all over and I am not trembling when he looks at me like that. I don't want this relationship.

'Got to go,' I say. 'I have to kill Leo before afternoon school starts.' His large bulk blocks the doorway and he grins at me. 'Move,' I tell him, and try to ignore the way my skin tingles as I brush past him.

'Thanks for your insights, Miss Marple. I'll bear them in mind. If you could just have a word with Anna . . .'

The man is impossible. I might as well have saved my breath. He's made up his mind who the killer is and that's that. As I run down the corridor, the buzzer sounds for afternoon lessons. Now I'll have to wait till after school to see Leo.

I'm still fuming two hours later as I stomp up the Observatory stairs, and I don't know who's making me more angry, Leo or Tom.

Leo has his back to me. He's talking to one of the Sixth Formers – a girl called Davinia. He's treating her to his view-over-London routine. Like the Devil on the mountain, showing Christ the kingdoms of the world.

'Got a minute, Mr Ratchett?' I say.

They both jump. The girl throws me an unfathomable look. Regret or relief?

'Davinia's doing a project on the City for her Leisure and Tourism GNVQ. I'm helping her identify some of our less well-known landmarks.'

I'll bet you are.

Suddenly the world is full of slimy middle-aged men leching after schoolgirls. Or maybe it's just my fears about Anna and O'Brien projecting out onto the rest of the world – like when you're pregnant and every second woman you pass in the street sports a big belly.

'Actually, sir, I promised to do some shopping for my nan after school, so I'd better go. Thanks for your help.' She slips past me.

Leo's smooth charm is absent today. 'Make it quick. I'm busy.'

'I can see that.' I look pointedly down the stairs after the retreating Davinia.

'Well?'

'I've just received a note saying my presence is not required after half-term . . .'

'Joanna wants to get back in harness sooner than she anticipated. A pity, but there we are.'

'And it has absolutely nothing to do with your antics at my house yesterday?'

'I'm sorry? You've lost me.'

'When you tried to blackmail me into your bed.'

'I haven't the faintest idea what you're talking about.'

'My contract's until Easter.'

'You signed one for this term, did you?'

The expression on my face must mirror the sinking feeling in my stomach. Leo smirks.

'Pity. Deal with the details, Rosa. Deal with the details.'

'You didn't even have the guts to tell me yourself.'

'Strangely enough, a Head Teacher usually has more on his mind than the termination of a supply teacher's contract.'

'Like perving after the Sixth-Formers, I suppose.'

Leo grabs my arm and holds it in an iron grip. 'There are strict laws governing slander in this country, Ms Thorn.'

I try unsuccessfully to shrug him off. 'There are laws governing common assault, too. And blackmail. And withholding evidence in a police investigation.'

As I wrench his hand away, my eye is caught by something out of the window. 'What's that?'

'What? A bevy of Sixth-Formers, perhaps, hanging from my window-sill by their fingernails?'

'Look.'

A column of smoke is rising into the air near the park.

'Probably one of our non-attenders amusing himself with stolen tyres and a box of matches.'

'Can I use your telescope?'

He makes no effort to help me focus it, but when I finally get a clear image I'm in no doubt as to what I'm seeing.

It's not burning tyres. It's a burning shed. And it's mine.

Leo listens to Rosa's feet thundering down the stairs. He refocuses his telescope and waits. A minute later he trains it on the flying figure, red hair streaming behind her, running down Albert Road. He smiles.

'Things at home not looking too good, bitch?' he murmurs. 'What a shame.'

He crosses to his desk and dials a number on his phone.

'A word, Fred, if you don't mind. My office. Five minutes.'

FORTY-FOUR

Hot, bright, glowing fire
Burning away nature's dross,
Cleansing and clearing.

I'm a fully paid-up member of the 'If God had meant us to run He'd have given us trainers on the bottom of our legs' brigade, but I cover the distance from school to home in a time which most people who know me would find inconceivable. When I rush into the back garden, I'm confronted by an inferno. The smoke is now a pillar of flame, crackling and dancing, throwing up vivid colours, blues, purples, greens, whenever the fire reaches one of Rob's store of paints. Thank God Larry insisted the work was removed to the gallery. As it is, I weep for the handful of sketches that were still inside a plan-chest waiting to be sorted. They'll be nothing but a heap of ash by now.

Just like Rob.

Then I remember. Danny and Dwaine – they spent the night in the shed. I try desperately to recall whether I've seen them at Churchill today, but however much I cast my mind's eye along corridors and in classrooms, I can picture neither of them.

I hear a voice, shouting. It's mine.

'Are you in there, Danny? Can you hear me?'

It's impossible to see into the shed. The flames are blinding-bright and the smoke is thick and deadly. In the far distance, I hear a fire engine. By the time it arrives it'll be too late. I shield my face with my arm, and try to move closer. The heat's intense. I'm forced back. I duck as an exploding piece of wood spatters around me, cracking like a rifle-shot. I try again and again, but each time, the scorching heat is too much.

Then my worst fears are confirmed. I see a movement inside the shed. I can't make out who it is, partly because of the smoke and flames and partly because the person's covered in a blanket. I see that he's dragging something.

A body.

He's pulling at the door, but the heat's warped the frame. I'm seized by a crazed obstinacy. I will not acknowledge the deadly power of the flames. I'm shouting, 'It's not hot! It doesn't hurt! I can't feel it!' I grab one of our cast-iron garden chairs and use it as a battering ram, hurling it against the unyielding door, ignoring the hot metal sizzling the skin off my palms, ignoring the flames singeing my hair. But the door won't budge. I take my chair and smash the window, trying to remove the major shards that remain. I don't want to save the boys from the flames in order to skewer them with icicles of glass. Time's gone into slow-mo, yet only seconds have passed. I climb onto the chair, hoping the soles of my shoes don't fuse with the scalding metal. I call out.

'Over here!'

There's a retching, rasping sound. Someone struggling for breath. I can't see through the thick smoke and flames, so I keep shouting. Finally I spot him. He's discarded the blanket. It *is* Danny, and he's dragging the inert body of Dwaine across the floor towards me.

'You lift. I'll pull him through.'

Danny's coughing too much to speak, but he nods.

It's not easy to push a dead weight upwards through a window, when searing heat's turning your clothes to black confetti, and your lungs are being kippered. However much effort Danny makes, he can't hoist Dwaine high enough. Eventually he sinks down, gulping in huge jagged breaths.

'Go away, Mum. The whole thing's about to collapse. Go. Please.'

I'm consumed with a rage as hot as the flames which threaten to destroy him. I will not lose another member of my family. No way is Danny going to die. I bellow at my son: 'Don't you dare give up. You push, I'll pull. Together – one, two, *three*.'

With a final burst of strength, Danny shoves Dwaine upwards, and I pull him through the window. I feel myself falling backwards off the chair and end up pinioned under the dead weight of his body. I try to push him off, but he's too heavy. I'm desperate. Danny's still in there. He hasn't the strength to climb through the window. He used the last of it saving Dwaine.

Then, inexplicably, Dwaine's off me. I scramble to my feet and run back to the window. I grab the chair, screaming with pain as the metal burns my flesh. Then I'm up and leaning through the window. Danny's slumped on the floor. He isn't coughing and retching any more. He's completely silent. I tip forward but I can't reach him.

'Get up, Dan. Please. Come on, you can do it. One last effort. Don't be a wuss. Please, Danny. *Please.*'

He doesn't move. I'm too late. He's dead. My little boy's dead. My beautiful Danny, with his father's eyes and his kindness and his sense of fun, is gone. The heat overwhelms me and I see no reason to fight any more. It all comes down to death in the end. I see Rob smiling at me and I think, If you can't beat 'em join 'em. I feel strong arms cradling me, bearing me up and away from this terrible place. The heat recedes, along with the awful roar of the flames, and for the first time in a long while, I'm at peace. There's a ringing in my head. I float on a tide of ethereal sound. I'm weightless yet cradled by a mysterious but gentle force. Images materialise and dematerialise around me: Baby Danny in a blue woollen hat. Anna playing 'Für Elise' on the piano. Me, aged five, being tossed in the air by my father, and Rob. Always Rob. Rob asking me to marry him. Rob wiping strawberry stains from my mouth. Rob painting, in a frenzy of concentration. Rob singing Caribbean lullabies to Anna . . .

Someone's calling me.

Leave me alone. I want to stay here, in my haven of peace and tranquillity. I don't want to be dragged back to a world full of pain and sorrow. I ignore the voice, with its strident, jarring tones.

'Mrs Thorn! Wake up, there's a good girl. Rosa? Can you hear me?'

There's whispering. Someone else is here. Someone who's crying.

'Wake up. I love you. Don't die. Please don't die.'

Someone's kissing my cheek. Someone full of sadness. Someone whose sadness matters.

'Wake up. Say something. Please.'

I open my eyes.

'Mummy . . .'

'Anna?' My throat hurts. 'Where am I?'

'In hospital.'

Reality crashes in. Danny's dead, in the fire. I'm in agony – I want so much to go back to my alternative universe. But I can't. I'm stuck here, in this crisp, bright hospital ward.

'Danny's dead.' Tears sting my raw face. Danny's dead.

But Anna's smiling. 'No, he isn't. He's suffering from smoke inhalation and minor burns, but otherwise he's fine. He's over there.'

I struggle up. There, in the bed opposite, black braids fanning across the pillow, my son is sleeping.

How could he possibly have escaped that inferno?

For a whole afternoon and night, Anna had paced the dingy ward, alternating between her mother and her brother. Her fragility tore at Tom's heart. Her pitiful exhortations to Rosa brought impotent tears to his eyes. He was desperate to give her the support she needed. Who else did she have except him? He'd been back to the hospital as often as he could, but it was difficult. The demands of the Petros case, particularly with the extra complications thrown up by yesterday's fire, meant that his off-duty time was minimal.

He'd walked into the ward for a quick visit just as Rosa was regaining consciousness. He watched Anna's joy as she smothered her mother in kisses. He moved towards them, then hesitated. There were times when families needed to be left to themselves. This was one of them. He slipped away quietly. There would be time for him later.

It was essential to keep calm. Dwaine knew that. When the nurses came, he feigned sleep. He watched Brice popping in and out. It was only a matter of time before he'd be along. He and Danny needed to decide on their story, but it was too difficult. Too public. They all thought he was drifting in and out of consciousness. He couldn't risk being spotted at Danny's bedside.

This wasn't meant to happen. He'd thought the nightmare of the last few months was over, but now all his sins had caught up with him, as his mum would no doubt tell him in no uncertain terms.

His mum.

He'd pretended to be out of it earlier, so after a while Charlene had gone away. But she'd be back. He had to act before she returned. He had to do something right now before things got even worse.

FORTY-FIVE

By the time the Fire Department had arrived at my house, Danny, Dwaine and I were all laid out on the grass, well away from the flames. The first fireman on the scene said there was no sign of anyone else. Someone had saved our lives and then vanished.

I was unconscious for twenty-four hours. A CAT scan shows no signs of brain damage – in fact, so desperate are they for beds, that they're letting me out later today. My hands are the main problem. Although they're bandaged so the air can't get to them, they're incredibly painful.

The good news is that Dwaine is also alive, and well, apart from a couple of burns. The bad news is that he's gone – he disappeared shortly before the police came to arrest him.

The other bad news is that a body was found in the remains of the shed; it was severely burned, but dental records showed it was Fax Max. Abrasions round his wrists and ankles indicate that he was tied up during the hours before he died, although there was no sign of any binding on the body.

I get all this information from Tom. Anna says he's been fantastic, that she wouldn't have known where to turn without him. What an isolated little unit we have become – me and my children. No grandparents or other relatives to help us through. Only Jess, who came yesterday, but couldn't stay because Lozz has a phobic aversion to hospitals.

And now Tom.

He's here with flowers and chocolates, looming over my bed, smelling of the outside world – too large and vigorous for this ward full of sick people.

He says they still don't have a clue who rescued us.

'Any idea who started the fire?'

Tom looks uncomfortable.

'You're not saying Danny's responsible? I know he had candles in there, but he's always very careful—'

'It's more serious than that. We think Dwaine might have started the fire deliberately, to kill Max Lucas. We also think he'd previously abducted him.'

Whatever I was expecting, it wasn't this.

'No way! Why on earth would Dwaine want to kill Fax Max?'

'That's what I have to ask Danny.'

'Danny? What's he got to do with it?'

Even as I ask, I know the answer. If Dwaine had kept Max a prisoner in the shed, then Danny knew, because Danny was there too. A fugitive from his mother and her lover.

'Let's ask him. Help me out of bed.'

Danny's in a side-ward now. When Dwaine disappeared, the police had Danny moved so they could keep him under surveillance. And there was me thinking my son was getting special treatment because he was a hero.

'I'd rather you didn't come, Rosa. Don't worry, I'll be gentle.'

'He's under eighteen. I've a right to be with him.'

'Yes, but—'

'Then let's go.'

Tom knows me well enough by now to accept that I won't be deflected, so we make our way down the ward followed by the avid gaze of the other patients, who are all bored out of their skulls and game for anything that smacks of drama and intrigue. I feel light-headed and I wish I were back in bed.

I'd talked to Danny earlier, but by mutual consent we'd avoided all painful topics. It was enough that we were alive. I think we both felt that Anna's joy at having her family safe shouldn't be spoiled by uncomfortable questions. But now I need to hear his story just as much as Tom does.

Danny's already dressed. He's leaving at the same time as me. An ambulance is to take us home. He gives me a wan smile.

'Wassup, Mum?'

'Tom has to talk to you. As a policeman, not a friend.'

'I'll make it as quick and painless as possible, Dan. I'm sorry to do this, but it's my job.'

'Get on with it then.'

'What do you know about the death of Max Lucas?'

'I couldn't get to him. It was too hot.'

'Did you know Dwaine Johnson was keeping him prisoner?'

Danny is silent.

'Did you?'

'Yes.'

'Did Dwaine kill him?'

'No.'

'Danny, your friend kidnapped Lucas. Now Lucas is dead and Dwaine's disappeared. What are we supposed to think?'

'Dwaine just wanted information.'

'What information?'

Danny sighs.

'What information?' Tom repeats, then: 'Look, Danny, if Dwaine hasn't killed Max then he has nothing to fear from the police. And he needs to be in hospital for his burns to be treated.'

'All right! Dwaine suspected Max knew something about Crystal and Athy. Max denied it. Dwaine didn't believe him. He decided to kidnap Max and starve him till he fessed up.'

'Why did Dwaine think Max was involved?'

'He didn't say.'

Danny's lying. Ever since he was small he's had a habit of scratching his left eyebrow when he's telling a lie. And that's what he's doing now.

'You're his best friend. Surely he'd tell you?'

'He just asked if he could keep him in the studio for a couple of days.'

'Weren't you there when Dwaine was questioning Max? What did he say?'

'He brought Max back the night after Athy was found. He didn't want me involved, so although we all spent the night there, he didn't talk to Max in front of me.'

'Why didn't he want you involved?'

'Dunno.'

Tom takes a different tack. 'How did the fire start?'

'Dunno. An overturned candle? Matches? I wasn't there.'

'There was electricity in that shed. Why use candles?'

'Because I didn't want Mum to know where I was. I was so gutted when I found you two together that I just wanted to be out of the house, and I didn't want her pestering me. If she knew I was in the shed, she'd have been down there trying to explain herself and I didn't want that. So I used candles when I had to, but otherwise stayed in the dark.'

'The fire wasn't started by a candle. The Fire Brigade found traces of accelerant.'

'Dad's paints and turpentine were in there.'

'It was a petrol bomb.'

Danny's eyes register total shock.

'Did Dwaine know how to make such a thing?'

'No, he fucking didn't. And since you know how it started, why ask? Are you accusing me as well?'

'I just want to find out exactly what happened yesterday afternoon.'

'I don't know. I wasn't there. I'd gone to buy food. We hadn't had anything to eat since the night before and I was starving. I didn't want to nick stuff from the kitchen and make Mum suspicious, and I also knew that Dwaine didn't want me there when he asked his questions. So I went shopping. When I arrived back, the place was already burning. I got a blanket from the house, soaked it in water, threw it over myself and went into the shed. I saw Dwaine cut Max free, but then they got trapped by a falling beam. They were both unconscious. I dragged Dwaine towards the door, thinking I'd get him out, then go back for Max. But the door wouldn't open . . .' Danny's very pale and his hands are trembling slightly.

'That's enough,' I interrupt. 'He's still suffering from shock. He's told you what you wanted to know.'

Tom gives Danny his most powerful interrogative scrutiny. Like a lighthouse beam piercing the darkness of deceit.

'Nothing else to say, Danny?'

'Leave it, Tom.'

I think he's going to pursue it, but he doesn't. He hasn't quite finished, though.

'You haven't told me anything which proves Dwaine didn't start that fire, so as far as I'm concerned he's still a suspect on the run. If he makes contact you must tell me. Otherwise you could be charged with perverting the course of justice. I'm sorry, Dan, but that's the way it is.'

Tom's only doing his job, but at that moment I hate him. Surely he doesn't have to be so cold and formal. Our friendly lodger's performed a vanishing act as successful as Dwaine's.

'Just go away, Tom,' I say.

He looks at me, an unreadable expression on his face.

'See you later,' he says, leaving me and Danny alone.

And I thought he was looking out for us – our only support in an alien world. Well, more fool you, Rosa. His first loyalty is to his job. Thank goodness I'd already decided to chuck him before all this happened.

But now – Danny. It won't be long before Anna's back to escort us home, and I've a few more things I want to ask my son.

'So, Sunshine, let's have the rest.'

Danny's a worm wriggling on my maternal hook.

'You didn't tell Tom everything.'

'Get off my back, Mum.'

'Something's been going on with you and Dwaine for weeks. I've tried to turn a blind eye, but now you're going to have to tell me.'

'There's nothing to tell.'

'Stop scratching your left eyebrow, then.'

'What?'

'Never mind. Danny, there's someone very dangerous out there. If you know anything, you *must* say.'

'I swear to you that Dwaine's problems have nothing to do with Athy's murder.'

'So you admit he's got problems?'

Danny chews his lip.

'What problems, Danny?'

'I can't tell you.'

'For God's sake! Dwaine's on the run, a suspected murderer!'

'He's not a murderer.'

'Then tell me the truth.'

Danny stays silent. Two minutes crawl by. Eventually I make a decision.

'I'm going to tell you something. You're not going to like it, or me, but that can't be helped.'

Danny looks up, startled.

'I followed you.'

Danny stares. 'You what?'

'I had to find out what was going on, and you wouldn't tell me so one night I followed you to a bar in Soho. Bertie's. I saw you meet Dwaine and argue with him. Then you left and I saw Dwaine take a package from someone. Later I realised it was Fax Max. And now he's dead.'

Danny's shaking his head in disbelief. 'You spied on me.'

'I'm not proud of it, but it's a measure of how worried I've been. I need you to tell me what's going on.'

'You're something else, Mum, you really are.'

He's looking at me like I'm dog-dirt on the bottom of his shoe. It's horrible.

'Go away.'

At that moment Anna arrives.

'Sorry I'm late,' she says in a rush. 'The queues in the supermarket were massive, but I wanted to cook you both a really nice meal tonight, so it was worth the wait.'

'Don't bother to tell Mum where you were,' Danny says. 'She knows anyway. As we speak, one of her army of spies'll be preparing a dossier of your day's movements ready for her to check later.'

Anna's too excited to take in the tension. 'The nurse says the ambulance is waiting. Mum, you're not even dressed yet. Hurry up. Let's get out of here.'

I've blown it. Not only am I none the wiser about Danny's activities, I've now forfeited his trust completely.

Spying on him. It was hard to credit. Mum had always been so trusting. He refused to acknowledge the reason why that trust had disappeared. If he looked too deeply at what he'd done, he'd have to admit that he couldn't blame her.

But there was no way he could tell her the truth.

It was easier to goad himself into such a state of moral outrage that leaving home for a while seemed the only option. Away from her he wouldn't have to keep up any deceptions. He could just finish what he'd started.

He thought about the night he'd met Dwaine at Bertie's. What a waste of time that had been. Then he felt the corners of his mouth twitch slightly. It was the thought of his mother ducking and diving down Greek Street in an effort not to be spotted. Rosa, with her height, her wild red hair and general sense of the dramatic was not the best person to travel incognito. Probably the only one who didn't spot her was him, deep in his own preoccupations.

He pulled himself together. What was he doing, condoning his mother's behaviour? He couldn't afford to forgive her yet. He scowled and threw some clean socks into his hold-all.

FORTY-SIX

Prey runs fleet of foot.
Now there is nowhere to hide
Soon hunter will strike.

Danny's gone to stay with Delroy, but before he leaves he tells Anna of my perfidy. So now she's wide-eyed with reproach and behaving as if it's me who's the killer. I can't do much for myself at the moment because of my hands, and it's the most irritating thing in the world to be ministered unto by someone exuding holier-than-thou compassion from every pore – 'It's a dirty job, but someone's got to do it' is the message coming over loud and clear. I'm glad she's at school today because I don't think I can take much more.

I'm trying to make a cup of tea without dropping the kettle when the bell rings. On the doorstep is a woman. Late thirties, perfectly groomed, voice frightfully top-drawer.

'Does Tom Brice live here?'

'Yes, but he's out at the moment.'

'Oh, I don't want to see him. Could you give him this?' She hands me a big brown envelope and I'm swamped by a waft of expensive perfume. Her make-up is immaculate in an understated way, and her coat is definitely not from British Home Stores.

'Who should I say called?'

She smiles. 'He'll know. Thank you so much for your help.'

She glides down the path and slips into a sleek blue Aston Martin driven by an equally sleek specimen of manhood.

It's the ex-wife, Felicity. I know it. I'm tempted to open the envelope, but then I remind myself of two things: firstly that my nosiness has got me into enough trouble with my children already, and secondly that since I don't want a relationship with Tom Brice, what goes on inside his envelopes is of no interest to me. I put it on the hall table and answer the phone which is ringing insistently.

'It's Jess. Welcome home. I feel awful about leaving you in that dreadful ward. How are you? Let me come round after school to help . . .'

There's something else. I know – I can hear it in her voice.

'Guess what?' she says.

'What?'

'Marion's been attacked.'

More violence.

'It happened last night. She'd gone up to the Observatory to get some papers and tidy up. Everyone else had left, but being Ratshit's little arse-licker, she often works unpaid overtime to keep up with his busy schedule. Anyway, apparently, another thing she often does is sit in the dark in his chair looking at London. Says she finds it inspirational. Personally I reckon she's imagining what she'd like him to do to her in that chair. So last night, there she is, fantasising away or whatever, when she hears a noise. She's about to get up when someone grabs her from behind, slips a cord round her neck and starts to fucking throttle her. What they don't know is that one of Marion's little hobbies is Judo, and she throws him off. He scarpers, leaving her floundering on the floor, and by the time she recovers, he's vanished. The police on the gate didn't see him – nobody did.'

'Is she all right?'

'All right? She's fucking loving it. She's holding court in the staffroom as we speak, wearing a very fetching purple silk scarf to hide the bruises. Ratshit's the one who's in a stew. Claims it had to be meant for him, since she was sitting in his chair and looks like a man. He's making noises about closing the school till the maniac's caught, but the Education Authority won't wear that, and the fuzz say it's not necessary. So he's stuck here with the rest of us, living life on the edge. Your policeman and his pals are giving everyone the once-over yet again. At this rate, it'd be simpler if they all moved in permanently. They could set up a Tardis in the middle of the playground.'

Leo has a point. In the dark, an intruder would assume the person in the chair was the usual occupant of the room. But why would anyone want to attack him? An image flashes through my mind: Leo spying through his telescope, knowing the business of the people of Consort Park better than they know it themselves.

In the cab, on my way to hospital to have my dressings changed, I face the fact that I am frightened. One dreadful event seems to follow another like some ghastly

Greek tragedy. What next? This is a question I'd rather not speculate about. I'll think of the weather, clothes, the state of the nation – anything.

At the hospital the nurse discards my soiled bandages and replaces them with new ones. If only it were possible to discard the soiled bits of my brain and replace them with pristine cells, ignorant of what's gone before.

As I'm leaving Outpatients, I bump into Charlene, who's still keeping vigil over Crystal. Her face is swollen from days of weeping. I hardly recognise her. She thanks me profusely for dragging Dwaine out of the burning building. I'm embarrassed by her abject gratitude.

'Come on,' I say. 'Let's have a coffee.'

Opposite the hospital is a French patisserie and I force her to choose the most outrageous cake in the shop, leading by example.

'How's Crystal?'

'Still the same. She just lie there wit' they tubes pokin' outta her body like she not human at all.'

'What do the doctors say?'

'They don't know nothin'. They say she could come out of it tomorrow, or next week, or never.'

'She'll pull through.'

'Maybe . . . But it my Dwaine I'm tinking of right now. I'm so scared, Rosa. What going on wit' that boy?'

I wish I knew, Charlene, I really do, because whatever it is, Danny's involved in it somewhere, too.

'Has he made contact?'

Charlene shakes her head. 'He a good boy. He ain't killin' nobody, not Dwaine. That Max, he a bad person, I know it.'

'How come?'

'I just get this feeling about him, right from when

he first come to the school. I tell Crystal to stay away from him.'

'Stay away from him?'

'I see him hanging around they girls all the time. Man like that ain't up to no good, I just know he ain't.'

'Did you ever see Dwaine with him?'

She is surprised. 'Max not interested in boys. Him want get him hands down girls' knickers. I tell him: "Max, you want I call your wife and tell her how much time you spend with little girls?"'

'What did he say?'

'He tell me mind my own business. I say if he botherin' my little girl it *is* my business.'

'And then what?'

'He say to chill out – he just making friendly conversation wit' them.'

'What do you think he really wanted?'

Charlene sucks her teeth. 'What do any man like that want with young girls?'

'Did you ask Crystal what they talked about?'

'Yes. She say he very boring and she and her mates run away when they see him coming.'

'Was she telling the truth?'

Charlene is about to leap to a spirited defence of her perfect child, and then remembers who she's talking to and shuts her mouth quickly. Then she says: 'I don't know. I don't know nothing no more. I just think Ratchett ought to look more carefully at the references of people he employ in him school. Look what happen wit' them poor babies wit' that Huntley monster.'

'What do you mean?'

'Ratchett give Max he job right at the last minute, and Marion let slip that he references a bit odd – but when she tell Ratchett he say not to bother, he'd deal wit' it.'

All staff who work in schools have to be checked by the CIB. If Max's references were dodgy, then Leo must be breaking the law, taking him on. I think about the assault on Marion. Everybody's taking it for granted that it was meant for Leo. And the person bleating this theory most loudly of all is Leo himself. But what if Marion *was* the intended victim? If Leo's involved with anything fishy, who knows more about his activities than Marion? He's her specialist subject in the *Mastermind* of life. Maybe Tom's wild theory about Leo isn't as far-fetched as it seems.

Charlene's waiting for me to say something. My suspicions are so absurd that I can't bring myself to voice them. Instead I tackle one of my other major worries. I'm probably putting my foot in it again, but I can't stay silent.

'About Dwaine. I'm very fond of him, and I no way believe the police are right that he killed Max, but . . .'

Charlene looks at me. 'But what?'

'I think he's on drugs. And I don't mean cannabis.'

To my surprise, Charlene doesn't flip her lid. She just stares at the table.

'Is he, Charlene?'

'I knew he was acting odd, and after a while I began to tink maybe it was . . . I tried to talk to him, but you know what they're like.'

'Believe me, I do.'

'He said I should mind my own business. But how could I when he out all hours, and looking so strange sometime, and not answering when I speak to him. So one day I search his room . . .'

Mothers of the World Unite! Another sly, conniving, untrustworthy parent. I stop myself from cheering.

'I found some white powder in a bag. I tink it cocaine or heroin. It was hidden under a floorboard. I couldn't ask him – I didn't want him to know I'd been peeking in he room. I thought about confiding in the minister after church, but he'd go straight to the police. I didn't know what to do. Then this fire happened, and now they are saying he killed that man, and he gone vanished. But Dwaine wouldn't hurt no one. He a gentle, gentle boy.'

Unless, of course, he's high as a kite. I don't say this to Charlene. What's the point? Instead I say, 'Do you know Delroy's mum?'

'Yes, why?'

'Because that's where I think he might go. Danny's staying there and I reckon Dwaine will try to contact his mates. Ask her to phone you if he turns up. And tell her not to call the police.'

'Why?'

'Because they'll bang him up, and then we'll never get to the truth. He and Danny are far more likely to talk to us than the fuzz. When we know what's going on, we can decide what to say when Dwaine does eventually turn himself in.'

'So you really don't believe he killed Max?'

'Of course he didn't. Dwaine's not a killer.' I wish I felt as certain as I sound. 'Now phone Delroy's mum. And don't worry.'

At home Tom's in the hall staring at some papers he's pulled out of Felicity's brown envelope. His face is grim.

'Anything wrong?' I say.

He just pushes past me out of the house.

His ex-wife clearly has a fabulous effect on him.

FORTY-SEVEN

Do I smell? Have I developed an infectious disease? I feel like one of the Untouchables. Even the one-eyed cat's sent me to Coventry. Danny's still at Delroy's. He communicates with Anna, but not me. And she's not speaking either. Just casting reproachful glances in my direction every now and again. Normally I'd have a moan to Tom, but ever since his ex-wife played postman he's been impossible. I know he's preoccupied with catching a murderer, but he's treating me like an unwanted stranger. Maybe his marriage isn't as moribund as he'd have me believe. But if so, I wish he'd talk about it. I may not want a relationship with him, but I'd still like him as a friend. Also, if I'm honest, my pride would prefer it to be me who calls the tune, not him.

I'm still at home nursing my wounds, and being alone all day is starting to get me down. The lowest point was yesterday when Boo rang, full of excitement about a last-minute casting. I had to turn it down because of my bandages.

Today I'm really depressed. Rob's with me all the

time. I can't push him out of my head. I berate him for leaving me with recalcitrant children, unemployment and the local killer. I keep thinking that if he were still alive, none of this would have happened. I try to psych myself into selling a painting, or at least asking Larry for an advance. But I can't. I know it's not rational, but Rob's paintings must be wholly mine until I'm ready to give them up. No half-measures.

By evening I'm stir-crazy. I go up to Anna's room and knock on her door.

'Who is it?'

'Who do you think. Can I come in?'

'I'm trying to sleep.'

A shudder of rage travels up from my gut to my brain, and I really want to pummel her out of this morass of non-communication. It occurs to me that never in my life have I had such a frequent urge to hit people.

'Suit yourself!' I shout. 'Do whatever you want. I've had it with you, with all of you. You can all just piss off!'

I storm out into the wet winter night and drive dangerously round to Jess's, trying to ignore the pain from my burns as I grip the steering wheel. I shouldn't be driving, but I don't care. Serve everyone right if I crash and burn. I spend the evening ranting to my friend about my life. Lozz, wide-eyed and solemn, stares as I burble on. After a while he snuggles up next to me, stroking my arm and murmuring, 'Poor Rosy, Lozz make it better. Lozz make it go away. Be OK in the morning.'

Jess doesn't interrupt and she nods in all the right places. After a couple of hours, as I say yet again, 'Am I going mad? Why do I wake up each morning with a pit of dread in my belly?' she rummages in a drawer and pulls something out. It's the Order of Service for Rob's cremation. She hands it to me.

'What do you see?'

I look at the poems and songs that I chose to celebrate my husband's life, and remember the day we said goodbye to him. I experience again the bizarre mixture of unbearable pain and spaced-out unreality that I had felt, standing in the soulless crematorium.

'I see two lives destroyed. Mine and his.'

'Look at the front cover.'

'His name and the date?'

'Exactly. The date.'

'January the twenty-eighth.'

'And what is today's date?'

'January the twentieth.'

'Precisely.'

'So?'

'You know what, Rosa? After January the twenty-eighth you might find things start to improve. I reckon your subconscious is building up to the anniversary of Rob's death and freaking you out.'

I test the idea for size. There's no blinding sense of revelation, but nor do I feel it's an absurd notion.

'It'd be great if you're right. It's rational – something I could cope with.'

A possible explanation for my jitters perks me up. We finish the night sniggering at Jess's account of Leo pacing the corridors of Churchill Towers, waiting for the sinister intruder to strike again and never accompanied by less than at least four Sixth-Form girls, known to the staff as the Praetorian Guard. I don't give Jess my version of Marion's assault – it sounds too far-fetched. I'd rather keep Leo as a figure of fun until proved otherwise.

I'm in a much better mood when I drive home. I want to apologise to Anna for swearing at her. It's not something I'm in the habit of doing, and it makes me feel bad. But her door's shut and her light's off. I don't fancy making myself even more unpopular by waking her, so I go straight to bed.

I lie awake, wondering whether Jess is right. Am I suffering from anniversary-itis? It's hard to access the feelings, but I suppose that's the point. If they were on the surface I'd know what they were, and wouldn't be drowning in dread. I'm drifting off to sleep when there's a knock on my door.

It's Tom.

'Can I come in?'

Do I need this right now? 'OK.'

He sits on the end of my bed. 'Did I wake you?'

'Yes.'

'I'm sorry. I couldn't wait till morning.' He clearly doesn't have my scruples about rousing people from sleep. 'I've been a big pain over the last few days and I wanted to apologise.'

'Apology accepted. Good night.'

'You're still pissed off with me.'

'And why would that be?'

'I've behaved badly.'

'Yes, you have. But I'm used to people behaving badly in my house at the moment. It's par for the course. Only difference is, you're old enough to know better.'

'Ouch.'

'I really am tired, Tom.'

'I had a communication from my ex.'

'I know.'

Tom's surprised. 'How?'

'I was here when she delivered it.'

'Did she say anything?'

'Like what?'

'I don't know. Anything.'

'No. She just asked me to give you the envelope, and then left in a rather expensive sports car driven by a rather expensive man. Why did it put you in such a bad mood?'

'It was the divorce papers. I knew they were in the pipeline, and I want this divorce to happen. Can't wait in fact – but . . .' He trails off.

'Go on.'

'It was still a shock, that's all. I spent a long time with Flick. Seeing our names on this official bit of paper – it just struck me as being very bleak, very sad. I've been feeling very sad, Rosa.'

He strokes my cheek. 'I don't want to talk about her. I'd rather talk about you.'

'Nothing to say.'

'Then maybe we shouldn't bother with words.'

He lies down, his body hard against me. I don't want this. I've made my decision. I can't give up Rob, not yet. But now, in the darkness, after days of being pushed away by those I love, my treacherous body betrays my aching spirit. My resistance melts away and I respond in spite of myself.

Afterwards I feel ashamed. Frailty, thy name is indeed woman. Then I fall asleep, and when I wake Tom's gone.

And so has Anna.

FORTY-EIGHT

Fallow Deer. *Dama dama.* For hundreds of years, hunted for its meat by the aristocracy. More recently, the presence of feral herds has been observed in many unlikely places. It is thought that these animals have escaped from protected environments and established their own breeding herds.

At first I think she's still sulking and gone to school without saying goodbye. But when I look in her room, there's her uniform, and her mobile, and none of her clothes seems to be missing. She must be around somewhere. I call her name. No answer. I phone Tom and ask if he saw her before he left. He says no.

'She's gone to school without her uniform, for some reason,' he suggests. 'Don't they do that sometimes?'

'Yes, but they have to pay fifty pence to the charity fund – she would have asked me for the money.'

'Maybe she forgot.'

'They only do non-uniform day at the end of term.'

'Phone the school.'

He's right. But I dither around for another fifteen

minutes. What sort of a mother doesn't know where her child is at breakfast-time? How can I reveal my sloppy parenting to my work colleagues?

Eventually the worry becomes too intrusive. I phone Churchill and speak to her Head of Year, who goes to check.

'She's not here. Is there a problem?'

'I'm not sure.'

I call Danny, but his mobile's switched off. I don't want to worry him, so I leave a noncommittal message. Then I call Tom again.

'Something's wrong.' By now, the niggling worry has blossomed into full-blown parental hysteria.

'She's probably bunked off school and gone shopping.'

'There's a killer on the loose and you're talking about shopping?'

'Calm down . . .'

'Don't tell me to calm down!'

'Is there any sign of forced entry into the house?'

'No.'

'Then she's gone somewhere of her own accord.'

'Wearing what? Her clothes are all here.'

'Come on, Rosa. I bet you couldn't list every item in your wardrobe, let alone Anna's.'

'No, but—'

'Wasn't she in a mood last night?'

'Yes.'

'It's obvious. She's giving you the finger by going on the razzle for the day.'

He's right. She's very cross with me. This is her way of making a statement. Like Danny and the shed. She'll probably sashay in later, telling me she had to go out at dawn to make certain she wasn't followed by her snooping mother.

Tom's still speaking.

'The police get this all the time – kids flouncing off, giving their parents heart-attacks. They always come back. It's only the ones with major problems who stay away.'

'That's what you said about Crystal and Athy. Look what happened to them.'

'Stop worrying. She'll be fine.'

'When are you back?'

'I'm on double shift today. We've had a sighting of Dwaine Johnson in Kentish Town. I'm going over to check it out this morning. Don't worry – Anna'll be back by lunchtime . . .'

There's a pause. 'Rosa?'

'Yes?'

'Thanks for – you know . . .'

An image of last night flashes through my brain. But Anna gets in the way.

'Rosa?'

'I'm still here.'

'Tell me what you're thinking.'

'I'm thinking that this isn't the time to talk.'

Another pause.

'No, but . . .'

'I just want to know where Anna is. I can't cope with anything else.'

'It's OK. Bad timing. We'll talk later.' Tom's voice resonates with reassurance. 'Anna wants you to worry, and you're surpassing her wildest expectations. She's fine. I'd bet money on it.'

Midday comes and goes. Anna doesn't. I try to remain

optimistic. I call Tom again. His mobile's on voicemail, so I leave a message. I'm about to call Danny but decide against it. I don't want to reinforce his view of me as a controlling mother who has to know where her children are every second of the day. I'm trying to see my earlier hysteria as just that. Hysteria. But it doesn't work. At half past one I call Consort police station. They say they'll send an officer.

It's Penny Black. Ms Cheerful.

'I'll take a quick look round – check she's not hiding under the bed.'

'You are joking.'

'Has been known. I'd also like a recent photo.'

When she's satisfied herself that there's no sign of Anna I ask her what happens next.

'We give it till the shops close. Then if she's still not back, I'll send this paperwork down to Willesden Missing Persons Unit, and pop something on computer for Scotland Yard.'

'Is that it?'

'With respect, if we sent out search-parties for every teenager who'd gone AWOL for a day, we'd have no resources left to catch all the muggers and thieves Joe Public's always complaining about. Keep us informed, and we'll take it step by step.'

Penny Black thinks I'm making a fuss over nothing.

'So if Anna's bumped off by the local killer, I'll let you know, shall I? Save you having to send your paperwork down to Willesden.'

Her face is studiously blank. 'Don't take this the wrong way,' she says, 'but I reckon all this murder business has made you see problems where they don't exist. Anna will be home before you know it. I'll mention it to the other members of the Community Action Team – tell them to keep an eye out for her.'

As I show her out, I realise I'm right about her: she doesn't like me. She never has. She's got me pegged as a neurotic fusspot. She'll go through the motions to find Anna, but I won't hold my breath.

It's now 2.30. Anna's gone shopping. She's spending her Christmas money in the sales. I run manically through her probable itinerary: Covent Garden, Oxford Street and, if time, a quick dash to Kensington High Street, although that's pushing it. I know she wants some boots. I envisage her trying on various pairs, parading in front of the mirror, her long legs the envy of shorter, stubby-limbed shoppers. In my mind's eye, she's now in Shelly's on Oxford Circus. As the afternoon wears on, ignoring my stomach which is doing a fair to middling impersonation of a tumble dryer, I tell myself that she mustn't have had much luck in town, and has undoubtedly peeled off to Kensington. I envy her stamina. I visualise her return, so excited about her purchases that she forgets her quarrel with me, and I anticipate spending a happy evening looking at her goodies. I resolutely ignore my hands which are permanently shaking.

By four o'clock I'm going insane. And something else is pounding away at my consciousness. Something that may be connected with Anna's disappearance.

Churchill Towers.

The school is the epicentre of something murky. I know it. Mick O'Brien might be Tom's chief suspect, but there are other avenues to investigate, and they all lead to Churchill.

Fred Borrage.

Whatever's happening at the school, Borrage is slap bang in the middle of it. And he's linked with Athy and Crystal through Fax Max. What if he's implicated in Athy's death, and thinks Anna knows things she shouldn't?

I decide to confront him. I don't know what I'll say. If he has taken Anna, he'll hardly tell me, but I can no longer sit here doing nothing.

Although it's only late afternoon, it's dark as I make my way to his office near the boiler-room. The students have all gone, and the alleyways round the back of the school are very badly lit. I'm glad. I don't want to be spotted. I'm lurking in the shadows when the boiler-room door opens and light floods out. Two men appear and make their way to Fred's office. One of the men is Fred.

The other is Guy Gropius.

FORTY-NINE

What do I really know about Guy?

I think of the many sessions in my kitchen, when one or other of his females has wept inconsolably over his latest bout of bad behaviour. I've heard more times than I care to remember about his selfishness, his irresponsibility, his lack of proper feeling. And about his boyish charm, that makes them forgive all his peccadilloes and welcome him back with open legs. Until the next time. Ultimately they all leave him, when it finally sinks in that Guy will never change. That with him, surface is all. Scratch that and what you find beneath is his ego, bright and shiny, reflected back at you endlessly.

Has Anna been secretly harbouring feelings for him? A teenage crush? I haven't seen any signs of it, but then I'm the mother who missed the fact that she was being terrorised by mini-monsters. To my knowledge she shares the satirical family view of Guy the Groper: the cultivated carpenter with a voice like liquid honey and touchy, feely hands who is in permanent hot water with his women.

What if he's noticed that Anna has grown, is no longer just the little girl next door? What if he tried out his charms and something went wrong?

He no longer seems such a joke. I think of all the furtive nocturnal activity at his house: people coming and going, Nikos Petros and his white van parked outside at all hours. And now here's Guy fraternising with Borrage, the man I'm convinced knows something about Athy's death.

Another thought hits me, with all the force of the wrecking ball that destroyed the old building and revealed Crystal's unconscious body: Guy Gropius, renowned for his detached attitude to life and other people's business, falling over himself to put Nikos Petros in the frame for his own daughter's murder. How out of character was that?

Before I confront him and Fred, I want to see what's going on in the boiler-room. I sidle across and try the door. It's unlocked. I don't switch on the light in case I'm spotted so my eyes take a while to adjust to the darkness. It's uncomfortably warm, a multitude of smells mingling in the gloom, the subdued roar of the boiler contributing an ominous soundtrack. After a moment I see irregular shapes against the walls. I can't make out what they are, but then I realise they're dustsheets, draped over things. I call Anna's name, but there's no one else here. I lift up one of the sheets. Underneath is a tower of boxes. It's too dark for me to see what's written on the side of them. I need to reach the top one and open it.

I'm feeling for something to stand on when I'm grabbed from behind, and a hand is clamped over my mouth. I try to wriggle free, but my assailant is very strong. He drags me back towards the door.

There's a click, and then the room is flooded with light.

'Bitch.'

I'm looking into the furious eyes of Nikos Petros.

'I thought you were being questioned by the police.' I don't mean to say this. It just shoots from my mouth.

Petros releases me while at the same time kicking the door shut. 'I was right. It *was* you who shopped me.'

'What?'

'You told the police I'd murdered my own daughter!' Petros looks half-demented.

'Why would I d-do that?' I'm stuttering.

'To get your own back for what Athenoula did to your girl.'

'No—'

His thick powerful hands grip my arms so tightly I can feel the circulation being cut off. He brings his sallow, unshaven face close to mine and I smell whisky on his breath. The comical Cockney-Greek accent is now Greek-Cockney and not in the least amusing. I wince as his spittle hits me.

'You think I could harm one hair on her head? I would have died for that girl. She was the only good thing in my life. And now I've lost her . . .'

His face contorts and he starts to cry. He relaxes his grip and I pull away, but his fingers tighten again. He smiles savagely. 'Now I think you, too, have lost your most precious thing.'

I freeze. 'What do you mean?'

'I hear you call your daughter's name. She, too, is gone perhaps?'

I ram my knee into his groin. He bellows and releases me.

'Where is she?'

He's doubled up, gasping, and I'm pummelling his fat back.

'Easy, Rose. Easy.'

I look up. Guy Gropius and Fred Borrage are standing in the doorway.

'Your psycho friend has taken Anna.' As I speak I want to unsay the words. What have I done? They're obviously all in it together. I'm no nearer to finding her, and I've shown my hand.

And there's three of them and one of me.

I scream. Very loudly. And lunge towards the door.

But Borrage seizes me, pressing my head against his chest to muffle my noise. I choke and heave. I can't breathe and I'm nauseated by his smell – stale sweat, tobacco and rancid stew. And the pressure of his gross bulk against my injured hands sends lightning bolts of pain through them.

Guy's talking. 'Fred, put her down. Relax, Rose. Sit down and tell us what's what.'

I'm plonked unceremoniously onto a dirty old chair. Borrage still blocks my exit, Petros remains on the floor nursing his groin, and Guy's crouching beside me. I can't work out what would be the clever thing to say – the thing that would take me to Anna. In the end I just blurt it out.

'I'm looking for Anna. She wasn't in the house when I woke this morning, and no one knows where she is.'

Guy frowns. 'Christ, Rose, you must be shitting yourself.' His concern seems genuine.

'She's the bitch who told the cops I done killed my little girl.' Petros spits out the words.

'I did not!' I wait for Guy to own up. But he doesn't, and his eyes ask me not to drop him in it.

He smiles at Petros. 'Rose wouldn't do that, believe me, Nikos. I'm glad the fuzz saw sense and let you out, mate. Welcome back.' His words are warm, affectionate.

Petros grunts. 'They don't have no choice. When they talk to the twenty people in the club I went to that night after I left your house, Guy, they know I have unshakeable alibi.'

Guy seems truly delighted that his friend's been cleared. 'You poor old sod. Fancy being arrested for murder on top of everything else.' He turns back to me. 'So, Rose, why do you think I'd know where Anna is?'

Have I made a mistake? Guy's no fool. I watch the questions fade from his eyes to be replaced by dawning recognition. He knows what I've been suspecting him of. I can't hold his gaze. I turn away and my eye is caught by the shrouded boxes.

The best defence is attack.

'Can you blame me, with what's been going on round at your place? Men coming and going at all hours, furtive mutterings in corners. Maybe Anna found out something you didn't want her to know.'

I'm babbling. Anything to steer him away from what he might have read in my face – that I suspect him of coming on to my underage daughter.

'I think we'd better tell her our secret, lads. Otherwise God knows what she'll accuse us of next.'

The lads don't look too thrilled. Borrage starts to speak, but Guy interrupts.

'You're right, Rose. We have been doing a bit of ducking and diving. But nothing like you're obviously imagining.'

He pulls off one of the dustsheets. The boxes

underneath contain well-known brands of whisky, gin, vodka and rum, and packs of cigarettes.

'Our little sideline,' he explains. 'Nikos and his mates go to Calais, bring back as much booze and fags as they can, and me and Fred help them store and distribute it. Technically it's for their own personal use, but hey . . .'

A Customs scam. Shady? Yes. Dodgy? Definitely. My business? Definitely not. In fact, I don't want to hear one more thing about it. Particularly in view of my close personal relationship with the Metropolitan Police.

'I get the picture. And I don't want to know. I'm off. See if Anna's home.'

The doorway's still filled by Borrage. His face is set and hard.

'My friend Guy's a very trusting man. You wouldn't do anything to betray that trust, Ms Thorn?'

'Are you threatening me?'

He leers. 'Perish the thought, miss. I'd be grateful, though, if you don't mention our little hidey-hole to the Head. We're only using it as a temporary measure. No need to bother him about it.'

I really don't like this man. He gives me the creeps.

'No need whatsoever, Fred. I never saw a thing.'

Fred steps aside, but then my arm is seized by Petros. I try to protect my burned hands.

'Do you swear on your daughter's life that you didn't tell the police I killed Athenoula?'

I see the pain etched into his face. How must it feel to lose your daughter in such horrific circumstances, and then be accused of her murder?

'Nikos, I am so sorry about Athy, and I know that you'd never do anything to harm her. For what it's worth, during rehearsals for the Christmas show, she was always talking about you. She so wanted to make you proud of her. She said you used to tell her what a brilliant dancer her mother was. She wanted you to feel the same about her. She said so – several times.'

Nikos starts to cry. Guy puts an arm round him.

'Let it all out, mate. Let it out.' He looks at me. 'Will you be all right getting home, Rose, or do you want a lift?'

What I want is to leave this place and the people in it as quickly as possible.

'I'm fine.'

'Anna's probably home already, wondering where you are.'

I hope he's right.

At the school gate I bump into Dave Alessi.

'Any sign of Anna?' he asks.

'No. I'm sure she'll be back soon, though.'

Whistling in the dark, they call it.

It occurs to me that Dave Alessi looks dreadful – as if he hasn't slept for a week. Then I forget him as I run home, hoping against hope that my daughter is back.

FIFTY

The house is cold, dark and deserted. There are no phone messages. It's now six o'clock. I call Danny. No joy. If he received my earlier message, he's not responding. Still punishing me for my transgressions. I continue my fantasy about Anna and retail therapy. The shops won't have closed yet. No need to panic.

I haven't eaten all day, so I force myself to make a sandwich and a hot drink. I stare out into the blackness of the winter garden. Then my heart leaps. Maybe Anna's sitting in her Pet Cemetery. Maybe she's been out there all day, brooding. This is the most foolish of foolish thoughts, but it persists. I'll have to check. I find a torch and set out.

Of course she isn't there.

I'm about to go indoors when I hear the most unearthly noise: a cross between a howl and a moan. It's coming from Singing Vic's shed.

I'm always amazed at the amount of thought the human brain can pack into a split second. How did Dave Alessi know Anna was missing? Where's Marge? What did Athy say to Vic at our party? Where does Anna fit in? Does she know about the IOU? Has she seen something she shouldn't? I remember Rob dying in the road, Singing Vic staunching his wound. The image changes. Vic's hand is over Rob's mouth, suffocating, not succouring him. Is that what I saw, or am I going mad?

Vic's locked Anna in his shed. It's her making that dreadful noise.

I use a garden chair to climb over the fence. I'm prepared to break down the shed door, but there's no need. It's ajar. A figure lies huddled on the floor.

'Anna?'

The figure doesn't respond. I shine my torch down.

Not Anna.

Singing Vic.

'She's dead,' he weeps.

My legs buckle and I'm on the floor alongside him, screaming, 'What have you done to her, you bastard?' I batter him with my fists. He doesn't defend himself.

'Nothing. That's the whole point. I tried to get the money for the treatment, but it was too little, too late. The cancer was too far gone. I failed her.'

He lies there, his face wide open to any more blows I might choose to rain down upon him. But by now, I've stopped.

'You're not talking about Anna?'

'Anna?' He starts to weep again.

'Rosa?'

It's Dave Alessi. 'Help me take him inside.' His eyes are sad.

'What's going on, Dave?'

'Let's get him into the house.'

We help Vic indoors, and make him comfortable on

the sofa. He's silent now. Dave sits beside him, holding his hand.

'Marge had a very rare form of bone cancer. The doctors told Vic there was no hope, but he did some research and found a new treatment in America that's had spectacular results. He's been trying to raise the money. He was almost there. Then after New Year, Marge suddenly deteriorated and had to be admitted to hospital. She died this morning.'

I'm devastated. 'Why didn't you tell me, Vic? Why didn't Marge?'

'Marge was a great one for putting her head in the sand,' Dave says. 'When she first started to feel unwell she told her doctor that she didn't want to hear anything remotely unpleasant. Vic was the one who knew the truth and he kept up the pretence that it was just a bit of arthritis.'

'Vic, I'm so, so sorry.'

'About the poker money, Rosa – I should have been straight with you, but I needed it too badly. I reckoned Rob would have understood.'

'He would. And so would I. And I also wish you'd trusted me about your love-life.'

'I couldn't tell anyone I was gay, in case they gave the game away to Mum. I never had the guts to come out to her – you know what she was like. It didn't matter. I got by – till I met Dave.'

He smiles at Dave, love shining through his grief.

'Dave wanted me to tell her. We rowed about it all the time. Eventually he gave me an ultimatum. Either I told her, or he'd leave me. I said I couldn't – she was too ill. I asked him to wait till after America. If the cure worked, I'd tell her. If it didn't, she'd be dead soon anyway . . .'

'Only I'd heard too many excuses,' Dave takes up the tale. 'I thought he didn't really love me. I told him we were finished. But we couldn't keep it up. One day, in school, we started talking again, and that was it.'

'That was nearly it in another way too,' Vic says, with a bitter edge. 'Athy Petros caught us kissing. She started blackmailing us. Said she'd tell Ratchett – make out we interfered with boys.' He grimaces. 'When that girl died, it felt like a dead weight being lifted off me.'

'Then Marge went into hospital. Vic knew she wouldn't be coming home, so he asked me to move in.'

'For the first time in my life, I felt like an honest man. Even though I was grieving over Mum.' His face crumples. 'How will I manage without her?'

I think of Anna. I don't know how I'd manage without *her*. She's been driven from my mind by the awful news about Marge, but now all my anxiety floods back. I fill in Vic and Dave.

'Have you seen her at all today?' I ask, but Vic's been at the hospital with Marge, and Dave hasn't clapped eyes on her.

'How did you know she was missing, Dave?'

'Her Head of Year – said you sounded a bit concerned.'

Rosa Thorn never thinks of the obvious explanation for things. Maybe she's back now. I have to go home.

'Vic, if there's anything I can do to help with the funeral, let me know.'

'Thanks. And I'm sorry about the money. I will sort it.'

'No, you won't. Gambling money's not real. Forget it.'

Dave gives me a hug. 'Don't worry about Anna. Tom's right. She's getting her own back on you by bunking off school. She'll soon be home, safe and sound.'

FIFTY-ONE

By eight o'clock I know I've been right all along. Why did I let anyone persuade me otherwise, when my gut instinct was screaming the opposite? All those wasted hours. I phone Penny Black.

'Do something, or I'll kick up such a fuss you'll wish you never clapped eyes on me.'

'Calm down, Mrs Thorn. She's now officially missing. I'll stick the information in the system straight away.'

'Stuff the the system. I want you to mount a proper search for my daughter.'

'It doesn't work like that, not at this stage. Don't worry. All the Home Beat officers have been told to look out for her. If she's in the area, someone will spot her.'

'I'm coming down to the station.'

'No. Your job is to stay put, in case she calls.'

Stay put when my little girl is out there with Athy's killer? I know Anna's disappearance is connected with what happened to those girls. And after my fruitless afternoon following up a series of melodramatic suspicions that have come to nothing, I have to face the fact that Mick O'Brien's back in the frame.

I'm desperate to see him lurking in his usual place, behind the trees, but tonight the park is dark and empty. Why didn't I ask Anna where he lives? The police came up with 'no fixed abode' when they tried to find him before – but everybody has some kind of abode, even if it's only a shop doorway. Who would know about Mick O'Brien's?

The Head Park-keeper. He took O'Brien on. There must have been some form-filling, if only for the payroll.

His house is in the park, which is now locked up for the night. And I don't know his surname so I can't look him up in the phone-book. Penny Black says to wait at home, but if I stay here one minute longer, I'll go bonkers. I grab my coat and cross the road. Desperation makes me bold. I'll climb over the railings.

I've never been any good at gymnastics, and however many times I try to heave myself over, I still remain firmly on the pavement side of the park. A well-built jogger is enjoying an evening run around the perimeter. The sweat steams off him, as if he's running in his own magic cloud. As he pants past, I grab his arm.

'Excuse me.'

His eyes register mad cow, bonkers bitch, and his voice adopts the neutral reserve of a Londoner used to dealing with inner-city insanity on a regular basis. He glances downwards to check that I'm not holding a knife.

'Can you give me a leg up into the park?'

He gives me another quick once-over. Am I concealing an iron bar about my person?

'Sure.' He sounds casual, as if he's always dealing with such requests, then makes a stirrup with his hands. There's a moment when I'm convinced I've impaled myself on a spike like poor Athy, but then a little extra shove from my rescuer takes me over.

'Thanks a million,' I shout up.

'Cheers. Take care. It's dark in there,' says my hero and jogs off, a cloud of virtuous nobility now mingling with his sweaty steam.

It *is* dark. There's no light at all, except for one solitary window in the Parkie's house. Away from the streetlamps I can hardly see my feet in front of me. I've stood here on the central green thousands of times, listening to the sounds of day: footballers shouting, tennis rackets hitting balls, children splashing in the paddling pool, the drone of Greg's mower cutting the grass, the occasional clatter of a circling police helicopter.

The noises of an urban park.

Tonight everything's different. This Consort Park, the place I've been avoiding for so many months, the place that's full of fears and forebodings, is suddenly revealed in its true incarnation. I feel like Alice on the other side of the mirror. I've entered into a forbidden world, mysterious and secret. Same trees, same grass, but everything transformed. It's wild here now. Strange. The park is no longer for people. It belongs to savage things. I disturb them as I grope my way towards the light. I can hear their rustlings, their crunchings, their frantic flight as I pass. Occasionally I see the gleam of a feral eye close to the ground. Squirrel? Toad? Mouse? Or something bigger? I'm the intruder here, crashing through the intimate intensity of their night-time existence. And even as they run from me, I sense other things are lurking and watching. Things that do not wish me well. Evil, holding back until it is time to strike.

It only takes me about thirty seconds to reach the

house, but it's long enough. I ring the bell. A woman's voice quavers, 'Who is it?'

'I need a word with the park-keeper about an ex-employee of his.'

'You shouldn't be here. The park's closed after dark, and the police are on patrol 'cos of the murder. I shouldn't let them catch you.'

'This man may have abducted my daughter. I need to know where he lives.'

'My husband ain't here.'

'When will he be back?'

'His dad's had a heart attack. He's gone to see him. I'm not expecting him back for a couple of days.'

I try another tack. 'Do you know Mick O'Brien? One of the gardeners?'

'Mad Mick? Your daughter don't want nothing to do with him. I wouldn't be surprised if he weren't the one who bumped off that poor girl.'

'Exactly. Would your husband have an address?'

'Mick was casual labour. Paid in cash.'

'So you've no idea where he lives?'

'In the gutter, I shouldn't wonder, the address he gave us for emergencies was false. Look, love, I hope you find your daughter, but I gotta go now. If I were you I'd get on to the police.'

So that's that. My brilliant idea hits the dust. I'm stuck for what to do next. I'm also stuck in the park unless I can persuade Mrs Parkie to leave her fortress and let me out.

'Could you unlock the gate for me, please?'

'Sorry, love. My husband don't like me to open the door after dark, 'specially after the murder. You'll have to get out the way you got in.'

I'm trudging back to the railings when I remember something: Mary the Hologram, rabbiting on about her friend who knew O'Brien's mum. Mary lives at the other side of the park, so I change direction, grateful that the bare winter trees enable me to use the houses around the edge as markers. I wonder where all these fabled police patrols are – the ones looking for Anna and the ones searching for O'Brien. I remember Granny's adage, 'If a thing is worth doing well – do it yourself'. It's up to me to find my daughter. I reach the railings near Mary's house and feel around unsuccessfully for something to climb on. Then I hear the sound of heavy panting. Lo and behold, it's my jogger again, still powering round the park. This is turning into a farce – *Carry on Consort*, with me as a skinny Hattie Jacques.

'Hello again,' I call. 'Could you help me *out* of the park this time?'

Pushing someone over railings is much easier than pulling them back, and my saviour is in a very bad mood, his Superman credentials in tatters by the time he finally hauls me over. My fear for Anna saves me from feeling embarrassed, however. No sooner am I on my feet than I'm running to Mary's house – leaving him doubled up, gasping and massaging his arms.

Mary's in and, as always, game for a gawp. Her bright little eyes widen with pleasurable shock as she hears my tale. She's adamant that a personal introduction to Mrs Hogan will best serve my purposes. No way will she pass up this opportunity to witness neighbourhood drama first-hand. This is pure gold for Mary. So we make for Dyne Road.

Mrs Hogan's very deaf. It takes me a while to get across what I want from her.

'Where did Mick go after his mother died?' I bellow.

'Sure 'twas to his sister Biddy, but then she threw him out on account of the violence.'

'Violence?'

'He was always a mammy's boy even though he led her a dance, and when she died he couldn't be doing with it at all and it turned his brain. He had nightmares something terrible, and sleepwalking, and one night he tried to strangle Biddy in his sleep. After that she told him he had to go.'

'Did she ever say where to?'

'She did not. She's always been ashamed of turning him away, y'see. She felt her mammy would blame her for kicking him out, but I said to her, "Biddy, it's you or him. Your mammy would understand".'

'Where does Biddy live?'

'Didn't she up and off to Dublin at Christmas, and I hear she isn't coming back.'

'Mrs Hogan, I'm desperate to find Mick. Have you any idea at all where he might be?'

'I wish I could help you, darlin', but I haven't a clue.'

I'm overwhelmed by failure. Then Mrs Hogan delivers a parting thought.

'Wherever he is, he'll have chosen somewhere safe for his rabbits.'

Excuse me? Did she say rabbits?

'Rabbits?'

'Oh yes. At least thirty of them. 'Twas another reason why Biddy kicked him out. He wouldn't keep them in hutches, you see. He let them roam all over the house and garden. The smell in poor Biddy's front parlour was something terrible, and the landlord was threatening to evict her after the neighbours complained they were digging through the fence and eating all the plants.'

Mick O'Brien won't be sleeping in a doorway if he has thirty rabbits to contend with. Mary and I are at the gate when the old lady calls out.

'Now I think about it, he did say something strange to me the last time I saw him.'

'Yes?'

'He was walking up the road moaning and muttering, and when he saw me he came right up and stared into my face. I was frightened, so I said the first thing that came into my head. I said, "How's your rabbits, Mick?"'

'And?'

'He laughed and said, "They're where no one can harm them, Mrs H. They're where the Saints go marching in".'

'Was that it?'

'Yes, darlin'. He carried on up the road chuckling to himself, and I said a prayer of thanks to the Good Lord that he'd left me alone.'

'What did he mean?'

Mrs Hogan gave me what my grandmother would have called an old-fashioned look.

'I think, my dear, he was telling me his rabbits were in heaven. I wouldn't like to speculate on how they got there, but I did notice the butcher in Alexander Street was selling stewing rabbit later that week.'

I walk Mary back to her house.

'Don't you worry, Rosa. Anna's a good girl. She'll be back in a brace of shakes, you'll see. Be sure to let me know if there's anything else I can do.' She's dying to phone her vast network of friends to tell them about

Anna's disappearance, and her part in the search. I say good night and walk home.

My house is still empty: a horrible emptiness that feels permanent. I sift through Mrs Hogan's words. Where do people go if they're chucked out of their home? Hostels? Not with thirty rabbits. And he couldn't keep them on the streets. The only certainty I have is that Mrs Hogan's wrong about him killing them. I don't know why I'm so clear about this, considering he's my chief suspect in the Pet Cemetery incident, but I'm somehow convinced that Mick O'Brien wouldn't butcher his own pets.

I phone Danny's mobile again, but it's still off so I leave yet another message. I call Tom. He's on voice-mail, too. I phone the police station and ask for Penny Black, but she's unavailable. I switch on the news to check that another girl's body hasn't been found in Consort Park. Nothing. Just news about disasters in far-flung places, flood warnings for parts of the South-East as a major storm heads our way, and an item on post-Christmas debt, broadcast from a shopping centre where people are being interviewed about their spending plans for the New Year. I watch, envious of them. There they are, pottering round the shops with nothing more pressing to worry about than whether to buy a discounted fish fryer, or whether to spare a few coppers for the visiting Salvation Army band, valiantly trumpeting God's word to Mammon.

The Salvation Army! An insistent thought batters its way into my overwrought brain. Who might be soft enough to take in a madman and his rabbits?

The Sally Army.

And they have a base in the Consort Park area. I

know because they used to stick polythene sacks for discarded clothing through our letterbox. Where is it? Who would know?

Mary the Hologram. Who else? I don't have her phone number, so I run round to her house. It's starting to rain: big drops spattering onto my face. I try not to take them personally.

Mary answers the door, phone glued to one ear. '... terrible troubles ... I'll ring you back, Maeve. Rosa!'

I ask her where the local Salvation Army operates from.

'Sure they did have the ould church in Disraeli Street – Saint Peter and Saint Paul. It used to be Catholic till the Salvos took it over – but they're long gone from there. That place is standing derelict now. A disgrace. The last Labour Council did it up – put on a new roof and all – and let the Salvos have it for a peppercorn rent. Then, when the Tories got back, they pulled the plug.'

'Where did the Salvos go?'

'Nowhere round here, that's for sure.'

Another brilliant lead scuppered. As I plod home, the sound of the Sally Army band echoes round my head. 'Oh when the Saints go marching in ...'

I stand stock still as an idea hits me.

Mick O'Brien told Mrs Hogan his rabbits were where the Saints go marching in. The derelict church is called St Peter and St Paul. The Salvos have gone. Maybe it's not them, but their abandoned building that shelters him.

The more I think of it, the more certain I am. It's probably quite dry inside if the Council re-roofed it. It's perfect. But where exactly is Disraeli Street? I run home and look it up on the A-Z. It's not far: tucked away behind the wholesale warehouse off the High Street. I leave another couple of messages for Danny and Tom on their respective voicemails, grab a torch and rush out. I dither about taking the car, but can't face it; my bandaged hands hurt too much. Besides, the time it takes me to park makes it quicker to go on foot.

I reach Disraeli Street in record time and, gulping for breath, stare up through the rain at the Church of St Peter and St Paul.

FIFTY-TWO

Black Rat. *Rattus rattus.* The invasion of the brown rat (*Rattus norvegicus*) in the seventeenth century has decimated the population of *Rattus rattus.* However, although nearly extinct, it can still occasionally be found in derelict, enclosed buildings.

The derelict building looms, enormous and lifeless, water pouring from its leaky gutters. St Peter and St Paul would have been the largest church in the area, built in the mid-Victorian period, when the outer villages of London were being subsumed into a massive conurbation, and the new citizens demanded their various houses of prayer. The Irish population in Consort Park was considerable, and a large Catholic church was needed to cater for them. The architecture's not the usual Victorian Gothic, but more reminiscent of a Methodist Hall. Something thrown up in a hurry to cope with a large influx of the faithful.

All the lower windows are barricaded with iron shutters. I climb a short flight of steps into a filthy porch, where pigeon excrement mingles with broken syringes, old rags, broken bottles, used condoms and the gnawed remains of a Christmas turkey carcass. The door's covered by a sheet of steel. No way in here. I examine the rest of the building. The church is surrounded by an area of scrubby grass which, like the porch, is rubbish-strewn and filthy. I squelch round the building, looking for an access point. No luck. I'm back at the underside of the porch, having done a complete circuit. What to do? It doesn't seem possible that anyone's inside. There's no sound or movement, other than the relentless beating of the rain against the shutters, and apparently no way in. Another bum idea. I'm becoming seriously soaked, and I'm freezing. The rain trickles down the back of my neck and even the bandages round my hands are damp. I lean back against the pillar which supports the porch.

And carry on going.

A sheet of corrugated iron, which I thought was nailed to the pillar, has given way and I find myself in a stinking space under the ground. Shining my torch onto the iron, I see the nails have been cleverly sawn through, so that from the outside it appears they are still attaching the sheet to the wall, whereas in reality it's a sliding door into the entrails of the building. I make out a tiny window, unshuttered and without glass. Just big enough to squeeze through, into the church.

The things I do for love, I think, as I drop to the floor inside the building.

I'm in a narrow corridor which leads to darkness at one end, and a flight of stairs at the other. By torchlight, I can see three doorways. I peer into the first one. It's stacked from floor to ceiling with altar candles, large and beeswax yellow. Several furry black things scurry across the floor into a hole in the wall.

Rats.

In the next room I strike gold: someone lives here. A filthy sleeping bag and a blanket are piled in one corner and various plastic bags heaped in another. The floor is sticky and slimy and as I cross the room, I slip. I drop the torch and am plunged into darkness. Then I look up and see stars: the glow-in-the-dark kind. Someone's covered the ceiling with them. I find my torch and switch it on. The walls are covered with photographs.

Of Anna.

Anna walking up the road. Anna in the park. Anna talking to Singing Vic. Anna laughing and tussling with Danny. Anna at our front gate arguing with me. There are close-ups, distance shots and all variations in between.

My first instincts about O'Brien were right. He has an insane obsession with my daughter. I stare at Anna, her life laid bare, every movement monitored, every shade and gradation of mood captured. He's invaded each small corner of her existence. It feels like the worst kind of violation. And it doesn't stop at our front door. Although the photos are all exterior shots, I now know for sure that it was him who broke into our house, and who destroyed the Pet Cemetery.

His interest is not benign. The man who committed such a violent act does not wish Anna well.

For the first time, the dreadful anxiety that's been plaguing me all day is not counterbalanced by the sensible part of my brain which has babbled of reasonable explanations, and anticipated the joy of seeing my little girl walk sulkily through our front door carrying bags full of Oxford Street booty.

This is not the wild imaginings of Rosa Thorn, drama queen. This is reality.

Anna has been abducted.

I am weak with terror.

I search the bags on the floor. One contains a couple of woolly jumpers, some ancient grey T-shirts and a pair of torn Levis. The second is full of mouldy vegetables: blackened carrots, withered cabbage and some rotten, stinking potatoes. The third is the most interesting: inside it is a cheap camera, a driving licence in the name of Michael Charles O'Brien, the much-fingered Death Certificate of one Nora O'Brien, a couple of uncashed Giros, and a tatty old book entitled *The Nature Lover's Friend* by James Jackson. There is one more thing. On the floor, by the door, is a leather-bound notebook.

I open it and see pages of cramped spidery handwriting. It's too difficult to read anything as tiny as this by torchlight, but there are wide margins and gaps down the pages. Poetry, perhaps – although I didn't think Mick O'Brien could string two words together, let alone master the art of versifying. There's only one word I can make out, and it occurs with sickening regularity on its own at the top of each page: Anna.

I have to find my daughter.

The urge is primal. Physical. Adrenalin floods my system as I rush from the room.

The third door leads to a warren of interconnecting small rooms, all completely bare except for little puddles of water oozing up from ornate cast-iron drain covers. The final room opens out into a kind of crypt – an architect's folly: medieval mystery grafted onto the stark simplicity of the main structure.

Most of the evidence for its ecclesiastical past has gone, but there are still tombstones set into the floor, and piled at one end, a garish Madonna with a broken nose and a kitsch Christ with a missing arm, a smashed leg and a great gash across His chest. I'm reminded of Athy's Crown of Thorns. Are the Madonna and her Son Mick O'Brien's morbid inspiration?

What now? I've searched all the cellars and the crypt. Where next? Then, hidden behind a pillar, I spot a large cupboard. I wrench open the door. Empty. I don't know where else to look. Then my eye is caught by one of the tombstones. It's the last resting-place of one Tobias McBride, Mayor of the Borough of Willesden and beloved husband of Ellen, 1801–1888, and it isn't properly in place. One edge is lifted up and rests on the floor. I can see a dark space in the tiny gap created by the misalignment.

Please God don't let Anna be in here.

It's colossally heavy and my hands burn as I grasp it. I can't budge it. I need some kind of lever. My eye falls on Jesus in the corner. One of His arms is missing, and an iron strut protrudes from the wrist. I'm sure He wouldn't mind donating the other arm to a good cause. I haul Him upright and smash the arm against the wall. But this Jesus is one tough cookie, and the holy arm stays firmly attached to the divine shoulder. Finally after the fourth attempt it drops off. I grab it before it hits the floor and smashes. Then I return to the hole and lift the stone up sufficiently to slip the arm under to jam it open. My hands are in agony, but I can't afford to dwell on that. Hoping that it's strong enough to take the weight, I press on Christ's bicep and lever the stone up several inches. I then put my shoulder beneath it and push with all my strength until the stone lid falls away from the grave.

The cavity is several feet deep. I can't see Tobias's coffin because it is covered with oblong, wrapped parcels. I pick one out and open it.

The parcel contains photographs of young girls, many pre-pubescent, some blossoming into early womanhood. They are all dressed in variations of school uniform, but the things they are doing bear no relation to scholarship. My mouth fills with bile. The photos are set in a classroom, complete with desks and blackboard. No concession here to the fact that schools use whiteboards nowadays – perverts obviously prefer an old-fashioned schoolroom. I assume this is a studio mock-up until, flicking through, I notice one print that has a window in the background. Through the window there's a playing-field with goal-posts, and some houses in the distance.

It's a Churchill Towers playing-field.

I must be mistaken. I trawl through the other shots and find several with the same background. These photographs have been taken somewhere in school – I try to work out where, but can't recall that particular view.

Then suddenly, I know: it's the derelict building, before it was torn down. I remember the night I heard strange noises coming from there. My ears weren't playing tricks after all. And who tried to convince me that I was imagining things? Fred Borrage. Who I subsequently saw talking to Fax Max, near the same building.

And what was Max holding? A camera. Which he tried to hide.

Fax Max again! The nasty little man turns up all over

the place, including dead in my shed. His grubby fingers have clearly been dabbling in a great many unpalatable pies.

And what is Mick O'Brien's involvement? Was he Max's gofer? Is this why he was stalking Anna – to persuade her to take part in this disgusting scheme? Not a love-struck suitor after all, more a big-game hunter?

I throw down the photos in disgust. Then I catch my breath. I'm looking at a shot I haven't previously noticed. A familiar face stares seductively back up at me.

Athy Petros.

Shaking, I examine the rest of the photos. Athy appears in several, and the ones of her are the most crude. Athy's doing things that would make her father weep for ever. And she's smiling as she performs.

I sit down, stunned, the rhythmic beating of my heart echoing in my ears. Then I realise it's not my heart which is making the noise. I've been here before: the grandfather clock at home. But this is no pendulum. It's something else. A faint, dull thump.

Am I imagining it? No. It's definitely there.

I scramble up, scattering the grotesque mementoes of Athy Petros, and pace the room, trying to place the sound. It seems to be located inside the empty cupboard. I open the door again, just to make sure.

Empty.

But the sound's louder in here. Or behind it.

The noise is coming from behind the cupboard. I try to pull it out, but it's mahogany – huge and heavy. I can't get a proper grip on it. I'll have to find help. I feel in my pocket for my mobile. Shit! I've left it at home.

'Anna!' I scream. 'Where are you?'

And I swear I hear something – very faint and weak, but almost certainly a voice. If it *is* a voice, then it could be Anna. And she might not be alone. O'Brien could be in there too.

Hurting her.

I have to stop him.

I try again to shift the cupboard, but my bandaged fingers keep slipping. Weeping with frustration, I kick it as hard as I can. Then I see a narrow gap between the side of the cupboard and the wall. If I could squeeze in there, I could use the wall as leverage. The space into which I must insert my body is less than six inches wide. Impossible. But desperation powers me and I force myself into the minute space. I can't breathe. I'm crushed between wall and cupboard. I don't care. With a monumental heave I push the wall with my hands and feet, while thrusting my bottom against the cupboard. Nothing happens. Then I hear again that faint, desperate cry. Superhuman power shoots through me. I make one supreme, final effort and suddenly the huge cupboard creaks, groans and slides along the wall.

I only move it a couple of feet, but it's enough.

Behind it is a doorway. I squeeze through the tiny space, still half-blocked by the cupboard, and once in there, I recoil. I'm sharing the darkness with a smell of vomit, urine and shit. And I've left my torch in the crypt.

'Anna?'

Maybe it isn't her. Maybe those little whimpering, scrabbling sounds belong to something else. Maybe O'Brien's killed my daughter and is waiting to entice me into his trap. In spite of the coldness of the crypt, I'm sweating, but I can't go back. If there's the faintest chance Anna's here I must find her. I need the torch, so I crawl back to the crypt and search the floor until I touch the cold metal.

The bulb flickers and dims. The battery's fading. I switch it off and feel my way back into the foulsmelling chamber, and around the wall towards the sounds. The pain from my burns has intensified and my hand trembles so violently that when I try to switch the torch on again, it slips and rolls away from me. As I grope for it, I touch something soft and mushy. I scream. Whatever is in the room with me screams too. Something bumps against me. The movement sets the torch rolling again, and as I hear its tinny sound I lunge towards it, hands outstretched. To my infinite relief, it's there, under my fingers. I switch it on, aiming towards the sound.

FIFTY-THREE

Underground princess,
Andromeda pinioned,
Waiting for the end.

It's Anna.

After all the hours of dealing with her dreadful and inexplicable absence, the sight of her is almost more than I can bear, and I'm sobbing and hugging her, feeling her familiar body against mine, kissing her, and murmuring inarticulate phrases of comfort.

My baby's alive.

Everything's all right again.

Then I calm down, and realise it's far from all right.

She lolls against the wall, wearing only her nightdress. It's filthy and torn, and her legs are blue with cold. Like her lips. At some point she's vomited, and bits of it are clogged in her hair. Her cheek is bruised and split. Her arms are outstretched. Each wrist is manacled to the wall.

She's barely conscious and stares without recognition, even when I turn the torch on myself so that she can see me. She mutters and bangs her fettered wrists rhythmically against the wall – the noise I mistook for my heartbeat.

I touch her face. She whimpers and shrinks away from me. She's very cold. Her breathing's shallow, and when I take her pulse its irregular fluttering reminds me of a dying sparrow I once found in the garden. She's been here less than twenty-four hours, but how long does it take for a half-dressed girl, with very little excess flesh on her bones, to succumb to hypothermia?

My joy gives way to panic. I must get her out of here, before she dies.

Before she dies? She's only fourteen. She can't be dying. I feel like one of those people describing near-death experiences, when they step out of their bodies and look down at themselves from the ceiling. It's happening to someone else, not me and Anna.

I train the torch on her manacles. They're shiny and new, and a crisp little keyhole stares up enticingly.

But I don't have the key.

I try to wrench the chains from the wall, but the mortar holding them in place is also new. And rock-solid. I feel the flesh on my injured hands splitting under the bandages. The chains stay firmly in place. If I had something heavy, maybe I could break them. I crawl into the main room again and look round. Once again Christ comes to my rescue. The metal rods holding Him together make Him the heaviest thing around. With difficulty I haul Him through the narrow gap. When Anna sees Him she screams and begins to babble. I think she's confusing Our Lord with O'Brien.

'I'm going to smash this down on your chains. It won't hurt, I promise. Don't look.'

Anna's addled brain somehow gets the message. She

closes her eyes. I pick up Jesus and hurl Him against the chains. He breaks into a thousand plaster pieces, and the fine dust almost chokes us.

The chains are still intact.

The torchlight flickers. I must conserve the batteries, so I switch it off. Anna and I are left in total blackness. We both start to cry. I try to do it silently, so as not to frighten her even more.

'Sweetheart, I have to get help. I'm going to leave you for a little while, and when I come back, I'll take you home.'

Suddenly Anna's voice, clear and strong, shouts, 'Don't go, Mummy!'

Now I'm sobbing out loud. I can't leave her. I hold her close, trying to warm her frozen body with mine, trying to infuse her spirit with my own lifeforce. I tell her repeatedly that it's going to be OK.

Eventually, she falls into a delirious sleep, and I'm free to go.

But what about O'Brien? I know, without a shadow of doubt, that he's coming back for her. I have to stay and protect her.

I can't go. But I must. If I don't, even if O'Brien doesn't come, she'll die of cold.

And not just that. For something else is in the room with us: water. Without me noticing, it's oozed up from the drain in the corner, and covers the floor to the depth of a centimetre. It's still rising.

I cover Anna with my coat. I kiss her and then I leave her and grope my way back towards the basement entrance. It probably only takes half a minute, but to me it seems like millennia before I see something glowing: Mick O'Brien's stars lighting the dark.

I've made it.

I'm not religious, but a childhood prayer keeps repeating in my head: *Lighten our darkness we beseech Thee, O Lord . . . Lighten our darkness we beseech Thee, O Lord.* I plunge forward and stub my toe. The pain's intense but I don't care, because I know that I've reached the stairs leading up to the main body of the church. That means the door to the outside world is on my right.

Then I hear a noise.

Upstairs in the church.

It's him. He's coming for her.

My heart starts its big bass drumbeat again. I have to stop him.

I start to climb. I'm on my hands and knees for safety – there's no bannister. The stairs are slimy with damp and my hands burn under their filthy dressings as I lever myself upwards. Then cold air hits my face. I must be near the top. I stand. My foot slips and I lose my balance. I grab at the wall. The pain from my hands is excruciating! I'm falling rapidly. If I go over the unguarded edge, I'll break my neck. I twist my body away from the drop. My foot catches underneath me and pain shoots up my leg.

Anna knew it was right that she was punished. He'd said so, and she agreed. She was a bad girl, no question. She tried to remember why she was bad, but it was difficult because of the pain. Pain in her arms and wrists, pain in her face where he'd hit her, pain in her head. And she was so cold. As cold as a corpse. Maybe she was dying. She didn't mind. Not really. Because if there was life after death, then she'd see Daddy and be able to say sorry. Suddenly she was drenched by grief: she remembered why she was so wicked . . .

In the park . . . She and Danny arguing – fighting over the Frisbee. Seeing Daddy . . . Her calling to him for help.

He'd always hated them squabbling. Mum said it was because he was an only child. He couldn't cope – couldn't see it didn't really mean anything.

He ran to stop the fight . . . straight under that car.

No one said it was Anna's fault, but she knew it was. And so did Mum. That's why she was always on Anna's case. Anna the walking disaster area.

No wonder Crystal and Athy were so mean. They saw right through her to the rotten core. He did, too. He always had. That's why she didn't really mind being in this dreadful place. It felt good to be punished at last.

Through the swirling mist in her brain, she thought that Mum came. Her face was contorted, twisted. Anna couldn't make out what she was saying, but she was obviously upset. Who wouldn't be – losing your husband because of the pointless stupidity of a fourteen-year-old girl?

Then it was dark again.

The only thing she couldn't cope with was the scuffling and squeaking in the corners of the room. She adored animals, but even she couldn't bring herself to love rats.

FIFTY-FOUR

Rabbit. *Oryctolagus cuniculus.* The rabbit is a home-loving creature which rarely strays far. The cropped grass around the burrow, combined with the rabbit's sharp olfactory, auditory and visual senses, make it difficult for predators to strike.

I think my ankle's broken.

Well, tough, Rosa. Anna's relying on you. She'll die if you don't save her. He must have heard my fall. So what's he doing? I crawl upwards and the pain's so intense I feel giddy. I despair. It's all over. I've failed to save my baby. Rob, wherever you are, if she comes to you, look after her. I couldn't. I'm sorry.

It's so easy to lose track of time. I've no idea whether it's two, five, ten or twenty minutes since I fell down the stairs. Then I hear the noise again. In the church.

Mick O'Brien.

I won't let him have my daughter.

By crawling on the side of my burned hands and one knee, letting the painful ankle drag behind me, I can climb without fainting. I bless the fact that the stairs are stone and don't creak. At the top is a doorway. Even in the blackness I can feel the change from small space to large. The damp, clinging air of the basement gives way to eddying currents of cold which swirl from different angles as draughts whistle around the vast empty space. The rain beats down on the shuttered windows, and I'm startled by a crack of thunder.

Then there's the smell. Acrid, yet sweet at one moment and in the next so vile that I heave. It's the smell of rotting food, like when we came back once from holiday to discover the freezer door open; the stench like that in a butcher's shop at the end of a hot day.

High on the end wall, unshuttered, is a rose window designed so that light would shine down on the raised altar. Since the church is deconsecrated, there's no longer an altar. But, caught in a beam of moonlight, is the dais on which it once stood.

On the dais is a pyre.

It's made from chairs, once used by the faithful, but now smashed and heaped up to form a mountain of wood.

There's something on the pyre. I look away. I know I'll have to see it sooner or later, just as I did with Athy. But not yet.

As I crawl down the hall towards the dais, I notice that the room is full of unlit candles – hundreds of them, all different sizes. I think I see a floor-painting around the base of the pyre – concentric circles like a mandala. The constituent parts of the circles are perfectly executed crosses, a mixture of browns and blacks and greys and whites and reds, with the shorter ends facing the middle.

Then I realise the circles are not painted images at

all. What I am looking at used to be living and breathing. They are Mick O'Brien's pet rabbits, their fur stained crimson with the bright blood which must have spurted out when he slit their throats. They've all been meticulously arranged. They lie on their backs, sightless eyes glazed over, front paws pinned out sideways to form the transverse arms of thirty little crosses, back paws fastened together with wire to keep them straight and true.

The stench makes my head spin.

He must have taken ages, perfecting his installation. I imagine him, beautiful grey eyes ranging round his handiwork, finally coming to rest, captivated by the thing on top of the pyre: his *pièce de resistance*.

I wonder which poor girl he's mutilated this time. Is this what he's planning for Anna? I take in the splintered wood. One large piece has fallen, and lies across two of the rabbits . . . Was *that* the the noise I heard? The wood is wet. He must have brought it in from outside.

Finally, I look at what's on top of the pyre. The room swims in front of me. There's a roaring in my ears and my body's consumed with heat. I'm going to faint. I put my head between my knees until the feeling passes.

The creature spreadeagled on this mountain of wood is not one of Mick O'Brien's victims.

It's Mick O'Brien himself.

FIFTY-FIVE

The circles of life
Surround the mountain of death
Enveloping all.

His malnourished naked body glows pale in the moonlight. Arms outstretched, his eyes stare sightlessly. I think of the phosphorescent stars in his basement hidey-hole, and imagine him lying shivering in the dank cellar, looking at his manmade firmament and dreaming.

What were those dreams? Did Anna have a starring role? How did she figure in his final scenario? What did he plan for her before he massacred his beloved rabbits, climbed onto his carefully constructed chair-mountain and slashed his own throat?

O'Brien's dead and no longer a threat. I can fetch help. I limp back down the stairs, and am almost at the outer door when I hear a cry.

It's Anna. Her voice is high and shrill. The pain in my ankle vanishes as I fumble and stumble back to the little chamber. My daughter sounds coherent. No longer delirious. And she's no longer in darkness.

Or alone.

By the light of a candle I see a figure looming over her. I launch myself onto his back, hitting him, clutching lumps of hair, trying to pull him away from her. I'm bellowing so much that it takes me a while to register the voice repeating my name.

'Rosa! It's me.'

The sense of relief is so profound that I collapse onto the flooded floor. My shaking hands, bandages bloody from the punishment I've just given them, drop, lifeless, to my sides.

It's Tom. His dear, reassuring face in the glow of the candle is like all the good things of the world rolled into one.

'It's OK, Anna. It's Tom.'

Then I'm trying to tell him everything at once. 'O'Brien's dead – he won't hurt her any more. I can't break those chains . . . We need to call the Fire Brigade.'

Tom's massaging her hands, frowning with concern. 'She's very cold,' he says. 'It's time to get her out of here, poor baby.'

His tenderness makes me cry. I'm no longer dealing with this nightmare on my own.

Then I see that he's clutching something. A bunch of keys.

He takes one of Anna's manacles, inserts a tiny key into the keyhole and removes the wrist from its iron prison. Then he frees the other. An icy chill sweeps over me.

'Tom?'

He crosses to me, taking my face in his hands. 'Be quiet.' His tone is reasonable, but his hands grip my cheeks like a vice. 'You're the most infuriatingly gobby woman I've ever met.'

He's teasing. I hear it in his voice – the gentle, bantering tone I know so well.

'Skip the humour,' I tell him. 'Anna could have died. It's no joke.'

Tom laughs, his hands still cupping my face. 'It's a joke all right.' The laughter doesn't reach his eyes.

Everything has a reasonable explanation. Everything can still be all right if I concentrate hard enough on thinking it so.

'Tom, we need to take Anna out of here. Let's go.'

His face is unutterably sad. 'It all got out of hand, Rosa.'

'What do you mean?'

'I've been so happy over the past few months, living with you and Danny and Anna.' His eyes are wistful. 'We've had some good times, haven't we?'

'You're scaring me. Stop it.'

'I wish I could. But you have to finish what you start.' His face darkens. 'If the Bradley girl hadn't been so greedy, I'd never . . . But on the other hand, in a way I owe her. If I hadn't wangled myself onto the team investigating her death, I wouldn't have come to Churchill and met Anna.'

Then Anna groans and I'm forgotten.

'Hush now, little one. Don't cry. Tears make your face all puffy, and we don't want that.'

He strokes her hair. I watch, numb with disbelief. He turns to me, his eyes bright with remembrance. His face is as it has always been, and yet it is completely different. For a moment, horror threatens to overwhelm me. I struggle to regain control.

He's still talking but it doesn't sound like him any more.

'I first saw her in the Science corridor at Churchill – nervous as a wild pony, tossing her hair around, trying to run away from me as fast as she could. There she was. Perfection. My golden Madonna. Not like all the other little scrubbers. I knew then, that everything I'd done in my whole life had been leading me up to that moment.'

There's a catch in his voice.

My inexplicable fears over the past months were justified: Anna *was* being stalked by a maniac. I was right all along. Except for one thing.

Wrong stalker.

'Why do you think I wanted to move into your house? I had to be with her. To eat and sleep under the same roof. Breathe the same air. Protect her . . .' His eyes gleam with compassion. 'I'm sorry I used you.'

Shame, fear and loathing creep over me like a dark stain. 'I let you into our lives to protect us from O'Brien.'

The mention of O'Brien's name is a mistake. Tom's face darkens. He turns to Anna.

'Why did you ruin things?' Then he shakes her, hard.

I try to stop him but he shrugs me off, and I fall into the murky water lapping across the floor. Anna whimpers.

'Why did you sneak off here with O'Brien last night? You've made everything ugly, letting that filthy gypsy touch you. You're all spoiled.'

He shakes her again. But her body is floppy and unresponsive. He holds her close.

'I could still forgive you. Tell me nothing happened with O'Brien?'

Anna is beyond speech.

I must placate him. 'If you love her, let her go. She needs medical help. See how cold she is.'

'Shut it.' He turns back to Anna. 'I want to know about you and O'Brien.'

Anna stares at him. Her yellow eyes gleam and I'm reminded of the feral night creatures in Consort Park. She says nothing, but I see contempt in her eyes. It means she hasn't given up. Tom sees it too.

'All this is your fault,' he hisses at her. 'And you won't even answer a simple question . . .'

Anna claps her hands over her eyes. But he prises the fingers away. Her cheeks are smeared with dirt. He gets out a handkerchief and wipes them.

'You can't hide any more. Everything's out in the open now. Everything's ready.'

Ready for what?

'Tom, please . . .'

He ignores me and finishes cleaning her face. Then he takes something from a bag in the corner of the room. The bag's wet but the water hasn't penetrated the contents. He unfolds a beautiful pale-blue robe which he holds up against Anna.

'Perfect,' he says, and smiles with a radiance that chills me.

'What do you mean?'

'Things have to be played out to their conclusion.'

I know what he's intending to do.

'She hasn't done what you think,' I say urgently. 'I'd swear to it. Anna's still a little girl. She's an innocent – not like Athy. Don't destroy her life before she's lived it.'

His answer is to strike me with such force that my head hits the stone wall. When I surface I'm in darkness and alone. My memory returns in a violent rush. I feel paralysed. Partly by despair, and partly by the icy water that laps around me. My head hurts. I might as well give up and die. Tom Brice made his intentions very clear.

Tom Brice.

My lover is a killer. A psychopath. And I brought him to our house, let him make love to me. And I enjoyed it. *What does that make me?*

Then I hear something. I can't make out what it is, but it jolts me out of my self-pity. Maybe Anna isn't dead. Maybe she's still somewhere in the building, waiting for me to rescue her.

I grope my way through the crypt and back to the corridor where I came in. Every movement is agonising.

The noises come from the church.

I haul myself up the stairs, retching at the top as, once again, I'm engulfed by the smell of spilled blood.

The church is bathed in soft candlelight and the air's filled with high-pitched squeaks. The moon shines in on Mick O'Brien, and around his head circle tiny black creatures. Bats.

He's no longer alone on Death Mountain. Alongside him, in a pale-blue robe, hair framing her face, is Anna.

My baby's dead.

But then I see movement. She's trying to wriggle free from the bonds which bind her to the pyre.

A figure flits to and fro, chatting as he lights yet more candles.

'You look amazing, Anna. Much more beautiful than the little Greek bitch. I thought she'd look stunning on those railings, but if I'm honest, she looked a bit cheap. In fact, that whole thing just didn't work for me. It was a mistake. Perhaps if I'd had more time . . .'

I must have made a sound because he turns round and gives me his boyish grin. The one I'd always found so beguiling.

'Doesn't she look fantastic?' he says. 'Like that Christmas angel her dad carved for her.' Then his smile fades. 'The symmetry's wrong.' He looks me up and down. 'Maybe, since you're here . . . if I cleaned you up . . .' He trails off, his face wrinkling in distaste. 'I suppose you'd be better than nothing . . .'

Tom's revolted by me. Everything's turned on its head.

I make a lunge back towards the stairs and freedom, but I'm slowed down by my ankle, and he's caught me before I've covered any ground at all.

'Just give up, Rosa. Go with the flow.' He sounds so reasonable. So normal.

He drags me over to a heavy, old-fashioned radiator, and chains me up with one of the manacles he used on Anna. Then he disappears downstairs. When I can't hear his footsteps any more, I call out to Anna.

She groans. Her eyes are closed and she's very pale.

'Anna! Wake up!'

She stirs and mutters.

'Anna!'

Her eyes open and scour the candlelit space in front of her.

'*Anna!*'

'Mum?' She's coherent.

'If he unchains me, I'm going to try and escape. If

I do, I want you to shout as loudly as you can. Someone in the street might hear.'

Anna sobs. 'He'll kill you.'

I hear him coming back up the stairs.

'Be strong,' I whisper. 'I love you.'

FIFTY-SIX

He's kneeling in front of me, sponging my face. It's a grotesque parody of the care and concern he's shown me during the past few weeks. He runs a comb through my hair.

'Your hair's like flames in a bonfire.' His eyes are full of regret. Maybe some remnant of goodness deep inside is struggling to surface. I cling to the thought.

'Was it all lies, Tom? Was everything between us a complete fabrication?'

'Whatever it was, it's irrelevant now.'

'Look me in the eye and say we didn't have something. Don't let me die feeling so degraded and humiliated.'

He stops combing my hair. 'What you need to do is shut up, and accept that I'm a very, very bad man. I'm way beyond the pale.'

'Nobody's beyond the pale. Not even you. I trust my instinct, and it's telling me that you felt something for me. All the talking we did, the way you always listened to my problems, the teasing, those two nights we had together – I don't believe it was all a pretence.'

His face is tight, angry. 'It has to be black and white, Rosa. Evil is evil. There are no half-measures.'

'People do evil things. It doesn't mean they *are* evil. Not completely.'

'Skip the psychobabble. What if I did care – so what? What if I told you things I'd never told anyone else – so what? What if it made me happy for the first time in my life being in your house, being with a family – not just Anna – you and Danny too? What does it bloody matter? It doesn't change a damn thing. I still used you. I still lied to you. I'm still going to kill you. It's all the same in the end.'

There are tears running down his cheeks.

For a moment I have an overwhelming urge to comfort him. It goes as quickly as it comes, but I capitalise on the feeling.

'What is it that's hurt you so much?'

I've blown it. His face changes, and I brace myself. But then, to my astonishment, his body goes limp. He makes a sound – a cross between a sigh and a sob – and curls up beside me on the stone floor. He's shaking.

'Shh . . . it's all right. It's OK.' With my one free arm, I make myself hold him. Like a mother.

After a minute, he puts his arms around me, and we lie there for a long time. I stroke his back and listen to his anguish. It's the hardest thing I've ever done – to comfort him while watching my daughter grow weaker and weaker as she hangs, helpless, next to the dead body of his last victim.

Eventually he pulls something from his pocket.

It's a snapshot of a small child in a summer garden. The child stares out, unsmiling. She's exquisite, with blonde curls and a perfect oval face. She wears a pale-pink silk dress, all ruffles, petticoats and puff-sleeves. The big blue eyes look familiar.

'I didn't know you had a sister.'

'She died when she was five.'

'I'm sorry.'

He tries to move away from me but I won't let him.

'Tell me.'

'What do you care?'

'I'm not like you. For me it's not all black and white. Maybe I do still care.'

'And maybe you're just playing for time.'

'Maybe. Does it matter?'

He smiles. It's still a great smile.

'No, I don't suppose it does. I'm the Piper – I call the tune, right?'

'Right.'

'We were playing in the barn. I pushed her . . . accidentally. She lost her balance – fell off the hayloft. Smashed her skull on the concrete floor . . . My mother never recovered.'

I look at Anna. She's listening too.

'She blamed you, didn't she?' I say.

Tom is silent.

'How old were you?'

'Four.'

'And you blamed yourself.'

He's trembling.

'It was an accident. You were just a baby.'

'Shut up! Look again.' He shoves the photo under my nose. I stare at the solemn little girl.

Suddenly it clicks. 'It's not your sister.'

Tom rams it back into his pocket.

'*It's you*, isn't it? It's you, Tom.'

'Ten out of ten.'

His face is a study of contradictory emotions – shame, fear, triumph, excitement – I find it impossible to read. But he wants to open up, and that's good. The more I get inside his head, the more chance I might find a way of saving us.

'Tell me about it,' I say again.

'Why?'

'I care.'

'Oh yeah?'

My mind races. I have to say the right thing.

'You can't turn love on and off like a tap. When my kids do bad things, I don't stop loving them. It makes me sad or angry or ashamed. But I still love them.'

'They're your kids. It's different.'

'Same principle. Once I love someone, that's it. No going back. It took a lot to let you into my life. It felt such a betrayal of Rob. But in spite of myself, it happened, and I'm stuck with it. I loathe what you've done, and I'm terrified of what you're going to do. But, unfortunately for me, I still have feelings for you.'

I see the uncertainty in his face.

'It could be a sort of confession. Like with a priest. After all, I won't be spilling any beans.'

'Won't you?'

'You're not planning to let me leave, are you?'

He shrugs.

'Why not tell me everything? You know you want to.'

So he does. And I try to stay calm while he talks of his unspeakable childhood.

His sister Lucy was the perfect child: beautiful, bright, and best beloved. When she died, Eunice Brice went mad with grief. She insisted on an open coffin for the child and kept it in the house for a whole week before the funeral. Each night of her vigil, after her husband had gone to bed, she woke four-year-old Tom and made him lie down beside his sister until dawn.

'She couldn't bear Lucy to be alone,' Tom tells me. 'I didn't understand why my sister was so cold. I couldn't sleep. I remember counting the embroidered flowers on her shroud.'

After the funeral, Eunice got religion – the High Church version of Christianity with incense and idols. She went to church every day, dragging Tom with her. For hours on end, she would pray to Christ and the Virgin to save the souls of her dead daughter and her erring son. At home, after her husband had left for work, she would make Tom, wearing nothing but a crown of thorns she had made from the flowers in her rose garden, prostrate himself in front of a crucifix of Jesus, while she beat his back till it bled, telling him it was a punishment for killing Lucy.

Little Tom fully concurred with his mother that he deserved the beatings. He had killed his sister – whatever that meant. He missed her dreadfully and would wander round the huge house and grounds looking for her, hoping that one day she'd reappear with one of her brilliant ideas for a game. His father explained the concept of death, but Tom didn't get it. He came to believe that Lucy was hiding in her room, which Eunice had locked up and refused to allow anyone to enter. One day he stole the key and crept in there. Still no Lucy. He searched everywhere – under the bed, behind the curtains, in the wardrobe. He buried his face in her clothes and tried to imagine she was in them. He pulled out one of her party dresses and held it against himself. He realised that if he blurred his eyes when looking in the mirror, he could almost believe he was Lucy.

Then his mother appeared.

'I was terrified. I thought she'd give me another beating. I remember the sensation of silk against my skin and a feeling of humiliation. I'd pissed in my pants.'

But she didn't beat him. She said, 'Put it on.'

Even at four years old, Tom was quite sure that he didn't want to wear a girl's dress. So he refused. But then something happened that hadn't often happened before.

Eunice gave him a big cuddle.

She told him that he was a good boy who wanted to make Mummy happy, and that Mummy would be very happy indeed if he just slipped into the dress. She took off all his clothes and popped the dress over his head. She hunted through the drawers, found a tiny pair of pink knickers and some white ankle socks with a little frill, and helped Tom to put them on, finishing off the ensemble with Lucy's pink ballet pumps. Finally she rushed off to her room and came back with some electric curling tongs. With a few tweaks she was able to turn Tom's shaggy thatch into Lucy's soft ringlets. When they were finished, it wasn't only Tom who was transformed. Eunice was radiant. She had her daughter back again. She led him into the garden and took a photograph.

After that, Tom became Lucy nearly every day.

I hear a noise. It's Anna, crucified by Tom Brice, but still weeping for him.

'Poor little boy,' she is saying.

Tom glances over at her.

'I loved it,' he says. 'My mother was nice to me when I was Lucy. I liked being her more than being me. Sometimes I'd sneak off when she wasn't watching and play my special Lucy game.'

He smiles.

'I called it Funeral Parlour. The woods near the house had their fair share of dead things – birds, squirrels and stuff. I'd collect them up, make little coffins out of cardboard, and bury them in the barn. Then I'd be Lucy, and sing hymns and cry over their graves. I devised some very complex ceremonies and rituals, and as time went by I enjoyed them more and more. Now and again I'd dig up the corpses, to see what had happened to them. I wasn't too keen on the putrescent stage, but when they were down to white bone, I liked that. It seemed to me very spare and pure. Sometimes I varied things by staging cremations. They were the best. I always felt – I don't know – purged, I suppose, after one of my fire festivals. I'd watch the flames lick at my cardboard coffins till all that was left was ash and bits of bone. Fantastic! If I couldn't find anything dead in the woods, I'd kill my own stuff. It was a great pity when it all had to stop. A great pity.'

His expression changes. It's brooding, hostile. Keep him calm, Rosa.

'What happened?'

'My bastard father ruined everything.'

Tom's father was a right-wing bigot with very defined ideas of how the world should be. When he walked into the barn one day with his gun and dog after a fun day massacring pheasant, and found his seven-year-old son in a frilly dress chanting Latin Mass over the maggot-infested corpse of a fieldmouse, he was not best pleased.

'I remember his face. It was purple and pop-eyed. His teeth were all yellow and his breath stank of shit. He was calling me names. Things I didn't understand – pervert, bum boy, shirt-lifter, brown nose. He knocked me down, and I knew he was going to smash the gun over my face . . .'

Tom's fists are clenching and unclenching.

'I grabbed at the gun. I remember feeling this incredible surge of strength. I saw the surprise in Father's eyes. He felt it too. It caught him offguard for a second and I was able to swivel the barrel towards him. The thing went off. In his face. Then the dog turned on me, so I shot her as well.'

In his voice I hear the frightened little boy. He looks at me with a mixture of shame and defiance, daring me to condemn.

'You were a child. It was self-defence.'

The eyes change again. The boy's gone. In his place I see a killer.

'I wanted him dead. I was glad.'

There is heat generated from the candles arranged around the church, but I'm shivering, and my mouth's dry.

'What about your mother?'

Tom laughs. 'She watched me do it. I saw her silhouetted in the doorway.'

I think of my one meeting with her. Small-minded, spiteful, provincial Eunice Brice. Maker of monsters.

'She was great. She took me back to the house and bathed me. We gathered together all Lucy's clothes and put them in a bag. Then she phoned the police and told them Daddy had shot himself. That night, when everyone had gone, we took Lucy's clothes and burned them on a huge bonfire. I'll never forget, clutching my mother's hand, feeling the heat and watching all the different reds and oranges melding together. Afterwards she said that Lucy was truly dead now, and that we would never mention her again.'

He runs his hand through my hair.

'There were no open coffins for my father. We cremated him. When the coffin slid behind the curtains, my mother bent down. I thought she was going to kiss me. Instead she whispered that Daddy would burn in hell. Later, outside, she pointed to the crematorium chimney and said it was the ventilation hole for hell . . . We've never spoken of him since. Or of Lucy. You and Anna are the only people in the whole world who know the truth.'

The look he gives me now is of such deep compassion that I know the game is over.

'But it doesn't matter, because as you so rightly pointed out, neither of you will be telling anyone.'

My attempts to soften him up have been a complete waste of time. He's going to do what he was always going to do.

FIFTY-SEVEN

Bat. *Pipistrellus Pipistrellus.* Britain's smallest bat, pipistrellus live in groups of up to two hundred, often in abandoned buildings. Their flight is a series of arcs and swoops as they hunt their insect prey.

He's brought a hold-all back with him, and from it he produces the dress he gave me for my birthday.

He unzips my jeans and tries to ease them down over my hips. I make no effort to help. I feel perversely pleased to be making life a little more difficult for him. But eventually he succeeds and turns his attention to my sweater. He has a problem here. In order to remove the sweater he has to free my arm.

This may be my chance.

But he's thought of this too, and while pulling the sweater over my head he covers me with his body, so that I'm unable to move at all. His hand is on my breast.

'Don't even think about it, Rosa,' he whispers. 'I'm one step ahead of you all the way.'

I feel something hard against my stomach. He has an erection.

I was right. He's not completely indifferent to me. I make myself cry – not difficult under the circumstances. I weep sorrowfully, soulfully, staring into his eyes, trawling for his soul. I trace the contours of his face, and I watch the struggle as man chases monster across his features.

'I can't bear the thought of what you had to go through . . .' I murmur, and see a flash of confusion on his face. 'I'm so mixed up, Tom. I still want you. So much. I want to take away all the pain, and love you till you're better. And yet I hate you . . . I just can't bear this muddle in my head. And I'm so ashamed to be saying all this in front of Anna. She doesn't deserve it.'

I look at Anna, but her head hangs down, her eyes are shut. Good. I don't want her to know what's about to happen next.

'I never felt like this before. Not even with Rob.'

He's caught. Almost. What else can I say that will disarm him completely? I have an idea, but it's high risk. It might rebound in my face.

'I do understand about Anna.'

'What do you mean?'

'Your feelings for her.'

His body stiffens. I've blown it. I should have known he'd never believe this particular fairy-tale.

'You're her mother, for God's sake. How could you?'

'I know.' I whimper. 'I must be as bad as you, but it's because I love you both that I know what it is about her that gets to you.'

'Oh yes?' His voice is hard, but I detect curiosity.

'Anna has a kind of purity. She's not like other kids of her age. It's as if whatever shit's flung at her, her innocence shines through. It's a kind of perfection. I understand you wanting that, especially now I know of all the innocent things that were taken away from you.'

'Psycho-twaddle again, Mrs Thorn.' He's still listening.

'But that's the problem. It's paradoxical. She *is* still a child. How can she possibly understand how you feel? You've frightened her.'

'I never wanted that.'

'I could talk to her and explain. She'd listen to me. I could make sure she did anything you want . . .'

As I say this, I gently thrust my pelvis into his belly. The erection's still there. His face softens, and for a moment I glimpse the old Tom.

'Do you really think she'd listen?'

'I know she would.'

I pull his head down and give him a deep kiss. I think of Anna and how much I want her to live. All I have to do is strike when he's at his most vulnerable. And I know, as any woman does, when that is.

The point of orgasm.

All I have to do is wait. But this is where things go wrong, and it's entirely my own fault.

As he thrusts into me, the revulsion I've been trying to contain gushes out and in one involuntary movement I throw him off. The strength of my loathing is so great that he falls backwards away from me. In a second I'm up and heading for the stairs. I ignore the raging pain in my ankle. This is my last chance.

I'm at the exit when he catches me. He rams me up against the wall, banging my head continually against it as he speaks.

'You conniving witch. You're like all the rest. Dirty

devious whores. Did you honestly think I'd believe a word you say? Don't insult my intelligence.'

With each blow I feel myself slipping away. Finally there's nothingness.

When I regain consciousness, it's like coming back from the dead. The first thing I'm aware of is that I can't move. I want to sink back into oblivion. My head hurts, but there's also a fuzzy warm feeling in there like a million bees buzzing in a hive. So peaceful . . . I've been here before, in this Land of Nowhere. This time I'll stay.

Then I hear a voice calling me. I ignore it, but it won't go away. It's becoming louder. It's the same voice I heard in the hospital after the fire. A very frightened voice.

Anna.

I open my eyes. I feel dizzy and black things fly about in front of me.

Bats. Their wings graze my face. I try to brush them away, but I can't move my arms. The smell of blood jolts me back to full consciousness.

I am high above the ground. Bound to the wood pyre in the Church of St Peter and St Paul. I'm wearing the emerald dress and my hair is loose. I turn my head. Next to me is Mick O'Brien's corpse. Beyond him is Anna. Her face is moon-pale and her voice weak, but she's alive, and coherent.

'Oh, Mum, thank God, thank God! I thought you were dead.' She bursts into tears. 'You haven't moved for ages.'

'Where's he gone?'

'I don't know.'

I look down. I'm tied so tightly that it's difficult to breathe.

'Let's shout. Someone outside might hear us.'

So we shout, and I curse the old church, because the sound doesn't penetrate its thick walls and shuttered windows. And even if it did, who in a big city takes notice of strange noises in the night?

Eventually we give up. Anna whimpers, 'We're going to die.'

'Don't say that.'

'Mum . . .'

'Yes?'

'Will you forgive me?'

'For what?'

She's crying. I twist my head sideways so I can see her properly, but her face frightens me.

'Just tell me.'

'You know.'

'No, I don't.'

'I killed Dad.'

Of all the things she could have said, this is the least expected. 'No, you didn't. He walked under a car.'

'Exactly. He saw me and Danny fighting over the Frisbee. I called to him and he ran out to stop us. If I hadn't he'd still be alive. I know that's what you think, and you're right. It's all my fault.'

'Anna, there's no way I think you're responsible for your father's death. That honour belongs entirely to the brain-dead car thief.'

'But if Dad hadn't heard me shout . . .'

'He was wearing his mp3 player – so he couldn't have heard you. You know how vague he was. He probably didn't even know you and Danny were in the park. He'd be thinking about his work, listening to music and imagining, like he always did, that the traffic would stop for him. When you were little, whenever he took you out without me, I was convinced he'd march you straight under a bus without noticing.'

Anna's face is pitiful. 'So you really don't think it was my fault?'

'No way. Have you been blaming yourself all this time?'

She exhales loudly, as if a baleful spirit is leaving her body. 'That's why I cut my arms,' she said. 'As a punishment.'

We think we know our children, but we know nothing. Anna has carried this guilt around for months, and I didn't have the first clue. Now her eyes fix on Mick O'Brien's dead face, so close to hers.

'Mick tried to warn me . . . He knew Tom was bad. He'd seen him in the park at night, doing horrible things to animals. And the night Susan Bradley died, Mick saw him bending over her, holding a knife.'

'So it wasn't suicide.'

'Mick didn't actually see him kill her, but he still had a bad feeling. Tom was the investigating officer, so it was easy for him to mislead everyone. When Mick found out that Tom was in charge, he left Consort Park because he thought Tom might have spotted him that night. Then he heard a rumour about a bent policeman running a porn racket, using under-age schoolgirls from Churchill Towers. He knew I was at Churchill, and he came back to protect me.'

'Why?'

'He said I was his best friend – the first person since his mum died who treated him like a normal human being.'

'But you hardly knew him.'

'I know. Poor Mick. Isn't it sad?'

She starts to cry again, but eventually she finishes her story.

'He saw Tom dump the cat on our doorstep. He was going to take it away so it wouldn't upset me, but then you came, so he ran off. He also saw him put the magpies in the porch.'

'Why would Tom do those things?'

'He told me – in the cellar. He needed to find a way of getting closer to me. He wanted to make you feel unsafe, so you'd have him as a lodger. You can imagine how Mick felt when he found that Tom had moved in.'

'Why didn't he tell us all this?'

'He was ill. Manic-depressive. It made him funny, particularly if he forgot to take his pills. Sometimes he felt so strange he didn't know what was real and what wasn't. Also, you hated him. He thought you wouldn't believe anything he said. After the Pet Cemetery thing I wasn't talking to him either, and he was frightened that we might tell Tom and put ourselves in even more danger.'

She's sobbing now. We both try to loosen our bonds, but we're tied securely. I can still move my hands though, and my fingers close around a small sharp piece of wood. If I could get Tom to climb up to me, maybe I could use it as a dagger, and disable him enough to grab his mobile from his pocket. I tell Anna, and she twists her wrists, trying to find something similar. I think about O'Brien. If he'd spoken up, Athy might be alive, and we wouldn't be here.

'Mick should have said something.'

'You wouldn't listen to him.'

'I might have.'

'Yeah, right. Anyway, he decided he had to break into our house to guard me. He found the unlocked bathroom window, and came in and out at nights.'

'Why did he wreck your Pet Cemetery?'

'You're not listening, Mum. That was Tom. When Mick was climbing out of the bathroom window that night, he heard noises near the railway line. He thought it might be the Consort deer, so he crept up the garden and hid behind the shed. But it wasn't deer. It was Tom. Mick said he'd never seen anything so weird.'

'If Mick O'Brien thought it was weird, then it must have been.'

It's hard to get my head around Mick O'Brien as saviour, not stalker. Then I see his broken body beside me and feel ashamed. He died trying to save my daughter.

'It was a full moon, so Mick could see Tom really clearly. He was ripping up all the graves. He'd smash each headstone, then dig for bones, and when he found them, he'd . . .'

'What?'

'He'd cradle them and kiss them, then throw them on the ground and trample over them. And Mick said that all the time he was doing it, he was singing some old Beatles song.'

I hear Anna saying these things, but they're just words. Too incredible to believe.

'Mick was guarding the house when Tom drove up with Athy's body and tied it to the railings. After he'd gone, Mick went to check if she was still alive. When he saw what Tom had done, he knew it was time to tell me everything and force me to believe him.'

'What took him so long?'

'I told you. You did.'

'*Me?*'

'You were so certain he was dangerous that you'd convinced me too. I did as you told me, and refused to talk to him or go anywhere near him. He tried to make contact by putting that cloak on the snow lady, with the note, but you took them away and didn't tell me about them.'

'Why didn't he tell the police?'

'Tom *is* the police. And Mick's never trusted them anyway. They wouldn't have believed him, particularly since Tom had planted the idea of Mick as chief suspect.'

I pictured Tom Brice and Mick O'Brien: the public-school policeman and the eccentric, wayward dropout. In a 'Spot the Psychopath' competition there'd be no contest.

'When did he tell you all this?'

'Last night. I woke up with his hand over my mouth. He'd broken in again, I don't know how. He said he had to tell me something, and that he couldn't do it in my house – that I had to come with him. I was scared stiff. I said no way, but then he stuck what I thought was a gun in my back and told me to do as he said. He brought me to the church. He's been squatting here for ages. It's a good place for his rabbits . . .'

Anna can't continue. Both of us are thinking of the slaughtered rabbits laid out with such chilling precision below us, and the dead young man trussed up between us on the pyre.

'He didn't hurt you?'

'No. He took me to his little room. The walls were covered with photos of me, which freaked me out. But he was very gentle and polite, so after a bit I calmed down. He was desperate for me to believe him. He said he didn't really have a gun and I was free to go, but first he wanted me to listen. Then he told me about Tom. I thought he was completely off his trolley. I was staring up at his stars, and planning my escape, when there was a noise and then Tom was in the room . . .' Anna breaks off.

'It's all right, darling, it's all right.'

'It's not all right. He cut Mick's throat – just like that. He grabbed him from behind, I saw a flash of something, and then Mick was on the floor and blood was spurting out, and there was nothing I could do.'

When she was little, I could always kiss things better. But now I can't think of one word to comfort her.

'I didn't do anything to stop him,' she sobs.

'It wasn't your fault.'

'I wouldn't go so far as to say that, Rosa. If the little shit hadn't wanted to get his grubby paws on her, he'd be alive right now. You shouldn't have gone with him, Anna. It most certainly *is* your fault he's dead.'

He winced at his own delivery. He sounded like the villain in the Christmas panto. He half-expected Rosa to shout, 'Oh no it isn't!' to which he'd have to counter with, 'Oh yes it is!'

In fact, the whole episode was taking on the ludicrous aspect of Gothic melodrama, what with the church and the candles and the bats. And the folk, dead and dying, on the pyre.

He was embarrassed by his own antics, but what could he do? Then he pulled himself together. This was how he'd planned things. This was what he wanted.

The Drama was all.

It wasn't the real Tom who felt uncomfortable with things – it was the construct he'd erected to bamboozle the world: Mr Normal, Mr Perfect Plod, Mr Getting-to-know-and-love-you-Mrs-Thorn. It was the construct who was responsible for these little leakages of conscience. He must be careful: let the genie of normality – dangerous, seductive normality – out of the bottle and who knows what could happen.

Still – gazing up at Anna's beautiful face, he wished it could have been different.

The killings were not something he'd planned. Not at first. They were something forced upon him.

Susan Bradley shouldn't have threatened him. He couldn't risk his job, or his little sidelines by leaving her alive to tell tales.

It had been ridiculously easy. Like killing the squirrels and mice in his childhood games. Easy and better: the knife slid much more smoothly into furless flesh. And once he'd experienced the rush that came with taking a human life, that was it. He was hooked.

But if he'd met Anna first . . . What? Her innocence would have rubbed off on him? Stilled those urges from the distant past? Prevented him from crossing the divide?

He didn't think so.

Sooner or later it was bound to happen. His whole life had been leading up to it. He remembered his distaste as he left Bradley's twisted body on the path, her throat still oozing blood. He hated to see her so lumpishly dead. It diminished the act; made it crude. He kind of knew then that there'd be another. Something more beautifully composed, where self-protection didn't drive him away, leaving things all messy and ugly.

And lo it came to pass!

Even then, if the Greek girl hadn't pushed it, he probably would have left her alone. She brought it on herself. But he had to admit he was glad. It gave him the chance to arrange things properly this time.

As for O'Brien, well, he had it coming. His slavering slobbering obsession with Anna had become ridiculous.

Ridiculously like his own.

Watching the agonised adoration in the man's eyes as he followed her up the road one day had been like staring at his own reflection. He knew then that O'Brien had to die. No one can look at their own pathetic weaknesses reflected endlessly back at them.

He looked at the pyre, relishing the pale nakedness of the central figure, flanked by the two women in their dazzling green and blue robes. It was so fortunate O'Brien was male. It fitted perfectly with the scenario he'd been carrying around in his head for so long.

As did Rosa.

She had to go. And not just because she knew stuff. She made him feel confused. His dalliance with her had been trouble in ways that he'd never envisaged. It showed him the life he could have had: full of intimacy, love and laughter. He'd thought that sleeping with her, in order to insinuate himself even more firmly into Anna's life, would be sickeningly unacceptable. But to his shame and horror, he'd enjoyed it, even though this betrayal of his darling meant he could hardly look her in the face afterwards.

So he had no problem with the disposal of Rosa. Good riddance.

But Anna . . . Anna would be a first. The first time he'd killed something he loved.

Almost the first time.

It made him ache – a sorrowful, all-consuming ache that threatened to engulf him, were it not for the equally strong pulse of unbearable excitement at the thought of what was to come.

He could see the loathing in her eyes. He'd blown it, big-time. And, he realised, he didn't care. Not any more. With the realisation came a bolt of pure energy that shot through his body, leaving him clear-headed, ready.

What mattered now was not the man he might have been, or the love he might have had. What mattered now was the ritual. The ritual was bigger than everything. The ritual would make things right.

Like it always had.

A small voice at the back of his skull told him to stop. He ignored it. Time to ditch the construct. Reality beckoned.

FIFTY-EIGHT

He stands below us, gazing up at his handiwork.

'What a sight,' he says. 'The Blessed Trinity. I know it's time to finish things, but you look so fantastic. Even you, Rosa.'

He takes something from his pocket – a leather-bound notebook. It's the one I saw in Mick O'Brien's room. It's not O'Brien's, after all.

He scribbles something with feverish intensity then begins to read. His voice echoes round the vast empty space.

'Time for the last things,
Oblivion for all thought,
On the hill of death.

'Very tricky, haiku – getting the syllables to match the sentiment,' he mutters to himself.

He's chatting about poetic form? My fingers still clutch the jagged piece of wood. If I could persuade him to show me the book . . .

'I didn't know you were a poet, Tom. What did you say it was?'

'Haiku. Must have a particular pattern of syllables. Five, seven, five.'

'You're very clever to be able to do that.'

'There's a whole book of them here. A chronicle of my life.' He smiles.

'Can I see it?'

He takes a couple of steps forward. Then he stops and laughs.

'Nice try. But I'm ahead of you all the way, Rosa. And I'm afraid, folks, that we've come to the end now.'

As he rummages in his pocket again I become aware that beneath the smell of dead flesh is another smell. I remember noticing that the wood was wet and wondering why the chairs had been left out in the rain.

It isn't rainwater. It's petrol.

He's going to have a bonfire.

Tom grins up at me and waves something in the air.

'Matches.'

'Let Anna go,' I plead. 'She won't tell anyone, will you, Anna?'

'Sorry, no can do.'

'I thought you loved her.'

'She's spoiled now that slime-ball's had his hands on her. But it doesn't matter. Fire purifies. She'll soon be perfect again.'

'The police will be here soon. They're searching for her. This is an obvious place to look.'

'No one's searching. I told Consort nick she'd turned up. Now shut it.'

From a dark corner of the hall he produces a can of petrol.

'Better safe than sorry,' he says, sprinkling it around the base of the pyre, over the rabbits. 'Nothing worse than a fire that doesn't catch. Your shed was a treat to torch. Went up in no time. Why you had to save that idiot, Johnson, I can't imagine. Never mind. At least I did for Max the Moron. Not one of my brighter associates. A bloody liability, if you really want to know. Always wanting more than his share.'

What's he raving about now?

'Just because he took the photos. Would you believe the little bastard tried to blackmail me? Shameful, I call it. I hope he died a painful death.' He grins again, disappears into the shadows and returns with a CD-player.

'Full volume, I think,' he says.

The music is 'Lucy in the Sky with Diamonds' by The Beatles. I've heard this song in many different circumstances throughout my life. No portentous shivers ran down my spine on any of those occasions. There was never the slightest inkling that it was to be the accompaniment to my death.

'This was played at Lucy's funeral. Since Anna meant so much to me, I'm prepared to share it with you both now. Your last song.'

I look across at my beautiful girl.

'I love you,' I tell her, with all of my heart.

Anna looks back steadily, the light from the candles reflected in her eyes.

'I love you too.'

Then Tom strikes the first match. A streak of flame licks around the pyre.

'Tom, please!'

Anna's screaming. And coughing. Tom is throwing lit matches one after another onto the pyre. Thick smoke is already rising. I hope it makes us unconscious before the flames reach us. I struggle to work free of the rope which binds me. Desperation makes me strong. I feel a tiny slackening, but there's no time. I'm coughing now and light-headed, and I can feel the heat on the soles of my bare feet. They say when you die, your life flashes before your eyes. Not in my case. I'm aware of only two things: an overwhelming wish to live, and an equally overwhelming urge to stop my daughter from feeling pain. Her face is contorted. I try to reach her, but I can't. *I'm sorry, Anna. I should have saved you from this.* Tom's singing along with The Beatles. His voice reverberates around the hall, triumphant, unrepentant. I don't want it to be the last thing Anna hears.

Then – just as I give up hope – comes an unforgettable, indescribable noise. Through the smoke, flames and flickering candles, I see three figures charging across the hall, roaring and bellowing. Two of them hurl themselves onto Tom, while the third's running into the flames towards me and Anna.

It's Danny. He's scrambling up the wood mountain, oblivious of the smoke and fire engulfing him.

In an instant he cuts Anna free. She flops into his arms, and nearly sends him crashing to the floor. He looks at me, trying to work out how to rescue two of us at the same time.

'Get down!' I shout, and for once in his life he does as I tell him.

The flames are unbearably hot now, and charring my skirt. Danny tries to climb back to me, but the heat's too intense. His face is a picture of despair. I'm not going to make it. I peer out towards the struggling mass on the floor and recognise Tom's attackers: Dwaine and

Delroy. Tom's lashing out – raging and ranting – but they have him under control. At least I'll die knowing he's been stopped. Danny is still trying to reach me.

'Go back,' I croak.

But he keeps on coming. He cuts me free, pulls me down, through the flames, and then I'm lying on the floor coughing my guts out. With each raw cough comes a huge sense of relief.

We're alive.

Then the nightmare returns.

Tom Brice has escaped his attackers and is heading straight for me. I've no courage left. I cover my head and cower. I'm shaking.

But it's not me he's interested in.

He begins to climb the pyre, clutching at the burning wood with his bare hands. The mountain of chairs is an inferno now. We're all seized by a weird paralysis as we watch him struggle upwards. Unbelievably he makes it, and straddling the summit, one foot resting obscenely on Mick O'Brien's head, he grins as the heat fries his face. He's still singing, even though the song has now ended.

Delroy breaks the spell and dashes forward. Dwaine grabs him.

'Leave it.'

I can't look any more. I crawl over to Anna, and put my arms around her. Danny joins us. The three of us stay huddled together until, eventually, the singing stops.

'Someone call 999,' I say.

'We already did,' says Danny.

I look up and see several fire-fighters running into the hall, followed by a crowd of police officers, including Penny Black. I shall never forget their faces as they gaze at the charred figures that can still be glimpsed through the conflagration at the end of the church.

Penny forced herself to remain professional, though she wanted to howl. How could she have got it so wrong? Dismissing Rosa Thorn as a neurotic spoilt bitch; secretly fancying the pants off a psycho. Her judgement was obviously deeply flawed. It was the South: she didn't understand folk down here. This carnage, this conflagration was probably the direct result of her crap policing. The sooner she went back up North the better. Then she'd never have to face any of these people again. Her resignation would be on the boss's desk by the end of this terrible day.

FIFTY-NINE

I don't know how we got through the next few days and weeks. It wasn't so much the interminable questions from the police, or dodging the media frenzy – 'Killer Cop in Church Massacre' – 'Consort Crucifixion Carnage'. It was more to do with regaining our grasp on reality, or rather, reclaiming our reality from the twisted mangled mess that Tom Brice had created. My first instinct was to distance myself by turning it into a story, keeping it between the pages of a notional book in the far recesses of my mind and pretending it was about fictional characters unconnected with us. But this didn't work. How could it? For we walked through the pages of our story every day: through the park and the streets, where Tom Brice and Mick O'Brien had roamed – predator and prey – both obsessing over Anna. Even our home, our supposed refuge, was steeped in memories of Tom. For me, Rob's old studio once more became a no-go area, and we seemed to be caught in a downward spiral of depression, unable to help each other avoid the vortex of horror that awaited us the moment we let our guard down.

I remember the turning-point.

We were in the sitting room one Saturday afternoon, watching some trashy daytime TV programme. We couldn't face going out into the world, yet we weren't enjoying being at home together. Life seemed reduced to one long wait, for something that none of us could define. Suddenly, Danny spoke.

'We could move.'

'What?'

'We could move house. Move areas. Get away from all of it.'

We looked at each other, testing the water. Yes – that was the answer. Start again somewhere new! We passed an excitable hour, galvanised into life, discussing where and when and how. We were arguing the relative merits of St Albans over Sunbury-on-Thames, when Anna shouted: 'Stop!'

Her face registered struggle. Danny and I waited, knowing somehow that what she was trying to articulate was important for all of us. Knowing she'd speak when she was ready.

Eventually she sighed, 'If we go, he'll have won. He'll have chased us out of our own lives. We can't let him do that.'

We all digested this.

'But he's here,' said Danny. 'Everywhere I turn he's here. I can't hack much more of it.'

'He's here because we're letting him be here. And that's wrong. This house, the park, the whole neighbourhood was around long before Tom Brice appeared. We were born here, Danny. We've lived here for ever. This place, it's the fabric of our existence. All those years with Dad, too. If we go, it's like giving up on him.

And if we go, our memories of Consort Park and this house will be of Brice and what he did, not of all the good times. Our childhood will be lost. We can't let that happen.'

She was right.

We sat in silence for a long time. Then Danny said: 'Mum, do you remember when you wanted to get Guy the Groper to put up new shelves in the kitchen, and Dad said it was a waste of money, that he'd do them instead. And he spent a whole week hammering and swearing, then two days after he'd finished, they all fell down?'

We all laughed, remembering Rob's incandescent rant as he viewed the splintered wood and smashed china.

'The floor's never been the same since.'

'There's a hole just under the table where one tile was smashed. I always stick my toe in it when I'm eating breakfast.'

'Show us.'

So we trouped into the kitchen and Danny showed us the hole in the floor, and we all laughed again. And suddenly the kitchen was full of Rob and us and our old life – our real life – and Tom Brice was a speck of nothing on the far horizon.

'This is what we should do,' said Danny. 'Our own exorcism. Let's go round every bit of this house remembering all the good things. Let's use our good memories to chase him away.'

And so we did. It didn't work all at once. It took time, and a huge effort of will. But gradually the old, precious memories blotted out the spectre of Tom Brice, and our house became our own again.

There were other exorcisms, too.

We've all three of us seen a very understanding therapist who's helped us go through everything. Anna continues to visit him. Her conviction that she was responsible for Rob's death is still taking its toll. We tell her constantly that it wasn't her fault, but something in her still can't quite give it up. I think she's lived with the notion for so long that it's become part of her. This, and all the other things have become so tangled together in her head, that she's going to need help for quite a while.

I struggle with my own demons. I sometimes doubt I'll ever be able to have another relationship. I continually rehash conversations I had with Tom, trying retrospectively to pinpoint moments when the mask might have dropped, remembering nuances of tone and expression that might have alerted me to his real character. I berate myself for being so naïve, for capitulating so easily to his spurious charm. I've lost all confidence in my ability to judge people. Or trust them. Jess says that the whole point about sociopaths like Tom is that they're able to charm their way into people's hearts, that they're ultra-skilled in the art of deception, but I know the way I feel and I can't see it changing. I don't want it to change. I'm content with my memories of Rob, who never deceived or betrayed me. That's the way I want things for now.

The part Danny and Dwaine played in our drama was another complicated skein that had to be unravelled to be properly understood. Immediately after the events in the church, Dwaine was closely questioned by the police about the death of Fax Max, and kept in suspense for several days about whether or not they were going to press charges.

One morning during our first post-Brice week there's a ring on the doorbell. We don't answer, thinking it's another reporter, but then we hear a familiar voice shouting through the letterbox.

'Dan, it's me! Guess what, they're not going to charge me with nothing. I'm a free man, bro.'

I rush to the door, determined to get there before Danny. When Dwaine sees me, he looks embarrassed. It's our first contact since the fire.

'Is Dan in? If not, I'll come back later.' He starts to walk off.

'Not so fast, Dwaine Johnson. It's truth time. You've told the police: now you can tell us.'

'Mum!'

Danny's come up behind me, with Anna in tow. He's outraged at the tone I'm taking, but I don't care. There are things I need to know.

'Right. What's been going on?'

Now it's Anna's turn to defend him.

'Mum, he saved our lives and you're treating him like a five year old.'

I look at the three young faces in front of me, two of them frowning in indignation, the third looking shifty. What I really want to do is scoop them all up and drown them in relief that we're all alive. But there are things that have to be sorted. Tom Brice wasn't the only actor in our drama. And I have the feeling that I'll get more out of them when they're still raw and wide open. I march them into the sitting room and sit them down.

'Danny, if you don't want me to interrogate Dwaine, perhaps you'd like to talk. Firstly – and this time I want a straight answer – are you on drugs?'

'No.'

'Is Dwaine?'

A long silence. Finally Dwaine speaks.

'I am – I was. Not no more. Danny's helped me get clean.'

It was the usual cautionary tale. First weed, then the progression onto something stronger. In Dwaine's case, cocaine.

'It started after my dad left. Smoking weed helped me forget what things was like at home . . . Then it got out of control and I needed something stronger . . . charlie. By the time Dan and me became mates I was pretty far gone. But once Dan saw how it was, he wouldn't let up. He kept on and on at me about how stupid I was, frying my brains and that. I didn't take no notice though. Then one night I was such a space cadet I nearly walked under a bus. After that he started following me to make sure I was cool. Couldn't get rid of him, could I?'

'Is that what all those late nights were about, Danny? Looking out for Dwaine?'

'Yeah . . .' Danny's looking uncomfortable.

'Wassup, bro?' Dwaine asks.

Danny can't look at him.

'It started like you said – me looking out for you,' he mumbles. 'I saw my dad die right in front of me. I wasn't about to let it happen to my best mate as well.'

'Steady, bro.'

Although Dwaine pretends to shy away from this soppy stuff, I can tell he's pleased. But Danny's still uncomfortable.

'It's just . . . you were so out of it for a while, I thought . . .'

'What?'

'The Pet Cemetery thing . . . it was so weird . . .'

Recognition sweeps across Dwaine's face.

'You thought it was me! You thought I was such a sick fuck that I'd dig your sister's animals up.'

Danny is writhing with embarrassment. 'You were so mashed, man.'

'Did you think I murdered Athy, too, an' left my own sister to die?'

'*No!*'

Dwaine stares at Danny. His breathing is heavy, rapid. His lips are pinched and a muscle pulses in his cheek. Then he slumps back in his chair.

''S'all right, man. I'm not surprised you thought that.'

'I know you didn't touch Athy and Crystal. D'you think I'd have helped you with Max if that's what I believed? And once you cut down on all the shit, then I could see there was no way you'd dig up animal graves either.'

'Why wouldn't you trust *me* to help Dwaine?' I want to know.

'Do me a favour, Mum! You'd have grassed to Charlene.'

I think about it. 'You're right. She needed to know . . .'

Dwaine interrupts. 'My mum did *not* need to know, believe me. With her thing about God and the Church, me being a junkie would have ruined her life.'

'She knew something was up. She found your stash. She just didn't know the best way to deal with it.'

'Anyway, Mum, we did it without you. He's clean now, aren't you, bro?'

Dwaine stares at me. 'My mum *knew*?'

'Yes.'

'Shit, shit, shit.'

'What?'

'I needn't have done—' He breaks off.

'Done what? It's truth time – remember.'

The expression on Dwaine's face reminds me of the time I caught six-year-old Danny stealing five pence from my purse to buy me a birthday present.

'Better out than in, Dwaine.'

After another long silence, he speaks.

'Brice somehow sussed I was a cokehead. Probably seeing me wired, when I came here for band rehearsals. He also knew, through you, how religious Mum is. One of his scams was drugs. He decided I'd be useful as a dealer – Class A shit. Heroin. If I refused, my mum would be told about my habit.'

I can't believe this.

'You knew that my lodger was a dope baron? And you didn't think to mention it?'

'I didn't know Brice was involved, till Max told me.'

'Max?'

'Max was Brice's front man. He was the one who blackmailed me into dealing.'

'That's why you were with him at Bertie's?'

'That's where I picked up my supplies. Then I'd unload it round Kilburn and take the profits back to Max.'

Danny interrupts. 'I knew there was something else going on with you. All those times you gave me the slip. Dealing – that's heavy shit.'

'Man, I was too ashamed to tell you.'

'So how did you find out about Tom?'

'It was after what happened to Crystal and Athy. I'd cut out the coke and I was getting my head together.

Max said something – I can't remember what – but it made me think he knew what had happened to the girls. He wouldn't tell me when I asked him nicely, so I decided to put on a bit of pressure.'

'We kidnapped him.'

This comes from Danny. With, I regret to say, a certain amount of pride.

'Wow.' Anna's impressed.

'Kidnapping's a criminal offence – not something to shout about,' I remind her.

'I think it's really cool. Max was such a perv,' says Anna.

'And a wimp,' Danny snorts. 'We came on like teenage hard men, tied him to a chair, made a few threats and he sang like a bird. Told us that he ran a porn racket specialising in photos of underage girls. Offered us a free supply if we'd keep quiet.'

'Let me guess: Fred Borrage was involved, and they used the derelict building at Churchill?'

The boys are gratifyingly amazed at my knowledge.

'How did you know?'

I look at Danny through narrowed eyes. 'I know lots of things, Daniel Thorn. It would be well for you to remember that.'

'Cut the drama, Mum,' says Anna. 'When did Max tell you about Tom, Dwaine?'

'The bastard said my sister was involved in the photos. I was so mad – I really wanted to hurt him, man. But I needed to find out who was the main man. It was obviously not him. He was shit scared of whoever it was, so I reckoned I had to make him even more scared of me. I knew Dan wouldn't be up for doing any real damage, so I persuaded him to go out, then had another go.'

'What did you do?'

'I came on like a crack-head psycho – out of control. He soon talked. He said Brice was the brains behind the porn and drugs racket and that he'd kill me if he found out I knew. Just like Susan Bradley. She'd been one of Brice's porn girls in a racket he'd set up at another school, and she'd recognised him. So he topped her, got himself put on her case, and then persuaded the other feds it was suicide.'

'What did he say about Crystal and Athy?'

'Max said he didn't know nothing except that Brice did it. He was shit scared, and it wasn't because I had him tied to a chair in your shed.'

Dwaine stops. Something has silenced him. I'm about to speak, but he holds up his hand.

'The bastard could have saved Athy – if he'd said something when Crystal was found. I looked at him, sitting in that chair, like some fat grey slug, and I thought of Crystal in a coma, and Athy . . .'

He falls silent again. We all wait.

'Man, I was nearly a murderer. As close as that. I was going to punch his brains out. I would've done. I would've smashed him into pieces, but then there was this crash, and a flash, and then the whole place was on fire . . .'

He slowly shakes his head. 'I nearly killed him . . .'

'But you didn't. You could have left him tied up in that burning building, but you tried to get him out. You're no murderer.'

'Yeah?'

'Even without the fire, you wouldn't have killed him. Something would have stopped you.'

'What?'

'Your conscience.'

'You think?'

'I know.'

A look of profound relief crosses Dwaine's face. Then he frowns.

'It was Brice who threw the petrol bomb. I saw his face at the window. He was smiling.'

'I'll bet he was. He liked fires.'

'I didn't know what to do. I couldn't tell the police. They wouldn't believe me about Brice, and I knew he'd have to kill me to shut me up. That's why I ran away. I wanted to warn you lot but I didn't know how. I couldn't come to your house and I thought the police would be able to trace any calls. I had to hope Dan would contact me . . .'

'Without you, Anna and I would be dead.'

He's shaking his head. 'Oh man, I nearly lost it . . .'

'But you didn't. Look at me, Dwaine.'

He doesn't want to. He's staring at the floor. I put my hand under his chin and tilt his face so he can see me.

'You're a life-saver, not a life-taker, Dwaine Johnson. Remember that.'

SIXTY

A month after being attacked, Crystal came out of her coma. She's back home now, and physically recovered, although Charlene says her left leg still drags a little when she walks.

I went to see her. Without Anna.

Charlene answered the door. 'Rosa!'

'I'd like to talk to Crystal,' I say.

'What about?'

'There are things I need to know.'

Charlene's face hardened. 'What things?'

'Things that only Crystal can tell me.'

'I'm not having my little girl upset. I want she to forget all about these last months.'

'We all want to forget. But I can't. Not until I know everything.'

'Not at the expense of my daughter.'

'Please . . .'

'It's not possible. I won't have she worried.'

I felt myself becoming emotional. It happened a lot at this time.

'Your daughter didn't worry too much when she was

burning my daughter's stomach with lighted cigarettes, and urinating over her school bag.'

Charlene, blocking her doorway, arms folded defensively, was outraged.

'That a cheap crack, Rosa Thorn. You should be ashamed of yourself.'

'Well, shame's something you must know a lot about.'

I think we may have come to blows. I saw several nearby curtains twitching in anticipation. But then Crystal appeared.

'Mum, I don't mind.'

Nice one, Crystal.

'You'll do as I say, my girl. If I say it no good for you to talk, then that's that.'

'I need to.'

After that Charlene had no choice but to invite me in.

Crystal was different from the brash child I remembered. This girl was subdued and quiet, eyes not meeting my gaze.

My mind went blank. The monster in my head turned out to be a thin, frail child with premature worry-lines round her eyes.

Eventually the words came.

'Just tell me why you treated Anna so badly.'

She sat, face impassive, body rigid. Then she started to cry. I watched the tears roll down her cheeks. I said nothing. I was happy to let her wriggle on the hook of self-disgust as she revisited the mayhem she'd perpetrated on Anna.

Payback time. Except it didn't feel as good as it did in my fantasies.

The seconds turned into minutes. It was too much for Charlene.

'You'd better go.'

'No!' The strength in the voice reminded me of the old Crystal. 'Anna was the new girl and Athy didn't like it 'cos Jamie Frost was comin' on to her an' everything, so we started making fun of her – name-callin' an' all. And the more she hated it, the more we hurt her. Specially since she wouldn't give in an' ask us to stop. I knew it was bad, but it was, like, excitin' to see how far we could push her . . . it was a buzz – like takin' drugs or somethin'.'

She shrank back, as if hoping to merge with the garish pattern of orange swirls on the sofa cover. She still couldn't look at me. Her voice sank to a mumble.

'Even when we . . . Even when we burned her she still didn't cry. She just lay there on the floor and looked at us.'

I couldn't take it.

'What had she ever done to you to make you do that?' I burst out. 'Had she been nasty to you? Or told tales on you? Or attacked you? *What?*'

'Nothing! She'd done nothing. It's just that . . . just that . . . She was so pretty and perfect, I wanted to get her – punch her – spoil her – make her rubbish like me. 'Cos I knew it was rubbish, what we were doing. And Athy felt the same, even though she never said so. I could tell.'

'So why didn't you stop? You knew it was wrong. How come you carried on?'

Crystal rubbed her forehead as if trying to eradicate the images that whirled around her brain.

'I don't know. I don't know. I'm sorry . . . I'm sorry.'

The girl's distress was pitiful. But Charlene didn't go to her. She was motionless. Only her eyes moved, flickering from side to side in pain and bewilderment.

'It was like we had a secret society or something where we dared each other to do badder and badder stuff. When we thought of the homework idea, I got great marks for the first time in my life, and that made me hate Anna even more because all the teachers were being nice to me about my work, and it wasn't mine. It was hers . . .'

She broke down completely now, rocking back and forth in misery, sobbing like a five year old. I knew I should go but there was more I needed to know.

'Tell me about Tom Brice.'

She shuddered, and I thought: I've gone too far.

'Those other things – the porn,' she began, but Charlene burst in.

'She didn't do any of that disgustin' stuff. It nothing to do with she. My girl have nothing to do with no porno.'

'Mum—'

'I don't want you pollutin' your mind with such wicked thoughts. You put them straight out of your head, Crystal, you hear?'

'Please, Mum, listen to me for once! I can't forget. It's there all the time. You won't talk about it and it's making me feel . . . kind of unreal – stuck. I need you to hear me. When you look at me, when you talk to me, it's like I'm some perfect cut-out doll that's nothing to do with the real me. Like if you admitted to yourself how bad I've been you wouldn't be able to love me any more.'

Charlene's eyes were fierce, but at last she swooped on her daughter, gathering her close.

'Girl, make no mistake, I know exactly what you did. And I pray every day that God forgive you. I don't see no perfect doll. I see my little one who done some very bad things. But it don't mean I don't love her no more. Lord, I'm your mother. Lovin's what mothers do. If you need to talk, then that's what we will do. Come on, get it off your chest.'

'Do you mean it?'

Charlene just nodded. So Crystal told her tale.

'Athy started to have lots of money, and she wouldn't tell me why. But I went on at her till she gave in. She said there were these mega-parties, with free alcohol, and cigarettes and . . .' She glanced up at her mother. '. . . And weed. Lots of weed. As much as you could smoke.'

Charlene sucked her teeth.

'Athy said they were held in the condemned school building, and she'd fix it for me to come. I was a bit scared, so I made up some excuse the first few times she asked.'

'Why were you scared?'

'That place was really spooky at night and I thought, What if it falls down on us? Also, I'd told Athy that I smoked weed and that, but really I never.'

Charlene couldn't resist. 'I should hope not!'

'Then she started calling me chicken, and said I wasn't her best friend any more, so I said I'd go. She made me swear on your life that I wouldn't tell, Mum.'

'May the Lord forgive me for speaking ill of the dead, but that Athy Petros . . .'

'When it came to the night, I was excited and scared all at the same time. The place was really dark and creepy, and I thought at first that Athy was winding me up, but then we did a special knock on a door hidden round the side. Fred Borrage let us in, and it was well cool. All these kids were there, some I recognised from Churchill, and others I'd never seen before, smoking and drinking and dancing.'

'And what did you do, missy?'

Crystal plunged on, ducking her mother's stern gaze. 'I had a puff of weed.'

'Lordy, Lordy, chile!'

'I only took a couple of drags. It made me feel a bit sick. Then I noticed there were no boys. I asked Athy why and she laughed and said did I want to earn some money. I said how and she said wait and see. She took me to this other room upstairs. There was a man guarding the door but he let us through.'

Crystal stopped. Her hands, nails bitten to the quick, were constantly plucking at her skirt.

'You want to stop?' Charlene asked in concern.

'No!' She took several deep breaths. 'It was horrible. This tiny Year Seven girl was having her photo taken – by Fax Max. She . . .'

I could see she was becoming distressed.

'We know about the photos,' I said. 'What happened next?'

'I wanted to get out, but the room was full of pervy men staring at the girl. The weed made me dizzy and I couldn't find the door. I panicked. I grabbed Athy and said I had to go. I tried what I thought was the right door, but it wasn't. Suddenly we were in this room that had nothing but a couple of chairs and a window in the wall. A bloke was looking through it into the big room with all the men. I realised it was a two-way mirror. The bloke was Brice. I recognised him straight away. So did Athy. She started this stupid giggling. He told her to shut up, but she just kept on. I wanted to go, but she wouldn't. She started winding him up—'

'How?'

'Asking if he was on surveillance like on the telly, and if he thought his landlady – you – would be interested in where he spent his spare time. I begged her to leave and I was so relieved when she said yes. But then she told Brice we'd need a cab home, and could he lend us five hundred quid.'

'Blackmail,' I said. Charlene was silent, shocked.

'Yeah. He went ballistic. He started calling Athy all sorts of really bad things, and then he hit her. Lots of times. I screamed at him to stop, but he took no notice. I tried to pull him off, so he hit me too. Then Athy collapsed onto the floor, and while I was trying to pull her up, he locked the door. He grabbed me and tied me to one of the chairs with some wire from his pocket. Then he tied Athy up, and left her on the floor. Then he left. I heard the key turn in the lock and I knew we were trapped. Even if we managed to untie ourselves we'd never break the lock – I could see it was very strong. We shouted and shouted . . .'

'Didn't anyone hear?'

I caught another glimpse of the old Crystal as she curled her lip at me.

'You must be joking. The music was really loud, and the men were getting all turned on by what was going on in front of Fax Max's camera – moaning and calling out and stuff. No one heard us. Then, after a bit, Brice must have got scared someone would hear 'cos he came back and gagged us. It was horrible. I couldn't breathe. I thought I'd choke and die. After ages and ages it quietened down out there. Then we realised we were on our own. It was so dark . . . and cold . . .'

I could see the worst bit was coming. So could Charlene.

'You don't have to do this, chile.' Her voice was gentle now.

'Yes, I do. If I say it out loud, maybe it'll leave my head. He came back again. He took Athy, and left me.' Crystal started to cry. 'He was doing things to Athy in the big room. I had my back to the mirror so I couldn't see what, but she was screaming and crying and he kept laughing at her. It was horrible. Then there was this gurgling sound and a bit later I heard a noise like something being dragged across the floor . . . and after that, nothing. At all. I tried again to untie myself, but I couldn't. I kept thinking: He's coming back for me next.

'But he didn't. I waited till it got light. I managed to get the gag off and I called out, but no one heard. I watched the light change on the ceiling, and eventually it got dark again, and I knew I'd been there a whole day. And that's how it went on. Light then dark, light then dark. I don't know how long for. He never came back, and neither did anyone else. I must have gone unconscious eventually because I don't remember the building collapsing or nothing . . .' Her voice faded away.

Charlene spoke. This time there was no mistaking the determination in her voice.

'You got what you came for, Rosa. You should go now.'

I had to agree. Crystal looked worn out. She gazed at me wistfully, wanting something I wasn't yet able to give.

But I could make a start.

'Thank you for that. I know how difficult it must

have been to talk, and I really appreciate it. I'm very sorry for what's happened to you.'

'Do you think Anna would see me – so I could apologise?'

Now it was my turn to go into protective mother mode. 'I don't know.'

As I walked home I thought: Over my dead body. But I changed my mind. That decision was Anna's to make. Not mine. Maybe I'd learned something about when to interfere in my children's lives, and when to leave well alone.

And so when Charlene invited us to tea one wet Saturday in late February, I relayed the message to Anna.

'You don't have to,' was all I said.

Anna was sitting by the window staring at the rain-sodden park. As if she were waiting for someone. Perhaps Mick O'Brien – long absent now from his sentry-post beside the chestnut tree. She traced the path of a raindrop down the window with her fingertip.

'I do.'

Like me, she had to confront her demons. For her, the months of bullying had been as traumatic as the ghastly twenty-four hours in the church with Tom Brice. She needed to see Crystal.

When we arrived, Crystal was lying on the sofa. She sat up quickly at the sight of Anna.

'Hi.'

There was a long pause. I could sense Anna's disinclination to speak. It was the same response I'd felt on my first visit. Let Crystal make the running.

'I'm sorry, Anna.'

'Yeah?'

'I'm sorry for the bullying and everything.'

Another pause, broken only by the ticking of Charlene's gold carriage clock on the mantelpiece.

'What exactly do you mean by "bullying"?'

Crystal looked stricken. 'The things me and Athy did to you.'

'What things?'

The girl was squirming. 'Come on, Anna . . . you know.'

'What are you sorry for exactly?' Anna's eyes were fixed on Crystal.

'Go on, girl. Make your peace.' It's Charlene.

'I'm sorry I made everyone be horrible to you. I'm sorry I pissed on your bag and your clothes and wrote all those things. I'm sorry I stole your dinner-money. And I'm sorry I made you do my homework all those times.'

Did she mean it?

'I'm really, really sorry, Anna.'

Silence again. It was endless.

Finally Anna spoke. 'Why did you do it?'

And so Crystal put herself through the whole thing again, repeating and enlarging on what she told me two weeks previously. I'm glad to say that it didn't trip any more easily off her tongue than it did the first time. Quite the reverse. Crystal seemed even more appalled at her own actions. Anna listened, all the time staring intently at her ex-tormentor. When Crystal finally stopped talking, there was another silence. Even longer and more profound.

Finally Anna spoke. 'Apology accepted,' she said. 'Where did you get that top? It's great.'

Crystal looked properly at Anna for the first time.

'Top Shop. I like your pendant. What's the stone?'

'Rose quartz. A present from a friend.'

A friend who saved her life. I'm glad I gave her Mick's gift. She wears it all the time.

Anna and Crystal will never be close. Crystal hurt Anna too much for that. But I'm glad my daughter found it in her to forgive. Today she has lots of friends who are helping her to come to terms with everything that's happened. And I hope that one day her nightmares will stop, and that she won't keep returning time and time again in her mind to the crypt of St Peter and St Paul, where a man she thought was her friend prepared to rape and kill her. I hope that one day I'll sleep through the night without being woken by her bad dreams.

SIXTY-ONE

On a dancing April afternoon Danny, Anna and I finally set Rob free. We stand on the cliffs overlooking Rhossili Bay on the Gower Peninsula, a place where the four of us once spent Easter. Staring down at the famous skeleton galleon, half-buried on the beach below, we say our goodbyes. It's taken us through the dark days of late winter and early spring to prepare for this moment.

I still wake sometimes, feeling the touch of Tom Brice's murderous fingers stroking my skin, and I shudder when I remember the delight they brought me. In deep night, images of his body on mine intermingle with images of the slaughtered. They come to me during the day, too. I'll be doing something very ordinary, and suddenly I'll see him slitting Mick O'Brien's throat. Or feel his body crushing mine, as he undresses me in the church hall in front of my crucified daughter. I'm told these things will pass. To imagine they'll be with me for ever is unendurable.

I'm delighted to say my teaching days have come to a halt for the time being. On the strength of my short-lived notoriety in the Tom Brice case, Boo's got me a small but vital role in a new eight-part series on the BBC. I play the neglected wife of an undercover policeman. In time-honoured TV fashion, she eventually kicks him out, leaving lots of opportunities for stressful scenes over money and child access which show him to be basically likeable but misunderstood. The odd similarities between this show and Tom Brice's life haven't escaped my notice. Except that, as I recently discovered, Tom's wife wasn't neglected, but regularly beaten to within an inch of her life.

Eunice Brice has sold her flat in Cheltenham and disappeared: no one knows where to. I wonder if she has any sense of her own culpability for Tom's actions.

Fred Borrage is in Wormwood Scrubs awaiting trial, and Leo Ratchett has resigned. His career as the nation's Top Totty Head Teacher is over. Mud sticks, and although there's never been any suggestion that he knew what was happening in his school, he's tainted by association. Rumour has it that he's writing his memoirs. I don't expect I'll figure in them.

I think he's lucky to be alive. Once Tom heard of his probing telescope, his days were numbered. The last thing Tom wanted was someone spying on his nocturnal escapades. The Praetorian Guard may well have kept him out of harm's way, after all. Without them, Tom, having mistakenly attacked Marion, might have made a second, more successful attempt on Leo's life.

Today would have been Rob's forty-second birthday. That's why we chose it to set him free. The sea is sparkling and the cliff where we sit is covered in pink armeria and golden celandines. Above us the terns shriek as they swoop and drift on currents of gusty air. Anna's holding the urn that contains what's left of her father.

'Ready?' I say.

Anna unscrews the lid of the urn. 'Fly free, Dad,' she says, and extending her arm over the cliff-edge, she inverts the jar.

For the briefest moment the air is filled with grey dust.

With Rob.

Then he's gone, whirling out to join the rest of the universe, away from us. Yet still with us.

Part of us always.

We stay on the clifftop until sunset, remembering him. Sometimes silent, sometimes tripping over words in our haste to conjure him, weaving our various strands together to form a cloth of remembrance which will shelter us through the dark times.

As the light fades and we prepare to leave, we hear a sound.

Perched on a nearby gorse-bush is a bird. Not the kind of bird usually associated with clifftops. It regards us with bright little eyes, head cocked to one side. Its crowning glory is its chest: a fierce deep orange.

A robin.